Landscape with Violence

Carter removed the cigarette from his mouth, and exhaled smoke, before he spoke.

He said, 'Flora, my dear. Listen very carefully to what I have to tell you. The men behind you – the four men, the four Americans – that each have an automatic pistol. Each pistol is loaded, and each man is prepared to use it. Given an excuse – any reason at all – and they'll shoot you.' Carter glanced at the fat man and the thin man, and added, 'And you. And you. Anybody!' He returned his attention to Flora, and ended, 'I don't want to see bloodshed, my dear. But they're desperate men, and they'll certainly commit murder . . . and without giving it too much thought.'

Flora Aimes did not faint, or collapse, or have an attack of the vapours, or anything like that. She was not that type of woman. She widened her eyes and, for a moment, disbelieved what she was hearing.

Carter saw the disbelief, and said, 'This is not some off-beat joke, my dear. I'm serious. Deadly serious. And so are they.'

Flora bent forward and rested the palms of her hands on the table top. She didn't *fall* forward but, nevertheless, the sudden weight, transmitted by her stiffened arms, made the coffee in Carter's cup move and slop a little over the lip.

Flora turned her head. Slowly.

The four Americans were seated at two tables. Each man had a gun in his hand; three of them were right-handed, and held their guns in that hand, and the fourth was left-handed. The guns (as Carter had said) were automatic pistols, square-shaped and deadly, and each pistol was held easily, but firmly; not aimed, but menacing. And the men who held the pistols looked as deadly, and as menacing, as their killing-tools as they watched Flora Aimes and waited for

JOHN WAINWRIGHT

LANDSCAPE WITH VIOLENCE

MAGNUM BOOKS
Methuen Paperbacks Ltd

A Magnum Book

LANDSCAPE WITH VIOLENCE
ISBN 0 417 04320 1

First published in Great Britain 1975
by Macmillan London Ltd
Magnum edition published 1979

Copyright © 1975 by John Wainwright

Magnum Books are published by
Methuen Paperbacks Ltd
11 New Fetter Lane, London EC4P 4EE

Made and printed in Great Britain
by Cox & Wyman Ltd, Reading

This book is sold subject to the condition that it shall not, by way of trade or otherwise, be lent, resold, hired out, or otherwise circulated without the publisher's prior consent in any form of binding or cover other than that in which it is published and without a similar condition including this condition being imposed on the subsequent purchaser.

TUESDAY, JUNE 25th

In retrospect, and while examining the cock-up under the magnification of hindsight, Harris put it in a nutshell.

He said, 'Y'know what I wish? I wish the stupid bastard who built those houses, *and* the stupid bastard who gave him planning permission, were down there with the stupid bastards who bought 'em.'

It was putting it strongly. Harris's excuse (at the time) was reasonable enough; he was tired, he was angry and he hadn't the foggiest idea what to do next. Short of sanctioning the slaughter of half-a-hundred innocent people—short of granting unconditional surrender to a man he didn't know, a man he hadn't even seen, but a man whose guts he hated with all the fury with which a detective chief superintendent of the mould from which Harris was cast is capable—short of all this, Harris was up a gum tree.

And Harris knew it.

Which (to a gold-plated jack like Harris) was one hell of an admission to make.

However...

Planning permission *had* been granted, the houses *had* been built, and innocent people *had* bought them and were living in them.

It was known as Robs Cully. 'Robs' as an abbreviation of 'Robert's', but without the apostrophe. 'Cully' as a shortened version of cul-de-sac... which it was. The builder, Robert Bottom ('Top people buy Bottom houses') had reached for small immortality via the subtle choice of a name for a new village. It was there, on the latest Ordnance Survey Maps, and no mere dealer in bricks and mortar could ask for greater fame than that.

And it *was* a village—it was more than a hamlet—because it had a church. The Church of St James, to be precise. Or, to be more precise, 'The Church of St James in the Parish of Raine', because the parent church was three miles away, at the ancient village of Raine and, if the truth be told, 'The Church of St

James in the Parish of Raine' was little more than a substantially built mission hall; a stone-walled, steep-roofed box containing a tiny altar, a pulpit, a font and an aisle with ten rows of hard-seated pews on each side; a House of God, by all means, but a House of God whose homage to its deity was rationed to a 10.30 a.m. Eucharist on the second Sunday of the month, plus weddings and baptisms, as arranged. No funerals; the tiny churchyard had become bone-filled years before and, these days, no fresh flowers were ever placed by the tilting headstones. It was a dead church; a place of bats and field mice—a place of wood pigeons and village cats seeking sanctuary in which to perform their yowling courtship. But it was a church, therefore Robs Cully was (technically) a 'village'.

There was a pub, *The Hind's Head*, originally a two-roomed ale-house. It had been extended and tarted up by a brewery combine with its eye on the main chance until now, and without much exaggeration, it could be described as a 'road house'. Admittedly, much of the Olde Worlde junk had 'Made in Japan' stamped in an out-of-the-way corner, the adze-marks on the beams were all pure ersatz and the warming-pans on the walls hadn't even seen the inside of an antique shop, much less the inside of a bed. But, despite these (and similar subtle con tricks) the overall impression was of age, but without the obligatory muck of antiquity. *The Hind's Head* was a popular enough noggin-shifter's gathering spot, both with the locals and with visiting anglers who sought the fish of the River Hewfraw, at whose banks the 'No Through Road' of the village ended. It served a moderately good pint, provided a moderately well-cooked meal and, if necessary, slept the handful of overnight visitors in moderately comfortable beds.

In the not too distant past—going back about twenty years or so—there had been no such place as Robs Cully. There had been the church, the ale-house, a communal pump alongside a patch of common ground and a huddle of tied cottages. On paper, it had been part of 'the Parish of Raine' but, to the parishioners of Raine itself, it had always been 'The Other Place'.

Twenty years ago, it had been a nothing. A nowhere. A spot which did not even merit the dignity of a name.

Then, Mr Robert Bottom had stumbled across it, rubbed his eyes and realised its potential.

It was a spec-builder's dream. It was made for people who

don't have to mess about with mortgages; people who don't have to borrow, before they can buy. Moderately rich people. The 'top' people who (according to the adverts) all bought 'Bottom' houses.

It was (virtually) an island, at the farthest point of a secret, steep-sided, blind-ended valley; a wind-sheltered sun-trap in summer, and a cosy corner of rural England in winter. The Hewfraw tumbled down from the tops, flattened out at the valley floor, then made a sickle-bow of racing, foam-spangled water. The points of the sickle were joined by Skew Beck—not noticeably less deep nor less fast-running than the Hewfraw itself—and the two waters combined to form a private island reached only (at that time) by a hump-backed ancient pack-bridge.

It was all there. The vision. All it needed for reality was money, influence and imagination.

Twenty years ago.

But, today, it was Robs Cully. The creation—the brain-child—of Robert Bottom.

Robs Cully; a river-swept hunk of real estate; an island of comfort, isolated (except for one very necessary road bridge) from the rest of the county; a place where water-bound privacy was sold as part of the amenities.

The tied cottages were still there, but no longer 'tied'; they'd all been gutted, re-roofed, pointed, colour-washed and centrally-heated, and they were now 'weekend cottages' for those who lived in cities, but who had cash enough to spend playing 'country gentlefolk' when time allowed. (But 'country gentlefolk', be it clearly understood, with fast cars, colour T.V., a yokel from Raine to keep the lawn and garden in good order and, *always*, extension telephones in every room ... just in case something happened, and the 'country gentlefolk' gag had to be abandoned in a hurry for the more sharkish role of finanacial gymnast!)

Not that the weekend cottages made up the bulk, or even much, of Robs Cully. The major part of this river-encircled island had been divided up into plots; each irregular-shaped and each with an area of between an acre-and-a-half, and two acres. And, on each plot, was a bungalow or a house; 'tailored to taste and built to your own specifications'; each different from the rest, each with its own individually-chosen garden layout and each (but, of course!) built only for the 'top' people.

Bottom figured that that island was the best gamble he'd ever taken.

He'd poured money into it; architect's fees, a thick layer of butter, here and there, as far as people with 'pull' were concerned, the fight with officialdom for a good access road, a decent bridge and mains services and (not least of all) the P.R. job of selling well-heeled smart boys the idea of travelling thirty, forty and, sometimes, fifty miles, to and from work, for the sheer joy of breathing fresh (albeit very expensive) country air.

One hell of a gamble.

But it had come off, spades!

And the result was Robs Cully, and just about the most loot-laden piece of land in the North of England.

And Robert Bottom's bank balance was proof that every blade of grass—every leaf of every tree—on that river-enclosed slab of real estate was worth its weight in pure gold.

6.30 a.m. . . .

Not that Barbara Pickering knew too much about gold or, indeed, would even have attempted to put a price upon 'Bottom's Place', as the rustics of Raine *would* insist upon calling Robs Cully.

Babs Pickering did not concern herself with such stupidities. She had (to use her own expression) 'enough to live on, but not enough to get me worried', and that was exactly how she wanted things.

She'd been born at Raine. She'd been schooled at Raine and had married at Raine. She'd lived at Raine, and had been widowed at Raine, and the widowing had not been the most painful experience of her life. She'd 'wed a wrong 'un' and had learned to live with him, but she was no hypocrite; when Old Nick had claimed his own, she'd been mildly grateful to fate for granting her a few years of peace before she, too, had clay tossed on to her coffin.

Meanwhile, she 'did' for people. She (like some of the other middle-aged-to-elderly ladies of the Raine and district community) was the proverbial 'little woman' who did the housework at one of the minor showplaces of Robs Cully.

She crossed the bridge which spanned the foamed waters of the Hewfraw; glanced over the parapet, without pause in her waddling stride and, with her country-keen eyes, saw the trout undulating in the shadowed quiet alongside what was left of the stones of the old pack-bridge. The fishing would be good that day; the fishing was good almost *every* day—the rock-strewn bed of the river made whirls and rapids, and dragged oxygen into the water, making the fish lively and eager for bait—there were better fishing rivers than the Hewfraw, but few stretches of any river were so consistently good.

A car came towards her, from Robs Cully, as she left the bridge for the road. A scarlet, low-slung Lancia. It sounded its horn in greeting, and she nodded an early-morning 'Hello' to the driver. It was Mr Mitford from *Green Gables*, and it was Tuesday and, every Tuesday, Mr Mitford had to be up and away; he had to reach Harrogate in time for the London Pullman—and London, in time for his weekly conference.

More than two hundred miles for a natter with his colleagues. For a 'cal', as Babs Pickering and her kind would have called it. And for why? Because they had 'brass'. Well, for her, they could have it; if that was what being 'well off' meant, they could have it, and they were welcome to it.

A corn bunting panicked at her approach. It swooped from the top of a trimmed hedge, curved upwards, then swerved and dived for cover behind the hedge it had been using for a perch. Babs Pickering smiled to herself. Buntings weren't too plentiful, these days. She could remember—and not so long ago—when they rose in yellow, wing-fluttering clouds as you walked the lanes; scores of them, rising and settling, as if playing timid tag from the safety of the hedgerow. The scientists had stopped all that. Insecticides had killed other things than insects; buntings, finches, wagtails—every seed-eating bird in the whole countryside—and by the thousand. But now they were coming back. Singly, and in pairs and, sometimes, in tiny colonies. Because these people— these rich folk, who lived in 'Bottom's Place'—hadn't yet grown so used to nature as to take it for granted. They believed in what they called 'preservation'; they saw more in land than corn and cattle-fodder. At least they had that much gumption.

Barbara Pickering's smile broadened.

With all their faults, the people who lived in Robs Cully weren't a bad lot.

The man watching from behind the curtains, at the upper window of *Yew Tree Bower* saw Babs Pickering hurry along the pavement, between the trimmed verges. He'd already seen the Lancia leave and head for the bridge.

Without taking his eyes from the road, he said, 'They're starting to move.'

'The mail. The milk. The kids off to school.'

The second speaker spoke from the bed. He wore yellow, shot-silk pyjamas and, over the pyjamas, a pale blue, 'shortie' dressing-gown. The dressing-gown was tied loosely, the pyjama jacket had the top button unfastened, and the curly black hair of his barrel-chest pushed, like undergrowth, as if trying to rid itself of the restraint of the smooth cloth.

He was what even the F.B.I. had once described as a 'tough baby'. Not crazy, 'Jack-"Legs"-Diamond-tough'. Not loud-mouthed, 'Al-"Scarface"-Capone-tough'. This one had once been *really* tough. He had never been a Godfather; he had no time for Godfathers. Godfathers (as far as James Edward Wolff, Jnr, was concerned) were elderly men, with reputations earned via the guts and death of their children and grandchildren; they were the inheritors of past glory, and pale shadows of the men who had made The Syndicate a law beyond, and above, the law. Spit at them, and they'd duck. *That* much for Godfathers!

Thus the opinion of James Edward Wolff, Jnr—who wasn't *quite* as young as he used to be ... and maybe not *quite* the strong man he figured himself out to be.

He said, 'Give it till thirty after nine. Then we move.'

The man at the window grunted an agreement.

'You know who we talk to?' asked Wolff.

'Chief of detectives. Some big-time bull called Harris.'

'You have his number?'

'Home and office,' murmured the man at the window.

'I hope,' said Wolff, wearily, 'he is not one of those heroic bastards. I hope he is smart enough to know when to *be* smart.'

'Does it matter?' asked the man at the window.

'No. I guess not ... not too much.'

'We knock a couple. He'll get smart,' said the man at the window, confidently.

Charlotte Douranby.

With a woman like her it *had* to be 'Charlotte'. No other name would have suited; no other name would have been appropriate. She had not 'come out'—she had not been 'presented'—

but this only because such nonsense was now a thing of the past. In the old days—in the *good* old, more elegant old days—things would have been vastly different. Daddy would have seen to that, and Mummy would have made sure. As it was, Ascot, Cowes, Henley and Wimbledon were the highlights of her year, with occasional West End first-nights thrown in for good measure, whenever Daddy could get hold of some decent tickets.

The rest was a bore; one monumental bore.

Even her two-year-old marriage was a bore. By this time, the biggest bore of all.

Roger. She'd married him (he didn't know it, of course, nor, come to that, and to be fair to her, did *she* know) but she'd married him because his name was 'Roger'. And Daddy's name was 'Roger'. And, like Mummy, she always called him 'Roj' ... and pronounced it 'Rawj'.

The Douranby part of the name had had a little to do with it, too. Mummy (who was up on such matters) mentioned that Douranby was the family name of the viscounts of Manderscroft, and, for a few heady weeks Charlotte had been *sure*. *Absolutely* sure! Then, gradually, the certainty had been watered down to wishful-thinking and now, after two years of married life, the wishful-thinking had weakened into daydreams.

Nevertheless, it was possible. It was still *possible*. These things *did* happen, you know.

And, as a first step she'd insisted upon naming their home, at Robs Cully, *Conte Lauba* which, she explained to Mummy—and very loosely translated—meant 'The Lodge of the Viscount'.

Meanwhile ...

She rolled her head on the pillow, flopped one bare arm clear of the brushed-nylon sheet and stared across the space which separated the twin beds.

Very quietly, she said, 'Are you still asleep, Roj?'

'Wha-a...' Roger Douranby opened his eyes, blinked, then said, 'What's that, my darling?'

'I thought you might be awake.'

'I am.' Roger Douranby grinned, and pushed a lock of his tousled hair clear of his face. He clenched his fists, put them to his shoulders and stretched. He said, 'I am, *now*.'

Charlotte rolled on to her back and stared at the ceiling.

She said, 'It's going to be another of those long, miserable days.'

'Oh, I dunno. You can...'

'Nothing to do. No excitement. No *anything*.'

He, too, rolled on to his back. He, too, watched the ceiling as they talked. Two people, holding the first conversation of a new day; not even looking at each other, as they talked.

He said, 'You should get a bit more involved, old girl.'

'Involved? In what?'

'Y'know ... social work. Get among people a bit more. Don't you think?'

'Take free soup to smelly old women,' she said, dreamily.

'Don't be silly, dear. That's not...'

'Visit lonely old men—dirty old men—and sit and talk to them, while they peep up my skirt.'

'Charlotte, old girl. Don't be...'

'I don't think I'm quite cut out for *that*, Roj.'

He said, 'That wasn't what I meant. And you know it. But I do think you should...'

'I think,' she said, 'I'll buy myself a pony.'

'A what?'

'A pony. Y'know ... a horse.'

'Now, why on earth,' he asked, 'do you want a pony? You can't ride.'

'I can learn.'

'And you already have two damn great dogs.'

'They are *not* "damn great dogs",' she said, with a touch of petulance. 'They're beautiful. They're two lovely Afghan hounds, and they're ...'

'Bloody expensive.'

'Don't be a bore, Roj,' she sighed.

He returned sigh for sigh, and said, 'I'm sorry, my love. If you like them, they're not expensive.'

'They're Afghan hounds,' she whispered, as if reassuring herself of certain facts. 'They're beautiful, and I love them. But, I think I'll buy myself a pony and learn to ride. I think I'd look rather fetching in jodhpurs.'

There was a silence. Not a closeness; not the brand of silence which bonds together more closely people who are already close. Just a silence which was an absence of noise—an ending of talk—that, and nothing more.

They both lay there, gazing up at the ceiling.

The silence lasted for about two minutes.

Then, she said, 'Roj, why on earth do you *have* to work up there, in that God-forsaken place?'

'It's where my work is, darling,' he said, and as he spoke he smothered a yawn.

'Up there, in that *awful* place. Tees-side!'

'It's where my work is, darling,' he repeated.

'Celia says...'

'Celia doesn't know what the devil she's talking about. Half the time, she talks pure, unadulterated cock.'

'She's not a fool, Roj.'

'*I* think she is.'

'She married a doctor—a specialist. She had sense enough to marry a specialist.'

'Bully for Celia,' murmured Douranby.

'I married a "civil engineer".'

'Quite, my love. But a very highly qualified civil engineer ... if I may be so bold as to remind you.'

'Civil engineer,' she mused. 'Civil engineer. Darling, it sounds so *awful*. Like a slightly superior, bureaucratic navvy. It isn't a thing to be *proud* of ... now, is it?'

'Actually, yes. It is.'

'Almost as if you used a shovel. A pick and a shovel. Almost as if you did *that*, for a living.'

Douranby linked the fingers of his hands behind his neck.

In a voice as musingly off-handed as his wife, and still staring up at the ceiling, he said, 'Charlotte, my love. Henry may be a doctor. He may even be a specialist, whereas I am only a "civil engineer" but—take my word for it, my sweet—as far as income is concerned, I could match Henry, pound for pound ... and still buy you two more Afghan hounds, *and* a pony, *and* a lot of other things. Count your blessings, darling. Be grateful it was Celia who married the doctor, and that it was you who married the—er—"bureaucratic navvy".'

'Pig,' she said, petulantly.

'As always,' he agreed, amiably.

'It's going to be one of those days. I can feel it.'

He chuckled, silently and as if at a secret joke.

'What time is it?' she asked.

He unlinked a hand from behind his head, reached towards the mock-antique table which separated the heads of the twin beds, and felt for the tiny alarm clock. He squinted at it.

He said, 'Half six.'

'Oh, my God! I hadn't realised there *was* such a time.'

Douranby replaced the clock and, teasingly, said, 'They'll all be up and about by this time.'

'Who? Who will? Who on earth...'

'Feeding their whippets and their racing pigeons.'

'Who? Who are you...'

'Fixing their chip butties. Scraping dripping on their flat-cakes.'

'Who? she said, irritably. 'Who on earth are you talking about?'

'All the other "navvies",' he grinned.

'You are a pig,' she said crossly.

'I've already said ... I know.'

'And this is going to be one of those days. I *know*. One of those dreary, boring, never-ending days. I just *know* it will be.'

'Go buy yourself a pony,' he suggested.

'Ye-es.' A half-smile bent her lips. Still watching the ceiling, she said, 'I'll give Celia a ring. I'll take her with me. She'll be pea-green with envy. *That's* what I'll do.'

'Where?' he asked.

'What?'

'Y'know ... where do you *buy* ponies, anyway?'

'Roj, you are an idiot. Sometimes, you're so *idiotic*.'

'You don't,' he observed, 'slip into Boots, the chemists, and ask to see the latest line in ponies ... or, do you?'

'Don't be an idiot, Roj.'

'I just don't know. That's all.'

'They'll be in the Yellow Pages.'

'Ponies?'

'Where to buy them. Somebody sells them. They'll be in the Yellow Pages.'

'Uhu. I suppose so.'

She moved; for the first time, she stopped watching the ceiling. She pushed the sheet and eiderdown towards the foot of the bed, sat up, took the hem of her flimsy nightdress and, in a single movement pulled it up, clear of her head, and tossed it on to the bedroom carpet. She was quite naked. She flopped back on to the pillow, bent her legs and assumed the classic position of copulation. She turned her head and smiled at Douranby.

'Roj,' she murmured.

'Very nice,' said Douranby, gently. Appreciatively.

'Make love to me, darling.'

'Did you take the pill?' he asked. 'We don't want...'

'I *always* take the pill, darling. In case of "emergencies".'

'Like this?' asked Douranby, with a tilt of an eyebrow.

He knew his wife. He knew her every mood. The mistake he made—the fundamental mistake which prevented it from being a complete and happy marriage—was in believing that 'knowledge' equated with 'love'. He made no move to leave his own bed but, instead, smiled at her near-animal eagerness. A smile which was both tender and mocking.

'*Roj!*' she whispered, urgently.

'A navvy?' he teased. 'A bureaucratic *navvy*? Charlotte, my love, your taste is slipping.'

'For God's sake, Roj!' The words were a breathless scream—soft, but imperative—and her whole body moved in tiny jerks, as she gasped, 'For God's *sake*. I want to have it off!'

The way she pronounced it, it should have been spelled 'Heave it awf'.

Wolff hoisted himself from the bed, jerked the cord of the 'shortie' dressing-gown tighter, and joined the man at the upper window of *Yew Tree Bower*.

'I think we eat,' he grunted.

'Sure.' The man at the window turned, to leave the bedroom, then asked, 'Anything special.'

'Coffee. Good coffee ... not the "instant" shit.'

'Sure.'

The man left the bedroom, and Wolff stayed by the window, watching the deserted, early-morning affluence of Robs Cully.

It was going to be a cinch. That, for sure. Back home—back in the States—it might have been less of a pushover. Not impossible, but less of a pushover. Back home, they had this thing about guns; every kid fancied himself as a top-class sharp-shooter. The fact that most of the finks couldn't hit a hog in a barrel didn't matter. They all had guns. Everybody! 'Licence to own' or 'licence to carry', every fink had a shooter. Even the street kids had zip-guns. Everybody!

But not over here.

Not even the cops.

Okay, down in the capital, some of the bulls rode around armed. Some, but not a lot. The bodyguard cops; armed and trained to hit what they aimed at.

But not up here; not in this hick corner of the U.K.

A few scatter-guns, maybe. Some of the farmers, around; could be they had some twelve-gauge shotguns and, maybe, a couple of two-two rook-rifles. But that was all.

But he figured he had more shooters here, in this fancy house—here, in *Yew Tree Bower*—than in all the rest of this gold plated dump with the stupid name. And not counting the guys housed-up in *The Hind's Head* place. And certainly not counting the guys who were coming in on the coach. Not counting them!

When they arrived—when things blew—this place would crap cubes of blue marble. *And* like it!

He smiled to himself. A smile which sat uneasily beneath the cold hardness of the eyes.

He murmured, 'Stick it, kid. You don't know it yet, but this is your last day.'

Barbara Pickering unlocked the rear door of the house called *Sunny Corner*. She used her own key. She let herself into the kitchen, and closed the door quietly, in order not to disturb her employers and took off first her hat, then her coat. She changed her shoes for the slippers she kept in the cupboard beneath the double-sink. She threaded her arms into the blue nylon overall-coat. Then she measured coffee into the percolator, added more water to its base container, then plugged in.

She padded around the kitchen, making preparations for her day's work and being careful not to make too much noise.

7 a.m....

Robert Hill swung his legs from the bed to the floor and felt, with his bare feet, for his slippers. He pushed his stiffened fingers through his hair, stood up from the bed and walked slowly from the bedroom, along the corridor and into the 'second bathroom'.

Why the hell have two bathrooms? I mean, for Christ's sake, *why*? Two bathrooms—four loos (two upstairs, two down)—and there was only himself and Jean. Just the two of them—no kids, no nothing—and two bloody bathrooms, and four bloody bogs!

Just the two of them, and six bedrooms, one lounge, one dining-room, one breakfast-room, one sun-lounge-cum-glass-sided-patio, one cloakroom, one study-cum-library, one 'sewing' room, two bloody bathrooms and four bloody bogs ... plus more heating, lighting, repair and rate bills than *that*!

Somebody was out of their tiny mind, and the name of that 'somebody' was Robert Hill, Esq.

He brushed his teeth, rinsed his mouth with some fancy, and expensive, mouth-wash Jean had been conned into buying, then wandered his way out of the 'second bathroom', along the corridor a few yards and into the 'second'—or, maybe it was the 'fourth' —toilet, in order to empty his bladder.

He aimed the stream of pee at the words 'Shanks of Glasgow' worked in tasteful blue lettering towards the rear, top of the W.C. basin. As always. It was a habit; a stupid, private, secret habit; it was, perhaps, a dirty habit. But, dirty or not, it didn't matter. It was *his* habit and something nobody knew about. To direct the thin jet of urine up the back of the basin—gradually and deliberately—and not to overshoot and make a pool on the carpet, and yet reach the words 'Shanks of Glasgow' before the pressure went.

A stupid, dirty habit.

Something, he supposed, he'd picked up as a kid. Like all dirty habits. Something he'd picked up in Leeds—in Hunslet—at Jack Lane School, with all the other kids of his generation. A row of them, in the school toilets, standing well back from the slate-slabbed stalls, legs planted firm and wide, bodies bent back at the waist and seeing who could piss farthest up the wall.

No—be damned for a tale!—kids of that age don't *have* dirty habits. They're not yet corrupted; they're still years too innocent. *Years* too innocent. They just do things—natural, young-animal things—and the adult world, which lost its innocence long since, and which is as corrupt as hell itself, decides that these things are 'dirty'. Because the decision-makers have forgotten, and the decision-makers don't know, that 'dirt' (like beauty) is in the eye of the beholder; that, to kids of that age, playing at who-can-piss-farthest-up-a-wall is just playing another game. Like football. Like cricket. Like conkers. Like all the other games of unsullied childhood.

Therefore his 'Shanks-of-Glasgow' game was ...

Christ Almighty, it was *stupid*!

That's all. Stupid, but harmless.

He shook himself and (again, as always) was reminded of that ancient joke he'd first heard (again) in those far off days. 'Newton's Law of Gravity'—it doesn't matter how long you shake it, the last drop will always go down the inside of your trouser leg.

Always!

He returned to the bathroom and ran water into the bath, while he shaved.

The tiny blades of the electric razor tickled the surface nerves of his cheeks and chin, his neck and his upper lip. The hint of grey stubble disappeared, and his face became smooth. More or less.

And that was another thing...

Electric razors. T.V. ads and Sunday supplements notwithstanding, an electric razor did *not* give a good shave. Did it hell as like! It took off the whiskers, but it didn't give the silk-smoothness of a good blade. A cut-throat, for example. Where the hell had all the cut-throats gone? The real blades, and the men who could handle them? The flip-flop, flip-flop of the steel on the leather strop. The sing—no exaggeration, you could actually hear the edge quietly *sing*—as it stroked the surface of tightened skin. And then, when you felt your cheeks. Smooth. 'As a baby's bottom' as they used to say. Like oiled silk. And you felt clean— polished—when you stood up from the chair.

But now—these days...

All this bloody money—a damn great house, two bathrooms and four bogs—and he couldn't even get a decent shave!

The bath was ready. He didn't have to test the temperature; elbows were out, the automatic thermostat made sure the bathwater was always at the right heat.

He turned off the tap, unplugged the razor, thumbed open the head and blew the hint of grey dust from the blades, closed the head and returned the razor to its wall-cabinet. He allowed his pyjama jacket and trousers to fall in a heap around his feet.

As he stepped towards the bath he caught a quick reflection of himself in the huge, tinted mirror which almost filled one wall of the bathroom.

Spindle-legged and pot-bellied (too much booze, too much food and not enough exercise); grey-haired, and going bald (too much worry, not enough relaxation and he was damned if he was going to wear a bloody wig); knobble-jointed and stoopshouldered (the arthritic curse of oncoming age and the pigheaded refusal to 'walk proud' and look like a blasted tailor's dummy).

But he could still take 'em. The fly-by-nights. The sharp-talkers and sharp-dressers. He could still prove (and in hard cash—the only proof worth a damn) that hard bargaining wasn't twisting; that good business meant being tough, but not heartless.

Those first few years.

Judas Christ!

That first hunk of Hunslet—his own midden—and he'd bought it, and everybody had said he was barmy. And, if that was being barmy, he only wished he could be officially certified. Then some more of Hunslet, then a piece of Holbeck, then Cross Flats, then into the posh district and Headingly. Then out of Leeds. Bradford. Huddersfield. Halifax. Wakefield. Harrogate. Then out of the county. Preston, St Annes and Blackpool. Darlington, Newcastle and Durham. Reading and Birmingham, Brighton and Margate, Hastings, Bath and Bristol. Everywhere!

He didn't *build* houses. Or offices. Or shops. He let other mugs build 'em then, when the market was right, *he* bought 'em. Then he rented 'em ... never sold. What he owned, he owned, and no bugger was going to tempt him to part. Bloody great lumps of England, and they were *his*. Freehold. Don't mess about with leasehold; leasehold meant nothing, but freehold meant forever. Forever. Unless, of course, the bastards at Whitehall played at 'compulsory purchase' ... and, by God, he'd had some rare old fights about that one, too.

But (compulsory purchase apart) what he had he owned, and what he owned he kept.

Not Rachmanism. The hell with Rachmanism; that was a mug's game. Property (like everything else) held its price whiever it was looked after. Held it, and increased it. Buy cheap, let it fall apart, and you end up by selling even cheaper. That wasn't business. That was being a bloody fool.

But, buy on a buyer's market, look after the place, choose your tenants, charge a good rent for good property, and that was *it*. The point came when you could sit back and pay other men to do the worrying for you. When bricks and mortar became a damn sight more stable than pound notes. When bank managers wanted to see *you*.

That was success.

From Hunslet to Robs Cully—from the outside 'lav', shared with three other families, to *Sunny Corner* with its four tiled and carpeted bogs—the hard way.

That was success.

As he stepped into the bath, he heard the post and newspapers arrive. He thought he heard Mrs Pickering pad across the hall to collect them.

He liked Mrs Pickering. A good woman. She gave a good day's work for a good day's wage, which made a nice change from a world over-stuffed with idle sods.

Wolff sipped coffee and smoked his first pipe of the day. He smoked an Italian pipe, with a leather cover around the bowl, and he smoked American pipe tobacco. To the Englishman's eyes, the tobacco looked wrong; it was in tiny, granular lumps and reminded him of breakfast cereal. It smelled wrong; it was aromatic, and the stink reminded him of the joss-stick stench of the old belly-dance dives.

The Englishman's name was Carter. Once upon a time, it had been *Major* Carter. Once upon a time. After he'd been court-martialled and cashiered his regiment had worked hard to forget Major Carter, but Major Carter had worked equally hard to forget both the court-martial and the cashiering. He was (he told people) a 'retired army officer', and some people believed him.

Wolff didn't.

Wolff growled, 'Hey, soldier-boy. I provide the bread, you provide the business. That way, we work together ... okay?'

Carter began, 'With well-disciplined troops...'

'My troops *are* well-disciplined,' interrupted Wolff. 'They are a damn sight better disciplined than any of the crappy bastards *you* ever ordered around. They step outa line, and ...' Wolff used the stem of his pipe to make a swift slashing gesture across the front of his throat. He said, 'That is the sorta discipline they understand. The sort they expect.'

'Yobs,' sneered Carter.

'Yeah ... yobs,' agreed Wolff, grimly. 'Mercenaries. That's what you'd call 'em ... right? Lemme tell you something, soldier-boy. They ain't in fancy uniform, but that don't mean a thing. They are the finest fighters ever to squeeze a trigger. They get paid good, they are expected to fight good. They are expected to die, if necessary ... and that, too, is okay by them. They do not need an "enemy". They do not need propaganda crap rammed up their ass-holes. Give them the dough, and they kill ... anybody!'

'Tearaways,' said Carter, contemptuously.

'Who do as they're told, first time of telling.' Wolff prodded the air with his pipe, leaned across the breakfast table and used a hard voice and hard words. He said, 'Lookee, soldier-boy. Lemme tell you just where you stand. I needed this place—this *Yew Tree Bower* dump—so I needed a front man. You. After that, you could screw yourself. Okay? But—okay—you sold me a certain idea. Maybe the finks who live in this place would listen to some guy who talked *their* language. Some smooth bastard who used big words to say big things. Maybe they'd listen, and see sense. Not that it matters, too much, but it might slide things along a little faster. Okay ... you earned yourself a position. But you take orders. You do not take over. You march in step, soldier-boy. And, if you keep in step, you take your dough. If not...' Wolff's lips moved into a slow, menacing smile. He growled, 'If not, *I* will not cut the tin pips from your shoulder, soldier-boy. I'll cut your goddam belly open, and spill your stinking guts all over the carpet. Okay?'

Carter moistened his lips, gave a single, quick nod, and said, 'Of course. Er—okay.'

'Great.' Wolff's smile stayed at his lips, but became mocking and contemptuous. He said, 'Eight-thirty ... right? You walk down to that *Hind's Head* joint, and you watch. The landlord takes his two kids off to school. You go inside, you let the boys there know. Then you stick around in case the landlady needs things explained in three-letter words. Okay?'

'A gun...'

'No guns,' interrupted Wolff. 'You don't need a gun. Just your mouth.'

'Damn it all, man! I'm to be trusted with a...'

'Johnny!'

Wolff bawled the name, as he half turned his head towards the door of the room. The door opened, and the man who had been watching at the upstairs window entered the breakfast-room. He was holding a Stirling sub-machine gun in his left hand. In his right hand he was holding a piece of oil-soiled cloth with which he was stroking the barrel of the weapon.

He said, 'Yeah?'

'Soldier-boy.' Wolff jerked his head towards Carter. 'Get him out of here. Feed the bum, and make sure he knows what he has to do. And he *don't* get a shooter ... okay?'

The man called Johnny said, 'Okay.' He motioned with the snout of the Stirling, and spoke to Carter. He said, 'Scrambled eggs in the kitchen, mac. Suppose the other guys have left any.'

Carter sighed. He held his temper and his contempt on a tight rein. He knew exactly what a Stirling S.M.G. could do. Exactly! He'd seen the end-result too many times. And he also knew that, at the word from Wolff, the man called Johnny would use the S.M.G. Without hesitation, and as off-handedly as normal men straighten their ties.

Carter stood up and walked from the room.

Wolff grunted, 'Fink!' and sipped some more coffee.

Henry Kempton whistled, as he lathered and showered. He was a good doctor, but a lousy musician; the tune was supposed to be *American Patrol* but, had his orchestra played so many bad notes, or changed key so often and so accidentally, Glen Miller (who originally made the piece a snippet of big-band history) would have either shot the band, or shot himself. Nevertheless, and even in its present tortured rendering, it was a happy piece of music, being whistled by a happy man.

Celia, his wife, joined him in the bathroom. She peeped around the shower-screen, grinned, and said, 'Holy cow! What a noise.'

'Wassat?'

'The noise.' Celia raised her voice a few decibels.

'Good music.' He moved around to let the jets take the last of the suds from his body. 'Best music ever. They don't play it, these days.'

She eyed him critically, and said, 'Hey there. You're getting skinnier every day.'

'Lean and hungry.' He turned off the shower and stepped from behind the screen. 'Fitness, little girl. It requires strong bones and hard muscles. Not fat.'

'And Daddy looks like something from a concentration camp.' She shrugged the bathrobe clear of her shoulders, tossed it on to a cork-bottomed chair, stepped under the shower and started the jets. She turned her back to him and, as she stooped for the soap, said, 'You should try to look like me.'

'Like you ... or *at* you?' He widened his eyes in an exaggerated ogle.

She straightened, returned an equally mock glare of disapproval, and said, 'Down Fido. I've a sneaking suspicion that *that's* what's making you lose weight.'

He towelled and she showered, as they talked. It was happy talk; married and contented talk. It was talk which meant little, except to themselves but which, to them, meant everything.

She said, 'What's today's programme, Dr Kildare?'

'Y'know. The usual. A couple of emergency operations. Save a handful of lives. Then—if I've time—make some major medical breakthrough.'

'Or?'

'Neurotic women and hypochondriacal men. As always.'

'Does anybody,' she asked, 'ever take you seriously?'

'They must do,' he admitted, cheerfully.

'I can't think why.'

'Look around you, child.' He towelled his back with a vigour which suggested an attempt at sawing himself in two. 'All this, and an occasional night on the tiles. And all paid for by private patients. We-ell ... most of it.'

'They must be mad.'

'I can assure you,' he said, solemnly, 'that *my* coloured sugar-water, and *my* glorified aspirins, are among the best in the country. If not in the world.'

She pulled a face, and the cascading water tumbled from her pouted lips and dribbled on to her chin.

He began to towel his hair, and said, 'There's a conference, this afternoon. Immediately after lunch.'

'Better aspirins? Different colour in the sugar-water?'

'I've been invited.'

'And why not? You being who you are, and what you are.'

'Some top-drawer German nut-cracker.'

'Stop it. You're making me envious.'

'Psychogalvanic reflexes ... no less.'

'Believe me, I'll be thinking of you ...'

'So, stuff it.'

'... every second. I'll probably end up with Charlotte, doing something ...'

'I'll tell 'em I have a fever, come home to collect you ...'

'... bloody stupid, as usual. But, believe me, I'll be thinking about ...'

'... then we can have a snack somewhere, then dinner at some sleazy strip-club.'

'... you every...' She stopped, pushed her head clear of the spray, and said, 'Come again?'

'A strip-joint.' He grinned at her from beneath the turban of the towel. 'Purely in the line of medical research, you understand.'

'Honest?'

'Mammiferous and pelvic observation, of a scientific nature.'

'Dinner and a night-club. *Honest?*'

'Honest,' he said, solemnly.

'There are times,' she said, happily, 'when I wonder why the hell I married you. Then something like this happens, and I know.'

'A strip-joint,' he reminded her.

'Great. So you like looking at boobs. Feed me well, and I'll sit around, drinking myself under the table, while you look at boobs.'

'And,' he said, dropping the towel, 'talking about boobs.'

The four men in the kitchen looked up as Carter and the man called Johnny entered. They said nothing. They merely lounged in various chairs, and looked. And yet, they spoke; they spoke with their eyes, and every eye sent the same message, loud and clear.

Hatred born of mistrust.

Carter was two things, as far as these men were concerned. He was a bastard who had once strutted around in uniform, therefore he was one of 'them'. He was also a bastard who happened to be a Limey, therefore he was a thing of suspect manhood.

The four men in the kitchen (and, come to that, the man called Johnny) were all of a kind. Sub-human. Animals. As they sat there, they reminded Carter of a quartet of big cats; tigers, relaxed but spring-steel ready to kill. Their eyes sent the message, but their eyes had no depths. Only surfaces. Hard, pitiless surfaces.

Carter suddenly realised that these men, and their kind, had oriental eyes. The shape was wrong; the shape of the eye was not the shape of the eastern eye. But the eye was the same. Without even the hint of human weakness; capable only of reflecting dislike and scorn. No love. No friendship. No trust. Such an eye could never translate that type of emotion into a look.

Oriental eyes in western men.

And every eye stared at him, and every eye sent the same cold message of hatred and mistrust.

The man called Johnny jerked his head in a tiny movement towards the Esse cooker. A percolator stood on one of its hotplates.

Johnny said, 'Coffee. It looks like the boys have finished the eggs.'

'That's quite all right.' Carter fought to hide his sudden fear. 'Coffee's fine. I'm not hungry.'

'Thirty after eight,' grunted Johnny. 'Check that end ... okay?'

'Yes. Er—okay,' muttered Carter.

The lawn of *Woodvine Manse* was dew-soaked. The moisture saturated Bill Elliott's slippers, worked its way through to his socks and was cooling to his feet.

Why *Woodvine*? Bill Elliott didn't know. He knew that plants grew in abundance in the garden; that they were everywhere and of many kinds. But he knew the woodvine was not one of them. Why *Manse*? Again, Bill Elliott didn't know. He knew the house had never been the home of a minister of religion. He knew it had been built for, and had been lived in by, himself, his son and his daughter-in-law. So, why *Manse*?

Why *Woodvine Manse*?

He'd often asked himself the question, stupid and pointless though the question might be.

His son Bill ('young Bill') had chosen the name, and had never given a reason. He hadn't been asked for a reason. He hadn't lived long enough to *be* asked.

And yet...

Despite the bereavement, within a fortnight of moving in, it wasn't an unhappy house. It wasn't 'the place where Bill died' ... even though he *had* died there. Maybe because they hadn't, at that time, lived in the place long enough for it to collect memories. Maybe because Bill wouldn't have wanted it to be an unhappy house. Bill had believed in happiness; those who 'live' and those who merely 'exist'. And Bill had been among the former. A little crazy; sometimes a little noisy, sometimes a little over-exuberant; sometimes drinking a little too much, sometimes driving a little too fast. He'd 'lived'.

But, no longer.

They'd moved into *Woodvine Manse* within a week of the pile-up. Elizabeth and himself. While Bill was still in hospital; linked up to plasma-bottles and deeply unconscious; smashed to hell and back, and with a Motor Manslaughter charge waiting for him when (if!) he recovered from his own injuries.

And—all right—they'd tried. They'd done their best. The surgeon had spoken the truth ('We aren't God, Mr Elliott.') but, for a short while, the truth had embittered him; the truth that their best wasn't quite good enough.

The unconsciousness had deepened into coma and, again, the words of the surgeon. 'Miracles. They sometimes happen, Mr Elliott. Every member of the medical profession can vouch for that.' (That was odd, too—the medical profession—the cold-blooded experts whose job it was to snatch life from death—the men and women who believed in the drugs and the scalpels—and, when the drugs and the scalpels didn't work, they fell back on religion—they fell back on God.)

So-o...

They'd brought Bill to *Woodvine Manse*. Not back to *Woodvine Manse*; he'd never seen the place, except in course of its erection. And they'd prayed for the miracle. Oh yes, they'd prayed. And on their knees, by the bedside. He and Elizabeth; the globe-trotting, teak-tough old reprobate, who'd made three fortunes and lost two, and the young wife who was now his daughter-in-law. They'd prayed, silently and for a long, long time.

But Old Man God must have been tuned in to another station at the time.

Twelve days after entering *Woodvine Manse* Bill went out of the coma, but at the wrong end. He died quietly and gently, and not at all like the way he'd lived.

But—another odd thing—there'd been a legacy. Bill had died but, in dying, he'd given them each a gift.

Elizabeth hadn't any family; no parents, no brothers or sister, no nothing. He, Bill Elliott, was also without kin; no wife, no brothers or sisters, no more kids (at least, none that he knew about).

But, when Bill died they *had*.

He had a daughter, and she had a father. Just like that! Like the throwing of a switch; like when you have the sights lined up and steady, plumb on that spot behind the shoulder muscle of a moose, and you know (you damn-well *know!*) that it's fresh steaks for supper. As certain as that—as absolutely sure as *that*—and without a single word being spoken, they became a two-person family.

So, maybe Old Man God had been half-listening, after all.

Bill Elliott shoved his hands deep into the pockets of his trousers and wandered back into the house.

Elizabeth had the breakfast ready.

She eyed his feet, disapprovingly, and said, 'You change your slippers, Pop.'

'Look, I'm not...'

'And your socks.'

'Hell's teeth. What's wet feet. I'm not gonna...'

'You are going to change your slippers, and change your socks,' she said, with finality. 'You're at an awkward age.'

He glared, and said, 'What the stink has age to do with it? What the stink sorta...'

'Change your slippers, change your socks. Then, come and enjoy your kippers.'

'Kippers?' His face brightened.

'Uhu ... after fresh socks and fresh slippers.'

'You're a minx, young lady. Y'know that?—you're a minx.' He chuckled, and added, 'A man couldn't ask for a more bitchy daughter.'

And, the way he said it, it was meant as the absolute compliment.

7 a.m. until 8.30 a.m....

Robs Cully emptied itself.

It was that sort of a village. Very few oldsters lived in Robs Cully; the houses were too big and the gardens were too sprawling; it needed a car, and the energy to drive comparatively long distances, in order to leave, and return to, the place. It was a young village, purpose-built and expensive, but tending towards gimmickry. It was a 'trendy' village, with energy to spare and money to spend. It catered for an income-bracket and a type and, whereas many middle-aged-to-elderly people were encompassed by that income-bracket, none but the young in heart could keep pace with, much less tolerate and understand, the type.

It was the sort of village Robs Cully had been built to become, and it was the sort of village it was.

The morning exodus lasted for more than an hour. The cars left the village, via the bridge, in a steady stream; good class cars; Jaguars easing themselves after the more expensive Austin models, Peugeots seeking road-space from Rovers, an Aston Martin and a couple of Mercs. The men took the big cars. The women used the runabouts; the Minis and the Simcas, the Triumphs and the Renaults. It was a two-car-family village, and the men had to go to work; and some of the women also worked, and others were hooked on the 'social' kick, and they left at about the same time; and the kids had to be taken to school, some by their fathers, en route to some office, others by their mothers who, having dropped the kids, returned towards the village.

It was a pattern. A daily emptying, and always at the same o'clock and, after the thickest wedge of motorised traffic had left the village, some of it began to make its way back, as mothers returned from taking their kids to school.

A pattern. Watched by professional men who knew how to watch such patterns; who had watched this particular pattern enough times to be certain of its weave; who knew that the best time to do what they planned to do was between eight-thirty and nine.

When Robs Cully was under-populated by men, over-populated by women, and ripe for a neat and temporary take-over.

8.30 a.m....

The thing started slowly, and without fuss, which is how all well-planned operations of a like kind start. The object was, eventually, to ring fire-bells, but the object was also to get things so far under way that, when the fire-bells started to ring, the blaze would be big enough to frizzle anybody foolish enough to try heroics.

Therefore, slowly and without fuss.

And at *The Hind's Head*.

The name above the door of Robs Cully's only pub read 'Rufus Aimes'. Rufus Aimes was the licence-holder. He was the man the brewery combine held responsible for the running of this, one of their star boozers, but everybody (including the brewery combine) knew damn well that *Flora* Aimes was the driving force behind the pub's success.

Flora Aimes was one of those rare people who can do the work of six normal folk, and still make it look easy. She didn't rush. She didn't fluster. She didn't shout. She just *did*. Everything! And (or so it seemed) all at the same time. Rufus, her husband, obeyed orders; he had gumption enough to recognise what he'd married, and gumption enough to know who knew best.

Flora ran *The Hind's Head*.

She did not believe in 'live-in' staff. They'd tried it twice and, both times, it had been a failure; for the first few weeks, fine—but gradually the 'live-in' member of staff had grown big ideas (one of them about Rufus, for God's sake!) and had deluded herself that *she*, and not Flora, was the dynamo which kept *The Hind's Head* running on oiled wheels. From then on, no more 'livers-in'. No, thank you! A cellar-man came each day, to give Rufus a hand at the daily task of getting the booze in a fit and proper state for consumption. A young twenty-year-old, who was ambitious and who had visions of becoming a West End chef, arrived at about three and helped with the preparation of whatever dinners were needed. The cellar-man took his place behind the bar each evening and, apart from these two men, everybody else was part-time; a handful of men and girls from Raine, all of whom were made to understand that their duties did *not* end at 'closing time'. They collected and washed the glasses, emptied the ash-trays, wiped down and polished the tables and the bar-counters and did a quick vac. job around the main rooms. Then (and *only* then) Rufus drove them back to their various homes in the shooting-brake. They were well paid, and they were expected to work hard, but nobody ever had the gall to complain because Flora worked twice, and three times, as hard as any of them ... and made it all look so damned easy!

Take this morning ...

Six breakfasts (ten, counting Rufus, herself and the two kids) cooked and served in a dining-room which was clean and tidy, and whose crockery, cutlery and table-linen couldn't be seriously faulted. And, at this moment, she was serving them (having cooked them) while Rufus whipped the kids off to school.

For the time of the year, six was a little unusual. At a squeeze, they could house eight, but that was expected only at the height of the holiday season. Three weeks—four weeks, at the most—around the latter end of July and the beginning of August. For the rest of the summer months it averaged out at something between two and three; keen anglers who knew about the Hewfraw and Skew Beck and (like most other anglers) kept their knowledge to themselves.

Six was a lot, for June, and four of them...

We-ell, fishermen came in all shapes and sizes, long and short, stubby and tall, but they all had a certain characteristic. 'Patience'. That was the only way to describe it. Slow-moving and deliberate. Not given to tantrums and obviously long-suffering. Fishermen were nice people, who had all the time in the world. It went with their sport, it showed in their eyes and it was their one common denominator.

But, four of *these* men...

They were Americans; that much was immediately apparent, whenever they spoke. They ordered 'scotch', and never 'whisky'; 'on the rocks' and never 'with ice'. They called the 'gents' the 'john'. They said 'yeah' instead of 'yes', and said it quite naturally and not (as sometimes happened when some young blood wanted to sound big) as a deliberate put-on. Once, she'd overheard one of them use the expression 'ass-hole'; not that the expression had shocked her at all, but it had sounded silly and prissy when compared with the average Englishman's full-blooded use of that same expression. The Englishman said '*arse*-hole' if, and when, he required the use of such an expressive vulgarism; Anglo-Saxon was his breed, and Anglo-Saxon was his language.

So-o...

All right, they were Americans, and Flora didn't have a complex either for, or against, Americans. And maybe this quartet was a bunch of Yanks visiting the U.K. on a round-the-country fishing trip. She didn't know. She hadn't asked, because it was none of her business. And not one of them had volunteered any information.

Which, again, was a little odd. Because, after a day's fishing, fishermen usually talked. They'd sat silent all day and, when they arrived back at *The Hind's Head* they uncorked all the pent-up conversation they'd denied themselves at the river bank. That was the normal way of things. Patient men, slow-moving men, bar-room-conversation men. That, in a nutshell, typified most anglers.

But not, it would seem, *American* anglers.

Carter strolled into the dining-room.

He smiled and said, 'Good morning, Flora,' and the way he

pronounced the name, it should have been spelled with an aspirate at its end.

'Major.' Flora returned the smile as she glanced up from where she was placing a plate of eggs, bacon, sausage and fried tomatoes before the fat man.

'Could you oblige me with coffee, my dear?' Carter strolled farther into the dining-room. 'If it's inconvenient, of course...'

'It's almost ready. Sit down, major, there'll be plenty for an extra cup.'

'I'm obliged, my dear.'

It was, of course, an act, but the act was so natural that it had long since stopped *being* an act and, instead, was genuine pseudo-reality. The 'my dear' bit; pronounced 'm'dear'. The ramrod back and the levelled eyes. There should have been a monocle, and there should have been a well-trimmed, toothbrush moustache. There was neither but, such was the completeness of the act, that the monocle and the toothbrush moustache were both there in spirit, if not in fact.

Carter pulled a chair away from the table and sat down facing the fat man and his skinny companion; the two non-Americans in the dining-room.

He drawled, 'You chaps don't mind, I hope.'

In a very amiable voice, the fat man said, 'Not at all, old son,' and, as he closed his mouth on the last word, popped in a forkful of egg and bacon and chewed away, happily.

Carter noted the two men, but without making a too obvious examination. He was of a generation which, as children, had read the boy's comic 'Chips' and these two reminded him of nothing so much as the two cartoon characters Weary Willie and Tired Tim; one of them beer-barrel fat, and the other beanstalk thin. Indeed, the fat man was more than *fat*, he was bordering upon the obese; his chins multiplied and increased rhythmically, as he chewed his food; his whole neck was a collar of blubber which seemed to drop from his bloated face, without the normal concave shape usual to a human neck; his apple-red cheeks bulged below his button-bright eyes and, above the eyes, there was little else but shiny skin. A few pathetic wisps of hair above and behind each ear but, apart from that, he was completely bald. His gut stuck out far enough to keep him at a slightly inconvenient distance from the table; he, virtually, had to reach forward with his podgy hands, before he could load the fork from the food on the plate.

And, as the fat man was fat, so the thin man was thin. Gaunt and hollow-cheeked; lantern-jawed and cavern-eyed; every cliche ever used to describe emaciation applied as far as the thin man was concerned. He looked like a stick-insect, and this despite the fact that he was shovelling food into his mouth with as much speed, and as much enjoyment, as his bloated companion.

They both wore open-necked shirts and unzipped windcheaters. Shirts of an eye-searing and floral design; shirts meant for 'with it' teenagers or (conversely) 'without it' middle-aged men who wanted to kid the world into forgetting the last ten, or twenty, years of living.

Stupid oafs, both—one thin, one fat—and, by no stretch of imagination, potential trouble.

Carter took a cigarette case from his pocket.

'D'you mind?' He raised a polite eyebrow as he asked the question.

'Nothathall,' muttered the fat man, through a barrier of half-chewed food.

The thin man swallowed, smiled, and said, 'When he's finished gorging himself, Lenny will light up and, whatever *your* cigarette smells like, what *he* smokes will make it positively aromatic. *And* he won't have the manners to ask.'

Carter murmured, 'Why not? I rather like the smell of pipe tobacco.'

'Cigars,' grunted the fat man.

'So-called,' added the thin man.

Carter chose a cigarette, snapped the case closed and returned it to his pocket. He took out a lighter, lighted the cigarette and was returning the lighter to its pocket when Flora arrived with the coffee.

She placed it on the table, in front of Carter.

Carter removed the cigarette from his mouth, and exhaled smoke, before he spoke.

He said, 'Flora, my dear. Listen very carefully to what I have to tell you. The men behind you—the four men, the four Americans—they each have an automatic pistol. Each pistol is loaded, and each man is prepared to use it. Given an excuse—any reason at all—and they'll shoot you.' Carter glanced at the fat man and the thin man, and added, 'And you. And you. Anybody!' He returned his attention to Flora, and ended, 'I don't want to see bloodshed, my dear. But they're desperate men, and they'll certainly commit murder ... and without giving it too much thought.'

Flora Aimes did not faint, or collapse, or have an attack of the vapours, or anything like that. She was not that type of a woman. She widened her eyes and, for a moment, disbelieved what she was hearing.

Carter saw the disbelief, and said, 'This is not some off-beat joke, my dear. I'm serious. Deadly serious. And so are they.'

Flora bent forward and rested the palms of her hands on the table top. She didn't *fall* forward but, nevertheless, the sudden weight, transmitted by her stiffened arms, made the coffee in Carter's cup move and slop a little over the lip.

Flora turned her head. Slowly.

The four Americans were seated at two tables. Each man had a gun in his hand; three of them were right-handed, and held their guns in that hand, and the fourth was left-handed. The guns (as Carter had said) were automatic pistols, square-shaped and deadly, and each pistol was held easily, but firmly; not aimed, but menacing. And the men who held the pistols looked as deadly, and as menacing, as their killing-tools as they watched Flora Aimes and waited for her reaction.

She turned to Carter, and gasped, 'Major, are you one of...'

'Take it easy, my dear,' soothed Carter. 'With sense—with a mere modicum of sense—nobody will get hurt.'

'Is this a...' Flora swallowed, controlled her voice, then said, 'Is this a robbery? Is that what you want? Is it a...'

'Not a robbery,' interrupted Carter, quietly.

'Then what *is* it? Why on earth are these men... Why on earth are *you*...'

'We—er—we require the use of *The Hind's Head* for a few hours. That's all.'

'I—I—I don't understand. I don't...'

Carter, always the perfect gentleman, stood up from his chair and held a hand to steady Flora Aimes.

He murmured, 'Sit down, my dear. Please sit down. It's not as bad—nothing like as bad—as it might look.'

Flora pulled her arms away from the touching hand but, nevertheless, lowered herself into the chair. She kept her head turned as she did so, as if fascinated—hypnotised—by the quartet of silent gunmen.

Then somebody burped. Very loudly.

It was incongruous. It was ludicrous. It was an 'in' joke from some black comedy. That, at this moment, with four obvious killers, four deadly weapons and four fingers hooked around four triggers ... and somebody was so utterly unimpressed as to find time to belch.

It was the fat man.

The tiny noise made two of the gunmen jerk their pistols into aim at the man who had made the noise then, for a sharded second of time, the two nervous gunmen looked crestfallen and returned their weapons to a relaxed, but ready, position.

'I beg your pardon, Mrs Aimes.' The fat man touched his lips with his napkin. He said, 'My wife would tell you ... I have the manners of a pig.'

And it was the last part of the remark which, in some subtle way, carried a message. Something more than the words themselves—something more than the apologetic tone in which they were spoken—but what that 'something' was Flora Aimes couldn't make out.

She couldn't make anything out.

She didn't *understand*!

She clenched her fists, moved her head from side to side as she looked at Carter, then at the four Americans, then back at Carter and, in a desperate voice, said, 'Look. What *is* this? What's going on?'

'Flora, my dear, you must...'

'I'm *not* "your dear", and I want to know what's...'

'These men are dangerous. Don't antagonise...'

'Don't be a bloody fool, Major Carter,' she snapped. 'This is my hotel—my home—and you expect me to keep calm when ...'

'Mrs Aimes, believe me. I know what...'

'All right! All right! You *know*. Now, tell *me*. Just what the hell's going *on*?'

'Tell her soldier-boy. It's why you're here.'

The newcomer stood, firm-footed at the door of the dining-room. He held a Stirling sub-machine gun at the 'ready' position. He spoke with authority and, without having to be told, Flora Aimes, the fat man and the thin man all knew that this one was at least one notch higher than the four gun-carriers, and quite a few notches higher than Carter.

The newcomer strolled into the room.

He drawled, 'Go ahead, soldier-boy. The dame, fatso and the skinny guy. They need to know. Convince 'em. Your way. Otherwise, we convince 'em our way.'

Wolff was bathed, shaved, talced, dressed and hair-oiled. He looked smart; New York smart, not London smart. The cut of the suit was just a *leetle* too snappy for the guardsman-style gent. The shoes were the wrong shade of brown. The shirt was nice—'conservative' nice—but the shape of the collar screamed 'transatlantic'. The tie was a dead giveaway; expensive, but unobtainable beyond the shoreline of the U.S.A.

Nevertheless, James Edward Wolff, Jnr looked (and felt) very smart.

He checked his wristwatch, and said, 'Okay. Johnny should have the *Hind's Head* dump wrapped up by this time. Any sign of the coach?'

The hood squinted out of the window, and said, 'Nope.'

They were still in the bedroom of *Yew Tree Bower*, but this time the window-watchman was a tall, slim hoodlum who carried a loaded shoulder-holster whose straps criss-crossed his white nylon shirt. He was without jacket, but not without hat; he was that sort of a man—he only removed his hat to bath and part his hair. He was a Texan—which was unusual, because the bad boys of the Sunflower State normally figure they don't need the hicks of New York to show them how to shoot straight—and he fancied himself as the poor man's Gary Cooper. That was the way he talked. 'Nopes' and 'Yeps' interspersed with an occasional nose-picking and the odd bum-scratching. Truth to tell he did, indeed, have a vague and superficial resemblance to the great 'Coop'; he had two arms, two legs, a body and a head ... but, beyond that point, the resemblance hit a brick wall.

Nevertheless, and because of his idiosyncrasies, this particular bad-smelling rose of Texas was known to his confederates as 'Cowboy'.

Wolff said, 'The other boys are ready ... right?'

'Yep.'

'And you have the bazooka thing ready?'

'Yep.'

'So, where the hell's the...'

'It's acommin',' interrupted Cowboy, in a real-live southern drawl.

'The coach?'

'Yep.'

'Great.' Wolff moved his shoulders, as if to settle the expensive jacket more easily on to his trunk, and said, 'Let's get rolling.'

Cowboy gave one last, 'Yep,' before turning from the window, collecting his coat from a chair and following his leader from the bedroom.

That was how it started. Slowly, and without fuss. That much, at least, to the credit of Wolff; that he could organise; that, given the lay-out, given a basic timetable, given a fifty-fifty share of luck plus men he could count on, Wolff could organise just about *anything*.

Even the invasion of a community.

The watchwords were 'simplicity' and 'ruthlessness'.

The mini-bus brought in the 'army' and the equipment. Ten hoodlums, plastic explosive, detonators, guns and ammunition. Including Carter, Wolff had twenty men, all ready willing and able. He had *The Hind's Head*. The next thing he wanted was the bridge; the link between Robs Cully and the rest of the world.

The bus slowed to a near-halt as it crossed the bridge. Two men jumped down and took with them plastic explosive, detonators, wire, and a battery. They scrambled down the bank and into the Hewfraw, waded through the tumbling waters and paused at each stanchion which held the road above the torrent. It wasn't hit-and-miss; they both knew the bridge and the structure of the bridge; they were both skilled men—engineers-cum-explosive-experts.

In five minutes, they were soaked to the skin but, in five minutes, they were climbing back up the bank, on the Robs Cully side of the river, and trailing wires linked carefully placed charges on each stanchion.

They ran the wires to the battery, which they'd left behind the slight shelter given by an elm. One of them thumbed the terminals loose while the other bared the ends of the wire by ripping it between his teeth.

One wire end was twisted around the negative terminal, there was a last quick glance to check that the bridge was empty of traffic, then the other wire was touched to the positive terminal.

And that was the end of a beautiful bridge.

There was surprisingly little noise; a muffled 'bwooph!' followed by the splash of great hunks of bridge hitting the surface of the Hewfraw. Top-class demolition boys don't go in for unnecessary pyrotechnics; they place their charges carefully, give a few chosen stress-points a little too *much* stress and let the sheer weight of the structure do the rest.

The bridge didn't 'blow up'. It shuddered slightly, then buckled; it almost lazily—in near-slow-motion—broke its own back and settled into the river.

One of the demolition men made a 'O' with the thumb and forefinger of his right hand.

The other murmured, 'Not bad. Not bad, at all.'

'C'mon. Let's find some dry clothes.'

They climbed the rest of the bank, then sprinted for the house called *Yew Tree Bower*.

Charlotte Douranby felt, rather than heard, the bridge go. *Conte Lauba* was not too far from the bridge, and the floor of the bedroom seemed to give a tiny, almost imperceptible hiccup.

Downstairs, the dogs set up a barking.

Charlotte was telephoning; she was the type of woman who spends a lot of time telephoning; the type of woman who, until the phone bill nudges the National Debt for size, doesn't count the Post Office as being worthy of serious consideration.

She was telephoning her friend, Celia Kempton and, until this moment, the subject matter had been ponies and the size, breed, colour and price thereof.

Charlotte said, 'What was that?'

'What?' Celia sounded surprised.

'That noise.'

'What noise? I didn't hear any...'

'No—not a noise ... not exactly a *noise*. Just that ... Damn those bloody dogs! They're kicking up hell's delight. I'll have to...'

Two things happened, at the same moment.

The phone went dead and the rear door bell sounded.

'I won't be a jiffy, Celia.'

Without realising it, Charlotte Douranby spoke into a dead telephone, placed the receiver alongside its rest, walked across the bedroom, unhooked a quilted dressing-gown from behind the door and, as she hurried downstairs, clothed her still-naked body in that one garment.

The Afghan hounds met her in the kitchen. They bounded and galloped around her, as they barked. Huge animals, but harmless; hunting dogs, spoiled and pampered by civilisation.

She said, 'Down Sheena. Down Shane,' but the dogs were, as usual, disobedient and danced around her all the more at the sound of her voice.

She opened the door, and the first man was inside before her senses had time to register either alarm or suspicion. He had a gun—a revolver—and the cylindrical extension to its snout was something Charlotte recognised from films and television plays.

It was the first silencer she'd ever seen. Come to that, it was the first *revolver* she'd ever seen.

She opened her mouth, took a deep breath but, before she could scream, the man spoke.

He snapped, 'Hold it, lady! Nice 'n easy—nice 'n softly ... then nobody gets hurt.'

The second man came into the kitchen, and closed the door behind him.

The dogs barked and bounded about at this unexpected presence of strangers. One of them ran at the man with the gun; it was not an attack—nobody in his right mind could have mistaken it for an attack—it was a friendly rush of canine exuberance.

The dog died.

The man with the silencered revolver tilted his weapon, and squeezed the trigger, twice. Twice, the revolver jerked in his hand. Twice, the silencer reduced the explosion to something less than the 'thup' of a tennis ball hitting the strings of a racket. And the dog was dead.

Charlotte stared at the crumpled, bleeding body of her pet; at the second Afghan hound, as it sniffed its puzzled stupidity at its dead companion. The shock hit her; it drained the blood from her face, glazed her eyes and made her whole body quiver.

She raised her head, glared at the man with the gun, and screamed, 'You bastard! You bast...'

The silencer landed across the side of her head and killed the last syllable, before it was uttered. Her legs bent first, then her body, and she sprawled, unconscious, alongside her slaughtered pet.

The second Afghan hound growled. Some instinct—some tiny

inheritance, from its past—identified this two-legged creature as an enemy. It growled, and bared its teeth.

It died, as quickly and as messily as its mate. Twice more, the revolver jerked in the man's fist. Twice more, the 'thup' was the only sound the weapon made. And the second beautiful animal gave a single, quick whine of pain, and was no more.

The gunman murmured, 'Goddam dogs.'

His companion said, 'We carry her?'

'We ain't hangin' around till she walks.'

'No. Just that...'

'What?' asked the gunman.

'Just that...' The gunman's companion nodded his head at the unconscious woman; at the opened dressing-gown. 'She ain't no clothes on, under that thing.'

'So?'

'Just that...'

'You never seen a piece of pussy before? Take a quick look... then look around for some car keys. We ain't gonna shoulder her all the way to the goddam gin palace.'

They were into the kitchen of *Sunny Corner* before either Robert Hill or Barbara Pickering realised they had visitors. The manner was the same, even though the men were different; smooth and practised. Open the door, step inside, level a gun and give a quick warning.

The man with the Colt automatic said, 'No hysterics, mac. That way, everybody stays happy.'

The second man was a youngster; handsome—*too* bloody handsome!—except for his close, bright-button eyes. He was grinning, and the grin was almost overflowing into a giggle. He was a combined homo-and-hophead, and Robert Hill recognised him, for what he was, at first glance. He'd seen too many, in his past life, ever to *not* recognise one immediately.

Babs Pickering gave a tiny squeak of terror and bit on to the knuckle of a forefinger.

Hill said, 'Don't get worried, Mrs Pickering. I know them.'

'Wassat?' The gunman eyed Hill, suspiciously.

'The type.' Hill curled his lip, and lowered his cup on to its saucer. 'Comedians. Like you, and the flower-boy you've brought along for moral support.'

The gunman grunted and something not too far removed from relief showed in his eyes.

The youngster's nostrils flared, and he jerked, visibly, as the insult hit him.

'Quieten it down, junior,' warned the gunman. He returned his attention to Hill, and said, 'There should be three.'

'Three what?' Hill played it dumb, if for no better reason than to show this duo of muscle-slingers that he didn't give a damn.

'Three *people*, mac,' said the gunman, softly.

'Where did you learn to count that far?' sneered Hill.

The gunman raised the snout of the Colt, squeezed, and the kitchen was filled with noise and falling plaster as the bullet smashed a hole through the ceiling.

Mrs Pickering rammed her knuckle hard into her mouth, to smother the near-scream.

'Three *people*,' repeated the gunman, gently. 'Let's keep it that many ... eh?'

Hill sighed, and said, 'My wife has her breakfast in bed.'

'Go fetch her, junior.'

'*No!*' Robert Hill pushed himself up from the table. The voice—the eyes, the whole expression—froze the gunman and the homo into momentary inactivity. Hill said, 'I'll go. She doesn't like strangers in her bedroom.'

'Look, mac. You wanna...'

'You start arguing with me, Yank, and you'll need more than a bloody gun,' snarled Hill. 'You—your kind—you're all vinegar and piss. Take the gun away, and the vinegar goes. I don't *need* a gun, bastard. I can take you ... you'd like to try me? You can empty the bloody shooter into me, as I come, and I'll *still* take you. Old as I am. I'll still live long enough to break your rotten neck.'

There was magnificence in the outburst. Suicidal magnificence, but not false magnificence. The gunman's eyes wavered. He knew —there wasn't a pinpoint of doubt on that knowledge—that Hill would try to carry out his threat ... and just *might*.

'Fetch her,' breathed the gunman, and this time he spoke to Hill. 'Don't try the phone. It's cut. Don't try anything fancy, else...'

He left the warning open-ended.

The youngster ended the warning for him.

He moved fast and smooth. He slipped the spring-knife from a hip pocket and, even as the blade shot from its housing, he stepped towards Babs Pickering, hooked an arm around her throat from behind and brought the needle-point of the knife to the side of her neck.

'Anything,' he said, with a grin, 'and she goes. Okay, tough guy?'

Babs Pickering looked as if she might faint.

'He won't harm you, Mrs Pickering,' said Hill, gently.

The youngster spat, 'Old man, if you think I'm...'

'He won't harm you,' rapped Hill. He stared into the youngster's eyes, and said, 'If he does—*anything*—I'll personally slice his balls off with that bloody knife of his, and stuff 'em up his arse so far they'll pop out of his nostrils.'

Hill turned his back on the two hoodlums and walked from the kitchen. He didn't hurry. He didn't *not* hurry. He walked at a normal, everyday speed, as if he was slipping into the hall to pick up the newspapers.

8.45 a.m....

The upstairs room of *The Hind's Head*.

It was a big room. Apart from the landing, toilets and two pokey little ante-rooms alongside the raised dais which was exaggeratedly known as 'the stage', the upstairs room stretched the length and breadth of *The Hind's Head* ground plan. It was known, officially as the 'Conference Room'; this, on the architect's plan, approved by the Licensing Justices when they granted permission for the original extensions. It had, at various times, been used *as* a conference room but, more often, as a room in which were held occasional dances and (once) a ratepayers' protest meeting.

It was equipped with chairs. Tubular-and-canvas chairs which, when not in use, were stacked in neat nests alongside the walls of the room.

The residents of Robs Cully were being brought to *The Hind's Head*, and were being shepherded into the 'Conference Room'.

The man called Johnny stood on the dais; an M.C. who kept order and decorum via the threat of a very ready Stirling S.M.G. The four 'fishermen' kept their backs to the walls, and their fingers around the triggers of their automatic pistols.

The residents, as they arrived, looked stunned, shocked, outraged, angry, disbelieving, terrified, worried or just plain numb—depending, not necessarily upon their age or sex, but upon their personal disposition.

The fat man and the thin man stood together, slightly apart from the rest, and to one side of the tiny stage.

The fat man figured that, at moments like this, the pasteboard scenery went for a burton, and what was behind the frontage was exposed for all to see.

They watched and, for most of the time, they were silent. But, spasmodically, they exchanged murmured remarks. Softly, and without lip-movement; their talk drowned by the rising hubbub as more people were gathered into the 'Conference Room'.

The thin man muttered, 'You know best, Lenny, but don't you think you should...'

'Leave it, Doc.' The fat man's eyes watched the people in the room as he interrupted. 'Let things ride at their own speed for a while. We don't yet know what the hell's happening.'

'You have a car?' asked the gunman.

Hill said, 'I have a car. Pinch it, and you'll be picked up before you've...'

'Just get it, mac.'

'You're bloody amateurs ... y'know that?' sneered Hill. 'You have one shooter, and one sticker, and you think you can lift property from some house. And you haven't even got a bloody...'

'It ain't a lift, mac,' said the gunman, in a flat voice.

'Eh?'

'Get them the car, Bob. For God's sake, get them the *car*.' Jean Hill was within touching distance of hysterics. She was a poor mate for a man like Robert Hill; a good wife, in all other respects but, at a time like this, a poor mate. Her voice rose a semi-tone, as she said, 'Bob, for God's sake! Don't—don't...'

'Easy, sweetheart,' soothed Hill. 'Don't let scum like this throw you.'

The youngster whispered, 'Old man, you're gonna go one step too far, and then...'

'Then I'll step on your neck, pansy-boy,' snapped Hill, 'and you'll wish you'd kept your bloody trap shut.'

'For God's sake! *Get them the car.*'

Jean Hill was tottering on the brink; despite the fact that she was fully clothed—that her husband had refused the two hoodlums even the urgency of not giving her time to dress properly—she shivered, as if an Arctic wind had caught her unawares. Her face was paper-white and her mouth twitched and writhed in an agony of nervousness and fear.

From where she was standing, with her back to the stainless steel sink with her hands gripping the cool, polished metal, Babs Pickering said, 'Don't be frightened, luv. Mr Hill's here.'

The elder woman spoke, as if to a child. Tenderly. Gently. And with absolute confidence in Robert Hill's ability to perform near-miracles.

'The car, mac,' said the gunman, harshly.

Hill nodded.

He moved towards the door, stopped, turned, then said, 'Keep that pansy well clear of 'em. Both of 'em. Anything—*anything*—and, I swear, you've seen your last sunrise.'

The youngster was going to say something.

The gunman shouted, '*Surrup!*', and the youngster closed his mouth and remained silent.

Hill smiled his contempt. He knew (and the gunman knew) that, Colt automatics notwithstanding—spring-knives notwithstanding—the biggest and the most dangerous man in the kitchen of *Sunny Corner* carried the name of Robert Hill.

The two men carried the unconscious woman into the 'Conference Room'. They dumped her, unceremoniously on to the polished floor. Everybody could see her nakedness beneath her unfastened dressing-gown, and everybody could see the ugly bruise at the side of her forehead, and the blood which seeped from the bruise and matted her dishevelled hair.

The rise and fall of voices stopped. There was a silence. It was as if, and for the first time, those present realised the full abomination of what was happening and the mad-dog mania of the men keeping them captive.

For a moment, a stout, middle-aged woman forgot her fear in the upsurge of her disgust.

She yelled, 'You disgusting *animals*. You foul, unspeakable *devils*.'

She ran forward, dropped to her knees alongside Charlotte Douranby, closed and smoothed the dressing-gown, tied the sash, then gently lifted Charlotte's head into the comparative comfort of her ample lap.

Flora Aimes joined the stout woman, and eased strands of hair from the stickiness of the blood-seeping bruise.

The thin man stepped towards the stage, and looked up at the man called Johnny.

He said, 'I'm a doctor.'

'So?' The man called Johnny seemed not to comprehend the remark.

'She needs attention,' said the thin man.

'Yeah ... maybe.'

'She'll have concussion. At least concussion.'

'Could be she asked for what she got, eh?' The man called Johnny lifted a sardonic eyebrow.

'Could be,' retorted the thin man, 'that you, too, will eventually get what *you're* asking for.'

'Could be,' agreed Johnny in a bored voice.

'Meanwhile, I'd like to see what I can do for her.'

'Be my guest, Doc.' Johnny moved his shoulders, indifferently. 'Just don't make anybody's trigger-finger itchy ... that's all.'

The thin man walked across the room, and joined the stout woman and Flora Aimes alongside the unconscious Charlotte Douranby.

The fat man stayed where he was, and continued to watch.

Rufus Aimes brought the shooting-brake to a halt and stared through the windscreen at what had once been a bridge; at what had, thirty minutes previously, been a very *good* bridge but at what was now a broken-backed and drunkenly tilted mass of concrete, tarmac and twisted steel.

He said, 'What the bloody hell!'

Aimes climbed from the shooting-brake and walked to where the first fracture of the bridge dropped into the foaming flow of the Hewfraw. He raised his head, and saw two men on the other side of the river. They stood, like himself, near the point where the road ended and the bridge *wasn't*. They were watching him —almost as if they'd been waiting for him—but he didn't recognise them. He knew everybody in Robs Cully, and most of the people who lived in Raine, but he didn't recognise these two men.

He cupped his hands to his mouth and called, 'What the hell's happened?'

'You from these parts, friend?' yelled one of the men.

'Aye. *The Hind's Head.* I'm the landlord. What the hell's happened, here?'

'Beat it,' yelled the stranger.

'What's that?'

'Blow.'

Aimes lowered his hands and frowned in puzzlement. It didn't make sense. I mean—what the hell—a perfectly good road bridge, shattered ... just like *that*! It wasn't as if it had rained. Y'know—a cloudburst ... summat like that. A couple of times—a couple of years ago, now—there'd been a freak storm, and the bloody Hewfraw ... Christ! It had gone mad. It had gone bloody *mad*. And people had wondered—y'know ... *wondered*. Whether the bridge might go. It was taking such an almighty hammering. Water—y'know, solid water—hitting the uprights at hell knows what speed. And people had wondered, for a few hours. Whether the bridge could take it. But—well—there hadn't *been* a cloudburst. Or a freak storm. Or owt! So, why the hell ...

'You gonna blow, friend?'

Aimes snatched his mind from speculation, and looked across the river

'Shove,' yelled the stranger.

Aimes cupped his hands to his mouth again, and bawled, 'Don't be bloody idiots, I *live* here.'

The answer he received was more than a little stupefying.

The second stranger (the one who hadn't spoken) put his right hand behind the left lapel of his jacket and produced a gun. A revolver. He crooked his left arm for a rest, raised the revolver, rested its snout against his bent elbow, squinted along the sights and fired.

Twice.

The first bullet hammered a hole through the radiator of the shooting-brake and, from the immediate and resultant noise, did terrible things to the engine. The second bullet shattered the windscreen, before it also shattered the rear window.

'Get it?' bawled the talkative stranger. 'Now, blow ... else you get the same.'

Rufus Aimes 'blew' ... fast!

He stayed just long enough for his jaw to drop, as he saw what had happened to his shooting-brake, then he turned and ran. He wanted to reach Raine, and as soon as possible. He wanted the village policeman.

They had some slight trouble at *Woodvine Manse*. Bill Elliott did not play by the rules; indeed, and on the face of things, Bill Elliott didn't even *know* the rules ... that, or he made his own rules up as he went along.

Bill was enjoying the last of his kippers, as Cowboy, accompanied by a tearaway with (of all things) a worried expression in his eyes, opened the kitchen door and entered.

Cowboy waved his revolver, and drawled, 'Reach!'

Bill Elliott looked up from his kippers, put on an expression of mild surprise, and came back with, 'Go shit yourself.'

Which (and by any rule-book) was all *wrong*.

Tearaway Number Two looked nonplussed. This was something they hadn't mentioned when he'd learned all about how to be a tough baby, in the exercise yards of various state penitentiaries.

Cowboy picked his nose, meditatively, with his free hand, waggled the revolver menacingly, and said, 'I ain't foolin', old timer.'

'Hang about.' Bill Elliott loaded the last of the kippers on to his fork, popped the morsel into his mouth and chewed as he spoke. 'Just let me finish this meal, and I'll give you "old timer". I'll land my boot up your arse-hole, five lace-holes deep.'

'Lookee ...'

'And if it's family jewels you're after, you're out of luck.'

'We ain't ...'

'Any diamonds you come across, let me know. We'll split, fifty-fifty.'

Tearaway Number Two began, 'Hey, Cowboy, shouldn't we oughta ...' but didn't have time to finish the question, it being damn near impossible to speak with a faceful of frying pan.

Bill Elliott said, 'That's my girl,' and, at the same time gripped the table, stood up and threw the table, contents and all, at the man with the gun.

Strictly speaking, it had been easy. Strictly speaking, these two particular hoodlums should have been carrying umbrellas, rather than firearms; they hadn't the brains to come in out of the rain.

Bill Elliott had deliberately riveted their attention; he had fascinated them into not noticing the presence of Elizabeth who, when they'd first entered the kitchen, had been shielded by the open door. Elizabeth (who could also juggle two and two until the answer was four) had stayed quiet and moved slowly; had stretched out a careful hand to reach the recently used frying pan, from the cooker. Then, she'd moved faster than she'd ever moved in her life.

And not once—not by so much as a flicker of an eyelash—had Bill Elliott signalled her presence.

Easy ... when you put it that way.

But (damn it all!) the two hoodlums were supposed to be *pros*!

For a few moments they learned how far short of perfection they were, the hard way.

Elliott followed the table and, as the pride of Texas staggered backwards, Elliott scooped up a chair and swung it in a sideways swipe. The revolver exploded and a Willow Pattern plate, propped on the shelf of a Welsh dresser at the far end of the kitchen, shattered. Elliott miscalculated slightly and, instead of clouting Cowboy with the edge of the chair's bottom, he hit him with the legs of the chair; it still hurt, and it still made Cowboy bawl like one of his home state's bulls, but it didn't down him. It knocked him sideways and, because it knocked him sideways, without putting him to sleep, Elliott lost the war.

Elizabeth was still belting hell out of Tearaway Number Two with the frying pan when, for a second time, Cowboy's six-shooter did what it had been built to do. It fired a bullet.

Nobody was aiming. Nobody was even deliberately squeezing the trigger. All that happened was that Cowboy windmilled his arms to keep himself upright, having stopped the legs of the chair with the side of his head, and his fingers contracted. And one of those fingers was around the trigger of the gun.

Elizabeth howled, jerked backwards, dropped the frying pan, spat out a very naughty and very unladylike word and clutched at her left shoulder. And, even as she did so, the blood trickled through and made scarlet rivulets across the back of her fingers, before dripping on to the lino-tiled floor.

Bill Elliott stopped the chair, midway through its return swing.

He snarled, 'You purple-pissing, Yankee bastard!' and gave his full attention to the wounded woman. He put his arm around her waist, eased the bloody fingers from her shoulder, and said,

'It's okay, honey. It's not too serious. It's too high up to be...'

'Why the hell,' she snapped, 'aren't you kicking the living stink out of these two germs?'

'Honey, you're...'

'You're an old fool,' she blazed. 'You're a stupid old...' Then, and because she was a woman, and when the shock came with a rush and buried the anger, she suddenly pushed her face into Bill Elliott's neck and jerked her whole body as she fought the sobs.

He held her, and repeated, 'You're okay, honey. You're okay, honey,' quietly; like a soft-spoken rote which would take away the pain and banish the misery.

The two hoodlums got themselves reorganised. Cowboy kicked away the table, rubbed the side of his face and gripped the gun more firmly. Tearaway Number Two wiped his mouth with the back of his hand, and the worried expression returned to his face when he saw the amount of gore he was leaking from a smashed nose and a belted mouth.

Something not too far removed from admiration lighted Cowboy's eyes as he looked at Elliott.

He drawled, 'Old timer, you sure have spunk. I ain't gonna blame you none for what you...'

'Why don't you stuff it,' said Bill Elliott, wearily. 'Take what you want. What you can find. Then just shove off. I have to phone for an ambulance, and...'

'That ain't possible, old timer.'

'Not possible. Why the...'

'Nope.'

'Why the hell *not*?'

'We cut the cables.'

'Oh, Jesus!' sighed Elliott.

'That's okay, Dad.' Elizabeth raised her face, and sniffed. She tried a wry smile for size, then said, 'I'll live.'

'Of course you'll live, but...'

'Sorry, pop. We ain't here to lift things.' And the truth was that Cowboy really *sounded* sorry. 'We're under orders, see?'

'Orders?' Bill Elliott frowned.

'Yep.'

'Whose bloody orders?'

'That ain't for me to say, old timer. Just that we pick you up, and deliver you to *The Hind's Head* saloon.'

'Us?'

'Yep.' Cowboy nodded.

'*Us?*'

'Yep.'

'Why the hell *us*?'

'Pop.' Cowboy tried to drive sense into this old bonehead who had the stubbornness of a Texan mule. He said, 'Believe me, I ain't allowed to say. Just that I deliver you, or plug you. And I mean dead, pop. You and the lady. I ain't saying I'm gonna enjoy doin' it. But I *am* saying I sure will, if I have to.'

'You're crazy,' growled Elliott.

'Nope,' said Cowboy. 'Just doin' what I'm here to do. That's all.'

'She needs a doctor, you crazy bastard. Can't you see she ...'

'Yep,' agreed Cowboy.

'So, why the hell can't we ...'

'We ain't raisin' hands on the deal, old timer.' Cowboy lined the revolver on to Bill and Elizabeth Elliott. He didn't look happy, but he looked determined. He said, 'I reckon there'll be bandages there. Somethin'. Like she says, she ain't dyin'.' He sighed, then ended, 'Lookee, pop, don't make me shoot a lady. It ain't somethin' I've a mind to do ... but I sure as hell *will*.'

Tearaway Number Two continued to mop blood from his nose and mouth. He used his hand and, periodically, flicked crimson droplets from his fingers. His face looked like something from a 'B' class horror film; horrible enough to bring on the giggles.

Bill Elliott turned to Elizabeth, and said, 'How about it, honey? Do we capitulate? Or does I sling these two goons out of the window?'

There was rough-hewn gentleness in the question. But it was a very serious question. It was asked in a voice, and by a man who, as Elizabeth well knew, would happily end his life charging his way towards an impossible goal for the sake of sheer cussedness.

'Neither.' Elizabeth raised the wry smile for a second time. 'Let's call a temporary truce, then belt their brains out when they're not looking.'

'Okay.' Elliott nodded solemn agreement. He turned to Cowboy and said, 'She's not walking. I'll get the car.'

'Yep.'

'And take that finger off the trigger. We have a truce ... at least till we reach *The Hind's Head.*'

Cowboy said, 'Yep,' and lowered the revolver.

And (for the sake of those who do not savvy such matters) there was nothing either stupid, or incongruous, about the lowering of the gun. Cowboy trusted Elliott, knowing that Elliott would honour that trust.

Not that everybody was like Bill and Elizabeth Elliott.

The 'Conference Room' was becoming, if not crowded, at least far from empty, and a woman was screaming. Tiny, meaningless screams which came with each exhalation of breath; kittenish meows of terrified and mindless panic, reminiscent of a bow being drawn lightly across the same violin string over, and over again. Never-ending. Nerve-nagging. And, in a subtle and insidious way, contagious.

She stood with her back to the wood-panelled wall, arms limp by her side, eyes glazed and unseeing and mouth slack and half-open. And the whimpering screams came, with every breath, and she was both deaf and blind to the entreaties of a grey-haired man, in pyjamas and dressing-gown, who pleaded with her to pull herself together.

The fat man watched the tableau, and scowled his worry.

He strolled nearer to the tiny platform, and raised a podgy-fingered hand to attract the attention of the man called Johnny.

'Yeah?' asked Johnny.

The fat man glanced at the screaming woman, and said, 'She'll start a riot, old son.'

'Uh?' Johnny looked suspicious and puzzled.

'It spreads,' explained the fat man. 'It's making everybody jumpy.'

'So?'

'If they all jump at the same time...' The fat man didn't bother to end the sentence.

'Somebody gets hurt,' growled Johnny.

'Somebody,' agreed the fat man. 'But they outnumber you. And by more than a few. You can't shoot 'em all with one bullet, son. One of 'em might grab a gun. Then somebody *else* might get hurt.'

'Who's side are you on, fatso?' asked Johnny suspiciously.

'Gumption,' said the fat man, quietly.

'Uh?'

The fat man said, 'It might be me who stops the wrong bullet. It might even be *you*.'

Johnny grinned, knowingly. He said, 'You're a wise kid, fatso. You value that fat hide of yours. You have sense.'

'Gumption,' repeated the fat man.

'Hey!' Johnny shouted across to one of the gunmen who had masqueraded as 'fishermen'. He motioned the snout of the Stirling towards the screaming woman, and called, 'Cork her ... right?'

The gunman strolled across the room. He grabbed the grey-haired man by the collar of the dressing-gown and sent him sprawling on the polished floorboards. He stopped directly in front of the screaming woman, and stared into her terrified face for a moment.

'Shaddap!' he bawled.

The woman's eyes came slightly into focus and widened even further. The tiny, frightened-animal screams continued.

'Cork her,' said Johnny.

The gunman nodded, without taking his eyes from the terrified woman's face. And still the whimpering screams came, with every breath.

The gunman raised his automatic. Deliberately. Slowly. Until it was pointing directly at the woman's face; until she was staring at its single eye, from a distance of less than twelve inches.

The gunman purred, 'The man said cork you. So, here it comes.'

He squeezed the trigger slowly enough for her to watch the movement.

The automatic exploded and, a split-second before the crash of the explosion, the gunman turned the gun slightly and the bullet smashed into the woodwork of the wall-panelling. The rush of air from the passing bullet plucked a lock of hair out of place alongside the woman's ear.

The woman stopped screaming.

She passed out and folded into an untidy huddle in the angle of the floor and the wall.

'Okay?' asked Johnny.

'Eh?' The fat man suddenly realised that he had been asked a question.

'Figure we're okay now, fatso?' Johnny curled his mouth into a sardonic smile.

'It was *one* way,' growled the fat man, drily.

8.45 a.m. until 9.30 a.m. ...

There is a saying, 'You can get used to owt.' The 'you' meaning the human animal, and the 'owt' being just that. Owt ... even being held captive in the 'Conference Room' of *The Hind's Head*.

The start-gun had been fired at seven o'clock, when Carter and Johnny had set out for *The Hind's Head*, from the house called *Yew Tree Bower* and, from then on, via the take-over of the hotel, the blowing of the bridge and the herding together of the inhabitants of Robs Cully in the 'Conference Room' the operation had gone like clockwork. A little muscle, maybe. A few guns fired. A swift smack across the kisser, if all else failed. But, what the hell! ... to kidnap a village (a whole *village*, even a village as small as Robs Cully) was no cheap crap throw.

And to pull it in two hours thirty—from nothing to the jackpot—took size. *Real* size.

Wolff—a man who did not please easily—was pleased.

The fat man—the man who was, in some odd way, an enigma within the captive community—was also pleased, but for a different reason. He was pleased because the half-hundred people, or so, were rapidly accepting an outrageous situation; they were 'getting used to it'; their initial fury was cooling to controlled anger—the terror was quietening to trepidation—they were beginning to accept the 'impossible' as a temporary, but inconvenient norm.

It pleased the fat man. It meant that fewer people were likely to make a quick grab for posthumous glory. Life was becoming a little quieter—a little less hectic ... and the fat man was a great believer in a quiet life.

There had, of course, been moments.

When they had dumped the near-naked, unconscious Charlotte Douranby on the floor of the 'Conference Room'; when, in their sudden indignation, the stout woman and Flora Aimes had ignored guns and tough guys, and hurried to give aid to the injured newcomer.

When the quintet of three men and two women had arrived; the slightly jumpy hoodlum and his effeminate pal, the fully clothed, frightened but more-or-less composed woman with her chunky, elderly and obviously less affluent companion, and the man with 'boss' stamped across his every movement.

The man had walked up to the dais and, with ice in his voice, had snapped, 'Tell me, are you the big fart in this general stink-up?'

Johnny had tilted the Stirling until it was lined up on the man's chest.

He'd drawled, 'Cool it, mac. Get back with the rest.'

The man had ignored the sub-machine gun; had apparently not even noticed it.

He'd rasped, 'My name's Hill. Remember it, germ. Remember it well. When you're dying, remember I'm the bloke who's going to spit on your coffin.'

Maybe (just *maybe*!) and for an eye-blink of time, some of the certainty had left Johnny's eyes.

Then he growled, 'Get back with the crowd, mac. I ain't gonna say anything twice.'

Hill had smiled.

Such a slow and confident smile. The smile of somebody who has weighed the odds, and knows he can't lose; the smile of the shark who has just spotted an unarmed and drowning man. That had been the nature of Hill's smile.

Then he'd turned, paused and, for a full two seconds, had deliberately exposed the broad of his back to the Stirling's muzzle. It had been a gesture. A deliberate insult to the potential power of death itself.

Then Hill had strolled across the room to join the two women with whom he'd arrived.

That had been one of the moments; a moment seen, and tabulated by the fat man; a moment from which an assessment could be made.

And the moment when Flora Aimes's temper had flared.

She and the stout woman had been knelt, fussing around the still unconscious Charlotte Douranby. The thin man—the doctor—was making a gentle examination of the head wound.

Carter—'Major' Carter—had joined the group. He'd gazed down at the unconscious woman for a moment.

Then he'd murmured. 'If there's anything I can do...'

'Oh, yes. There is.' Flora Aimes had straightened from her crouched position. She'd stood, feet wide and nicely balanced, and less than twenty-four inches from the half-smiling Carter.

Then, she'd said, 'As a very personal favour, you *could* do something.'

'Yes, my dear. What?'

'Drop dead.'

And, as she'd said it she'd hit him.

Okay—women can't *hit* ... they can only slap and claw. But this one could. She was fit and healthy, and in the very prime of her life, and she was roaring angry. She had just about everything going for her.

The clenched-fist roundhouse she'd brought up from waist-level had carried every last ounce of meat on her whole body. And—equally important—Carter hadn't been expecting it.

But he'd known all about its arrival!

It had landed flush across his mouth—bang on to his still-smiling lips—in a sideways slash which had knocked the smile into outer space, skinned the lips, sprayed blood and loosened a couple of front teeth.

Carter had staggered back and clapped a hand to his mouth.

Then Flora Aimes had raised her voice, and had spoken to all the people in the 'Conference Room'.

She'd said, 'Most of you don't know ... so listen. This animal—this "Major Carter"—is one of *them*. He's on their side. He's one reason why we're all here. Because *he* let them in. Remember that. Everybody! "Major Carter" from *Yew Tree Bower*. When this thing's over—whatever it is—don't forget to tell the police. Tell them *that*, first of all.'

From the dais, Johnny had said, 'Hey, lady. Back to the Florence Nightingale kick ... eh?'

Then Flora had looked at Johnny, and said, 'Just one thing, Mr Hero. A thing you'd do well to remember. I don't know who *you* are. I don't think any of us know who *you* are. But we all know Carter. And *he* knows who you people are.'

A sound had risen and died away, at her words. A soft hum; beyond true description, but a little like the noise made by a dynamo, switched on then immediately switched off.

The fat man had seen and witnessed the incident. Had heard the rise and fall of the sound. And the fat man had known that Flora Aimes had sentenced 'Major Carter' to death, merely by her words to the man called Johnny. The importance of what she'd said—the necessity for the certainty of his silence—was there, and the fat man had seen it reflected in Johnny's face. The fat man had wondered whether Flora Aimes realised what she'd done ... and had decided that Flora Aimes knew *exactly* what she'd done.

And that, too, had been a moment; one more moment seen and noted by the fat man; one more item upon which to base a future assessment.

It was during this period (between 8.45 a.m. and 9.30 a.m.) when the police first learned of what was happening in Robs Cully.

'The police', in the person of Police Constable 2728 Wallace Clemens.

Clemens was a village flatfoot but, despite this, he was no 'P.C. Plod'. He was a village copper for the best reason on God's earth. Because he *liked* being a village copper. Ask him, and he'd have told you; the village bobby carried more immediate weight than the chief constable. In *his* neck of the woods, he *was* the chief constable. Other coppers didn't count. Four villages, Raine, Robs Cully, Low Barkley and Frinton—plus all the farms and dribs and drabs of cottages and hamlets between—and they were all *his*. From murder to riding a bike without a rear light; from High Treason to dogs fouling the footpath. Everything! And the decision was his, whether to 'caution', report for summons or arrest. He worked what, in police lingo, was known as 'a discretionary beat'; which was one way of saying that, as long as he drove around in his mini van and/or was officially at the beck and call of the public, and at the receiving end of radio waves eight hours out of each twenty-four, *he* could decide which eight hours might serve best purpose.

(In point of fact, of course, Clemens—like every other fuzzman—was on tap twenty-four hours out of every twenty-four and, when he thought about it, counted this major inconvenience as part of the job, and one of the 'hidden perquisites' which solemnfaced ladies and gentlemen conveniently forgot, whenever they were called upon to evaluate the cost, in mundane pounds and pence, of a moderately efficient Police Service.)

However...

P.C. Clemens was a happy man. And why not? He was a born copper. He had beef, but didn't sling it around until, and unless, all else failed. He used his mind, before he used his mouth. He chose his friends carefully. Without being slow, he gave the impression of deliberate and considered movement. He knew when to listen, when to stop listening and when to tell the other bloke to shove it.

He listened to Rufus Aimes and, at the same time, donned his uniform tunic and slipped his feet into shoes.

Then he chipped in, with, 'The bridge gone?'

Rufus agreed that the bridge had 'gone'.

'And a couple of men, on the Robs Cully side, taking pot-shots at you with a handgun?'

Again, Rufus Aimes couldn't argue with the summary.

'Right.' Clemens walked to the telephone, dialled a number and spoke into the receiver. He said, 'Raine Beat here, sergeant. A complaint. The bridge across the Hewfraw's collapsed, and there's a chap here—Rufus Aimes, landlord of *The Hind's Head* —tells me some men are shooting at him from the Robs Cully side of the river. I'm on my way. I'll radio the details in, when I have them. Time the complaint at—er—let's see... ten past nine.'

Just like that.

The official jump-off for one of the most hair-raising episodes in the history of the force, timed at 09.10 hours ... as off-handedly as *that*.

There had also been the moment when Cowboy, Tearaway Number Two and Bill Elliott had helped Elizabeth Elliott into the 'Conference Room'.

Comedy. A little black around the edges, perhaps. But comedy, nevertheless.

The cloth at the girl's shoulder was blood-soaked and her face was pale; but the pallor was from pain, and not from fear. Tearaway Number Two looked a little like a refugee from an abattoir; his face wore a mask of drying gore, and the gore had spilled down the front of his shirt and his jacket. Cowboy limped slightly, from where the table had belted his shin and, moreover, his revolver was back in its shoulder-holster.

That had been the group which had staggered into the 'Conference Room'. Plus, of course, Bill Elliott. And, whatever else, Bill Elliott hadn't staggered. He'd left Cowboy and Tearaway Number Two to guide and assist Elizabeth into the room.

Johnny had stared, then barked, 'What the stinking Christ...'

'It's okay.' Cowboy had grinned, a little sheepishly, then added,

'It's okay, Johnny. We grabbed a wildcat by the whiskers ... that's all.'

'A wildcat?' Johnny's mouth had curled into contempt.

'Yep.'

'An old soak like ...'

'If you really *want* to know what your teeth taste like,' Bill Elliott had roared. 'If you'd really *like* to swallow a few pints of your own blood...'

'Cool it.' Johnny had used his Stirling S.M.G. argument.

'Nope.' Cowboy had done a slow, sad shake of the head. 'He don't scare, Johnny. He don't have the sense to scare.'

And the fat man had walked across to Elliott, and positioned himself between the Stirling and the fuming man who did not have the 'sense' to be afraid.

'Easy, old son,' the fat man had murmured. 'Just for a while... eh?'

'Who the hell...' Bill Elliott had begun.

'Just for a while,' the fat man had repeated.

'If you think...'

'I think that—for the moment—*they* have the edge. They have guns, and real bullets.'

'It won't be the first bloody...'

'For you, maybe not.' The fat man's murmured whisper had carried life-or-death urgency. 'But for other people. Think about *them*. Shorten the odds a bit ... that's all I'm asking.'

Bill Elliott had snorted; not a snort of defeat, but a snort of angry acceptance of a good argument.

He'd turned and walked to where Elizabeth was sitting on one of the chairs, leaning forward and holding her shoulder.

He said, 'How is it, honey? Bad?'

'Pretty painful.'

The thin man had joined them, and said, 'D'you mind? I'm a doctor.'

'Thank Christ for small mercies.'

Elizabeth had asked, 'Look ... do you know what's *happening*?'

'No.' The thin man had shaken his head. 'Just that these people aren't bluffing. Whatever it is, it's serious. Now ... let's have a look at that shoulder.'

And Elliott had muttered, 'They don't know *how* bloody serious. So help me! Give me one chance—just *one* chance—and I'll have some bugger's liver served up with fried onions.'

And this, too, had been an episode—a moment—from which the fat man had built possible schemes, and made calculated assumptions.

By 9.25 a.m. they were all in the 'Conference Room'. The frightened and the angry—the fatalistic and the outraged—they'd all been gathered in from their fancy houses in Robs Cully, and the car park around *The Hind's Head* was well filled with cars.

Johnny still held the tiny stage, with the Stirling S.M.G., but the watching gunmen, around the walls, had now been doubled. Eight gunsels, each watching for the first sign of revolt; each expecting some sort of trouble, and each ready to send bullets into whichever person started that trouble.

And the odd thing was that the captives were getting used to the situation.

Crazy?

Anybody who knows human nature would not ask the question. Only so many tears can be shed, only so many cuss-words can be used. After that comes a form of acceptance. Apathy, if you like. Numbness, if you will. A philosophical acceptance of something which can't be changed.

And especially is this so with the middle and upper-middle classes. Unlike the poor, who have nothing to lose—who rebel and keep rebelling, and who pin their future to the promises of anarchists—the middle and upper-middle classes complain, grow angry, become frightened ... then shrug their shoulders, and stop worrying.

It goes with the life-style.

And that life-style was what Robs Cully was all about.

It was why about fifty people—mostly women, with a scattering of middle-aged-to-elderly men—sat on chairs, or milled around, aimlessly, in the 'Conference Room' of *The Hind's Head* and, for the most part, just waited.

Charlotte Douranby, back to consciousness, but with a swelling bruise on her temple, sat on a chair in a group which included the stout woman, Celia Kempton and Flora Aimes.

Robert Hill and Bill Elliott—obviously buddies of long-standing—stood in a corner, glowered at their captors and, no doubt, planned plans which were both hare-brained and suicidal ... while the fat man kept a wary eye on them.

The thin doctor examined Elizabeth Elliott's shoulder wound, helped by Jean Hill and a gaggle of would-be-assistants who merely got in the thin man's way.

Carter sat on the edge of the dais, and dabbed his broken lips with a stained handkerchief. Occasionally, he glanced up at the man called Johnny—fearful, and pleadingly—but Johnny's expression was as cold and as deadly as the Stirling with which he dominated the room.

The fat man watched. Noted all these things then, apparently to pass the time, took out a packet of cheroots, lighted one and added a stench reminiscent of smouldering straw to the atmosphere of the room.

But the 'acceptance' was the main thing. It was the blanket which seemed to kill all hope of retaliation, and all but a handful of the people in the 'Conference Room' had hidden themselves beneath that blanket rather than terrify themselves by gazing at a frightening reality.

Indeed, few of them seemed to notice the sound of the distant explosion from the Carl Gustav.

P.C. Clemens and Rufus Aimes heard it. *And* saw it. *And* saw the result of the explosion.

They'd arrived in the mini van, at the wrong side of the bridge, and they'd climbed from the van, walked to the edge of the bridge and stared across at the two men on the opposite bank.

One of the men was holding what, at that distance, had looked like a length of drain-pipe and, as Clemens and Aimes had walked to the bridge end, this man had lowered himself to a prone position, widened his legs into a steadying 'V' and pointed the 'drain-pipe' at the police mini van.

Clemens had asked, 'Them 'em?'

And Aimes had replied, 'Aye. Them's 'em.'

Then Clemens had cupped his hands to his mouth, and called, 'You two. What's going on over there?'

Which was when the 'drain-pipe' had stopped being a 'drain-pipe' and become what it *was*. A Carl Gustav, 84 mm. short-range anti-tank weapon. More commonly called a 'bazooka'.

It all happened so suddenly that the sequence of events was as near simultaneous as touch is to feel. The belch and crack of the bazooka, the pressure of wind as the shell passed within twelve feet, the smash of steel on steel as the shell hit the mini van and, finally, the bellowing roar of flame as the petrol tank went up. One-two-three-four. But not four separates. Four split-second parts of a single whole.

Clemens gasped, 'Bloody roll on!' dived for Aimes's knees and brought them both to the ground in a rolling, bruised tangle of arms, legs and bodies on the verge, alongside the road. Later, Aimes swore Clemens had saved his life; that the billow of flame and the sing of flying metal as the mini van turned, from a motor vehicle, into a make-do-and-mend anti-personnel bomb would have caught him (Aimes) and certainly injured, and possibly killed him had not Clemens performed that hastily improvised rugby tackle.

For a 'saver of lives', P.C. Clemens was uncommonly shaken.

He peeped above the crook of his arm, watched the two men on the opposite bank, then muttered, 'Christ! They mean *business*.'

'For God's sake. I've already told you what they...'

'Aye. I know. Hang on a bit.'

'Look! I've already said they...'

'All *right*.' Clemens twisted his head, stared at the blazing remains of the mini van and blew out his cheeks. He said, 'Let's get out of here.'

'What?' Aimes seemed surprised—shocked—at the suggestion.

'Out of here,' repeated Clemens.

'You're not going to...'

'What the hell do you *want* me to do?' The question was laced with angry impatience. 'Ask 'em for their names and addresses?'

'You're a bloody copper, mate. You're a...'

'Fine.' Clemens moved his head in a single nod, towards the broken edge of the bridge. 'You go up there, Aimes. You tell 'em. Stand up there, and tell 'em ... that *I'm* a copper. I'll stay here, and watch bits of you fly past when they train that bloody bazooka thing on *you*.'

'You can't...' began Aimes.

'I'll tell you what I can do,' cut in Clemens. 'What both of us can do. Crawl back, along this verge ... down. Well down. And pray. Then, when we're round that first bend, you can run like hell for the nearest phone. Send a three-niner to D.H.Q., and tell 'em what's happened. That I'm at the scene, and that I need assistance. A *lot* of assistance. And as soon as possible. That, for the moment, I'm busy making damn sure no other cars get within range of 'em ... but that, for the moment, I haven't the faintest idea what the hell goes on.'

'I—I suppose,' sighed Aimes, shakily.

'I do a damn sight more than "suppose",' grunted Clemens. 'I *know*. C'mon ... let's get crawling.'

9.30 a.m. ...

Harris.

Introductions are called for, if for no better reason than that the war—the 'shooting war'—started at exactly 9.30 a.m. This being the time when Harris learned of the parlour games being played at Robs Cully.

Detective Chief Superintendent Harris. Have no doubts. Or, if you *have* doubts, check with the man himself. Harris figures himself to be on first-name terms with the Almighty.

Head of County Constabulary C.I.D. Again, if you have doubts, check with the man, personally. A force, at least ten furlongs clear of any other force in the field ... including the pansy boys of the Met who, even given a compass, couldn't detect their way from one end of a drainpipe to the other. And monarch of the elite of this elite force ... but naturally!

Married, with no kids. Ask his wife, and *she'll* tell you. Strictly speaking a 'bigamist'. Married to a woman, and 'married' to his job, and consistently far more considerate of the latter than he is of the former.

Harris.

A lot of people call him a bastard.

A lot more people call him a damn good cop.

Harris was having a shave when the telephone bell rang.

He muttered, 'Damn it to hell,' placed the razor on the rim of the wash-basin, left the bathroom for the bedroom, picked up the receiver and said, 'Harris.'

A nasal-toned voice said, 'Hiya.'

'What?'

'You Chief of Detectives?'

'Eh?'

'Harris?'

'Speaking,' grunted Harris.

'Chief of Detectives ... right?'

'Who is this?'

'You *Harris*?'

'If not,' said Harris, nastily, 'somebody has just had one hell of a night with his wife.'

'Wassat?'

'Who are you? Who's speaking?'

'It ain't important ... not for now.'

'It had *better* be important.'

'Don't get tough with me, copper.'

'Are you going to tell me who you are?' barked Harris.

'That I ain't ... not yet.'

'Fine. Goodbye.'

Harris dropped the receiver back on to its cradle.

From the bed, Mrs Harris murmured, 'Who was it, Bob?'

'One more bloody nut.'

Harris hurried to the bathroom, before the lather dried.

In *Yew Tree Bower*, Wolff glared, disbelievingly, at the dead receiver, and snarled, 'That guy is a goddam nut.'

'Yep?'

Cowboy sat on a chair, rubbed his still-aching shin and added a question mark to one of his favourite utterances.

Cowboy was once more (to use his own vernacular) 'ridin' herd' on the boss. Johnny was busy controlling *The Hind's Head*. A couple of boys and the bazooka were guarding the broken bridge. The rest of the outfit were strung around the joint; some in the 'Conference Room' with Johnny; some double-checking that all the houses had been emptied; some keeping an eye on the Hewfraw and Skew Beck, in case some goofy character tried to swim across.

Meanwhile...

Wolff drawled, 'Okay. He wants it rough, he can *have* it rough.'

Wolff dialled the number, again.

Harris answered.

Wolff snapped, 'You want I should stiffen a few bastards, before you unstop your ears, Harris?'

'Eh?'

'If that's the sorta deal you want, that's okay by me, copper.'

There was a pause.

Then, Harris said, 'Let's start with fundamentals. Who are you? Where are you? And what the bloody hell are you talking about?'

'Wolff,' snapped Wolff.

'And what is *that* supposed to mean?'

'James Edward Wolff.'

'It still doesn't mean anything.'

'You know my boy, copper. Ric—Ricardo Wolff.'

'Eh? ... Aaah.' Harris made remembering noises. 'Yes, I know Ricardo Wolff. A cheap little hook, with big ideas. He thought he could...'

'You put him away, copper.'

'That I did,' agreed Harris.

'Seven years.'

'And cheap at the price, for what he was trying to do.'

'Now, get him out,' snarled Wolff.

'Eh?'

'*Get him out!*'

'Any time,' said Harris, sarcastically. 'Just you name the place. How you want him delivered—with, or without, pink ribbon—and I'll deliver him personally.'

'I mean it, copper.'

'You've been reading the wrong sort of paperbacks, Wolff. Try the comic strips. They'll make you laugh more than...'

'You know a dump called Robs Cully?' cut in Wolff.

'Robs Cully?'

'Yeah. A dump alongside a river called the Hewfraw.'

'Robs ... Oh, aye. Robs Cully. In Beechwood Brook Division. It's a...'

'I don't give a snot-nosed damn which police division it's in. You *know* it?'

'Uhu. I know it.'

'I hold it,' said Wolff, coldly.

There was another pause.

Then Harris said, 'The—er... You mean something, Wolff. The meaning isn't clear. You "hold" it. Just what the hell does *that* mean.'

'You listening, copper?' Wolff allowed a cold smile to touch his lips.

'I'm listening,' growled Harris.

Wolff said, 'Great. So, listen good. I ain't gonna send any

illustrated postcards. I *hold* Robs Cully. I have some boys with me. I've blown the bridge. And every punk in Robs Cully has a gun in his belly, and *my* boys are working the trigger. Anything funny—anything clever—and you are gonna have to draft in more grave-diggers. Okay?'

'I'm listening,' said Harris, gently.

'I want my boy sprung. That's the deal,' rasped Wolff.

'How the hell d'you expect me to...'

'*That's the deal!*' Wolff almost screamed the words into the receiver. 'I dunno how—I don't give a fink's toss how ... just *do* it, Harris. You put him away. Okay ... you spring him. I want him delivered here, within twenty-four hours. Otherwise, I start blasting. And nobody—*nobody!*—is gonna walk away from this place alive. Do I make myself clear, copper? Do you get it?'

'That you're mad,' growled Harris, grimly. 'If it isn't a bluff. If you've really...'

'It ain't no bluff, copper.'

'In that case...'

'You figure Eddie Wolff is kidding, copper. You ever think he's bluffing. You think that, copper, and you have trouble on your hands. You get that? Eh? You *get* that?'

'Robs Cully,' said Harris, slowly.

'That's the dump. And I got...'

'I *know* what you've got ... what you *say* you've got.'

'And, like I say...'

'I'll be down there,' interrupted Harris.

'Look, pig, you ain't gonna pull no smart-assed tricks. Not...'

'One thing I'm *not* going to bloody-well do,' snapped Harris. 'I'm not even going to contact the prison authorities, on the strength of a disembodied voice at the end of a telephone wire. You be ready to meet me. To talk. To air your muscles ... supposing you have any. Just be ready, Wolff. Robs Cully ... I'll be there, in an hour.'

Once more the phone in Wolff's hand went dead, as Harris replaced his receiver.

Wolff's mouth twisted as he, too, returned the receiver to its rest.

He said, 'So-o ... now he knows.'

'Yep.'

'Now the whole damn world knows.'

'Yep.'

'Let's go, Cowboy.' Wolff jerked his head. 'Let's go pick who we're gonna stiffen first.'

Cowboy stood up from the chair. He didn't say 'Yep' and he didn't say 'Nope'. He was just happy that his shins didn't give him as much hell.

Harris stared at the telephone. Frowning. Breathing long, deep breaths.

His wife looked up at him, from the bed.

'Something wrong?' she asked, sleepily.

'Something *very* wrong,' muttered Harris.

'What? What is it?' The concern in his voice brushed away the last of her drowsiness.

'Robs Cully,' murmured Harris. He seemed to be talking to himself, rather than answering his wife's question. 'Wolff—Ricardo Wolff ... we put him inside, about a year ago. Dope ... we had a tip-off. One more try to get the U.K. distribution organised. Wolff was ... Anyway, we nailed him. Seven years ... and bloody lucky to get away *that* easy.'

Harris stopped talking.

His wife frowned up at his face, then said, 'I don't see what that has to do with...'

'Robs Cully,' said Harris, heavily. 'That was his father Ricardo's old man ... claimed to be. He says he's...'

Harris choked on the word.

'Yes?' encouraged his wife.

'"Taken" is the word he used,' growled Harris. 'He's "taken" Robs Cully. Blown the bridge. Isolated it. Hijacked it—that's what it boils down to ... hijacked the bloody place. With a gang of Yankee tearaways.'

'Oh God!'

'I believe him.' Harris's voice was not much more than a rasping whisper. 'I *have* to believe him—pending verification ... I daren't *not* believe him. It had to come. God damn and blast it! It *had* to come. But why the hell here? Why the hell in *my* area?'

Those who knew Harris—correction, those who claimed to know Harris—would have been shocked at the weary defeat which touched his words. At the droop of the shoulders. At the suddenly old and bitter expression which sat on his face.

His wife knew him. *Really* knew him.

She threw the bedclothes aside and, as she swung her feet on to the carpet, she said, 'I'm coming with you, Bob.'

'What the hell! I don't need...'

'If it's true.' She felt, with her feet, for her slippers. 'You'll need everybody. Not just policemen. There'll be people—like a rail disaster—people with relatives in the village. You'll need somebody to *tell* those people. To keep them informed. Let them know what's happening. I can do that. I can help.' She paused then, in a very solemn voice, said, 'I'll take orders, Bob. Don't worry—I won't argue... I'll take orders.'

Harris nodded, without speaking.

His wife hurried to the bathroom.

Then, like the throwing of a switch, Harris became another man, a different man. Cop—*all* cop... the Harris the rest of the world knew.

He lifted the receiver and dialled a number. And the bite was in his voice when he bawled the instructions along the telephone wire.

'... that's the place, Robs Cully. Beechwood Brook Division ... I want every man, from the chief superintendent down, at Raine ... Raine—that's the nearest village—I want them there, as soon as possible ... That's an order, inspector. They obey orders in this force, inspector. They obey orders—they obey *this* order—or God help 'em ... Get 'em down there, ready to meet me within the hour ... And get the chief constable out of bed, too. I need *him* at Raine, too ... I don't give a damn what he asks—how many questions he asks—just get him there ... Tell him I say so. Tell him I wouldn't be asking if I didn't think his presence was necessary. Very necessary...'

And, as Harris was belting instructions from the top, Rufus Aimes was yelling blue murder from the other end; from a telephone in the hall of a farmhouse, midway between Robs Cully and Raine. Unfortunately, and because he was a 'civilian' and a near-incoherent 'civilian', and because the sergeant at the other end of the telephone wire was a mite on the dumb side, the conversation hadn't the snap and sparkle of Harris's conversation.

'A bazooka,' wailed Aimes. 'For God's sake! Don't you know what a bazooka...'

'I know what a bazooka is, lad,' said the sergeant, in a very world-weary voice. 'When we were advancing against Jerry...'

'Oh, my Christ!'

'... we saw plenty of bazookas. We used 'em. It's what...'

'Sergeant. I've no doubt you were a blasted war hero.'

'... stopped the Panzers, lad. I've seen more bazookas...'

'It's important, sergeant. It's *important*.'

'... than you've had hot dinners. And I'm inclined to doubt whether...'

'*SERGEANT!*' Aimes almost cracked the diaphragm as he screamed the word. Then he grabbed his voice and, in a very hard—very deliberate—tone, said, 'Sergeant. In there—in Robs Cully—there is something happening. Something I don't like. Now I, too, know a bazooka when I see one. I know the bridge has gone. I know I've been shot at by men with guns. I know a police van has been blasted to hell and back with a bazooka. And I also know that my wife is in there, somewhere. Now I want action, sergeant. D'you understand that? Action! Now! And, if you arse around telling me how you won the bloody war, instead of giving me that action and if, as a result of you arsing around, anything happens to my wife, God help you. I mean that, sergeant. *God help you.*'

'Oh!'

'I'm making myself clear, I hope, sergeant?'

'Hang on a bit...'

Along the wire Aimes could hear mutterings, and a couple of 'yes sirs'. Then the sergeant came back and, this time, with a very different tone of voice.

The sergeant said, 'It's all right, Mr Aimes. We've—er—we've just had confirmation. Y'know... confirmation.'

What sort of "confirmation"?'

'That—y'know—summat's happening at Robs Cully.'

'You blithering idiot,' breathed Aimes.

'Eh?'

Aimes seemed to have difficulty in breathing. As if he'd just ended a long and strength-sapping race.

He gasped, 'Sergeant, you're an idiot. D'you know that? You're a prize twat, of the first order. It's men like you who make the police force stink.'

9.45 a.m. ...

Wolff walked into the 'Conference Room', and everybody knew the boss-man had arrived. He was the tiger to Johnny's wild-cat—the Hitler to Johnny's Hess—and it was as obvious as *that*. He walked the length of the room; he walked in a straight line, and everybody parted, to let him pass. He climbed on to the stage, and, like a bit-player when an international star steps forward to take a bow, Johnny moved to the rear and to one side.

There was an air of off-handed, but ruthless, arrogance about the man. A personality as strong, and as immediate, as a jolt of electricity. And every man and woman in the 'Conference Room' felt it, and knew that here was something (somebody) the like of which they had never met before. Fascinating, but evil. A man other men might wish to emulate ... but unique.

For a moment, he stood, silent, on the dais.

He looked at his audience, and every member of that audience felt a personal scrutiny; a split-second stripping of the soul and an exposure of every secret thought and every secret fear.

He spoke, and they all listened. They concentrated, as if to catch every word and every nuance; as if what this man was saying was a form of salvation and a key to eternity.

He said, 'No kids. My boys tell me the kids are outa this place. That's okay ... I don't play war with kids. You people, you're all here. There ain't nobody left in this Robs Cully dump except you ... and you're all *here*. Okay. A coupla the boys have dynamited the bridge, so nobody's goin' anyplace. Everybody behaves themselves, nobody gets hurt. Anybody gets fancy, and I ain't responsible. My boys have orders to shoot ... and they'll shoot. They don't *mind* shootin'. It don't bother them any. Just so's you'll know ... okay?'

He permitted his mouth the luxury of a quick, twisted smile before he continued.

'Thirty after nine, tomorrow morning. That's the deadline ... see? My boy—my son—he's inside. Seven years. That's what the stinkin' coppers hung round his neck—seven years ... about a year back. We-ell, they're gonna get my boy out, folks. They are gonna deliver him here—to me, at this Robs Cully dump—and before thirty after nine, tomorrow morning.

'They do *that*, and we walk outa your lives, and you all go home and tell your friends you've met Eddie Wolff. They *don't* do that ... and nobody tells anybody anythin'!'

He paused. He took his time examining the various expressions on the faces of his audience.

Then he growled, 'Okay ... any questions?'

Hill spoke.

He said, 'The obvious question. Do you *really* think you'll get away with it?'

'Yeah.' Wolff nodded ... as if the question had been a stupid question, and hardly deserving of an answer.

'You're crazy,' murmured Hill.

'Hey, mac.' The smile came again. Slower, this time, and with cruelty tagged at each end. He said, 'You'd better hope not ... eh? 'Cos, if I'm crazy, you're dead ... right?'

Wolff stepped down from the tiny stage and walked from the 'Conference Room'.

Nobody stood in his way.

Nobody said another word.

9.45 a.m. until 10.20 a.m. ...

The chief constable's name was Grafton.

He was a joke; he was everything a chief constable shouldn't be; he was so damned self-opinionated he almost snapped his spine whenever he had to bend to tie his own shoe-laces. He broke sound-barriers, but got nowhere. He made more noise than a herd of stampeding elephants, but said nothing. For a copper, he was a little guy and (like so many little guys who are acutely aware of their duck-sized stature) he drove a car as big as an aircraft-carrier; he drove it fast, he drove it dangerously—it was his car, and it was his county constabulary ... so who the hell was going to drop the boom?

Grafton, and his antics, scared blue crap out of every young, grass-green recruit. The older men opened both ears—one to let it in, and the other to let it out—and mentally blew him one long, silent raspberry ... then, when he'd disappeared over the skyline, forgot him and went about their law-enforcement business.

Some forces had such chief constables.

Grafton was one of them.

And (to a man) they are a pain in the crotch to every Head of C.I.D., and Grafton was a pain in the crotch to Harris.

Harris said so. It was no time for polite chit-chat. It was not an occasion for meaningless bonhomie, therefore Harris spoke his mind and didn't pull any punches.

He said, 'Get off my back, Grafton ... *sir*. I need you. I need the rank you carry. If this bastard Wolff has...'

'If!' Over the telephone wire, Grafton made that single, tiny word sound like a firecracker.

'Are you prepared to accept the risk ... *sir*?' rasped Harris.

Mrs Harris hurried into the hall, from the kitchen, she placed a cup of hot coffee on the hall table, alongside the telephone. Harris nodded his quick thanks.

Grafton bawled, 'Harris, I think you're jumping the gun. I think you're panicking. I think...'

'That'll be the day,' snarled Harris.

'What?'

'When you *think* ... *sir*.'

Harris took a sip of the coffee while Grafton exploded. Harris allowed himself a few seconds in which to enjoy the taste of the coffee, and ignored the noises coming over the telephone wire. Then he lowered the cup on to the saucer, and cut in on Grafton, mid-stream.

He snapped, 'With respect, chief constable ... shove it! I've already arranged for men and vehicles to be at Raine, as soon as possible. I've authorised the issue of firearms. I've checked that Wolff's son—Ricardo Wolff—is, at the moment, in Wakefield nick. I need *you* to contact the governor—or anybody else, necessary—and arrange for his release, if it comes to stick and lift. I also need *you* to telephone around—army camps, air force bases —and get me a helicopter standing by. If—all right, *if*—Wolff means business I need a few cards up my sleeve. That's what I need ... *sir*. That's the situation, as of this moment. Now, I'm on my way to Raine. Now! If you want to chew my balls off, that's where you'll find me.'

Harris dropped the receiver on to its rest.

He finished the coffee in one last, long gulp.

Mrs Harris said, 'I'll be out there in an hour or two...'

'There's no need...'

'When I've collected some other people who might want to help.'

Harris shrugged.

He pecked his wife on the cheek, hurried out of the house and towards the garage.

The fat man said, 'I—er—I'd like to leave the room. D'you mind?'

Johnny frowned down at the obese, half-smiling man, and didn't understand.

'A leak,' explained the fat man. 'Y'know ... the call of nature.'

'I dunno...' began Johnny.

'For heaven's sake! A man's got to pee,' protested the fat man, plaintively. 'I've held it. I can't hold it much longer.'

'Hey lady!' Johnny called to Flora Aimes. 'Where's the nearest john?'

'Toilets,' supplied the fat man.

'Where?' asked Johnny.

'There's—er...' Flora gestured with her arm. 'There's two off the landing. The main toilets are downstairs. One off the...'

'Those just outside are fine,' interrupted Johnny. He motioned to one of the gunmen, and said, 'Fatso wants a piss. Go with him ... uh?'

The fat man looked mildly outraged—mildly embarrassed— and said, 'Look ... You don't have to tell *everybody*.'

'It's okay, fatso.' Johnny grinned. 'You don't have somethin' nobody else has. Everybody pisses, at some time. You're no different.'

'That bloody sergeant,' grumbled Aimes. 'Buggering about, wasting time. On about how he won the war, instead of...'

'He's getting things moving?' cut in P.C. Clemens.

'Aye ... *now*.'

'Good.'

'After—what was it he said?—summat about "confirmation". What the hell *that* means. Somebody else must have...'

'As long as things are moving,' soothed Clemens. 'That's the main thing.'

'The main thing,' corrected Aimes, grimly, 'is that my missus is on the other side of that river. And I dunno what the blazes is happening. And I'm worried. Mate, I am bloody *worried*.'

'Aye.'

Clemens was watching the road leading towards Raine. He was watching an approaching pedal-cyclist.

Clemens waved an arm, the cyclist stopped, rested one foot on the road, alongside his machine, frowned his non-understanding at Aimes and said, 'Wot's oop, Rufus?'

Rufus told him, and the cyclist's eye widened.

He said, 'Bloody 'ell! Tha'll be worried abaht t' wife, I reckon.'

Clemens allowed the duologue to continue, but without taking too much notice. Clemens was worrying his way through a mess of other thoughts.

Men with guns, for example. Men with a bazooka—and men capable of *using* that bazooka, in order to destroy a police vehicle. Why? If not as a warning—as a demonstration—for what other reason?

A bridge, for example. A perfectly sound, well constructed bridge with its back broken. Blown. Demolished ... or, if not demolished what? And *if* demolished, why?

And another thing...

Two men—two men, with guns and a bazooka—and no other sign of life. Okay, Robs Cully was no Piccadilly Circus, but neither was it a cemetery. There was usually *somebody* around. Taking a stroll. Walking the dog. It was a place where 'retired' people lived—where 'professional' types lived—people who were a little bored, whose wives were a little bored, and people who tended to mooch around if for no better reason than to kill time. The 'coffee-morning' crowd.

And the bridge had gone.

And a bazooka had been fired.

And yet, nobody. *Nobody!* That was the puzzler; that was the worrying aspect. That not a soul, other than the two men, had been in sight. It was wrong—all wrong—and it didn't fit in with normality. People who organised 'action groups' at the drop of a hat; who'd once kicked up hell's delight and fought the local authority to a standstill, for the sake of a single electricity pylon; who didn't give a damn how much money they squandered, just so long as their world stayed *their* way. And a bridge had gone, and nobody was even there *looking*.

It wasn't the way Robs Cully worked.

So-o...

Inside his brain Clemens shifted the muck of possibility and probability, and sought what few gems of 'fact' he could come up with. Speculation was useless at this point. Truth—what he *knew*

—was the only thing that mattered.
And what he 'knew' scared the hell out of him.

The fat man returned to the 'Conference Room'. The gunman who had accompanied him to the toilet took up his previous position against the wall. The fat man waddled towards the stage, and Johnny grinned down at him, sardonically.

'Okay?' asked Johnny.

'Eh? Oh!—ah ... yes.' The fat man exchanged the grin for a half-smile. 'Much better now, thanks.'

'You got bladder trouble, fatso?' Johnny seemed genuinely interested.

'Er—we-ell ... yes, as a matter of fact, I have. A little.'

The fat man sounded very self-conscious as he made the admission; as if the ailment was something of which to be ashamed.

'Yeah. My old man,' said Johnny, sombrely.

'What?'

'Always wantin' to piss. All night. All day. Y'know ... always with a leakin' washer. I guess it comes with age ... uh?'

'I—er—I suppose so,' agreed the fat man.

'A goddam nuisance,' grunted Johnny.

'Aye—it is ... sometimes.'

'Any time, fatso,' said Johnny off-handedly.

'Eh?'

'You wanna leak, just say. Okay?'

'Oh! Er—thanks ... thanks a lot.'

The fat man smiled his appreciation.

Johnny returned his attention to the people assembled in the 'Conference Room'.

It filtered through, into Clemens's busy mind, like a thick liquid working its way through litmus paper. The conversation between Rufus Aimes and the pedal-cyclist.

Clemens knew the cyclist; a middle-aged Yorkshireman who carried the uninspired name of Sam Wilson. The presently-employed cellar-man at *The Hind's Head*. A Raine man, born and bred, who knew every field and every path and short-cut for miles around. Who knew the Hewfraw and Skew Beck better than most. Not a popular man, with Clemens, because Wilson was also a part-time poacher, and a man who could tickle a trout from its basking place and into a frying-pan with all the ease and skill of a cardsharp selling a sucker a stacked deck.

Sam Wilson knew the river; its every mood and its every inch. Clemens quietened his dislike for the man, and said, 'Hang on a minute.'

The other two stopped talking.

'What you just said ... there's a way across?' asked Clemens.

'Aye.' Wilson nodded.

'This side of the falls,' volunteered Aimes.

'Where?' asked Clemens.

Aimes said, 'Look—you know the falls? ... the pool, just before Skew Beck branches off?'

'Uhu.' Clemens nodded, slowly.

'Right,' said Aimes. 'Well—this side of the pool—right at the far end of Robs Cully—there's some rocks. Not rapids—the kids call 'em that, sometimes ... but not really *rapids*. You know 'em?'

'I know them,' said Clemens.

'There,' said Aimes. 'Stepping stones. We-ell, not exactly *stepping stones*, but...'

'If tha knoaws 'ow,' grunted Wilson.

'Tricky,' said Aimes.

'But if tha knoaws 'ow,' repeated Wilson.

'And do *you* know how?' asked Clemens.

'Many a scoare time,' growled Wilson. 'There's nowt to it ... if tha knoaws 'ow.'

Clemens pondered the problem for a moment, then he spoke directly to Wilson.

He said, 'Look—we've had our differences ... agreed. But let's forget them for the moment. Agreed?'

Wilson moved his head in a single nod.

'Something's happening in there,' said Clemens. 'Hell knows what, but ... I dunno. Just *something*. Something a damn sight worse than an odd pheasant—an odd partridge ... something a damn sight worse than *that*. And I need to know what it is. I have to know!'

'Aye. I reckon,' agreed Wilson.

'You know my home telephone number?' asked Clemens.

'Aye.'

'Look—what I want you to do is this. I can't order you—I won't try ... but I'll say "please", if necessary. Get in there. Use those stepping stones, and...'

'They aren't real stepping stones,' interrupted Aimes.

'There's nowt to it,' growled Wilson.

Clemens said, 'Get across, that's all. Mooch around. Find out what the hell's happening, then telephone my home. Tell my wife ... if anything's really wrong, she'll know who to pass it on to. Okay?'

Clemens asked the question and waited for an answer.

Aimes said, 'I'll go. I know where...'

'Tha'll noan,' interrupted Wilson. 'Tha'll break thi neck.'

'Look—my wife's in...'

'I'll go.' Wilson swung his leg clear of the machine, and wheeled the cycle on to the verge. He leaned it against the hedge. He said, 'There's nowt to it. But tha 'as to knoaw 'ow.'

Clemens sighed, and said, 'I'd go with you, but somebody has to stay here and stop traffic. Unless it's somebody in uniform they'd...'

'Not *thee*.' Wilson grinned, and there was a measure of contempt in the curl of his lips. 'Tha'd never *get*. Them bloody grut feet.'

Aimes began, 'All right, I'll...'

'One of us,' insisted Wilson. 'It's reight. I'll let thi knoaw wot's 'appenin'.'

He nodded a gesture of temporary farewell, trotted along the verge, back towards Raine, vaulted a gate leading into a field beyond the hedgerow and left Clemens and Aimes worried and silent.

The fat man stripped the cellophane tube from one of his cheroots. He fingered-and-thumbed the cellophane into a tiny ball, looked around, saw the sand-filled fire bucket, strolled towards it and dropped the ball of cellophane on to the surface of the sand.

It was such an innocent series of movements—such a natural sequence of unimportant actions—and that it took the fat man beyond the conversational hearing-range of either Johnny, or the nearest positioned gunman seemed quite incidental.

The fat man patted his pockets and frowned his annoyance.

He said, 'Er ... excuse me.'

'Eh?' Robert Hill turned his head.

'A light.' The fat man spread gherkin-shaped fingers, and smiled timidly. He said, 'Sorry ... but I seem to have run out of matches. D'you mind?'

Hill scowled small annoyance. He'd noticed the fat man; noticed the jazzy shirt, and the near-apologetic, lickspittling manner in which he'd spoken to the bastard with the Stirling S.M.G. Hill had noted these things, and had mentally earmarked the fat man as a barrel-gutted, yellow-bellied slob; of a type he'd known; of a type he'd met. Of a type to make complete men puke.

Hill said, 'Ask somebody...'

'Please!' The vacuous grin stayed on the fat man's face—the tone of voice remained as timid as ever—but, for a split second, the eyes changed. They remained round and slightly bulbous but, momentarily, there was a glint. It was there, then it was gone ... but, it undoubtedly had *been* there.

Hill stepped nearer to the fat man, and handed the fat man a box of matches.

The fat man lighted his cheroot.

He held the cheroot firmly in his teeth, to prevent any giveaway wobble. His lips hardly moved. He spoke with his tongue and his throat; a deep-toned half-whisper—a mutter—which carried as far as Hill ... but no farther.

'Go to the toilet. Behind the cistern, there's a note.'

The fat man finished lighting his cheroot, handed the matches back to Hill, and said, 'Ta.'

Hill grunted, and walked away.

The fat man strolled back, to within hearing distance of Johnny.

Beechwood Brook D.H.Q.

It was known locally, and irreverently, as 'The Fuzz Palace'. It had been designed (obviously!) by some berk who, up to that moment, had designed building blocks to be used by kids. It was angular, it was concrete, it was glass, it was flat-topped, it was square-cornered. You name it—if it means 'ugly' it described Beechwood Brook D.H.Q.

Inside, it was a little like a Mecca ballroom. Acres and acres of polished parquet floor-space. Yard after yard of counter-desk tops. Hidden lighting. Broad and shallow-stepped stairs. And lifts, for God's sake ... lifts! There was even a roof patio.

It had everything ... except coppers!

Normally, coppers tended to lose themselves in its umpteen

corridors, countless rooms and ante-rooms, offices and canteens, stairs and interview rooms. You damn near needed a compass, or a street map, to find your way around.

Normally.

But not today.

Today, every copper in creation seemed to have converged upon Beechwood Brook D.H.Q., en route to Raine.

Blayde—the chief superintendent who'd stepped into Ripley's shoes—held them in check in the huge Charge Office, and silenced their speculative murmur as Harris strode into the room.

Harris wasted neither time nor words.

He said, 'Right—here's the situation. Robs Cully. It's been isolated ... it's an assumption we have to accept as a fact, pending verification. It's been isolated, and certain comedians—one comedian in particular—is trying terrorist tactics. He wants a man released from prison, or else ... I'm told the local man—Clemens—is already down there. That guns are being used, and that an anti-tank weapon has already knocked Clemens's van for a burton. I'm told the bridge has gone ... presumably demolished. That makes Robs Cully an island. There are people there—members of the public—being held hostage. So-o, until we know *exactly* how much is bluff, and how much isn't bluff, we go gently. Very gently! No medals ... understand that? I want no medals, at the cost of innocent lives.

'If we need guns, I have 'em with me. Rifles, revolvers and tear-gas. I don't want to use them, but if we *have* to we have them. I want the qualified marksmen to get together and be ready ... if I need 'em, I don't want to have to *find* 'em. I also want some idea about who's in Robs Cully. Chief Superintendent Blayde'll detail a couple of men. They'll check the electoral roll. Who, and where, everybody lives. Who's likely to be away at work ... and they'll contact 'em. Don't scare 'em. Just make sure they get to know *officially*, and without the news being tarted up to make it sound ten times worse than it is. Tell 'em we have the situation under control ... and that's *all* they're to be told. The one thing I don't want is panic.

'We work from Raine. There's a village hall. That's going to be the Incident Centre ... but in contact with here. That's where I want you all to go. Now. I'll join you there, shortly. Meanwhile, no heroics. No medals ... right?'

The murmur of assent was a little like gentle applause.

Harris turned to Blayde.

In a quieter voice, he said, 'Policewomen, superintendent. The kids'll be at school, but they'll get to know. Bound to. I need policewomen to keep 'em calm. The one thing we *don't* want is screaming kids around our ankles.'

'I'll see to it,' said Blayde.

'And Clemens?' asked Harris.

'Yes?'

'What's he like?'

Blayde said, 'Steady. Sensible. He won't go off at half-cock.'

Harris grunted approval, and said, 'Does he know the place?'

'It's his beat.'

'That means damn-all,' said Harris, irritably.

'With me it does.'

'I've known men,' insisted Harris, 'who've worked beats for donkey's years, and they still don't know...'

'Not with *me*,' snapped Blayde. 'Clemens knows the beat. He's not a native, but he knows the beat.'

'I hope you're right,' grunted Harris.

Blayde said, 'There's a plan.'

'What sort of a...'

'An architect's plan. A man called Bottom—Robert Bottom— built Robs Cully. He had to get planning permission. He had to submit a plan to the local authority, showing the whole set-up. Where every house is.'

'Right. We'll have...'

'I've already got it.'

'Oh! In that case, let's have...'

'It's in the Duplicating Room.' Blayde jerked his head. 'I'm having a dozen copies run off. And a dozen copies of a large-scale Ordnance Survey map of the district. Five minutes ... they'll all be ready.'

Harris eyed the newly-appointed Beechwood Brook chief superintendent quizzically.

He said, 'Did you know Ripley? ... your predecessor?'

'By sight,' said Blayde. 'Not well.'

'You'd have liked him,' growled Harris. '*He* hated my guts, too.'

Blayde said, 'They tell me he was a good copper,' and the remark was as deadpan as Blayde's face. It could have meant anything ... up to, and including, a direct insult.

Wilson travelled at a steady jog-trot. Knees bent and head lowered, to keep the hedge and a field-length between himself and the Hewfraw The midsummer midges kept pace with him, spiralling and dancing around his close-cropped hair, but they were insects of his world and he accepted and ignored them. He passed within two strides of a hare's tufted hide; for a split second, they saw each other—eyes meeting eyes—and the creature tensed its hindquarters, ready to race for safety ... then Wilson was past, and the hare relaxed in his hiding place.

Wilson knew, and loved this countryside.

It was his habitat; his true world. He worked in the cellars of *The Hind's Head* for money; he humped crates and barrels around, for money. It was one way of getting it—as good a way as any, and better than some—and money was something people had to have. But *this* was his home ... the open air, the fields, the hedgerows, the river. He'd dreamed of being a gamekeeper— he'd even applied a few times, in answer to adverts in *The Field*—but, every time, he'd been short on references. They'd all wanted 'good references' ... and a handful of 'Previous Convictions' for poaching didn't count. It made him a criminal; it branded him as 'dishonest'.

'Dishonest' my arse!

These bigwigs—these 'landed gentry' clowns—they were as thick as two short planks. Bloody gormless. They couldn't *see*. A man who could take game from the toes of a gamekeeper was a better gamekeeper than *that* gamekeeper ... but they just couldn't *see*.

Poachers ... that was the only blasted word they could say. 'Poachers'. And what was 'poaching', anyway? It wasn't stealing. It wasn't *pinching* anything. It was just getting there, first; beating the game, *and* beating the gamekeeper ... *and* beating the coppers. It was knowing things—y'know ... knowing which patch of kale the pheasant always fancied—knowing which long grass the partridge always used as a nesting place—knowing which hole, in which wall, the hare always went for—knowing which net was going to catch the rabbit when he raced for his burrow. Knowing fox-tracks from dog-tracks. Knowing pigeon-droppings from starling-droppings.

Knowing things ... things gamekeepers *should* know, but often don't.

The bloody fools!

They hadn't the gumption—these bigwigs—they hadn't the gumption to realise it—he'd have made a damned good gamekeeper. No poacher on earth would have pulled the wool over *his* eyes.

And now ...

We-ell—now bobby Clemens wanted a favour. And who did he ask? Who was the only man capable of getting into Robs Cully without being seen? Who was the only man capable of outwitting whoever was ...

Whoever was *what*?

Wilson stopped. He squatted on his heels and leaned his left shoulder against the wide bole of an elm. He eased forward slightly, until he could peer through the slanting gap where the foliage of the hedge kissed the broad trunk of the tree. Across the slope of the meadow, to where the Hewfraw raced and foamed around half-submerged boulders. To the right; to where the still surface of the pool formed a smooth platform at the foot of the waterfall. Beyond the water, to the far bank, where ...

Where *what*?

Summat was wrong in there; in the village. Summat was amiss. And Mrs Aimes was in there, somewhere; Flora Aimes ... one of the few women Wilson respected. And summat ... summat just *might* be happening to her. Summat bad. Summat awful.

'Cos ...

Wilson's eyes glinted. He muttered, 'By God! Whoever tha is, tha'll pay ... tha'll pay, bloody dearly.'

He eased himself out, flat on his belly, then wriggled forward towards the low gap in the hedge; the gap only he knew about; the gap which would take him into the meadow—then down to the water's edge—then across the boulders and into Robs Cully ...

Hill zipped his fly, pulled the chain of the toilet, then allowed his fingers to feel gently along the narrow space between the cistern and the wall.

The note was there, where the fat man had said it was; folded and wedged, midway up the back of the cistern.

Hill palmed the note in his right hand, and stepped towards the washbowl.

From beyond the partly-closed door, the accompanying gunman said, 'Hey, mac. Don't take all day ... uh?'

Hill growled, 'I wash my hands when I've had a piss. D'you mind?'

'Yeah?' The gunman sounded mildly surprised.

'It's an old English custom.'

Hill turned on the taps, bent over the washbowl and unfolded the note.

It read...

> *I need to know reliable men. Not too many. Just talk to them. Don't tell them anything, yet.*
>
> *Lennox*—DETECTIVE SUPERINTENDENT.

The words 'Detective Superintendent' were underlined.

Hill shoved the note into his trouser pocket, and began to wash his hands under the running taps.

Police Constable 2728 Clemens felt a little happier. He was no longer alone. Two squad cars, blue lights revolving their warning to approaching vehicles were parked, one at each side of the road leading to the broken bridge. A duo of Road Traffic constables and a Road Traffic sergeant added the weight of their authority to his own, and the steady build-up of vehicles and pedestrians, originally destined for Robs Cully, could now be handled without too much sweat.

Clemens left the Road Traffic men arguing with a couple of pedestrians and the driver of a butcher's van, while he stood on the verge and exchanged ideas with Rufus Aimes.

'What's happening, Wally? What the hell's *happening*?' Aimes's voice was a worried croak. 'My missus. She's in there, and I dunno what...'

'Wilson'll get in, and let us...'

'Bugger Wilson!' Aimes was on the point of cracking. 'My missus is in there, mate. And men with guns. And a bloody bazooka. And I don't give a damn about whether Wilson gets in or not. It might be too late. Somebody might...'

'Easy, Rufus,' said Clemens, gently.

'Oh, aye. "Easy"—it's easy to say "Easy" when you're not...'

'She's not alone.'

'*I'm* not with her.'

'We'll get her out.' Clemens put false conviction into his tone. He made himself sound sure. Certain ... a damn sight more certain than he felt. He said, 'We'll get 'em all out, Rufus. But we need your help.'

'How the hell can *I* help, when I'm out here, and ...'

'You're from in there,' said Clemens.

'Eh?'

'From in there,' repeated Clemens. 'This thing—whatever it is—it just didn't *happen*. Somebody didn't just pick Robs Cully ... just like that. Blow the bridge up. Start shooting. Y'know ... just like that. It didn't just *happen*.'

'I'm sorry. I'm not ...' Aimes shook his head in puzzlement.

Clemens said, 'There's a reason. There's planning.'

'Maybe. But I dunno what ...'

'Somebody organised it.'

'Who?'

'That,' said Clemens, 'is what you can tell us.'

'How the devil can I ...'

'Somebody,' mused Clemens, grimly. 'Guns. Dynamite ... whatever they used to blow the bridge. It isn't "English". Y'know— not like they do over here. At least, not often. Yankee, maybe. It's more like ...'

'Those bloody Americans,' breathed Aimes.

Clemens was a wise man; he knew when to talk and when to listen.

He waited, then listened.

'Four of 'em,' said Aimes, heavily. 'Fishermen—y'know ... that's what they said. Come to think about it, they were funny fishermen. They usually—y'know ... the usual sort. They catch summat, bring it back, then ask Flora to make it into a meal for 'em. Y'know ... sorta eating what they've caught. Sometimes it tastes lousy. I *know*—sometimes, I wouldn't serve some of the fish some of 'em bring in ... but they *do*. And make on it's good grub. Even if it almost chokes 'em.'

'But not these four?' asked Clemens.

'Not a thing.' Aimes shook his head; partly in answer to Clemens's question, partly at the realisation of his own stupidity. 'Out all day, and not a bite ... that's about the size of it. Bloody funny fishermen. I shoulda *known*.'

'American?' asked Clemens.

'Aye ... Yanks. We get 'em, sometimes. The odd one ... maybe two. First time we've had four. But—y'know ... they pay, don't cause too much trouble. It's what we're there for.'

'Names?' asked Clemens.

'Eh?'

'They'd book in. What names?'

'Oh—er—lemme see. Miller—one of 'em's called Miller. Then there's an Ellington. And the other two—er—lemme see—oh, aye ... Kenton and Goodman.' He looked at Clemens's face, and added, 'False, I reckon ... eh?'

Clemens took a deep breath then, in a weary voice, said, 'We-ell, now Rufus. One, I could have swallowed. Maybe two. But *four*! Miller ... Glen Miller. Ellington ... Duke Ellington. Kenton ... Stan Kenton. And Goodman ... Benny Goodman. Christ Almighty, Rufus. What d'you want 'em to call themselves? Frank Sinatra and Bing Crosby?'

'All right. All right.' Rufus Aimes closed his eyes in self-disgust. 'I'm a mug. Don't rub it in.'

'Not the two who shot at us?' checked Clemens.

'Eh?'

'With the bazooka—the two who shot at *you* ... they weren't two of the four staying at *The Hind's Head*?'

'No. They were ...'

'That makes six.' Clemens rubbed his jaw. 'They were Yanks too, by the sound of their talk ... wouldn't you say?'

'Yanks,' agreed Aimes. He stared at Clemens, and his face was twisted with almost unbearable worry, when he said, 'Look—Wally—what about Flora? I can't just stand here and wait. I've *got* to know. Damn it all! Six of the bastards. I dunno what the hell's happening, but...'

'Flora's okay.' Clemens qualified the remark, by adding, 'I'm pretty sure Flora's okay.'

'How the hell can you be...'

'It wouldn't take six. They wouldn't blow the bridge. They wouldn't blast a police van to hell. Not just for Flora. No offence, mate ... but not all *that*, just for Flora.'

'All right.' Aimes spread his hands. 'So, what the blazes ...'

'I dunno.' Clemens stopped rubbing his jaw, and cupped his hand around his chin. 'They had to stay somewhere, I suppose ... so-o, *The Hind's Head*. But it's summat else. Somebody else. I dunno what ... but not your wife. She just happens to *be* there.'

'Just happens to *be* ...'

'Somebody else,' reflected Clemens. 'Who? Who lives in Robs Cully? ... Who's worth all this trouble? Who owns anything worth all this trouble?'

Aimes said, 'I don't know. I don't care. I don't give a single damn about anybody—anything—in Robs Cully, except Flora.'

'You're lucky.' The come-back carried a hint of bitterness. 'I'm paid to give a damn about 'em all. And everything.'

Clemens turned and hurried towards the nearest squad car.

On the way, he paused to speak to the Road Traffic sergeant.

He said, 'A little bit of info. Not much ... but I'd like to radio it through.'

'Sure. Go ahead.'

Clemens glanced back at Aimes, and said, 'Watch him, sarge. His wife's in the village. At the moment, he's just about daft enough to get himself killed.'

In the 'Conference Room' of *The Hind's Head* the half-hundred, or so, inhabitants of Robs Cully mooched around, sat on chairs or gathered in low-murmuring groups.

Disbelief, outrage, shock, anger and fear ... those were the main feelings. They were abstract feelings, but they fused and fought for supremacy and, in their fusing and fighting, gorged upon each other and built up an atmosphere soup-thick with suppressed emotion.

Charlotte Douranby—a loaned coat over her dressing-gown— sat on one of the chairs, alongside the wall. She held a folded handkerchief to the ugly, discoloured swelling at her temple. With her other hand she raised and lowered a cigarette to and from her mouth in quick, jerky movements.

A handful of women fussed around Charlotte Douranby— among them Celia Kempton and Flora Aimes—but Charlotte seemed unaware of them. She stared into space and, periodically, whispered, 'Roj. Why doesn't Roj come? Where's Roj?'

Another, and slightly larger, group centred itself around Elizabeth Elliott. Elizabeth was stretched out along the seats of four chairs; on a makeshift stretcher. The thin man, who was a doctor, busied himself with the shoulder-wound, while Bill Elliott stood to one side and scowled ineffectual fury. Robert Hill, Jean Hill and Babs Pickering were among those anxious, but unable, to help. Jean Hill held Elizabeth's hand and squeezed it, comfortingly, whenever the thin man's probing made the younger woman wince.

Hill touched Bill Elliott's elbow.

Elliott turned his head and frowned a question.

Hill moved his head and eyes in the tiniest of gestures.

'What?' asked Elliott.

'A minute,' said Hill, softly.

'What about?'

'Just a minute,' repeated Hill.

'Look...'

'Please,'

Annoyance touched Elliott's expression for a moment, then he stepped away from the group.

Hill stood alongside him, and murmured, 'No half-cock action, Bill.'

'What the hell sort of...'

'I know you.' Hill's voice was calming, and little more than a whisper.

'Hey ... you two.' Johnny spoke from the stage. The Stirling S.M.G. stared at Hill and Elliott with its single, unblinking eye. Johnny said, 'Don't start pricking any private boils ... eh?'

In the silence following the words, there was the sound of a chuckle. The fat man's belly wobbled in time with his mirth.

Johnny switched his attention to the fat man, and growled, 'Funny?'

'The turn of phrase, old cock.' A melon-wide grin went with the explanation. 'Americanisms ... they fascinate me.'

'Yeah?'

'Colourful.' The fat man gave another, quick chuckle. 'A highly expressive language.'

'Could be.' Johnny's mouth twisted, momentarily, then he returned his attention to Hill and Elliott. He said, 'Just so we can all hear, fellas. Talk about the climate ... something like that. Right?'

'You're wrong, son.' Once more, the fat man diverted Johnny's attention from Bill and Elliott.

'Uh?' Johnny looked perplexed.

'In America ... the climate,' explained the fat man, cheerfully. 'On the continent—everywhere else in the world ... the climate. But we don't have "climate" here. We have *weather*. It changes every day. Almost every hour. It's "weather". It's not "climate".'

'You some sort of a nut, fatso?' growled Johnny.

The fat man shrugged and smiled, good-naturedly.

Somebody said, 'The stupid, fat oaf. He's out of his mind,' and the remark held a neat mix of disgust and disapproval.

'You're making yourself unpopular, fat man,' observed Johnny drily.

'How would you people put it?' murmured the fat man, ruefully. 'You can't win 'em all ... that it?'

'Right,' agreed Johnny.

He glanced across the room.

Elliott had re-joined the group around Elizabeth.

Hill hadn't moved. He stood, feet planted firmly apart and hands deep in the pockets of his trousers; head lowered and eyes gazing pensively at the floorboards.

The grass smelled good. And the earth, too ... it, too, had a good smell. Sweet, yet tinged with the background pungency of cow-smell; where the beasts had waddled to the water's edge to drink. Better than all your Paris perfumes, or your fancy after-shave concoctions. The smell of the countryside—the *real* countryside ... and you had to get your nose down, almost to soil-level, before you knew it was there.

Wilson loved the smell—he loved the open country—and, especially, he loved the open country, and the smell of the open country, in mid-June.

In mid-June, the sun had had time to round off, and complete, what Spring had started; time to do that, but not time enough to weather-bake the earth like an over-done steak. Wilson liked his countryside to be the way he preferred his meat; not cooked to a cinder, but warm and with the blood following the cut of the knife. Moist and tender ... like a good, ripe woman. Not cold and frigid. Not dry and acrid.

Like a good, ripe woman ...

He parted the stalks of long grass and watched, narrow-eyed, across the boiling surface of the Hewfraw.

A cat—a smooth-furred, well-fed tabby—strolled, tail in the air, along the low, whitened wall of one of the weekend cottages. It paused, lowered its nose to a patch of lichen, then continued its regal saunter.

The cat was the only living creature in sight.

Wilson brought his gaze nearer to where he lay in the grass;

to the river, and the zig-zag of half-submerged boulders which—if you know the pattern and were quick-footed enough—were 'stepping stones' from bank to bank.

They were there; remembered as a route he'd taken, more than once, when 'authority', in the shape of an angry farmer, or Police Constable Clemens, had come too close for comfort. But slippery. Treacherous. Always wet with splash from the foaming water.

Without taking his eyes from the river, and the farther bank, Wilson bent his legs, one at a time and, reaching down with his right hand, removed the shoe and sock, first from his right foot, then from his left. He flexed his freed ankles and wriggled his toes. When he hit the wet surface of those rocks, his toes were going to be necessary ... as necessary as fingers to a climber.

He bent his legs until he was in a crouching position, gave the far bank a last, quick scan, then raced for the nearest boulder.

They drove to Raine in Blayde's car. It was a Simca, and it headed a small cavalcade of squad cars, police vehicles and cars driven by both uniformed and plain clothes coppers.

It was a little like a well organised 'police raid'; controlled speed, with each vehicle tucked tight behind the rear of the vehicle in front.

Blayde drove, with Harris sitting alongside him.

'I don't go for guns,' said Blayde, bluntly.

Harris twisted his lips, and said, 'Is it important?'

'It drops us down to their level.'

'Whether, or not, you "go for guns"?' amplified Harris.

'To me,' said Blayde.

'And, is *that* important?'

'To me,' repeated Blayde.

'Aye ... well, it would be.'

The antagonism was far deeper than the Uniformed-Branch-C.I.D. thing. These two men truly disliked each other. They were rank for rank—both chief superintendents—and, when rank of that size makes war, the underlings with any sense start worrying ... because *they* are the ones who are going to bleed.

'What d'you suggest?' asked Harris, sarcastically. 'A pillow-fight? Telling 'em what naughty boys they are?'

'We can afford to be brave,' said Blayde. 'If it's as bad as we think, we're on the right side of the river ... we can *afford* to be brave.'

'Ripley...' began Harris.

'Ripley's dead,' cut in Blayde. 'He'll become a legend ... because he *is* dead.'

'If you bobby this division as well as *he* bobbied it, you'll...'

'And better.'

Harris turned his head, stared hatefully at the profile of the hatchet-faced Blayde, and growled, 'You're going to win all the popularity contests going, superintendent. You are going to be the pin-up boy of Beechwood Brook. Knock Ripley enough times, and you'll...'

'I am already gut-sick of that name.' Blayde watched the road ahead, as he spoke. 'Ripley was a passably good policeman. No more than that. He was a fool. He believed in guns. As a result of that belief, he was crippled ... somebody shot back.'

'He was a damn good...'

'As I understand it—from what everybody tells me—*you* weren't his best friend ... while he was alive. Since his death, you've had a regrettable lapse of memory ... or, so it seems. Or are you saying you—even *you*—can be wrong?'

The hatred in Harris's eyes intensified for a moment. Then he returned his gaze to the windscreen and breathed deeply through flared nostrils.

Blayde glanced up at the driving mirror.

Immediately behind the Simca, and being driven by a Road Traffic sergeant, Harris's Rover kept perfect position in the motorcade. And (as Blayde knew) in the rear of the Rover were the weapons; the rifles, the revolvers, the tear-gas cartridges.

Blayde's lip curled fractionally.

Harris spoke.

He said, 'Ruth's coming.'

'What!'

'Ruth ... she'll be at Raine.'

'You're not serious. Even *you* can't be as...'

'She volunteered. There'll be a problem. Relatives. Next-of-kin. She wants to help.'

Blayde murmured, 'Christ! That's *all* we need.'

'Aye ... I thought you'd like to know.'

Harris's remark was, in some strange way, the culmination of the exchange; a verbal kayo carefully, but ruthlessly, delivered and guaranteed to end the fight.

The fight ... or the first round!

The hoodlum with the silencered revolver—the hoodlum who'd been one of the pair to enter *Conte Lauba*; who'd knocked Charlotte Douranby unconscious and killed the two Afghan hounds—watched from the curtained window of the weekend cottage.

He was interested in what the goddam fink was fixing to do. Just what this bare-footed kook figured he was hatching. Dancing around, like a goddam ballet-hoofer. Like a goddam fairy. Arms waving around, for balance, and zigging and zagging up and about the stones ... and, all the time, getting a little nearer.

It was time for a real look-see.

The hoodlum left the window, walked to the door and left the cottage.

The fink saw him, and stopped; stopped, just about half-way across the river, arms windmilling as he steadied himself on one of the stones.

They watched each other for a few moments ... for the space of a dozen heartbeats.

The hoodlum's lips bent themselves into a slow smile as he eased a hand behind the skirt of his jacket and slipped the silencered revolver from its hip-holster. He raised the gun, in a two-handed grip, and brought it slowly up to eye-level.

The fink made as if to move, then changed his mind and stood, motionless.

The hoodlum increased the trigger-pressure. The hammer eased itself slowly away from the chamber, and the striking-pin tilted slightly ... like a man drawing back his fist.

The revolver whispered its 'thup' noise and jerked slightly.

The fink's left leg was knocked backwards, before the fink lost all balance, folded and dropped into the racing water. For a moment, he was lost from sight. Then he surfaced, grabbed for, and clung to, a rock about twenty yards from where he'd gone under.

The hoodlum strolled to the low, whitened wall of the garden. He used the top of the wall as an arm-rest; to steady the two-handed grip with which he still held the revolver.

He aimed very carefully.

He fired two shots.

The first chipped the rock, before flying off in a whining ricochet.

The second opened the fink's skull, at a point just above the bridge of his nose, and sent bone, blood and brains into the clean waters of the Hewfraw.

NATHANIEL WILSON ... R.I.P.
To be born of a dead mother; to be born of a mother who perished in giving you life, then to be brought to young manhood by an elderly, spinster aunt has certain Dickensian overtones.

You are grateful ... grateful to the unknown woman who died, that you might live.

You are also bitter ... bitter at a fate which demanded such an outrageous price.

As a child, you are not as other children. They have parents. You have a childless woman, who is your guardian. They have love ... all of them, and at some time, know what it is like to be loved. You have something less than love ... an 'acceptance' which is allied to a 'duty', but which includes very little true affection.

You grow suspicious. As the years tot up—as teenage milestones are passed—you become wary of a world which has dealt you a hand from a stacked deck and, with the arrival of manhood, your pattern of life is fixed.

You are a dour man. Like Kipling's cat, you 'walk alone'. You claim freedoms peculiar to yourself; the freedom of utter independence; the freedom to examine every man-made law, and decide whether, or not, it applies to you; the freedom to go where you will and, if necessary, across land other men claim as theirs.

The freedom to reject other men's gods and, in their place, erect a god of your own. A goddess. A personal madonna. A woman you never knew and who, as you sucked air into your puny lungs for the first time, breathed her last.

She was immaculate. She was perfect. She was without flaw.

She was why you have never married; why, with few exceptions, you hate all other women. They fall short. They are incomplete. They lack her beauty, lack her wisdom, lack her infinite love.

Other women—most other women—are like sows. Like bitches. Like mares. They are objects of copulative necessity ... female animals, who stand upright and who, unlike other female species, face their sires as they couple.

Poor, poor Nathaniel Wilson.

Go to her—go to your dream madonna, and pay homage .. but, as you go, be prepared to know what Hell is.

She will tell you.

She will grin, as she tells you.

She was the whore of the village ... she will name a dozen men, any of whom could have been your father.

Poor, poor Nathaniel Wilson ... R.I.P.

10.20 a.m. ...

Wolff stroked the flame of a lighter across the surface of the American tobacco which was packed into the bowl of his Italian, leather-covered pipe. It was a slow, deliberate and assured movement; the movement of a man in complete control of a situation.

Wolff looked assured ... but was not quite as assured as he looked.

Ask around, and they'd tell you. Ask at all the hot-spots—from New York to 'Frisco—from Minneapolis to New Orleans—and they'd tell you. James Edward Wolff, Jnr could move—but *move*! He could raise a cloud of following dust in any company. He picked up a telephone, he talked and things happened. Ask around, and they'd tell you ... they'd tell you all about Wolff, and the way he worked.

So-o...

What was with this Harris bastard? How come *he* wasn't setting his goddam shirt-tail alight?

It worried Wolff ... just a little.

Okay—he hadn't worked the Limey landscape before. Okay—maybe they *were* a shade or two different from the U.S. cops.

But—Jesus!—by this time the sirens should have been howling. The lights should have been flashing. The whole stinking force should have been squatting on their collective ass, hiding behind trees and prowl cars, shooters in their fists and wondering what the hell to shoot at.

There was a pattern. Y'know ... like a well-run barn dance. The music played a certain rhythm, and folks did certain things.

But these damn Limeys didn't *know* the goddam pattern ... like they'd never heard the music before.

Blow one of their vehicles to hell—just to make sure nobody figures all this as one big bluff—and what happens? ... nothing.

Nothing!

Not even a stinking telephone call.

So-o...

Wolff was just a mite worried.

He stood in the sun lounge of *Yew Tree Bower*, smoked fancy tobacco in his fancy pipe, stared out at the deserted village and wondered what the hell was happening out there, beyond the river ... if anything!

'You get a feelin'?' he growled, without removing the pipe from his mouth.

'Uh?' Cowboy creased his face into an expression of non-understanding.

'A feelin',' repeated Wolff. 'Y'know ... that somethin' ain't quite on the rails?'

'Nope,' said Cowboy, honestly.

'I get the feelin',' muttered Wolff.

'It ain't but nerves, boss,' volunteered Cowboy.

'You wanna smack in the banana-chewer?' snarled Wolff.

'Uh?' Cowboy looked startled.

'You just say I ain't got nerve again ... that's all. You're gonna be able to string your goddam teeth into a necklace.'

'I ain't meanin' that,' protested Cowboy. 'Y'know ... that you ain't got more than what you rightly need. Your kid, though ... uh? It ain't but natural that a daddy should worry about his kid.'

'Yeah.' Wolff sounded slightly mollified.

'It ain't but natural,' repeated Cowboy.

Wolff glared his impatience at the empty landscape for a few moments, then said, 'That Carter cat ... does he keep juice in this place?'

'Yep.'

'Fix me somethin'.'

'Sure.'

'Somethin' long and strong. Scotch, maybe. With ice.'

'Yep.' Cowboy moved towards the door leading from the sun lounge to the body of the house.

Wolff growled, 'And with more muscle than wet ... okay?'

'Yep.'

'That Carter cat' was having trouble. He was making discoveries about himself, and the discoveries were not comfortable discoveries.

For example ... that he was scared.

To use the language of these animals with whom he had allied himself, Flora Aimes had 'fingered him'. Short of the onset of rigor mortis, he was already a dead man. He knew the man called 'Johnny' ... knew his full name, and that he owned a house, a wife and four kids, in Springfield, Illinois. That the police of Houston could give chapter and verse about the hoodlum who answered to the name of 'Cowboy'. That, of the four men who had been paying guests at *The Hind's Head*, one was a professional trigger-man from Carson City, Nevada, and two of them were brothers whose home town was Little Rock, Arkansas.

Wolff? Of course he knew Wolff—who Wolff was, and where Wolff held his various headquarters ... but *that* knowledge wasn't important. Wolff didn't give a damn, because Wolff was rich enough, and powerful enough, not to *have* to give a damn. Wolff dealt in corruption in high places and, what the hell Wolff did, there was a thick wall of dollar bills between James Edward Wolff, Jnr and justice.

And this, too, was the way Wolff worked.

He 'bought' men; he paid for them, by the hour and by the job. He wasn't a typical mobster, in that he headed no identifiable 'mob'. These men—these hooligans who were holding Robs Cully at gun-point—were his temporary employees. No more than that. He owed them no loyalty, and what loyalty they owed *him* was on a strict C.O.D. basis.

It was safer that way.

Safer for James Edward Wolff, Jnr.

Nobody—not even the most conscientious F.B.I. agent—could start nibbling away at the bottom of the pyramid, in the hope that, eventually he'd bring the whole edifice crumbling. The damned edifice wasn't there! Just the peak—Wolff, himself—held firmly in place by hard cash, plus a reputation untarnished by even the hint of a double-cross.

But, come the end of the 'job' ... ah, come the end of the 'job'!

Nobody owed loyalty to 'Major' Carter. Nor did anybody trust him. Johnny, Cowboy, the trio of make-believe fishermen—men he'd come to know, and come to know about ... they owed him damn-all.

Except, perhaps, mistrust.

Except, perhaps, a bullet to keep his mouth shut.

It was a very uncomfortable feeling—a comfortless realisation—and Carter was probably the most unhappy person in that 'Conference Room'—which was saying something.

He walked to the stage, and cleared his throat, before he said, 'Er—Johnny.'

Johnny raised an enquiring eyebrow.

'I need some air,' said Carter.

Johnny kept the eyebrow cocked, but his mouth closed.

'These people hate me.' Carter glanced at the other occupants of the 'Conference Room'.

'That I'd say,' agreed Johnny, drily.

'I need some fresh air,' said Carter quietly. Desperately.

'They ain't gonna hate you any the less, soldier-boy.'

'For God's sake! Can't you understand?'

'You ain't runnin' no place, mac. You ain't...'

'I'm not running *anywhere*. Just a breather ... that's all.'

'For what?'

'It's—it's stifling in here. They'll—they'll...'

Carter ran out of words. There was no valid argument capable of penetrating the skull of this sub-human who controlled every life in the room.

'That they will,' agreed Johnny and, as he spoke, he nodded, slowly. 'They live, you're crow-meat, soldier-boy. You are crow-meat.'

'Please!' pleaded Carter.

'It ain't gonna help.'

'Just to get away from it, for a while. Just for a little while, to get away from the hatred.'

'You're soft-centred, mac ... y'know that?' Johnny grinned contemptuously. 'That shell you live in ain't so thick. And, inside, you're shit-soft. Y'know that?'

Carter nodded, miserably.

'*Kerrist!*' Johnny pursed his lips and made a spitting motion of his disgust. Then he glanced across the room, and called. 'Hey ... Pinky.'

One of the gunmen looked up.

He was Cowboy's erstwhile companion; one of the two who had entered *Woodvine Manse;* the man whose face had received frying-pan treatment from Elizabeth Elliott. His face still carried the marks, and dried blood still streaked his upper lip and chin and stiffened the front of his shirt and jacket.

He ambled across the room, towards the stage.

Johnny said, 'Take soldier-boy for a walk, pal. He needs to get some stiff-upper-lip crap back into his system. All these jerks not likin' him ... it's makin' him nervous.'

Pinky nodded, and said, 'Sure.'

'And watch him,' warned Johnny. 'Anythin' fancy, and cool him ... right?'

'Sure.'

Carter and Pinky walked from the 'Conference Room'.

They were watched every inch of the way, and the accumulation of hatred could almost be felt.

Raine village hall ... officially designated 'Raine Community Centre'.

Go into any not-so-modern village hall, and five gets you ten it will level peg with 'Raine Community Centre'. A place of cobwebbed corners and finely-layered dust; of cheap colour-wash covering near-crumbling plaster; of scuffed floorboards and chipped paintwork; of a postage-stamp-sized stage and stained, torn-and-stitched curtains; of inadequate heating and poor lighting.

Raine village hall.

Harris wrinkled his nose, and grunted, 'The "Incident Centre" ... some "Incident Centre"!'

Blayde waved a hand towards a mountain of stacked chairs and trestle-tables, and gave orders to a sergeant and a group of uniformed coppers who had crowded into the building, behind the two chief superintendents.

He said, 'Set them up, sergeant. U-shaped, from the stage. Enough chairs. And search around for a blackboard—something of that nature—to use as a notice-board.'

The little man with steel-rimmed spectacles looked worried.

He said, 'Look—I think you'd better...'

'What?' barked Harris.

'I—er—I'm only the caretaker, you understand. I haven't the authority to...'

'We have,' interrupted Blayde.

'Oh!'

'Telephone?' said Harris.

'There—in there.' The caretaker waved a fluttering hand towards two doors leading from the main hall. 'The Committee

Room ... there's a telephone in there. And, next door ... that's the kitchen.'

'What we need,' said Harris, sarcastically. 'We'd be lost without a kitchen.'

'There's a kiosk, outside,' said Blayde.

'Aye ... I, too, have eyes.'

'Two telephones.'

'If we don't run out of coins,' said Harris.

Blayde said, 'I'll get the number, then station a man there. I'll have D.H.Q. call us—at the kiosk—every fifteen minutes.'

'It'll help,' admitted Harris, grudgingly.

The little man repeated his plea.

He said, 'Look—I think you'd better...'

'I think *you'd* better go back home,' growled Harris. 'Back to bed.'

'I wasn't in bed. I was...'

'What the hell you *were* doing. Go back, and do it.'

Harris turned his back on the caretaker and strode towards the Committee Room.

10.25 a.m....

In the 'Conference Room' they heard the ringing of the telephone bell. They heard it gradually. Nobody heard the first ring; the 'burr-burr' eased itself into the background hum of muttered talk then, as each in turn realised that, downstairs, a telephone was ringing, the talk thinned out into silence.

The ringing continued.

Flora Aimes walked up to the stage, and looked up at Johnny.

'We'd better answer it,' she said.

'Uhu.' Johnny shook his head.

'They'll wonder.'

Johnny said, 'It ain't important, lady. They already *know*.'

Flora chewed at her lower lip for a moment, then shrugged and turned away.

The telephone bell continued for another two minutes.

Then it stopped.

It was a little like the cutting of a life-line, and a small sigh of disappointment seemed to whisper its way through the 'Conference Room'.

'Okay, folks?' Johnny grinned at the assembly. 'Everybody

relax. Nobody ain't "at home". *Nobody* ... right?'

The grin stayed on his face as he surveyed the captive community.

Then it wiped itself clean, and was replaced by a scowl, as the distant 'burr-burr' started up again.

Harris glared at the wall of the Committee Room and muttered, 'Where the blazes *is* the bastard?'

He could hear the ringing tone in the earpiece, and knew that the telephone at *The Hind's Head* was working properly. He knew damn well he'd dialled the correct number once but, just to make doubly sure, he'd replaced the receiver and re-dialled.

He glanced up at Blayde, and said, 'Clemens ... you're sure you got his message right?'

'I don't get messages wrong,' said Blayde, flatly.

'All right. What about Clemens? Could he have...'

'He passed on what he learned from Aimes. That the Americans were at *The Hind's Head.*'

'This germ Wolff?'

Blayde moved his shoulders.

'In that case, how the hell...'

'Do you know what Wolff looks like?' asked Blayde.

'How the blazes do I know what...'

'Nor does Aimes. Nor does Clemens.'

Harris breathed heavily, gripped the receiver, and rasped, 'Why the deuce doesn't somebody answer?'

The fat man (who was known by his thin companion, and by Robert Hill, to be a character called 'Lennox' and, moreover, a character who carried the rank of detective superintendent) blinked, owlishly, at Johnny.

'It—er—it might be important, old son,' he remarked.

'Shove it, fatso,' muttered Johnny.

'The bloke,' expanded Lennox.

'Uh?'

'Y'know ... the bloke who was here, about an hour ago.'

'Which goddam bloke?'

'The boss,' amplified Lennox, mildly. '*Your* boss ... the bloke who told us what all this was about.'

'Wolff?' Puzzlement creased Johnny's forehead.

'I wouldn't know, old cock.' Lennox spread his hands. 'Just

that, whoever it is, he's pretty insistent. It's urgent ... whatever it is.'

Indecision chased a series of expressions across Johnny's face. He gave a tiny nod—as if to punctuate the making up of his mind—and looked across the room to where one of the gunmen stood guard, near the door. He took a breath, before speaking.

'Er...' Lennox beat him to the punch.

'Yeah?' The annoyance of indecision returned to Johnny's face.

'If it isn't,' said Lennox.

'If it ain't what?'

'Wolff.'

'So?'

'We-ell ... y'know.' The fat man showed the palms of his hands again. 'If it's somebody else.'

'So?' repeated Johnny.

Lennox grinned, self-consciously, then said, 'Y'know? don't take offence—but the accents...'

'What about the goddam accents?'

'Hollywoodish,' explained Lennox. 'Y'know—gangster movie talk. Anybody from outside. They're not going to *believe* it.'

'That's their worry, fatso.'

'It's—er—worth thinking about,' insisted Lennox, gently.

'Okay—so, I've thought about it—now I'm gonna...'

'Let me go,' volunteered the fat man.

Johnny stared his disbelief, then said, 'You nuts? You have some sorta hole in your head, fat man?'

'Not alone,' said Lennox, hurriedly. 'Good lord, no ... not *alone*.' He widened his mouth into a moon grin, as if the idea of him going downstairs, alone, to answer the telephone was too ludicrous for serious consideration. Then he said, 'No—I mean with whoever answers it. Then, if they don't believe, I can tell 'em. Y'know ... in proper English.'

'Which spitball language you figure *we* talk, you fat gink?' Johnny glared, as he asked the question.

'Y'know what I mean,' said Lennox, plaintively.

The telephone bell continued to ring.

Johnny called to the man near the door.

He said, 'Hey, Dutch. Answer the blower ... uh?' He hesitated, then added, 'An' take this belly-heavy bastard along with you.

Just in case some screwy Limey don't understand his own goddam chatter.'

The grass was close-cropped, and as well-kept as a bowling-green, where it ended at the river's bank. Trees—flowering cherries, almonds and rowans—marched, in orderly Indian-file along the turf and between the tarmac path and the water's edge. It was a tiny, but very select, promenade which encircled the whole of Robs Cully; one of the 'amenities' for which the residents of Robs Cully paid through the nose.

Carter strolled, hands in pockets, along the path.

The man called Pinky walked about two paces to the rear and, in Pinky's right hand, there was a gun. It was, by any normal revolver-automatic-pistol standard a very oddball-looking gun. The *Gun Digest* described it as a Dardick Series 1500; calibre .38; fifteen-shot; three-inch barrel; fixed ramp front sight, adjustable rear sight. In layman's language, that meant it fired fifteen bullets through a barrel a mere three inches long, and the bullets were housed in the stock of the weapon. It was an angular gun; all but, with a fiddling little snout and an exaggerated trigger and trigger-guard.

It was one hell of a killing instrument. Not popular ... perhaps because it lacked the more conventional shape of the average automatic pistol. Virtually unobtainable within the shore-line of the United Kingdom ... because you needed exceptionally strong powers of imagination to visualise its use as other than a man-killer.

Pinky carried it loosely, and easily; ready to tilt it and send one of its .38 slugs through the spine of Carter at the first hint of heroics.

Carter was aware of Pinky's presence. He was also aware of the Dardick ... and knew enough about firearms to know that, strange as it looked, the Dardick was no water-pistol!

He worked to push the gun, and the gunman, out of his thoughts.

It was necessary—a simple matter of life or death—that he didn't return to the 'Conference Room'. Johnny had allowed him out ... this once. But there wouldn't be a repeat. This particular moment of the operation was one which was not going to be repeated; the 'waiting time'—the period when things either stood up, or fell down ... the time when every movement had to be played by ear.

But get this time over—let Wolff be told 'Yea' or 'Nay'—and every subsequent action would be crystallised by that answer. There would be nothing, or there would be wholesale slaughter.

So-o ...

Carter didn't want to die. He started with that simple, no-messing proposition. That 'Major' Carter, or what the hell he cared to call himself; that whether or not, it branded him a coward; that his once-upon-a-time chosen profession dealt with sudden death. That—all these things notwithstanding—*he didn't want to die.*

And, to Carter, the 'Conference Room' at *The Hind's Head* was the equivalent of a death cell.

James Edward Wolff, Jnr removed his pipe from his mouth long enough to take a deep swig of iced whisky, and snarl, 'Why 'n hell can't that gold-plated bull move his gold-plated ass?'

Robert Harris—detective chief superintendent—Head of County Constabulary C.I.D.—held the telephone receiver hard to his ear, listened to the ringing tone at the other end of the wire, and muttered, 'Where the bloody hell is that stupid bastard Wolff?'

The telephone was in the bar; at the end of the curved bar-counter. It rang away, merrily, as if this was its sole reason for being invented (as, indeed, it was) and as if it was prepared to continue ringing until its bell wore out, or its clanger dropped off.

The man called Dutch hurried into the bar.

Lennox waddled along, behind.

Lennox said, 'Ah ... booze.'

'Wassat?' Dutch paused, en route to the telephone, to catch a repeat of the fat man's remark.

'Wallop.' Lennox waved oversized fingers at the array of bottles, beyond the counter. He said, 'I could do a drink, old son. How about you?'

'Yeah ... why not?'

The fat man changed direction slightly, lifted the bar-counter flap and examined the variety of drinks available.

Dutch leaned against the bar, kept an eye on the fat man, and lifted the receiver from its rest.

He said, 'Yeah?'

'Is that Wolff?' Harris's voice crackled across the telephone wires.

'Whossat? Wolff?'

'Is that Wolff?'

'Naw. This ain't Wolff.'

'Is that the bloody *Hind's Head*?'

'Yeah. Why?'

'There is,' bawled Harris's voice, 'a lunatic called Wolff, there. He...'

'Wolff ain't here,' growled Dutch.

'Brandy?' asked Lennox, politely. He reached for a bottle on one of the upper shelves. 'This is good stuff... I can vouch for that.'

'Yeah... great.' Dutch nodded his approval.

'Great *what*?' yelled Harris. 'What the hell sort of an answer is...'

'It wasn't meant for you, pal,' countered Dutch.

'What wasn't meant for me?'

'Wolff ain't around,' said Dutch.

'He told me to telephone him.'

'Sure... that follows.'

'Judas Christ! What the hell sort of conversation *is* this?'

'You phoned, pal. I didn't.'

Lennox fished glasses from under the counter and poured brandy from a fancy bottle; a bottle with a long neck and a bulbous body; a bottle made of very heavy glass.

'I want to speak to Wolff,' shouted Harris. 'God in His high heaven! How many more times do I have to say it?'

'Wolff ain't around... I keep tellin' ya.'

'Get him,' roared Harris. 'Get the stupid bastard. Tell him I'm here, waiting to...'

'That ain't possible, pal.'

'Why not? Has he dropped dead?... I hope.'

'Hey pal. You wanna ease the yap. Okay?'

'Cheers?' Lennox raised his glass.

'Yeah... cheers.'

Dutch (whatever his other name was)... the tough baby.

Dutch (whatever his other name was)... the trigger-man.

Dutch (whatever his other name was)... the mug!

He didn't know it, of course, but he was facing a con who had conned some of the best cons ever to sell a common-or-garden sucker a gold brick. He was up against a man who could give O'Toole lessons in extempore acting.

He didn't know all this.

But he learned ... fast!

He learned as he placed his revolver to hand, on the surface of the bar-counter; as he reached for the glass of brandy; as the bulbous body of the heavy glass bottle smacked the side of his skull, and the long, thin neck of the bottle snapped; as he made a belated grab at the revolver, and the sharded glass of the neck of the broken bottle was driven into the back of his hand and held it pinned on the bar-counter top.

Lennox's hand reached the revolver first.

The muzzle was held steady, within an inch of Dutch's upper lip, and Lennox murmured, 'Not a whisper, son. Not a peep. Otherwise...' The fat man shrugged, resignedly. 'It's a rough game, laddie. And you know the rules.'

Dutch took a deep breath, eased his hand away from the bar as Lennox released the pressure on the snapped neck of the bottle.

In a voice which was little more than a whisper, he said, 'Y'know, fat man. They are gonna crease you slowly for this. They are gonna fry you, medium rare.'

'Maybe.' Lennox smiled; and, this time, it was a smile and not a grin. He said, 'Don't let it worry you, sonny. If you start it, you won't hear any of the screaming.'

Dutch allowed the rest of his breath to come out in a long, heavy sigh.

He had been around. He was a wise man, as far as his own brand of wisdom was concerned. He knew voices, and when voices meant the words which those voices spoke. And, although it came as a surprise, amounting to a traumatic shock, he knew that this fat, slob of a body was wrapped around one of the toughest hombres he'd ever had the misfortune to meet.

And, if the voice needed ratification, the eyes in the full-moon face provided ratification enough, and the ratification was underlined by the rock-steady revolver held in the pudgy paw.

Lennox said, 'About two yards away, son. Then turn round. Feet apart and hands clasped behind your neck. I don't want you to shout. You don't want me to shoot you. We'll do a deal ... you don't do one, and I won't do the other.'

Dutch murmured, 'You're hot property, pal.'

'Medium rare,' smiled Lennox.

Dutch exchanged the smile for a twist of the lips, then obeyed orders. The blood from his hand dripped on to the rear of his collar and stained the back of his jacket.

From the receiver, hanging at the end of its wire, Harris's voice still squawked unintelligible questions.

Lennox reeled in the wire, raised the receiver to his face, and said, 'Put a bung in it a minute, cock. You have a new party on the line.'

'Who the hell's *that?*' barked Harris.

'That,' said Lennox, 'is my question.'

'Eh?'

'Your name, old son. To whom have I the pleasure of addressing my remarks?'

'Are you trying to be funny?' Harris's voice was explosive with pent-up fury.

'Not at all,' said Lennox.

'You know damn well...'

'That I do not. This is a telephone ... not a television set.'

'Harris,' roared Harris. 'Detective Chief Superintendent Harris, of the ...'

'Nice to hear from you, Bob,' interrupted Lennox, cheerfully. 'Lennox, here.'

'*Who?*' The outrage, the anger and the frustration gave way to incredulity.

'Lennox,' repeated Lennox.

'Sweet creeping Jesus!' breathed Harris. 'What next?'

'You know what's happening, in here?' Lennox's voice was uncommonly serious.

'What the devil are *you* doing in there?' asked Harris.

'Fishing. I'm on a fishing holiday, with Doc Pearson ... we got caught up in this pantomime. You know what's happening?'

'Aye. A bastard called Wolff.'

'He has everybody holed up in *The Hind's Head* ... in an upstairs room. Something about his son being inside.'

'Seven years,' explained Harris.

'Or until nine-thirty, tomorrow morning ... unless you want everybody here to wear a wreath,' said Lennox, sombrely.

'As bad as that?'

'Just as bad as that,' emphasised Lennox.

There was a silence which eased itself into all of ten seconds then, when he ended the silence, all the shout and bounce had left Harris's voice and he was back to what he was paid to be ... a very high-ranking and very objective cop.

He said, 'Put me in the picture, Lenny.'

Lennox said, 'Yankee trigger-men. I'd say about two dozen, counting those holding guns on the civilians and those needed for this sort of operation. Wolff's the boss. There's also a bastard called Carter ... lives here. Ex-army. He's in with 'em.'

'Anybody hurt yet?' asked Harris.

'Two—both women. One with a knock on the skull. The other with a shoulder-wound. Pearson's fixing them as well as he can.'

'They're not playing Ludo,' grunted Harris.

'Or bingo,' agreed Lennox. 'Take things easy, Bob. They'll have the bridge covered. When you cross, you'll have to...'

'There's no bridge,' interrupted Harris.

'Eh?'

'They've already blown it.'

'Aye.' Lennox nodded, slowly ... as if the news was a verification. 'They would.'

'So?' asked Harris.

Lennox said, 'I'll take a quick squint. There's a comedian here—you've already had words with him—I'll have to...'

'He's still there?' Harris sounded surprised. A little worried.

'But safe.' Lennox chuckled. 'I borrowed his gun. We have a working arrangement. He won't pull any fast ones, and I won't pull any triggers.'

Still with his back to the fat man, Dutch muttered, 'Just for now, gut-boy. Just for now.'

'Don't run too many risks, Lenny,' warned Harris, quietly.

'Do I ever?'

'And we'd better talk. Wolff ... where the hell do I contact Wolff?'

'Dunno.' Lennox pondered a moment, then said, 'Carter's place ... it seems an obvious first choice.'

'What's it called?'

'Don't ask *me*.'

'You won't know the telephone number?'

'Right ... I don't know.'

'I'll find it,' said Harris. 'I'm here ... Raine, three-two-two. Get what you can out to us, Lenny. Keep your fingers crossed.

We might be able to chase this monkey up a stick, yet.'

Lennox said, 'I'll be in touch.' He dropped his voice a semitone and, very sombrely, added, 'And Bob—take my word for it —these boyoes really *don't* give a damn.'

'I've already said ... watch yourself,' growled Harris, and hung up.

Lennox replaced the receiver.

Dutch stood patiently, hands still clasped behind his neck, and waited. Lennox had already reminded him ... he knew the rules.

The rules still applied.

Lennox walked from behind the bar-counter, eyed the back of the gunman's head for a moment, then belted him across the skull with the barrel of the revolver.

For his size and shape, Lennox was very nimble on his feet.

He side-stepped smartly to allow the hoodlum room enough to fold into an untidy heap on the carpet.

Carter stopped. His gunsel escort also stopped and brought the odd-shaped Dardick handgun a little more in line with Carter's spine.

'What...' Carter nodded to where the Hewfraw eddied around a promontory at its bank. 'What on earth's *that*?'

Pinky flicked a glance at the tiny headland, then muttered, 'Search me.'

Carter stepped off the tarmac path and walked across the grass to the water's edge.

He breathed, 'Good God!'

'That' was, quite obviously, a dead man; a dead man who, except for shoes and socks, was fully-clothed; a dead man, floating and bobbing on the surface of the water, with the back of his skull opened and exposed to show shattered bone and blasted brain-tissue.

Carter closed his eyes and, in a whisper, repeated, 'Good God!'

'Somebody got him,' observed Pinky, without emotion.

Carter kept his eyes closed, and nodded.

'He ain't one of ours,' said Pinky.

'No.' Carter opened his eyes, forced himself to look at the corpse again, swallowed, then said, 'He—he isn't one of ours.'

'Wolff'll wanna know,' said Pinky.

'I—er—I suppose so,' said Carter, wearily.

And, slowly, within Carter's mind, the transformation took place. Like the gradual lighting of a stage; as slowly, but as certainly as a sunrise ... it came and, eventually, it filled his whole intelligence.

Not 'manhood'. Manhood was a quality Carter had, for too long, scorned; it was something he equated with idiots—something on a par with the fallacy of blue blood and *noblesse oblige* —something as stupid as 'honour' or 'integrity' ... a weakness in other men which, for too long, he'd taken advantage of. Therefor, not 'manhood'.

Nor 'courage'. Courage brought pain. It sometimes brought death. It occasionally brought medals ... and, too many times, the medals were awarded posthumously. Courage was, to Carter, another name for 'madness'. Another name for 'crass stupidity' ... therefore, whatever else, not 'courage'.

But something.

Self-preservation was certainly part of it; the near-certain knowledge that, if things just *happened*—if he allowed things to happen—he'd end up like this 'thing' which flopped, bonelessly as the ripples nudged it ... which bumped, soundlessly and sickeningly, against the bank of the Hewfraw.

Self-preservation was certainly part of it ... and a major part.

But (and to be charitable) self-disgust was in there, somewhere, too. Some tiny knob of self-disgust, which had made itself felt at Pinky's throw-away remark. 'He ain't one of ours.' *Ours!* Meaning Wolff, and his scum—and including *him* ... Carter. The pronoun had been meant to embrace Wolff, and every man employed by Wolff—including *him* ... Carter.

God Almighty!

That one word—that single pronoun—triggered off the transformation.

Pinky nudged him in the ribs with the snout of the Dardick, and said, 'C'mon, buddy. Wolff'll wanna know.'

'We should—er ...' Carter worked for time; time to remember the hints and wrinkles of unarmed combat; time to wish he'd taken more notice of the instructor. He said, 'Shouldn't we check?'

'Check?'

'Who he is?'

'He ain't one of us ... so, who cares?'

'Wolff might like to know.'

'Naw. He should worry. He ain't one of our boys.'
'Nevertheless...'
It was now, or never.
The muzzle of the Dardick was touching the cloth of his jacket, at rib-level, on the left side.

Carter swung his left arm back, then forwards. Fast! He caught Pinky's wrist on the forward swing (which was what he'd meant to do) and, at the same time, grabbed the wrist with his right hand. And, even as his fingers tightened in a two-handed grip on the gun-wrist, Carter twisted his body to the right, dropped to one knee, yanked the gun-arm forward, stood upright and used his own shoulder as a fulcrum against the elbow of the gun-arm. Pinky screamed fractionally ahead of the snap of the elbow and, suddenly, the Dardick pendulummed on the useless forefinger, as the trigger-guard caught against the top joint.

Carter released the wrist, brushed the gun off its finger, turned and (for no reason, other than that the perverted lunacy of pain-inducement was within him) crashed a shoed toe into Pinky's crotch.

The gunman went down; one arm helpless, the hand of the other arm holding his groin. He curled on the grass and whined his pain.

And Carter kept kicking. Head—shoulders—arms—ribs—spine ... anywhere and everywhere, until the gunman was quite unconscious.

Unconscious ... perhaps even dead.

Carter didn't give a damn, either way.

10.35 a.m. ...

Neither of them wasted time on pleasantries.

Harris said, 'Is that Wolff?'
'Yeah ... you Harris?'
'I'm at Raine,' said Harris.
'So?'
'Raine, three-two-two.'
'So?' repeated Wolff.
'In case you need me.'
'I don't need *you*, pig ... I need my kid.'
'The chief constable's on his way.'
'That don't interest me none.'

Harris said, 'We need his authority.'

'I don't need a damn thing, pig,' snarled Wolff. 'I got all I need. I got Robs Cully, and every sonofabitch in the goddam place. And—get me Harris—we trade. Ric, for them. And before thirty after nine, tomorrow morning. Otherwise you have grief, copper ... more grief than you can handle.'

The gunman's name (his *real* name—not the name he'd entered in the register of *The Hind's Head*) was Beaumont ... Hugh Beaumont. Which (as the cops of his home town, Rapid City, South Dakota, agreed, to a man) was something of a cockalarky name for a short-arsed fink who figured himself as a latter-day Dillinger. 'Hugh' (according to the boys sporting the badges) was a pansy name. 'Beaumont' (according to those same boys was) an even more pansy name. Which (by logical and mathematical progression) made 'Hugh Beaumont' a pansy-pansy name and, all his adult life, Beaumont had worked hard to counter this most unjust slur upon his manhood.

He was a two-gun man ... the only two-gun hoodlum in the whole Robs Cully operation. More than that (and something which was unusual, even in the world of 'shooters', 'gats' and 'pieces') he was a twin-Luger man.

The Luger (so-called—although it is, these days, made by any God's amount of various firearms manufacturers, under licence, but *not* by the firm which originally put it on the market) is the ultimate in semi-automatic pistols. It is some gun! It is accurate, reliable and very, *very* deadly. It is the one handgun any 'torpedo' feels happy to own; the greatest 'equaliser' ever to become part of a hit man's hand.

And Beaumont had *two* ... maybe as a means of balancing the two pansy names he'd been bugged with.

He came down the stairs, a Luger in each hand.

He was obeying Johnny's instructions to 'See what the hell that Dutch creep is hangin' around at. An' tell him to go easy on the lush-juice.'

A simple instruction, and a short, but pleasant, change from standing around in the upstairs room watching the mugs crawl around and feel sorry for themselves.

Hugh Beaumont—big guy—tough guy ... but, even the biggest and the toughest can, at times, be suckers.

He rounded the bend in the stairs, walked down the few

remaining steps and gradually slowed to a halt. He stared. He could hardly believe his eyes.

I mean ... what the stinkin' Christ!

There, on the carpet, to his right, and pretty well in the middle of the entrance lounge leading to the bar. Some sorta juggling act. Some sorta balancing routine ... and for *what*?

What sorta loop-brained idea was it to take forty—maybe fifty—glasses and build 'em into a stinkin' pyramid? Waist-high, and just standing there. Looking like, at the first breath of breeze, they might topple. What the hell sorta crackbrained notion had gotten itself into Dutch's skull?

Beamont lowered his foot from the bottom step, walked slowly to the small mountain of glasses, stared down at it and muttered, 'What the...'

At that point in the remark Lennox stepped briskly, but silently, from under the angle of the stairs and repeated his skull-belting routine.

Beaumont folded forward and the pyramid of glasses collapsed under his falling weight.

Lennox chuckled to himself, scooped up the two Lugers and made for the rear door of *The Hind's Head*.

Carter gazed at the boiling waters of the Hewfraw. In his right hand he held the Dardick. To his left, and behind him, the unconscious Pinky stained the turf with the last of his life-blood. In front of him—within a yard of his shoes—the bare-footed corpse slopped around on the surface and, with sickening regularity, nudged the bank.

And, not for the first time in his life, Carter wished to hell he'd learned to swim.

The waters of the river scared him. They weren't like ordinary liquids. Like the liquid in a glass. Like the liquid in a bath. These waters were alive and furious; they boiled, they spat, they fought a never-ending war with each other. They were terrifying waters; waters strong enough and angry enough to make even a good swimmer pause.

And Carter couldn't swim.

He heard, and saw the bullet slice a scar across the bark of the almond tree at the same time as he heard the whipcrack of the shot. It was a miss—a two-yard miss—and, whoever was firing was either too far distant for accuracy, or a rotten shot ... probably both.

He gasped, 'Oh, Christ!' forgot the river, forgot the floating corpse, forgot the battered Pinky and sprinted, at a crouch, for the cover of the nearest building.

11 a.m. ...

There was a log.

There is *always* a log. Give the cops an incident of any size and, one of the first things they do, they 'open' a log. A time-table. A booking-in and booking-out. A recording of everything ... from the o'clock when the main suspect breaks wind, to the time of day when the cuffs are clicked into position. Everything!

It is necessary. Like statistics, it can mean anything. It can be used as a means of justifying future commendations. It can also be used (and exactly the same data) as a means of demanding a resignation. It is, if you like, a documentary launch-pad and, from it can be fired either satellites or rockets.

There was, therefore, a log.

The entry in the log read ... '11.00 hrs. C.C. arrives I.C.'

Grafton had arrived at the Incident Centre.

A detective sergeant was busy pinning a map of Robs Cully on to a rectangle of hardboard, propped against an easel which somebody had rooted from one of the tiny lumber rooms behind the postage-stamp-sized stage. The Incident Centre was still sparsely furnished and inadequately staffed; a couple of trestle-tables, a handful of rickety chairs, the easel, hardboard and an ancient Olympia typewriter was about all the equipment at hand; less than a dozen men, plus three policewomen, worked hard at creating a nerve-centre from which to combat whatever was happening at Robs Cully.

Already, however, there was a log. It was (for the moment) being meticulously kept by one of the policewomen, and she it was who entered, '11.00 hrs. C.C. arrives I.C.'

'Harris!' barked Grafton, as he strode into the village-hall-cum-Incident-Centre.

'Er—sir?' The D.S. turned from the easel, verified with his eyes what his ears had already registered—that the Grand Panjandrum was breathing down his neck—and straightened to a quick, token attitude of attention. He pointed to one of the doors leading from the main hall, and said, 'Over there, sir. That—er—Committee Room ... it's a Committee Room, Chief Superintendent Harris and Chief Superintendent Blayde are using it as a ...'

The D.S. stopped speaking as Grafton moved beyond earshot.

Grafton didn't knock.

The impression was that, had it been possible without inflicting upon himself bodily hurt, he wouldn't even have wasted time turning the knob. Technically speaking, he 'entered' the Committee Room ... graphically, but more accurately, speaking, he *exploded* upon the two chief superintendents.

Blayde said, 'Good morning, sir.'

'I want you out of here, Mr Blayde,' snapped Grafton.

'I beg your pardon, sir?'

'Out of here ... I want a word with Chief Superintendent Harris. Alone!'

Harris watched the exchange from where he was sitting, at a battered table-desk upon which was a telephone. He watched with hooded eyes and with a hint of sardonic distaste touching his lips.

'Alone?' Blayde asked the question in a quiet voice, which rode a tone as expressionless as a concrete cube.

'I have things to say,' rasped Grafton.

'About Robs Cully ... I hope,' observed Blayde mildly.

'Blayde. I don't intend ...'

'About getting this man Wolff's son out of prison.'

'What I wish to say to Detective Chief Superintendent Harris, is none of your business, Blayde. I'm asking you to ...'

'Indeed, it *is*, chief constable,' interrupted Blayde.

'What!'

'Beechwood Brook. That's my business, sir. Everything about Beechwood Brook, everything that happens in Beechwood Brook, everything that's *said* about Beechwood Brook. It's my division ... therefore, it's my business. At this particular moment, innocent members of this community—*my* community—are being held hostage. Everything else is of secondary importance. Everything! You can, of course, order me away from here. Out of this room. Away from any one part of this problem. You have the authority, chief constable. Exercise that authority, if you think fit ... but know that my resignation will be on your desk, before the day's out. That I won't question the wisdom of your decision. But ...' Blayde paused for a fraction of a second, stared eye-to-eye at the chief constable's face, then ended, 'I'll make damn sure the Home Office question it.'

It stopped Grafton.

Not merely what was said but, equally importantly, the voice in which the words were delivered. There was no 'if-you-I-may' quality about the delivery of the words ... every one carried an unqualified 'if-you-I-*will*' threat.

Harris cleared his throat.

Blayde waited.

Grafton glared, then sniffed.

Harris growled, 'Let's all cool down ... shall we?'

Blayde waited.

'We have work to do,' continued Harris. 'Squabbles can keep.'

'Wise,' murmured Blayde.

Grafton filled his lungs with air, held it for a moment, then let the air out slowly. It was a long, long sigh. It contained frustration and the tail-end of a monumental anger ... but not defeat.

Grafton said, 'You're right, of course. Squabbles can wait ... *must* wait. But there'll be a reckoning. Remember that. Meanwhile—both of you—put me in the picture ... and come up with some ideas.'

The thin man—the friend of Lennox, whom Lennox had identified to Harris as 'Doc Pearson'—walked across the 'Conference Room', stopped at the stage and looked up at Johnny.

He said, 'I need things.'

'Uhu?' Johnny's grunted question was devoid of any true interest.

'Bandages.'

'Rip somethin', doc. We don't have bandages.'

'Antibiotics. Sulphonamides.'

'You crazy?' Johnny's voice was bored.

'That girl.' Pearson glanced to where Elizabeth Elliott sat nursing her shoulder and surrounded by Bill Elliott, the Hills and a couple of women in Elliott and Hill's age-group. 'Her shoulder's bad.'

'Whose fault?' Johnny shrugged.

'She's been shot.'

'So? Who ain't ... at some time.'

'You're an ape,' said Pearson, disdainfully.

'Yeah ... they tell me.'

'Septicaemia. It's not only possible ... it's likely, if we don't get antibiotics.'

'So?'

'Don't you care?' exploded Pearson. 'Don't you bloody-well *care*?'

'We-ell, now...' Johnny eyed Pearson cynically. He smiled, without humour, then said, 'Since you have smoke comin' outa your ass. Since your goddam fanny seems to be gettin' itchy. Since you ain't grabbed the true size of this thing. Since all these things, I will draw you pictures, doc. To me, you ain't a bag of beans. One at a time, or all together ... you ain't a bag of beans. Don't ask me that some crazy snotball who don't know better is gonna get hurt. Don't ask me that I should give a damn. You're wastin' everybody's time, doc. That crap ... I had it belted outa me, years ago. That's what it is ... crap! You are dyin', doc. Ever think about that? You, me—both ... dyin'. Everybody. We are all busy as hell, easin' ourselves into a hole in the ground. That's all. And, come one day, we are gonna touch bottom ... everybody. Okay? So, things ain't important any more, see? Antibiotics. Guns. Gunshot wounds. Nothin'—what the hell it don't matter a damn ... it is gonna happen, anyway. So, I figure—y'know ... why not let go, and just drop?'

'Your philosophy?' Pearson looked up at Johnny with something not too far removed from sympathy.

'Ain't it right, though?' asked Johnny, softly.

'Perfect ... as the philosophy of a dead man.'

'Y'know—could be you're right, doc,' agreed Johnny, heavily. 'Could be you are so damn right.'

JOHN LINCOLN SPURGEON ... GUNMAN.

'Lincoln' because you were born, and still live, in Springfield, Illinois; resting-place of the great 'Abraham' of the same name.

But you are no 'Honest Abe'. You are no political giant—no historical colossus—no ...

What are you?

You, whom these people know as 'Johnny' ... just what the hell are you?

You are a freak, and a fake, and a madman.

What else?

To be what you are and, at the same time, pretend to be what you are not, is to be two people. It is to tear yourself apart. It is schizophrenia run wild; a deliberate and conscious schizophrenia ... and a personal choice which, in time, must become a hot-bed of self-hate.

In Springfield, Illinois, you are respected.

Almost two-hundred miles south-west of Springfield, in Chicago —in the good old 'Windy City' of corruption, sudden death and tough guys—you are also respected ... but for other reasons.

In Springfield, the respect came with your birth; it was a legacy from the respect earned by your parents. By their parents. By your whole family.

Sane people bestow that respect upon other sane people, and upon the children of sane people. Which is why your own wife, and your own children, are respected.

You are (according to the good people of Springfield—as far as your wife is aware—as much as it concerns your children) a 'representative'. You are a travelling salesman. You are a trusted employee of one of the town's main arms manufacturing firms. Successful. Well-paid. A man of no mean consequence.

You travel a great deal—sometimes abroad—which means you are away from home more than most men ... but, even this is a sign of your expertise and, because of this obvious expertise, it adds lustre to the respect which you command, in the town of Springfield.

But, in Chicago...

In New York...

In Detroit...

In a score of other towns and cities...

In all the places where you are known simply as 'Johnny' there, too, you command respect. There, too, you deal in fire-arms. There, too, you are a 'travelling salesman' ... a salesman who offers death, at the right price.

One of these men is you. The other is a pretence.

Which?

One is a good husband and a fine father ... the other is a butcher of fellow-men. One loves his wife, his kids, his parents ... the other carries around with him an emotional vacuum.

You have a good home ... a place of happiness and laughter.

You have twelve notches on your gun-butt ... a dozen graves, each filled with grief and wetted by tears.

Who are you?

Are you John Lincoln Spurgeon?

Or are you merely 'Johnny' ... the man who has neither soul nor surname?

Johnny said, 'Talk sense, doc. Y'know ... talk sense.'

'I'm talking sense,' insisted Pearson.

'Uhu.' Johnny shook his head.

'I'm a trained medical practitioner. I know what I'm talking about. If she doesn't get...'

'Look, where we gonna get antibiotics—that sorta junk—in a dump like this?'

'She needs something more than I have at hand.'

'Okay ... she ain't gonna get it. She shoulda thought about that when she jumped Cowboy and Pinky.'

Pearson said, 'I have a first-aid kit, in my room.'

'Easy, pal.' Johnny's mouth moulded itself into a sarcastic grin. 'I ain't no four-year-old kid, doc. I ain't lost no marbles. Your buddy—fatso—he's gone. But not you, too. I ain't *that* dumb.'

'My room,' said Pearson, 'is number fifteen. Send one of your gorillas...'

'They don't like being called names, doc.'

'... It's on the bedside table. A small, black case, marked "First Aid" ... assuming any of them can read.'

Johnny tilted the Stirling, warningly.

'If I say "please"?' said Pearson, softly.

'She ain't gonna die,' said Johnny. 'I seen flesh wounds, before. She ain't gonna die.'

'Please?' said Pearson, gently.

'She ain't gonna *die*,' repeated Johnny.

'She's in pain ... and it'll get worse.'

'And you figure your box o' tricks can help?'

'A little.'

'Yeah?'

'There's some morphine,' said Pearson. 'It will ease the pain.'

'Some first-aid kit,' observed Johnny.

'I'm a qualified medic,' Pearson reminded him.

'Yeah.'

'I like to be ready for emergencies?'

'Yeah.'

'Road accidents—things like that ... they happen, without warning.'

'Yeah ... I guess.'

'Therefore...' Pearson moved his shoulders. 'I carry basic medical requirements around with me. My own first-aid kit. Always. Is that so surprising?'

'Okay, doc.' Johnny twisted his lips, again. 'I buy it. Don't push the sell any harder.'

Pearson said, 'I need that stuff, to ease the girl's pain.'

'Okay.' Johnny nodded. Convinced, but still not completely without suspicion. 'When Beaumont comes back with Dutch and Fatso, I'll send one of 'em for the box.'

11.10 a.m....

The odd thing was that Grafton shifted all the trees and, for the first time, Harris and Blayde were able to have a clear view of the wood.

There may have been reasons. Good reasons.

Grafton was *not* a 'policeman' ... not within the definition of that word, as understood by the two chief superintendents. He was a bureaucrat, with a bureaucrat's mind. He was just that shade more objective than a man, within whose police area an abomination had been committed—and who took that abomination as a personal insult to his own crime-fighting ability—and a man, new to a division, and in whose division had occurred the first giant-sized criminality with which he had to cope—and who, because he now filled the shoes of an already legendary copper, was a little over-eager to prove himself.

Maybe these things.

Maybe, also, because he was a 'desk man', whereas the other two were 'street men'. The chasm is wide; it is the gulf between theory and practice.

But practice—year after year of practical, down-to-earth coppering—can bring its own weakness and its own blindness. It solidifies into a set procedure. A given series of cast-iron rules ... as unswerving and as close-knit as the contrapuntal weave of a classical fugue. The rules have been tested and re-tested, and they work. Always! Given a killing, and the rules will, eventually, sniff out the murderer. Given a rape, and those same rules will, in time, identify the rapist. They will pinpoint the house breaker, corner the arsonist and—when occasion demands—stand the traitor in the dock.

But...

As Grafton said, 'You're both approaching it from the wrong angle. This isn't a crime that needs *detecting*. We already *know*. Wolff has fifty innocent people, at gunpoint. He means business ... you say he means business.'

'He means business,' grunted Harris.

'And he has every trump card,' said Grafton.

Harris and Blayde spoke together.

Harris growled, 'I'm damned if I'm going to stand by and be dictated to by a gun-happy...'

Blayde said, 'Chief constable, we can't allow a man like Wolff to get away with...'

'*Shut up!*' Grafton put anger and disgust into the exclamation. He snapped, ' "The preservation of life" ... remember that? The first article of the Police Oath. Nothing about your stupid little prides. Nothing about "unless somebody gets us over a barrel". *Lives ...* that's what we're interested in. What the devil some armchair strategist might come up with. What the devil the newspapers say about "breaking under pressure". They'll say it— never fear ... they'll all be infernally wise, after the event. But they don't have to make the decision. Nor do you, Harris. Nor you, Blayde. It's my decision, and *I'm* making it. He can have his blasted son ... and good riddance. In exchange for fifty innocent people, he can have his damned son any time he likes.'

'As easy as *that*,' murmured Harris, scornfully.

'No ... *not* as easily as that,' countered Grafton. 'I haven't the authority. I wish to God I had ... but I haven't. That's one thing Wolff must understand. Must be *made* to understand.'

'How?' asked Blayde.

'By talking to him. By explaining the time-consuming difficulties.'

'Oh, he'll listen,' said Harris, sarcastically. 'He's a great one for listening. Start fannying about "official channels" and he'll drop the receiver before...'

'Not by telephone,' interrupted Grafton. 'Face to face.'

The two chief superintendents waited.

Grafton paced the tiny Committee Room as he talked. He spoke quietly, but with the edge of authority on his voice. He asked questions. He gave orders. He outlined each step of the proposed action carefully—meticulously—before he moved to the next.

For once—probably for the first time in his life—he became what he *was* ... a genuine, one-hundred-per-cent chief constable.

He said, 'Telephoning. We start by telephoning. The prison ... to put the governor in the picture. Then, next-of-kin of everybody in Robs Cully. I want them ...'

'They're already being told,' cut in Blayde. 'I have a team at Beechwood Brook D.H.Q. ... they're working on it.'

'Good.' Grafton nodded his satisfaction. 'In that case, we need a Reception Centre. Somewhere where we can feed information —genuine information—to be given to people who have the right to know. I don't want rumours. Rumours spread panic ... and we can do without panic.' Grafton glanced around the room, and said, 'This place. This village hall ... it'll do nicely.'

'It's earmarked as Incident Centre,' growled Harris. 'There's nowhere else we can ...'

'We don't *need* an Incident Centre,' snapped Grafton. 'It's what I've been trying to get over. This room ... all right. This telephone ... we can use *that*. But the rest of the building ... we don't *need* it Harris. We're not collecting information. Building up a crime file. Harris, get it into your head. We aren't *detecting* anything. We're *preventing*—if at all possible ... we're preventing wholesale slaughter.'

'I'd better ...' began Blayde, then stopped.

'What?' asked Grafton.

'Bumf,' said Blayde, bluntly. 'Cartloads of it, on the way from D.H.Q. An Incident Centre—y'know ... everything in triplicate. I organised men to ...'

'Cancel it,' rapped Grafton. 'We're not fighting this thing with paper.'

'We're not fighting ... *period*!' snarled Harris.

'You're damn right, chief superintendent!' Grafton turned on his Head of C.I.D. and exchanged disgust for disgust. 'This isn't a war. Not when they have guns and hostages. We're capitulating ... as of this moment.'

'They're breaking the bloody law. They're ...'

'Harris, one more word out of you—*one more insane argument*—and I suspend you from duty. On the spot. Now—do I make myself clear?'

Harris held on to himself. The pressure needed almost purpled his face and sent a vein in his forehead throbbing; it tightened his jaw muscles and made his nostrils widen and quiver; it fisted his hands and whitened the knuckles ... but, nevertheless, he held on to himself.

In a quieter, but very deliberate, voice Grafton repeated the question.

'Detective Chief Superintendent Harris ... do I make myself clear?'

'I ...' Harris choked for a moment then, in little more than a whisper, said, 'The responsibility's yours. It's why you're here.'

'Not mine,' said Grafton, grimly. 'Not yours. This is a Home Office decision. The responsibility rests with the Home Secretary.'

'And if he doesn't agree?' asked Blayde.

'He will.' Grafton smiled. Not a nice smile—not a happy smile —but a very sardonic and very confident smile. He said, 'He's a politician. He's susceptible to pressure ... they all are.'

'From you?' mocked Harris.

Grafton said, 'From the mass media. Television. Radio. Newspapers. The lot! I want them all notified, and given a free hand. Tell them—hammer it home—the choice ... his *only* choice. Some tinpot little American criminal who was caught hawking heroin in this country—and who can be refused future entry into the U.K.—or half a hundred law-abiding citizens ... most of 'em women. That's the choice. The Home Secretary's choice. Give it to the news-boys thick, fast and heavy. *Make* him choose ... and make him make the *right* choice.'

'Tactics,' murmured Blayde, not without a hint of admiration.

'Chief constables have their uses, sometimes,' grunted Grafton.

Wolff scowled at the blackened tobacco in the bowl of his cold pipe. He poured near-neat whisky down his throat, then raised his eyes to look, for the umpteenth time, beyond the glass to the sun lounge and along the main road which led from the smashed bridge into, and through, the deserted village.

He muttered, 'There ain't much we can do.'

'Nope.' Cowboy lounged in one of the cane chairs. Hat tilted to the back of his skull, jacket open and shoulder-holstered revolver in plain view.

'The waitin' spooks me,' murmured Wolff.

'Yep,' agreed Cowboy.

'They gotta be doin' *some* goddam thing.'

'Sure.'

'They ain't gonna just sit on their ass, and do nothin'.'

'Nope.'

'Goddam it!' Wolff turned and spat his irritation at the other man. 'Why 'n hell can't you talk like you *wasn't* some cheap Tom Mix?'

'Uh?' Cowboy blinked.

'This thing ain't some piss-assed horse opera.'

'Lookee, boss,' protested Cowboy, 'we pulled a neat hold-up, here. We got this whole shebang hogtied ... there ain't a thing worth frettin' about.'

'You horse-orientated twat!' snarled Wolff.

'What d' I do? What d' I say?' wailed Cowboy, plaintively.

'Forget it,' said Wolff, heavily. He drained the glass of whisky, and said, 'I ain't one for sittin' around, waitin' ... that's all. Here ... make with some more booze.'

Cowboy said, 'Yep ... sure,' and pushed himself from the comfort of the cane chair.

Beaumont returned to the 'Conference Room'.

He walked as well as he was able ... but with a slight totter, and with a still-slightly-dazed expression about the eyes. With his left hand he held the back of his skull. Momentarily, and with his right hand he steadied himself against the jamb of the door. His face was criss-crossed with scratches and shallow cuts, where he'd kissed and smashed the pyramid of glasses in his fall, and tiny threads of blood trickled and converged in the natural creases of his features.

Very quietly—very coldly—Johnny said, 'What the hell!'

Having paused at the door, Beaumont gulped air then continued his way down the room, towards the stage. He walked like a man gently drunk, but trying to act soberly ... like a parson who's had one too many.

He reached the stage, looked up at Johnny, winced as he moved his head, then explained 'what the hell'.

It amounted to very little.

A view of some balanced glasses ... then lights-out. A regaining of consciousness, and the realisation that he was two Lugers short of his normal ornamentation. A look into the bar, and the discovery that Dutch, too, was in Dreamland ... and without shooting equipment. And that the fat guy had disappeared through a knot-hole in the floorboards.

And that was the total of 'what the hell.'

'Great.' Johnny's voice was flat and hard. 'So, now we have a fat-gutted fink wandering around with three shooters in his belt. That's great. That is *all* we need.'

Beaumont sighed, and nursed his head.

Johnny stepped forward and, in a single, fluid movement twisted, turned on the balls of his feet and slashed the snout of the Stirling from right to left, across Beaumont's face at nose-level. Beaumont screamed as the foresight tore a path through flesh and cartilage. The gore gushed, like a turned-on tap. Then Beaumont's knees buckled and he folded into a bleeding heap in front of the stage.

Pearson said, 'Did it help?'

'Yeah ... it helped,' said Johnny, harshly.

'Of course. With you, it would.'

'Don't push it, friend.' There was soft, terrifying madness in the words. 'Do not *push* it ... not even the thickness of paper.'

Pearson hesitated a moment, then said, 'The first-aid kit ...'

'Are you makin' funnies?'

'*He* needs it, too.' Pearson motioned towards the unconscious Beaumont.

'He's bleedin',' said Johnny, icily.

'He's injured ... badly injured.'

'He's bleedin'. When he stops bleedin', he's dead. Who the hell cares? Who the hell cares if every bastard in this room dies?'

Carter knew he was being hunted.

He'd been seen; watched when he'd disarmed Pinky and watched when he'd smashed his shoe into the sprawling gunman's helpless body; watched when he'd picked up the fallen Dardick and watched when he'd glared his disgust at the raging waters of the Hewfraw.

Watched—seen ... then shot at.

Therefore, hunted.

Hunted—but not cornered ... no, by God, not *cornered*!

He was a trained soldier. He'd been on Battle Courses. He knew the basics of hit-and-run jungle warfare. And he could handle firearms ... he could handle firearms one devil of a lot more efficiently than any backstreet Yankee yob.

He settled the grip of the Dardick snugly into the palm of his hand, eased gently forward on his belly—pulling his flattened body along by 'walking' with the elbows of his bent arms—and worked his way between the rows of neatly caned-and-wired raspberries. His elbows made shallow indentations in the well-worked soil and the toes of his shoes left scratchy furrows; the mulched soil smelled rotten—like farmyard manure—within inches of his nostrils; tiny, low-flying insects settled on his face and made him itch. He was miserable, he was scared, he was disgusted ... but, most of all, he was angry.

By God, yes! He was good and mad. The thought that *he*—a professional soldier, and a gentleman—had been treated as an equal (and even an inferior person) by a gang of undisciplined Yankee crooks was an insult. An insult to his honour and an insult to his upbringing.

They needed a short, sharp lesson ... and he was the man to give 'em it. He could out-think, out manoeuvre and out-smart any of 'em ... any, or all, of 'em.

And the first step was to demonstrate what battle-tactics *really* meant.

He reached the end of the twin rows of raspberry canes, paused, then gently eased his head forward until he could view the terrain.

He was in the kitchen garden of *Conte Lauba*—the Douranby place—and within a hundred yards, or so, of *Yew Tree Bower* ... where that slob Wolff was still, no doubt, throwing his weight around.

Into *Conte Lauba*. That was the first objective. Into the house without being seen. Then a secret barricading of the doors, to prevent surprise. Then a telephone; to notify the authorities, outside Robs Cully, that they had a field-commander on the spot (within the camp of the enemy) who could, and would, direct operations from inside the attack zone; who could keep an eye on the opposition headquarters, check what action was being taken and switch the plan of attack, accordingly.

But first ... 'view the terrain'.

At ten o'clock—the rear of the house; french windows leading into a sun lounge; a porch, beyond which was an open door ... careful of that open door, it might mean enemy troops already in occupation!

Eleven o'clock—a gap and, beyond, a rose garden and a trimmed hedge; then the double-garage with a row of cold-frames built up to its rear.

From noon to three o'clock—the kitchen garden; neat rows of young vegetables; peas, already twigged, and runner beans, already staked and netted; the sort of garden seen in catalogues ... but this one was real.

From three o'clock to six o'clock—a herb garden, followed by a lawn, surrounded by soft-fruit bushes of which the raspberry canes were a part.

He moved his head to the left.

From ten o'clock round, once more, to six o'clock—the rear of the house; a flagged patio leading from the french windows and down to the lawn.

Nothing! No living creature. No sound. No movement. He was the last man on earth ... and it was time to move.

He eased himself into a sprint position, curled a finger around the trigger of the Dardick, then sprinted, zig-zag for the open door, beyond the porch.

Pinky was not quite dead.

Almost ... but not quite.

The last of his life-blood oozed from one ear, where Carter's fear-maddened kicking had fractured the bones of his skull; it stained the close-cropped grass before being sucked in by the good earth beneath. It masked the side of his face from his smashed nose and lacerated face, and thickened as it slowly drenched his jacket and shirt with crimson.

Nevertheless, Pinky was not quite dead ... but almost.

The fellow-hoodlum reached out a foot, hooked a toe under Pinky's shoulder, pushed and rolled the dying man over and on to his back.

Pinky moaned softly as the added pain penetrated the depths of his unconsciousness and touched his dying with an excess of agony.

Then the agony went ... and, with it, life.

PERCIVAL 'PINKY' MARTIN ... R.I.P.
To be born a sucker; one of a family of suckers, and the biggest sucker of the litter. To have four brothers, all older than you and all (for three memorable months) locked away in a quartet

of state penitentiaries at the same time. To have three sisters—again, all older than you—and all of them out-and-out hookers; a trio of tramps, experts at street-walking and renowned hawkers of pussy.

Suckers, all ... and you are the runt. And, from the moment you opened your mouth for that first bawl, the cops had your number.

They knew ... with that background, and from that family, what else?

Son of a hoodlum—son of a hustler—with hoodlums and hustlers for brothers and sisters ... what else?

The cops of Syracuse, New York State, rubbed their hands and waited.

Nor were they disappointed.

A knifing, before you reached puberty. A zip-gun hold-up at the age of seventeen. An attempted rape, a mugging and two filling-station stick-ups before your twenty-first birthday ... you worked hard to make lost time on the other members of your family!

So-o ... the bulls panned you. But good. You became their own, personal mascot. Whatever happened—suppose some dumb jerk parked alongside a hydrant—it was enough. You were hauled in for questioning.

Questioning!

Jesus, they smacked you around like you were the greatest craze since the yo-yo. You spent more time in the precinct house than you did in your own home; and every time a cop passed— bull or uniformed—he landed you a belt in the mouth ... or in the gut ... or around the head. It became a habit. A ritual. Something everybody did.

One of the pigs comes into the station ... great, belt Pinky as you pass. Another bull goes off duty ... okay, but his day is not complete until he has smacked Pinky on the way out.

It became as regular as that.

As monotonous as that.

And, first you became punchy—then you got the message ... you were not too popular with the law-enforcement guys. Your future—doing the thing you'd been born to do—was very limited within the law-enforcement area of Syracuse.

And ... remember?

Remember the big idea? The idea big brother Steve came up

with? That—just to show the pigs you weren't yellow—just to show the bastards you weren't taking it on the lam—it might be wise, and very tough, to call in at the precinct station and give the sons of bitches one last horse's ass of a goodbye.

Some goddam idea!

Jesus and all His saints ... they kept you there all day, and all night. They took turns at slamming you against every goddam wall in the place. They hit you with every damn thing they could lift. If they could have taken the stinking roof off the building, they would have hit you with that!

And, when it was all over—when you were hauling yourself up from the floor for the millionth time—the captain of the bulls had strolled from his office and had spoken hard words of warning.

'You can crawl outa here now, Pinky. And keep crawling. Crap on somebody else's doorstep, from now on. A hundred miles from here ... never an inch nearer. You come closer than that, boy, and we'll bury you. I swear, we'll bury you.'

The big idea—brother Steve's big idea ... but you (as always) was he the sucker. He had the big idea ... but you took the big lambasting.

And (goddam it) it almost soured you. It almost made you go straight.

For close on two years you behaved yourself ... more, or less.

You drove trucks, you heaved garbage, you washed dishes. You bounced at small-time dance halls, hosed down at slaughter-yards and swept floors at bowling alleys. A thousand and one jobs in a thousand and one towns—from Buffalo south to Charleston, west to Atlanta, south to Palm Beach, then north all the way to Sioux City, Iowa.

And, in Sioux City you met Cowboy ... and, with him, a rebirth.

That was four years ago. Four years of stick-ups and small-time bank hold-ups. Four years of a good partnership, with a man as footloose as any maverick from his home state. You were hired, as a twosome, by some of the mob outfits. You worked duo, and unhindered by any loyalty other than a loyalty to each other.

You horsed around the edges of the protection game. You stole a few cars. You cracked a handful of drugstores. Nothing too big—nothing to move the feds into action—nothing some state line couldn't cancel out.

You lived. Sometimes crummy—often in some two-bit rooming

house—but always with the dream. The dream of the zinger. The dream of the big heist. The dream of the last jackpot ... and, after that, Disneyland forever.

Cowboy, your buddy. Cowboy, your pal. And Cowboy knew Wolff. And Wolff had a kid. And the kid dropped himself, in some U.K. hick town. And Wolff had this big idea ... everybody in the whole goddam world has big ideas!

One big idea ... and the cops tore you apart to see what made the cogs go round.

This big idea ... and the last of your life drips in a final drop of blood on to the grass of a two-bit river island which ain't even in the land of your birth.

Everybody has big ideas.

The only idea you ever had—and it wasn't so big—was to trot through life nice and easy ... a little bent, maybe, but not a big enough nuisance to cause any other guy to have nightmares.

So-o ... Percival 'Pinky' Martin. Sucker.

Percival 'Pinky' Martin ... R.I.P.

Noon...

In fifty minutes, Grafton had changed the whole face of the police operation. It was no longer an 'enquiry' ... indeed, it had never *been* an 'enquiry'. It was now (if it was anything capable of official tabulation) a 'disaster'. It was treated as such; basically, along the lines of a rail crash, or a plane crash ... but (for the moment) without the attendance of the Fire Service.

'At 'Raine Community Centre' things were...

We-ell, now...

Blayde strolled into the main hall from the Committee Room and, for a sliced second of time his mind hiccuped back to the early fifties—to the East Coast floods—to Mablethorpe, and a certain Sergeant Blayde who, along with hundreds of other coppers from a score of forces, had been drafted in to assist in a town smashed by the tides and half buried in sand. Coppers, civil engineers and the W.V.S. Like the Holy Trinity those three organisations had joined to form something bigger, and stronger, than nature itself.

The coppers had protected the deserted town. Eight hours on duty, eight hours off; patrolling streets of shattered shops and houses—patrolling in pairs and, sometimes, each pair responsible for a single street; eyes skinned for the army of looting bastards to whom the stricken town was a prime target; manning road-blocks around the whole area; burning every rule-book ever printed to get the lorry-loads of gravel down to the beach and into the makeshift sea-wall before the next high tide. Fourteen days of it ... and every copper who experienced that particular detail came out of it a new, and more complete, man.

The civil engineers—every major firm in the country—had thrown men and machines along that tiny coastline; working round the clock, to tame the sea; slamming steel piles into the sand; bulldozing thousands of tons of ballast into position; doing the impossible ... hourly!

But the W.V.S. had been the real heroines. Everybody admitted it. Without the W.V.S. what had been done could never have been done. The way they worked ... one team took over, and worked solidly, *non-stop*, for forty-eight hours, then that team was pulled out and replaced by a fresh team. Forty-eight-hour shifts. Christ Almighty ... they'd made the men look ninnies! And every minute, day or night, there'd been hot drinks, soup and sandwiches ready for the taking. There'd been a dance hall, towards the rear of the town, and the W.V.S. had set up shop there ... and, for fourteen days, mealtimes hadn't meant a damn thing ... no gas, no water, no electricity, nothing! ... so, no mealtimes. What the hell was a mealtime anyway?

The W.V.S. had changed *that* attitude. They'd said (in effect), 'Come and get it. Day, or night ... it's here for the taking. It's here for the eating.'

And that battered old dance hall had become the heart of the whole mad operation. Men, grey with fatigue, had dragged themselves to the counter, collected bowls of steaming soup, mugs of hot tea and plates of sandwiches; they'd wandered to the tables, slumped into a chair and re-charged themselves. At any time—day, or night—for fourteen, never-to-be-forgotten days.

The men had licked the elements.

But the women had kept the men alive.

The W.V.S. ... without 'em, it couldn't have happened.

And, for a moment, 'Raine Community Centre' slammed a quick memory of a Mablethorpe dance hall into Blayde's mind.

Wolff paced the sun lounge and, from the sun lounge, into the more conventional lounge, beyond ... then back into the sun lounge, to stand and scowl, unseeing, at a point beyond the glass of the french windows.

'Where is the bastard?' he breathed.

'It ain't done in a hurry, boss,' soothed Cowboy, from his resumed position in the cane chair.

'Something screwy is happenin' out there,' snarled Wolff.

'It ain't possible,' murmured Cowboy. 'You have the drop. They ain't gonna...'

'You *know* that?' rasped Wolff, nastily. 'You—you have a hot line to God, or somethin'? ... you *know*?'

'Nope.' Cowboy reverted back to his role of poor-man's 'Coop'.

'So why not shove your goddam talk up your Texan ass?' said Wolff.

It was a rhetorical question, and Cowboy treated it as such. He didn't answer it.

'I ain't gonna phone,' muttered Wolff. 'Holy cow! I ain't gonna phone *him*.'

'Nope.'

'*I* call the shots in this goddam game.'

'Sure.'

'Not that Harris pig. *I* call the shots.'

'You call the shots,' agreed Cowboy.

'So, what's with the stupid fink? Does he figure this is some sorta bluff? Is that it, maybe? Does he figure I *ain't* gonna stiffen every mother-suckin' creep in this whole dump, if I don't get action?'

Cowboy sighed, and returned to his original remark.

He said, 'It ain't done in a hurry, boss.'

Wolff breathed heavily, then growled, 'I need a drink.'

'Lookee,' protested Cowboy, 'you ain't gonna help none by fillin' your guts with...'

'A drink!' exploded Wolff. 'I wanna get gassed, I get gassed ... okay? I don't need no sonofabitch preachin' temperance crap at me ... okay?'

'Okay.' Cowboy once more heaved himself from the cane chair.

'The bottle,' rasped Wolff.

Cowboy shrugged and said, 'Yep ... the bottle it is.'

Lennox moved from house to house. He moved with infinite care knowing that, by this time, a brace of unconscious gunmen would no longer be unconscious; that the ungodly would, by this time, know that they were three guns light of their original count ... and one man on the loose who just might start slinging bullets around.

In which case, these jokers wouldn't hesitate. They'd shoot first, and apologise afterwards.

He kicked each door open—all the way back to the wall—before he entered a room; standing to one side of the doorway, and waiting for the sound of the explosions and the arrival of the slugs. Before entering any room, he waited then sprinted across the open doorway ... giving any potential opponent the opportunity of a snapshot which, in turn, would be the visiting card Lennox was waiting for.

It was one way of living dangerously ... but, arguably, the least dangerous way of any in the present situation.

He searched each house, room at a time. Every corner. Every cupboard. Even under every bed.

Then he moved on to the next house.

He had certain things going for him. Notably the fact that every inhabitant of Robs Cully had (or so it seemed) demanded the sort of privacy usually reserved for hermits living in the middle of woods. Hedges were everywhere. Trees were in abundance. Walled-in patios and sun-traps were plentiful. Not counting pavilions, greenhouses, sheds, garages, cabins, swimming pools with changing booths, fancy dog-kennels, stables and, in one rear garden, a gaudy orange-and-blue tent.

And Lennox was *very* careful.

He moved only when he was damn sure ... and having *made* damn sure. Then he moved fast, but not far. From hiding-place to hiding-place, in a zig-zag, drunken pattern which, sometimes, took him away from the house he was making for in order to give a more circuitous, but safer, route.

A revolver and a Luger weighed down the pockets of his windcheater, and the second Luger was gripped firmly in the pudgy paw of his right hand. He hated the bloody thing—he hated *all* guns—but the rules of this particular game demanded guns and, if he *had* to have a gun, a Luger was as good as any, and better than most.

He'd already spotted Wolff's men. Four times. Patrolling, maybe ... or, maybe, out searching for a pot-bellied copper who's slapped down two of their number and made off with three of their weapons.

No matter ... he'd seen *them* first. And he'd waited.

And now he was moving—a few yards at a time—towards one more house ... a house which (although Lennox didn't know this carried the fancy title of *Conte Lauba*.

By noon, the police marksmen were in position along the outer banks of the Hewfraw and Skew Beck. They kept well back; hidden from sight, behind hedges and in coppices; an encirclement of firepower ... just in case.

Fourteen men—nine armed with B.S.A., bolt-action rifles and five armed with .38 Smith and Wesson revolvers—and, with each trained marksman, a companion equipped with binoculars. They lay on their stomachs, or squatted on their haunches, and watched, waited and hoped. They hoped it wouldn't build up into a war; hoped they were wasting their time.

Each marksman could handle his firearm expertly. Could, given a moderate sighting, hit what he was aiming for. But—hell!—this wasn't the range. These weren't going to be dummies. This time, it was the real thing—flesh and blood—a living target. And every second of their training had been geared towards *killing*. The golden rule ... if guns *have* to be used, they must be *used*. Nothing fancy. No messing about trying to wound. When the British copper has been driven to the point where he *must* use a gun then, at that point, he is justified in killing. Therefore, aim to kill ... the chest, or the guts. And, if possible, kill him before he even *sees* you.

One of the marksmen moistened his lips, and said, 'Christ, I could do with a smoke.'

'Aye. Me, too.' His companion answered, without taking his eyes from the stretch of the opposite bank they had been detailed to watch.

'I wonder...' began the marksman, then stopped.

'What?'

'Y'know ... whether we'll be needed.'

'Somebody must think so. Else we wouldn't be here.'

'Oh, Christ!' muttered the marksman.

His companion still watched the opposite bank, nodded once, then said, 'I know.'

'It's—it's not like the range.'

'No. They warned us, though ... that it wouldn't be.'

'Still...'

'Worrying won't help.' The man with the binoculars raised them to his eyes, and fingered the focus-wheel to obtain a clearer image. He muttered, 'Sooner them, than us.'

Kempton looked up as the middle-aged woman knocked, then opened the door without waiting to be told to enter the examination room.

She was a well-kept woman; slim and younger-looking than her years; with an air of polite and calming efficiency. She wasn't a nurse, but she *looked* like a nurse ... and the spotlessly white, belted overall added to the desired effect.

She said, 'Excuse me, Mr Kempton...'

The skinny, yellow-skinned old man wearing a string vest looked suddenly embarrassed and hurriedly re-zipped the trousers he was just about to remove.

Kempton frowned mild annoyance, said, 'Excuse me, Mr Fording,' then turned to the woman and asked, 'Yes, Miss Bain. What is it?'

'The—er—the police.' The middle-aged woman sounded at loss for words.

'What about the police?' Kempton's frown became less mild.

'They—er—they'd like a word with you, sir.'

The skinny man concentrated his attention upon Kempton's face and looked suspicious, and not a little cross.

'The *police*?' Kempton's frown changed from one of annoyance to one of non-understanding.

'They'd like a word with you, sir.'

'Are they here? In the Reception Room? Is that what you're trying to tell me?'

'No, sir. They're on the phone ... through to the Reception Room.'

'In that case—if it's *really* urgent—put them through to here. I can...'

'No, sir!' The middle-aged woman fluttered her hands a little; as if, had she been a weaker woman, she might have actually *wrung* them. She stammered, 'It's about—it's about your wife, Mr Kempton. It's urgent. I—er—I think you'd better...'

Her voice trailed off into miserable silence.

The skinny man said, 'Oh!' and his expression changed from one of suspicion to one of interested concern.

Kempton controlled the muscles of his face. He remained

silent for a few seconds—until he was sure he could also control his voice—then, he said, 'Thank you, Miss Bain. I'll take it in your office.' He turned to the skinny man, smiled, and said, 'If you'll excuse me a moment, Mr Fording. I'll be back.'

'No—it's—it's...'

Kempton stood up, smiled again, and said, 'Some misunderstanding, I'm sure. I won't keep you waiting, Mr Fording.'

'It's all right, doctor. It's—it's quite all right.'

Kempton nodded a token 'thank you' and hurried past the middle-aged woman and out of the examination room. The middle-aged woman followed him, closing the door behind her.

The skinny man blinked at the closed door a couple of times, shook his head in puzzlement, then hitched his trousers a couple of inches higher.

There was an atmosphere of near terror in the 'Conference Room'.

Until the return of Beaumont there had been a lot of self-delusion; the brand of self-kidology which comes, almost as a matter of course, with a certain tide-mark of wealth. Everything had a price tag. Okay ... some things were expensive. Okay ... some things needed a certain amount of back-door horse trading. And okay ... life held certain pin-pricks of minor inconvenience which even money could only blunt. But loot—given time— could breakwater any wave of disaster ever thought up by man.

Consciously, or unconsciously, these people had believed this. They had truly believed that even evil had its price; that, given a big enough cheque, even *it* could be bribed into going away.

They were learning!

Barbara Pickering...

A few hours ago Babs Pickering had been a well-contented, closing-up-to-elderly widow. Glad to be rid of a ne'er-do-well husband. Not rich, but owning her own cottage at Raine and employed by people who *were* rich and giving value for money, therefore settled and satisfied and, in effect, part of *their* wealth. Healthy, but not scared by the thought of death ... death, to her, being the other end of birth and, as such, no more terrifying than birth. An ending, as opposed to a beginning.

But she'd always visualised death as something which happened in bed. At home, or in hospital. In comfort, and without pain;

the continuation of a drug-induced sleep.

Not this. Not bullets. Not agony, inflicted by strange men to whom the infliction of agony was the only form of valid argument worthy of consideration.

To die this way wasn't right. It wasn't human ... or decent ... or proper. Even animals—even a pet dog, or a pet cat—even beasts, about to be slaughtered—had the right to a better ending than *this*.

The terror crept up on Babs Pickering—like the blush on the face of a virgin—and, although she fought it with her own brand of down-to-earth logic, it gradually increased and dried the spittle from her mouth and caught her throat, and pitched her voice a semi-tone higher than normal whenever she spoke.

Jean Hill ...

Jean Hill had had a good life. She knew it. She appreciated her good fortune. She knew that ten thousand other women, who had had her start in life—ten thousand other one-time-shop-assistants in one of a chain of shoe shops—would have gladly (eagerly) have exchanged places with her ... even at this moment.

She also knew her own weakness. Her major weakness. The weakness of an inbuilt sense of insecurity. She couldn't help herself—she'd spent half her life feeling ashamed of this weakness—but it was something of which she'd never been able to rid herself. Even today (as she well knew) when they could both well afford the good life—and, moreover, afford it without even touching the capital amassed by her husband's property deals—she still suffered this nagging fear of insecurity.

Money. She wanted money ... and yet, contradictory as it seemed, she wasn't *greedy*. It was just that, as far as she was concerned, money was just that. Money! Not figures on a bank statement. Not more figures on the pages of a ledger. Not so many zeroes, written down by some cold-blooded accountant. *Money* ... pound, and five-pound notes ... cash, that she could actually *handle*; that she could count, and tuck away in her billfold; the weight of which she could feel in her purse.

She'd never written out a cheque, in her whole life ... she wasn't even sure she really knew *how*.

And yet it was there; she knew, perfectly well, that it was there. Every penny, and every possession, 'joint'. From the moment of their marriage, when they'd both been in their early twenties, and Robert had (even then) had the shine of a world-beater in his eyes, there'd been a complete and absolute sharing; nothing 'his', nothing 'hers' but everything 'their' ... everything, to the last brass farthing, 'joint'.

It had been Robert's way of licking this stupid 'insecurity' thing ... and the one thing he *hadn't* been able to lick.

She'd loved him. Wrong ... she'd worshipped him, and still worshipped him. And, whatever she felt for him, he'd returned. She was his goddess. Always had been, and always would be ... but, even this, had added to the silly, illogical feeling of insecurity.

They had to die. At some time, they *both* had to die and, in the secret hours, after midnight, she'd stared into the darkness and contemplated the near-unthinkable. Her, without him ... lost, and a prey to all the wickednesses and lonelinesses which must come to a woman who had handed her whole life to one man. Him, without her ... crazy (he'd certainly go crazy!) and bitter and, because of what he was, self-destructive to the point of suicide.

Insecurity ... it all stemmed from that one, stupid mental block of which she couldn't rid herself.

She'd prayed. She'd prayed—for one thing only, and the granting of a single last request—that they'd both go together. Suddenly, and without knowing anything or feeling anything. How? Any way, dear God ... but without pain, and hand-in-hand.

And now, this.

Her terror fed upon itself. Not at the thought of death. Not even at the thought of potential pain ... physical pain. But because she knew Robert; knew Robert would only take so much; knew that the limit had almost been reached.

And then he'd die. That man—that animal who stood on the stage, and threatened the whole room with his sub-machine gun—and the men under his command would kill her Robert. And they *would*. Because that was going to be the only way they could stop him.

And then...

Jean Hill bit upon the inside of her lower lip in an effort to ward off the panic which rode on the terror which filled her thoughts.

Blayde murmured, 'Hello, Ruth.'

'What?' Ruth Harris looked up, smiled a smile which carried

a touch of surprised embarrassment, then said, 'Oh! ... hello, Jim.'

'Long time,' said Blayde.

'A *very* long time,' she agreed, gently.

'Er—Bob said you were coming.'

'Yes. I thought the womenfolk might be able to help.'

'Quite.' Blayde nodded.

The lay-out of the trestle-tables had been altered; from the U, from and back to the stage, they had been straightened into a long counter, with spare tables spaced around the room and chairs drawn up to them ... reminiscent of a certain dance hall, at Mablethorpe.

Women were spreading cloths along the trestle-table counter; white cloths, some of which were table-cloths and some of which were freshly laundered linen bedsheets. The women numbered about a dozen; of a dozen different ages and a dozen different shapes and sizes ... but each one was a copper's wife, and each one was there to help her man.

Cups—dozens of thick, heavy cups, borrowed from some works canteen—were being made ready; were being placed in tidy, geometric ranks at one end of the counter. Behind the counter were two crates of bottles of milk. A baking-bowl stood alongside the cups, and the bowl was more than half-filled with sugar. A lesser bowl held spoons. Two of the women were busy buttering sliced bread, while a third woman wafered corned beef and turned the buttered bread into sandwiches.

So like—so very like—a dance hall, at Mablethorpe ... so very many years ago.

'Plenty of helpers,' observed Blayde.

'I could have had more.' Ruth Harris smiled. 'You never know. We may need a reserve team.'

'Like ...' began Blayde, then closed his mouth.

'What?'

'It doesn't matter.' Blayde's habitually hard expression softened, momentarily. 'Women. Some other women ... once. It reminds me. That's all.'

In the tiny kitchen, alongside the Committee Room he'd just left, Blayde could see two women busying themselves with an ancient hot-water geyser and a brown, enamelled, gallon-sized teapot.

'I—er—I didn't know,' said Ruth Harris, timidly.

'What?'

'About this being your division. Who'd taken Mr Ripley's chair.'

'Oh ... that?'

'I didn't know,' she repeated.

He eyed her quizzically, and said, 'Or?'

She looked puzzled.

'Wouldn't you have come?' he amplified.

'Of course I would.' For a moment, she looked cross.

'Ye-es ... of course you would,' he agreed, soothingly.

At the end of the counter nearest to the hall's entrance, two policewomen had propped a hand-written sign on the white cloth. The sign read *ENQUIRIES* and, already, the policewomen were seated and sorting through typewritten foolscap lists; making marginal notes and hieroglyphics before storing the sheets neatly into manilla folders.

'You—er...' She hesitated, flicked a quick smile across her lips, then said, 'You haven't married.'

'You've kept a check?' he countered.

'A woman's curiosity.'

'But, of course.' His smile was a little twisted, but not bitter. Not sardonic.

'Why?' she asked.

The question was innocent-sounding, but pastel-tinted with a faint mixture of timidity and female guile.

His smile expanded until it became a grin. The grin grew, until it reached the maturity of a soft chuckle.

She said, 'You haven't been—what's the expression?—"carrying a torch"?'

A keen ear might have caught some slight disappointment in the tone of her voice.

Blayde said, 'You married the best man, Ruth.'

'Oh, I know *that*,' she said, sharply.

'Not,' he amplified, 'the best man in the world. Of the two of us—that's what I mean ... and that isn't saying much.'

'Oh!'

'Is it?' he taunted, gently.

'Robert's a good man,' she snapped ... and now there was defensive anger in her voice.

He stared into her eyes for a few moments. At first, without expression then, gradually, the stare became cold and scorn-filled.

He said, 'Don't apologise, Ruth. That's what you're doing ... apologising for the man you married. Don't. Don't apologise for a man like *me*. We're both bastards. The only difference is, I *know* it.'

Flora Aimes ...
Flora Aimes, too, fought to control the mounting terror.

She wasn't a 'career woman'—not what the world means by the expression 'career woman'—but she claimed, with some justification, to be a 'working wife'. *The Hind's Head* was a well-run, respectable hotel. It was a success, and its success (and even its respectability) was a direct result of *her* effort and *her* business-sense.

Rufus ...
We-ell, Rufus was a good enough husband. He was an excellent father, thank God—and he was a good enough husband ... and no woman had the right to expect (much less demand) *everything*!

A couple of times, he'd rolled his eyes at other women; with the wrong wife, he'd have slipped off the rails. But he hadn't *had* the wrong wife. He'd had a wife who understood him; who knew what he was, and what he always would be. A 'follower' ... but never a 'leader'. He waffled; he couldn't make decisions for toffee. He hadn't the guts. He hadn't the necessary self-confidence. He was a child, grown tall—which was, maybe, why he and the kids had a world of their own, in which she was something of a stranger—and, like so many children, he had this great belief that, if you ignored problems long enough they'd go away.

Fancy talk—fancy phraseology—but it wrapped up a basic truth ... that she had a weak husband.

Okay, so she had a weak husband. Which was as good a reason as any for not wanting to die.

With her out of the way, he'd run wild. Any tart who showed him a few inches of thigh would have him in the palm of her hand. He'd be panting and drooling—eager to get up there, between her legs ... and the hell with the consequences.

He'd be sorry afterwards. Truly sorry ... when it was too late! When the kids had been forgotten. When the spare cash had all been spent on some hot-arsed floozie. When reality lashed out, and kicked him downstairs and into the cellar.

He'd be sorry ... truly, and genuinely, sorry.

But, by that time, what about the kids.

Rufus loved his kids. It was arguable that he loved them even more than she did. But he didn't *consider* them. He wasn't capable of being objective—of sitting down, and saying to himself, 'If I do this, *this* will happen ... therefore, I mustn't do it.' —because his nature was a 'present' nature ... it ignored tomorrow. Today—this hour, this minute—that was as far as Rufus could ever see. He was the sort of man whose eternity stretched no farther than *now*.

So, if she went, what about the kids? Come to that, what about Rufus?

She didn't want to die, and her reasons for wanting to live were not selfish reasons ... but they were no less violently urgent reasons because of their unselfishness. They did nothing to quieten the fear of death which crept, like a plague, through the hostages held in the 'Conference Room'.

Charlotte Douranby ...

The object of the exercise ... to live.

What matter that these men were animals? ... they were still *men*. What matter that they had broken into her beloved *Conte Lauba*? ... it could be cleaned, repaired and re-decorated. What matter that they had shot one of her pets? ... Afghan hounds were going out of fashion, anyway. What matter that they'd terrified her? ... they hadn't yet *killed* her. What matter that one of them had knocked her unconscious? ... bruises mend, and headaches go away.

The object of the exercise ... to live.

She had money. She could offer them money, in exchange for her life; but if money was the bullet-proof shield offering protection from this creature, Johnny, and his henchmen, they were *all* safe. Every hostage had money. Many of them had more money than she had. Therefore, it wasn't money ... money *wasn't* the bullet-proof shield.

So, what else?

What else, bearing in mind the object of the exercise?—the *only* object of the exercise? ... to live.

Her body. Not dead, but alive. Herself ... the one possession peculiar to herself. The one thing nobody else in this terrible room could offer ... Charlotte Douranby.

It would not make her a whore. Why should it make her a whore? Others—others, in this room—had men-friends. Lovers. Followers. Admirers. And others *would* have ... if they dared.

It was 'civilised'. It was 'modern'. It even helped marriages to work—that's what some of the experts claimed ... that it even *helped* marriages to work. So, Roger would understand ... as a 'civilised' man, as a 'modern' man, he'd understand. He'd prefer that to attending her funeral. For God's sake! He'd prefer *anything* to attending the funeral of his slaughtered wife.

Because...

The object of the exercise ... to live.

It wasn't as if...

I mean...

She could do it. There wasn't any doubt about that. She could *do* it. She could 'satisfy' them ... even *these* creatures. She could please them ... please them enough to allow her to live. As payment. The only payment she'd ask ... which meant she wouldn't be a *whore*.

Because...

I mean...

Last January—at the New Year's Eve Party, at the Mitfords—at *Green Gables*. All right ... they'd all been a little squiffed. All right ... when Tony Mitford had said, 'C'mon—who's for a nice little orgy?' nobody had taken him seriously. He hadn't *meant* it seriously. Not at first. It had been a joke—a not-very-funny, drunken joke—until somebody had answered with, 'Okay ... why not?'

Who the hell *had* answered? Who the hell *had* been responsible?

She didn't know ... and it wasn't important.

Just that it had happened; that everybody had been a little squiffed, and very 'modern' and very 'civilised' ... and, anyway, wife-swapping was the 'thing', and the experts claimed it helped marriages to work.

Funny, that ... she'd drawn Tony's name out of the hat. Tony ... a man she'd had something of a crush on. (Unbeknown to Roger, of course ... not that Roger would have minded.) Tony ... the man who'd started it all by his not-very-funny, drunken joke.

She couldn't remember—odd, that, but she couldn't remember

—who Roger had drawn. Just some woman. Maybe the red-head —the cousin of somebody, from Lancaster—who'd been shoving her tits under his nose all evening. Maybe he'd drawn *her*—he'd never said, never told her ... and she'd never asked.

But she remembered. She'd *always* remember ... Tony!

The bedroom. The other couple ... 'Let's make it foursomes —two pairs to each room—it adds to the fun.' The initial shyness. The pretending not to watch the other two; the pretending *not* to ... but not being *able* not to. Then the excitement. The sudden realisation—the sobering shock—that you were naked. And Tony was naked ... as were the other two.

Then, the hell with the other two. The hell with being 'civilised'! The hell with being 'modern'! The hell with *everything* ... except the contorting, and the gasping, and the clawing, and the biting.

And Tony's whispered moan of, 'Blow it now, girl. Blow it *now*!'

And she'd 'blown it' ... as never before.

Afterwards—hours, weeks, years, afterwards—Tony had turned to grin at her. Shamefacedly, but also admiringly. Still naked, but spent.

He'd reached across, patted her cheek, and whispered, 'Sweetheart, I've had as many rides as the next man ... but never, *ever* one like that. You have my word. That was a New Year's present I'll *never* forget.'

So-o ...

She could do it.

She had something nobody else in this room could offer— something peculiar to herself ... and the object of the exercise was to *live*.

Blayde returned to the Committee Room and re-joined Grafton and Harris.

Grafton was lowering the telephone receiver on to its prongs. He said, 'Right. We're under way.'

'The Home Office?' Blayde queried.

'If you hadn't wandered off ...' began Harris.

'A call of nature,' lied Blayde. 'It happens ... to normal people.'

'Wakefield Prison.' Grafton answered Blayde's question. 'The Home Office already have a man on his way north.'

'Speed ... for Whitehall,' murmured Blayde.

'Figuratively speaking.' Grafton corrected himself. 'He's flying. I'll have a squad car meet him, at the Leeds-Bradford Airport. Meanwhile, Wolff—young Wolff—is being brought here.'

'And the old Wolff?' asked Blayde.

'Let him sweat,' growled Harris.

Blayde said, 'He won't be alone, of course.'

'Eh?'

'There are people in Robs Cully. *They'll* be sweating, too.'

'If they've any sense, they'll know we're ...'

'They'll be worried, Harris.' Grafton backed Blayde's observation.

'Look—they'll know ...'

'The only thing they'll *know*,' snapped Blayde, 'is that they're hostages. Expendable ... and being held by men prepared to *expend* them. The philosophies of the situation will, for the moment, be escaping their notice. They're on the wrong side of that bloody river!'

12.10 p.m. ...

'Damn!' Carter glared his disgust at the dead telephone, hurled the useless receiver on to the carpet of the bedroom, and muttered, 'Damn! Damn! Damn!'

Every blasted telephone in the house dead. Of course, they *would* be. Wolff was a puffed-out yob, but he wasn't an idiot; he'd have given very specific instructions to his bully-boys. Cut the link with the outside world. Don't give anybody an opportunity to raise the alarm.

Basic precautions.

Basic enough, even for a yob like Wolff.

Carter walked to the window. He peeped through the horizontal slits in the half-closed Venetian blind; watching for some sign of movement across at *Yew Tree Bower*.

The Dardick was where he'd tossed it, prior to checking the bedroom telephone. It was there, on one of the beds ... staining the brushed-nylon sheets with a smear of gun-oil.

Carter watched; he caught an occasional glimpse of Wolff in the sun lounge of *Yew Tree Bower*—a quick, on-and-off sighting through the branches of ornamental trees and bushes. Wolff moving around. Wolff looking agitated about something. Wolff waving his arms a little. Wolff talking to somebody ... somebody Carter couldn't see.

Carter bent his knees and squinted between some of the lower slats.

A voice said, 'Interesting ... is it?'

Carter whirled, tensed his legs for a dive for the bed and the Dardick, then froze as Lennox waved the Luger in his face.

'Naughty,' warned Lennox. The fat detective bent forward, over his own stomach, scooped the Dardick into his free hand, and said, 'I'm collecting 'em, son. I'll soon have a full set.'

Carter straightened his legs, relaxed, blew out his cheeks in a long sigh, and said, 'Thank God!'

'For what?' enquired Lennox interestedly.

'That—y'know...' Carter waved one of his hands in a vague gesture. 'That you're not one of them.'

'Them?'

'Wolff's crowd.'

'Y'mean *your* lot?'

'Oh, for heaven's sake, man. You don't think...'

'Easy sonny.' Lennox pointed the Luger at Carter's navel, as Carter made as if to move towards the middle of the bedroom. 'I don't enjoy shooting people—I'll grant you that... but, in my line of business, I have to do lots of things I don't enjoy.'

'I'm—I'm not with Wolff,' said Carter, urgently.

'No?' Lennox looked curious ... and disbelieving.

'Not with *Wolff*,' repeated Carter.

'You could have fooled me, cocky,' said Lennox gently. 'This morning—in the boozer—when you pitched stumps for this little game. You put up a hell of a performance.'

'Oh!'

'For somebody who *isn't* with Wolff,' emphasised Lennox.

'I—I suppose...' began Carter, then stopped.

'Go ahead,' said Lennox. '"Suppose" a little ... we aren't pressed for time.'

'That you think I'm on their side,' mumbled Carter.

'Rather more than "think",' corrected Lennox.

'After this morning, I mean. Y'know ... after this morning.'

'That,' said Lennox, 'is exactly what *I* mean. "After this morning". And, come to that, *since* this morning.'

'Yes,' said Carter, heavily. 'You would—of course you would ... everybody will.'

Lennox watched Carter's face, as he asked. 'And *weren't* you?'

'This morning,' agreed Carter, wearily. 'But not now.'

'No?' Disbelief was still thick upon the question.

'They'll kill me,' said Carter, simply.

'Probably.'

'*Certainly*. It's the only "safety" their kind can understand.'

Lennox nodded silent agreement.

'After what Flora Aimes said. After what she did.'

'She shouldn't have done it. Is that what you're saying?'

'No.' Carter shook his head, slowly. Miserably. 'She—she did what...' He dried up, again.

'What she *had* to do?' suggested Lennox.

'What she should have done,' sighed Carter. 'What any right-thinking person would have done. But—y'know ... it signed my death warrant.'

'I think,' said Lennox, 'she knew that. In fact, I think that's why she did it.'

'I—I suppose...' Once more, Carter couldn't find the words. He waved a hand towards the beds, and muttered, 'Look ... may I?'

Lennox waggled the Luger, and said, 'As long as you don't forget *this*.'

Carter almost smiled. He walked from the window, sat on the edge of one of the beds, clasped his fingers together, between his knees, stared at the carpet for a few moments, then spoke without looking up.

He said, 'There's a dead man, floating in the river.'

Lennox didn't reply.

'He's not one of Wolff's men,' said Carter, in an expressionless voice. 'He's—I dunno ... I think I should know him. But I don't know. He's floating, face downwards—near the bank—and...' He swallowed then, in a soft-spoken rush, said, 'The back of his head's been blown off.'

Lennox said, 'But you think you know him ... right?'

'I should.' Carter looked up, into Lennox's eyes. 'You wouldn't understand, I suppose, but ... Things. The build. The—er—the general shape. If you'd had experience. In the forces—something like that—you'd know what I...'

'I know what you mean,' said Lennox.

'He's somebody I should know. Somebody I *do* know. I'm sure of it ... if I could see his face.'

'You saw him?' said Lennox.

'For God's sake. I've just told you. I...'

'While you were taking a pleasant stroll along the river bank?'

'Well—yes ... you could put it like that.'

'Odd,' mused Lennox. 'Y'know, old son, I find it *rather* odd. Here's you ... sweating cobs, because Wolff's lads are likely to bump you off. With some justification, I'd say. In your shoes, I'd tend to think in a very like manner. I wouldn't—if you don't mind me saying so—make any long-term plans. Champion. I'm with you, that far. Give, or take, an odd question without a satisfactory answer, here and there, I'm with you up to that point. But the rest...'

The fat man shook his head in sombre disbelief.

'You saw them,' said Carter. 'You were there ... in that upstairs room.'

'Uhu,' agreed Lennox.

'I had to get out. I needed air. I had to get away from them all.'

'*Which* "all"?' asked Lennox, innocently. 'Wolff's "all"? Or the rest?'

'The Robs Cully crowd. The people I'd—I'd...'

'Betrayed?' suggested the fat man, quietly.

'All right ... *betrayed*!'

'Ah!'

'But that doesn't mean...' Carter argued haltingly, but desperately, from what he knew was an impossible premise. He said, 'Look—you were *there*. You felt it—you *must* have felt it ... unless you're a complete oaf.'

The fat man grunted.

Carter continued, 'I had to get out. I had to! Good God, you heard me. How I pleaded with that animal, Johnny. How I begged him to let me get some air. Then—when he did, with that yobbo Pinky—how I...'

'Ah, yes,' murmured Lennox. 'That Pinky bloke.'

'What about him?'

'One of the—er—odd questions without a satisfactory answer. I mentioned 'em. When is he due to arrive?'

'Who?' Carter stared.

'Pinky.'

'Oh!' Carter swallowed, then said, 'I broke his arm.'

'Really?' Lennox's face registered wide-eyed amazement.

'Yes.'

'Just like *that*?'

'Unarmed combat,' said Carter. 'I know a little about it ... having held the Queen's commission.'

'I'm sure,' said Lennox, pointedly, 'Her Majesty'll be highly delighted, if she ever learns of your part in this little cock-up.'

'I broke his arm,' insisted Carter. 'That's how I got the gun. I took it away from him.'

'And?' pressed Lennox.

'And what?'

'Where is he, at this particular moment? Dashing back to the boozer? Organising search parties? At a guess, what would you say friend Pinky is up to, right now?'

'Dying,' said Carter, flatly.

'Of a broken arm?'

'I—er—I *punished* him. I proved who was the best man.'

'Having disarmed him, of course,' said Lennox, mildly.

'Of course.'

'How?'

'I put the boot in, old boy. I put the boot in.'

The pseudo-innocence of the question invited—and got—the mock-arrogance of the answer.

The fat man said, 'I see,' and there was a silence.

Carter seemed to pull himself together. He looked up at the fat man, with a mix of curiosity touched with contempt, then said, 'And you?'

'Me?' Carter's question seemed to puzzle Lennox.

'You're around too, old boy,' explained Carter.

'Oh! Ye-es ... I'm around, too,' agreed Lennox.

'For what reason?'

The fat man chuckled, and said, 'To collect guns ... or so it seems.'

'No. I mean ...'

'I know what you mean, sonny.' Lennox's voice was soft and, suddenly very serious. 'I didn't have to kill anybody.'

'No. You wouldn't. A man like you ...'

'Kidology,' explained Lennox. 'A couple of headaches ... nothing worse.'

'I can't see *you* killing anybody,' said Carter, and there was some of the old arrogance in the remark.

Lennox said, 'Just don't stake your own life on that opinion, cocky,' and moved the Luger, promptly.

'No ... I don't think you'd use that thing,' said Carter.

'It'll be your blood, laddie.'

'You're not that sort of a man.'

'Never trust first impressions, Carter.'

'You're not the type.'

'Sit still.' Lennox held the Luger rock-steady, then said, 'For starters—and don't spare my blushes, son—what sort of a man *am* I? ... in your considered, and very expert, opinion?'

'Lazy,' said Carter, airily. 'The—er—"executive" type. Some plush office, somewhere. Bags of "Yes-men". Probably the director of some tin-pot little firm making useless articles for the masses. Newly rich ... at a guess. More money than brains. Certainly more money than guts—and, by that, I mean manliness ... not bodily circumference.'

'Not bad,' murmured Lennox.

'Am I right?'

'For a man who's just admitted betraying his friends ... not bad.'

'But I *am* right?'

'Y'know—for a man who's also admitted kicking another man to death—to committing murder ... not bad.'

'I *am* right ... aren't I?'

'A bit out.'

'All right. Tell me,' said Carter.

Lennox smiled. A slight smile, and a sad smile, and a smile which hadn't the strength to climb as high as his eyes.

He said, 'Copper. High-ranking, working copper. Deputy Head of a County Constabulary C.I.D. Detective Superintendent. And —Carter, you miserable little insect—we'll start counting the pips in this particular pomegranate from *there*!'

Elizabeth Elliott ...

The terror which crept through the 'Conference Room' touched her, but she brushed it aside. Her mind brushed it aside, with something not too far removed from angry irritation.

She wanted to live.

Sweet Jesus and all His saints, she wanted to live ... and, by hell, she was *going* to live. Of all the people in this room—of all the silly, stuck-up madams, the sexy, po-faced bitches, the gormless, gold-plated she-men, of them *all*—she had the best reason for wanting to live.

Because she'd once wanted to die!

She'd been in The Pit. She'd touched rock-bottom and, for a few months, had stood, up to the nostrils; in shit. She knew! She'd experienced the other thing.

If anybody really wants to know what the other end of the see-saw is like, okay ... let 'em spend a few months in a New Orleans cat-house. They'll know. They'll come out at the other end—*if* they come out at the other end—either a zombie, or a re-birth ... and, for every re-birth, count a thousand zombies.

That was being down, mister. And that was where *she'd* been.

It made you puke—y'know that?—it made you bloody-well puke ... all the concentrated hypocrisy capable of being wrapped up in one neat bundle beneath a single man's skin. The midden so many so-called 'respectable' men called a mind. These berks in this room—these two-faced bastards—who had the gall to walk upright and call themselves human.

That film—that Brando thing ... *Last Tango in Paris*. Sweet Jesus, the yapping some of 'em had done about it. Some of these scared bastards here, in this room. 'Disgusting' ... that's what they'd said. That's what they'd yelled from the housetops ... having sat through, and *seen* the bloody thing.

These men—not the same men, but the same *sort* of men—not the same men, but equally 'respectable' men ... y'know what? They'd parted with money. Big money. They'd sat on seats—not particularly comfortable seats—and they'd sweated, and panted, and strained forward for a better view. And at what?

Missus, that's your man. And he was there, watching. And what he was watching was something, by comparison with which *Last Tango in Paris* was like *Mary Poppins*. And what he was watching wasn't shadows across some cinema screen, lady. What he was watching was live—up there, on a stage like the one in this room —and it was a performance of which I was a part. A very important part. A very central part. A very disgusting and de-humanising part.

And, missus, your husband was out there, in that audience, watching ... and enjoying himself!

Sweet Jesus and all His saints ... thank Christ for Bill!

Bill had known. He hadn't seen—maybe if he'd *seen* it would have been different—but he'd *known*. Hell, you can't marry a man—not a man like Bill—and keep a thing like *that* from him. He'd known ... he hadn't given a damn ... and, after she'd told him, he'd kissed her and, thereafter, hadn't even mentioned it.

Except to Pop—he'd told Pop ... he'd always told Pop everything.

At first, it had angered her. A sour and secret anger, which she'd kept to herself; that Bill (of all people) should have run to his old man, and spilled his guts about...

Then, she'd understood, and the anger had melted.

It was something unique in her experience. Something she'd never encountered before; something she hadn't guessed even existed. Not father-and-son. Not even buddies. Something more basic—more fundamental—than even that. They were the same person—just that, and nothing less than that ... the same *person*, straddling two generations.

And thank God for the knowledge. Thank God for the understanding.

Because, when Bill had died Bill *hadn't* died ... which may sound crazy, but was no less than the truth.

Bill was still here. Another Bill ... but the same Bill.

Which was why she wanted to live.

Which was why she was not—repeat *not*—going to allow the pain from this damn shoulder to show in her face. Because her pain might spark off Bill's don't-give-a-damn fury ... and, this time, Bill might *really* die!

And that prat on the stage—that prat with his sub-machine gun—wouldn't know whether it was Shrove Tuesday or breakfast time. And all the lesser prats, with their shooters in their hot little hands ... they'd get blown out of the windows by the breeze!

But Bill might die.

Therefore, she wanted to live—she *had* to live ... if only to keep Bill from killing his ever-loving, pig-headed self.

A third man died as a result of the lawlessness perpetrated against the residents of Robs Cully.

It was a peripheral death—a mere spin-off ... but, despite this, the man was no less a corpse.

The site foreman called the news to Roger Douranby; that 'The coppers are on the phone, Mr Douranby. They say it's urgent. Summat about your wife.'

Douranby was aloft, checking the positioning of strut-girders on a partially built fly-over, at the time. The cat-walk was a bare twelve inches wide, and the waist-level hand-rope had been out in all types of weather and, as a result, had some rotting strands in its twist.

Douranby turned quickly, lost his balance and grabbed the rope. The rope parted, and Douranby fell from the cat-walk and ended his fall across the cab of a parked dumper.

The medics fought to mend his smashed spine. They knew, from the start, that he'd never walk again, but they fought to repair the damage well enough to allow him to live.

They failed ... maybe because Douranby *wanted* them to fail.

The drug-quietened pain left him, six weeks later, in one of the men's surgical wards of a Darlington hospital.

It was a spin-off death to what was happening at Robs Cully.

But (and for all that) Roger Douranby became no less a corpse.

'Right.' Grafton reached a hand towards the telephone. 'Now ... I'll talk to this Wolff character. Convince him it has to be an eyeball-to-eyeball thing. Him, and me. Otherwise...'

'Not you,' interrupted Harris.

Grafton left his hand resting on the receiver, and said, 'I carry the authority, Harris. The top man goes in, and talks to *their* top man. Anything less, and it doesn't mean much.'

'Somebody,' said Harris, 'has to soft-soap the Home Office. That's not my *forte* ... and you know it.'

'You have my backing,' said Grafton. 'I've driven 'em down a hole. All you have to do is keep 'em there.'

'They'll pull weight,' growled Harris. 'I can't order *them* around. Anyway ... Wolff contacted *me*. I'm the man he wants to do business with. Any eyeball-to-eyeball stuff, and I'm the man he might believe. He doesn't even know you exist.'

'Nevertheless...' began Grafton.

Blayde said, 'Not you, chief constable. Harris is right. You're needed out here ... just in case Whitehall sends the wrong man.'

'Thank Christ for *some* degree of agreement,' grunted Harris.

Blayde smiled, and said, 'You're out-voted, sir.'

Grafton removed his hand from the receiver, looked at the two chief superintendents for a moment, then said, 'There may be sense in what you both say. It's possible. But I'm not ordering anybody. And I'm not asking for volunteers. Whoever crosses that river does so with his eyes wide open. No heroics. No bluster. He goes, on the strict understanding that, when he gets there, he's the *least* important person in Robs Cully. He obeys orders—to the letter ... if necessary, orders given by Wolff.'

'That lets Harris out,' murmured Blayde.

'What the hell,' blared Harris, 'is that supposed to mean.'

'Harris,' said Blayde, wearily, 'unless you agreed with 'em, you couldn't obey orders from Archangel Gabriel himself.'

'Look—just because I happen to have a mind of my own...'

'And a mouth of your own. And a temper of your own. And an opinion of your own. Harris, I wouldn't trust you to shoot a mad dog ... not until *you'd* decided it was mad. You're everything you shouldn't be, for a job like this. You also have a wife ... and I haven't!'

'What the hell's *that*...'

'Not that you'd be much of a loss ... to any woman,' continued Blayde, coldly. 'But she'd go through the motions. She'd wear mourning ... and black doesn't suit her.'

'Wolff wants *me*,' blazed Harris. 'What the hell my wife has to do with this thing I don't know. Why the hell bring *her* into it ...'

'Would you go, Blayde?' Grafton cut in on Harris's tirade.

'It's my division,' said Blayde, simply.

'That's not the question I...'

'If anybody else goes—if, for example, Harris is allowed to cross that river and balls everything up—I'd take it as a personal affront.'

Harris began, 'And I'd take it...'

'Shut up, Harris!' Grafton didn't waste time on pleasantries. He spoke directly to Blayde but, at the same time, seemed to be voicing his own thoughts. He said, 'Uniform ... these animals tend to place some importance upon rank, and the uniform of that rank. There's also this man Lennox. Harris knows him.'

'I don't,' said Blayde.

'Therefore,' mused Grafton, 'we'd better have somebody at this end capable of assessing Lennox's information ... assuming he can keep out of sight, and can get in touch. Harris can stay at this telephone.'

'That makes me indispensable,' snarled Harris, sarcastically.

'What we get to know from Lennox, we might be able to use. We'd better have a code—something basic, and simple ... something we can both understand, assuming we're allowed to communicate with each other, and assuming that, whatever we say, we'll be listened to.' Grafton paused for a moment, then continued, 'Rank means it's true. "Mister" means the opposite ... that's the best we can do at such short notice. If I address you as "chief superintendent", what I say thereafter is authentic. If I address you as "mister", what I say thereafter is the opposite of what is going to happen. And with you. "Chief constable" prefixes the truth. "Mister" prefixes an untruth. Agreed?'

'Bloody Boy Scouts,' muttered Harris.

Blayde said, 'Got it. With a careful choice of words, it should work.'

'Anything else?' asked Grafton.

'Ye-es.' Blayde paused, then said, 'I know Robs Cully. Better than you—better than Harris, here—but I don't know it intimately. The people who live in the various houses. The sort of people they are. The cul-de-sacs. Which house—supposing anything goes wrong—can give best cover ... the best escape route. It's knowledge we might need. In certain circumstances, vital knowledge.'

'To know where to run,' added Harris, quietly. Contemptuously.

'Exactly.' Blayde took Harris's contempt, and turned it into a valid argument. 'If running becomes necessary, to know *where* to run.'

'Who does know?' asked Grafton, gruffly.

'Clemens—P.C. Clemens ... it's his beat.'

'I'll not order any man to...'

'Nor will I, sir.'

'Nor ask him to volunteer.'

'Not that, either,' agreed Blayde.

Grafton waited.

Blayde said, 'I'll show him a plan of the place. Ask him for information ... names of householders, and so forth. If he makes the offer, without prompting...'

Blayde moved his shoulders.

'Without prompting,' insisted Grafton.

'*Mister* Blayde,' murmured Harris.

12.20 p.m....

Wolff dropped the receiver back on to its rest.

'They are nuts,' he breathed, harshly. 'Y'know that? These crap-assed Limey cops ... they're *nuts!*'

'Yep,' agreed Cowboy ... not knowing what the hell he was agreeing with, but having sense enough to realise that a half-drunken Wolff was no man with whom to enter 'meaningful discussions'.

'What 'n hell is a goddam "chief constable"?' Wolff tipped more booze down his throat, straight from the bottle. He varied the question slightly, and said, 'Some big pig—okay ... but some sorta police commissioner, maybe? That what the punk is?'

'Yep,' said Cowboy, from the point of view of safety.

'Y'know that?' Wolff's eyes narrowed. 'Y'know that, for a fact? That all this "chief constable" balls means police commissioner?'

'Wa-all—er ... nope,' admitted Cowboy, reluctantly. 'I can't say I rightly *know*. It ain't a thing I'm likely to ...'

'Okay ... so keep your stupid chewer zipped. Okay?'

Cowboy shrugged.

'He wants clearance,' muttered Wolff. 'He ain't gonna talk—he ain't gonna do one damn thing ... not without his own guy here. He's outa his skull. Don't he know? Don't the crap-assed fink *know*? We have people here. We ain't playin' games. We ain't puttin' up no fancy bluff. If I don't get my ...'

The hoodlum opened one of the french windows and entered the sun lounge.

Wolff roared, 'What 'n hell do *you* want?'

'Pinky's dead,' said the hoodlum.

'So?'

'I found him. Smashed up. Stiff ... like he'd been beaten-up.'

'So?' repeated Wolff. 'Maybe we ain't rounded all the creeps into the booze-hall. Maybe some tough baby is prowlin' around some place. Warn the boys ... don't run to me with your goddam troubles.'

'Yeah, but ...' The hoodlum frowned his puzzlement. 'Y'know. Pinky's dead.'

'Beat it!' shouted Wolff. 'So Pinky's dead. Screw Pinky. He was a fink—he was half dead all his goddam life ... who cares?'

The hoodlum muttered, 'Okay,' and left the sun lounge.

Wolff slopped whisky into his mouth, wiped his lips with the back of a hand, and bawled, 'Judas Christ! Ain't I enough ...'

'I care,' said Cowboy softly.

'Uh?'

'You asked who cares. I care. Pinky was my buddy.'

'So, now you need a new buddy,' sneered Wolff.

'Maybe I need a new boss,' said Cowboy, dangerously.

'Hey.' Wolff's voice dropped to a low pitched purr. Except for his lips, his whole body was motionless. 'You gettin' screwy ideas, punk?'

'Yep.' Cowboy met stare with stare, and contempt with contempt.

'Could be you're already livin' on hocked time,' warned Wolff.

'Could be,' agreed Cowboy, flatly. 'Could be I also ain't too happy with the town drunk runnin' things.'

'Is that a fact?'

'Could be I'm hankerin' after a change.'

'You ain't big enough, punk.' Wolff's lips curled. 'That saddle-sore ass of yours. It ain't within a hundred miles of *this* goddam saddle.'

'Could be,' drawled Cowboy. 'It's just that I ain't yet convinced. But—lemme tell you somethin'—Pinky was my partner. And I figure he was a whole lot nicer guy than a high-stinkin' louse, name o' Eddie Wolff.'

'You're dead, man,' whispered Wolff. 'You are already stiffening.'

'Ain't that a fact, though? ... one of us, for sure,' agreed Cowboy, quietly.

Broken down into its component parts...

Moments of explosive violence never can be, of course, but (presupposing the impossible) broken down into its component parts, each split-second slice of that particular moment of explosive violence went like this.

Wolff flicked his wrist, and sent the whisky bottle cartwheeling at Cowboy's face. At the same time, he launched himself sideways and backwards, towards the dubious shelter of a high-cushioned divan at the rear of the sun lounge. He also grabbed at his hip pocket, wherein was housed a pearl-handled derringer ... the only firearm a big-shot, like himself (a big-shot who could buy a whole army of trigger men) allowed himself to carry around.

Cowboy saw the bottle and moved his head. The bottle grazed the side of his jaw, then smashed itself against the back wall of the sun lounge. Cowboy also moved his hand; his right hand, towards the shoulder-holster at his left armpit. To say that the right hand moved 'fast' would be a gross understatement; the man, of whom the hand was a part, came from an area of the world renowned (justifiably, or not) for its fancy gun-play; an area which had bred legends in the art of the 'draw' and in which much of its present generation worked hard at perpetuating those legends. Cowboy was one of them. Unlike Wolff, he didn't *grab*. The movements of the hand, arm and fingers were as co-ordinated and as swift as smooth rubber along polished ice. As the hand snapped around the stock, the trigger-finger took up the first pressure and, before the Colt .45 revolver was fully clear of the holster, the thumb was holding back the hammer.

The roar of the Colt was merely a continuation of—the conclusion of—the whole, silk-smooth movement.

Wolff took the heavy slug in the gut. It smashed a rib, and sent him tumbling into a corner of the sun lounge, before his own hand had even reached the hip pocket.

Cowboy drawled, 'Could be that saddle ain't so tall, after all.'

Wolff sprawled and stared homicidal loathing at the man who had toppled him from his perch. He couldn't talk; his teeth were clamped into the flesh of his lower lip as a counter to the mounting pain and, already, a trickle of blood crept from the corner of his mouth and dripped from his chin.

Grafton made it 'official'.

He stood on the steps of Raine village hall, with Harris on his left and a little behind him, and gave the first Press Conference of the day.

It was a newshound's dream; Open House to every reporter ready to lick his pencil and open his notebook. There was a solid arc of T.V. cameras and held-out hand-microphones around the shallow steps leading to the door of the hall. And the timing was immaculate ... hot news for the 1 p.m. radio put-outs and the afternoon television newscasts; perfect for the evening editions, and with space in which to contact all the self-styled 'experts' who might add controversy for the entertainment of viewers, readers and listeners.

Nor was it the usual, meaningless police-pap which, ninety-nine times out of every hundred, left everybody wondering just what the hell *was* happening.

Grafton gave it to them, straight from the shoulder.

He said, 'Approximately fifty people—mostly women, and some elderly men—are, at this moment being held hostage in Robs Cully. Their lives are being threatened by a band of criminals, led by a man called Edward Wolff. We—the police—have been given an ultimatum. That Wolff's son—Ricardo Wolff—must be returned to his father, before nine-thirty, tomorrow morning.

'Ricardo Wolff. For your information, he was sentenced to seven years' imprisonment for a drugs offence. That was about a year ago. He's an American citizen ... as is his father. As, indeed, are the men who are under the orders of his father, at this moment. This means that Ricardo Wolff, his father—all of them —can be deported from the United Kingdom, and refused re-entry, for the rest of their lives.

'There is, therefore, no choice. Wolff can have his son ... and, as a personal opinion, good riddance! I refuse to even consider any other possible option. I refuse to place a single innocent life in possible jeopardy, for the sake of an undesirable alien like Ricardo Wolff.

'The Home Office know my views. They approve of those views ... for obvious, and humane, reasons. A Home Office official is on his way here, at this moment. Ricardo Wolff is also on his way here. The sooner the exchange can be made, the better.

'That's the situation, ladies and gentlemen. That's the decision. Have any of you any questions?'

The I.T.V. camera moved in, and the accompanying interviewer called his question fractionally ahead of his colleagues.

He said, 'Chief constable, what's likely to happen if there's a reversal of your decision.'

'There won't *be* a reversal,' snapped Grafton.

'But, if there is?'

'Wolff has threatened to kill hostages,' said Grafton, grimly. 'I believe him. I can't afford *not* to believe him. I'm told, by the American authorities, that he's a man capable of carrying out his threat. To answer your specific question, then ... if there's a reversal of this decision, innocent people are likely to be murdered.'

'We understand the bridge has been blown up.' The B.B.C. Radio man chipped in, before the I.T.V. interviewer could hog all the questioning period.

'It was a planned attack,' said Grafton. 'The bridge *was* blown. Robs Cully is isolated ... it's an island.'

'What steps are being taken to rescue the hostages, chief constable?'

'We're meeting Wolff's demands.'

'Chief constable, wouldn't you say that was a somewhat negative attitude...'

'Have you any plans to cross the river, with police, and...'

'What would you say to your critics, chief constable, who'll argue that if these people get away with this sort of...'

The questions came in bundles, as each man and woman thrust forward a possible point of view.

Grafton held up his hand.

When the babble of questions had died into silence, he said, 'I'll take criticism from the people who are at present being held hostage. Whose lives are in danger. They matter ... nobody else! A senior police officer—Chief Superintendent Blayde—is on his way to act as my personal representative, in any negotiations with Wolff. There are certainly no plans to cross the river in force. The primary object of the Police Service is to save lives. Not to engage in pitched battles, at the expense of...'

'It sounds as if one of your friends has shot somebody,' said Lennox, drily.

'They're not my "friends". I've already...'

'Fellow-murderers.' Lennox corrected himself.

The fat man had crossed to the window, at the sound of the shot, and was dividing his attention between the slots of the Venetian blind and Carter, who still sat on the bed.

Carter compressed his lips, then said, 'God knows how you reached the rank of superintendent, but...'

'Sonny,' warned Lennox, 'you already have more fertiliser than you can handle. Don't dump even more on to your lap by being saucy.'

'I object to...'

'Who's across there?' interrupted Lennox. 'Who were you watching, when I arrived?'

'Wolff.'

'I don't see him. I don't see anybody.'

'In the sun lounge. He was moving around. Just glimpses of him ... that's all.'

Lennox glanced between the slats of the blind.

'I can't see anybody.'

'He was there,' insisted Carter.

'Whose place is it?'

'Mine.'

'Aye,' grunted Lennox, 'it would be.'

'Look, I keep telling you...'

'And I don't believe you.' Lennox hefted the Luger as a silent reminder of who was running things. He said, 'How do we get across there?'

'Wha-at?' Carter widened his eyes.

'It's your place.'

'I know. But...'

'Back doors. Approaches. Without sending him a visiting card.'

'You're mad. You're a lunatic, man.'

'Aye.' Lennox nodded, solemnly. 'You're in a room, with a homicidal maniac, laddie. A homicidal maniac, with pockets filled with guns. Now, be advised—humour him ... how do we get across there?'

'How do I get there?' asked Blayde.

A photostat copy of the architect's plans of Robs Cully was spread across the bonnet of a squad car. The Beechwood Brook chief superintendent was asking questions, and Police Constable 2728 Wallace Clemens was answering them. Both men were using forefingers to clarify the questions and the answers.

'*Yew Tree Bower*,' said Clemens.

'Is that its name?'

'Yes, sir. Major Carter's place.'

'Major Carter?' said Blayde, innocently.

'Ex-army ... so he says.'

'You don't believe him?'

Clemens chose his reply carefully, and said, 'I can't *dis*believe him, sir.'

'But?'

'He's—er...' Clemens hesitated, then said, 'He's very stereotype. Y'know—he pushes it a bit much, sometimes. That's only an opinion, of course.'

'Of course.'

'I could be wrong.'

'Indeed,' agreed Blayde. 'But that's where he lives?'

'Yes, sir. *Yew Tree Bower*.'

'And this place?'

'*Green Gables*. That's where the Mitfords live. She's away, at the moment. Spain, I think ... holidaying, with her parents. He'll be in London, all day.'

'Really?'

'Tuesday,' explained Clemens. 'Every Tuesday, he drives down to London. Some conference, or another.'

'I see.' Blayde traced his finger along the map. 'Now ... supposing I want to get from here—*Yew Tree Bower*—to here—*The Hind's Head*—what's the best way? Not the obvious way. The least likely way ... the way nobody would *expect* me to take?'

'We-ell...' Clemens rubbed his jaw.

Blayde said, 'Don't rush it, constable. It's urgent, but we don't want any mistakes.'

'There's a way through *Conte Lauba*.'

'*Conte Lauba?*'

'Here ... where the Douranby's live. At the back, there's a garden—a vegetable garden—and a lawn. Then a hedge. There's a gap ... not much of a one, but it's there. I've used it as a short cut, when I've been checking unoccupied property. It's about two yards in, from the angle of the garden ... here. It leads into Mitford's place—y'know ... *Green Gables*. Then, if you make for the rear of the aviary—Mitford's hobby, he breeds prize budgies—you'll find a...' Clemens stopped. He frowned, looked at Blayde, and said, 'Look, sir, is it fixed?'

'Fixed?' Blayde's expression was one of complete non-understanding.

'That *you* go?' amplified Clemens.

'Yes, constable, it's fixed,' said Blayde.

'I mean...' Clemens waved a disgusted hand at the map. 'All this. It doesn't mean much.'

'I can map-read, constable,' said Blayde, gently.

'I'm not saying you can't, sir, but that isn't the same. These short cuts you're looking for ... they aren't *on* the map. Even the names of the houses. You'll be wasting your time, looking for the name-plates. No offence, sir ... but you're the wrong man.'

'I'm the man who's going.'

Clemens swallowed, moistened his lips, then said, 'Alone?'

'I beg your pardon?'

'Alone, sir. Is that strictly necessary?'

'The plan,' said Blayde, carefully, 'is for me to go alone.'

'All right. Can the plan be changed?'

'How?'

'To include me,' said Clemens. 'I'd obey orders, to the letter.

I wouldn't...'

'That is understood, of course,' said Blayde, flatly.

'I know the place. Better than any map.'

'There are certain—er—"facts of life",' said Blayde. 'For example, that the place is stiff with armed criminals ... we estimate about two dozen. For example, that none of them would hesitate ... they're all capable of killing a police officer. For example...'

'For example, sir,' cut in Clemens, with a wry smile, 'that it's a very dicey proposition, and that either of us—or both of us—could be carried back, feet first. I know that, sir. I've already been shot at, with a bazooka, and I didn't enjoy the experience. But, if the plan *can* be altered, I'd like to go. I know the place better than you. I know the place better than *them*. There's also a man in there, somewhere—a local man, called Sam Wilson—he went in, on my behalf, to find things out ... and I should have gone myself. For the sake of my own conscience, I'd like to make sure he's still in one piece.'

'The plan can be changed, slightly,' said Blayde, quietly.

Clemens said, 'With respect, sir ... it'll be a much better plan.'

'Who's that?' asked Lennox, suddenly.

Carter stood up from the bed.

Lennox showed him the Luger, and warned, 'Just to look, Carter. Just to tell me. No Military Medals ... not today, Josephine.'

Carter joined Lennox at the window. He peered between the slats. He watched the hoodlum walk along the side of *Yew Tree Bower* and into the sun lounge.

'Well?' asked Lennox.

'They call him Bobs ... that's all I know.'

'Bob?'

'No ... *Bobs*. It's short for something, I suppose. nickname, perhaps. They have rather ridiculous names, as you may...'

'They call you "Carter",' said Lennox, nastily. 'So far, I haven't noticed a horse.'

Carter looked cross, but said nothing.

'Tell me about Bobs,' said Lennox.

'There's nothing to tell. He came, yesterday ... with Wolff, and five others.'

'Came to Robs Cully?'

'Yes.'

'Not to *The Hind's Head*.'

'No ... of course not. To *Yew Tree Bower*.'

'Which is?' purred Lennox.

'My place,' said Carter, heavily. 'But that doesn't mean...'

'Back on the bed, chummy.' Lennox waved the Luger to emphasise his instructions. 'Start working out what it *does* mean. Much else, and we'll need a ready-reckoner to work out exactly how many crimes you *have* committed.'

The man carrying the unusual name of 'Bobs' looked, with interest, at the quietly moaning Wolff, before turning his head, frowning his non-understanding, and saying, 'You bump him, Cowboy?'

'He ain't dead yet.' Cowboy held the Colt .45 as easily as an artist holding his palette ... but ready.

'He's goin'.' Bobs made the observation, as an expert. 'One in the basket don't take too long.'

'Pinky?' said Cowboy, quietly.

'He's stiff.'

'Sure?'

'Yeah ... I figure.'

'I wanna be sure.'

Bobs moved his shoulders, philosophically.

'You sure?' Cowboy pressed his question.

Bobs said, 'Jesus ... he *looked* stiff.'

'How?'

'Some sorta smash-up.' Bobs moved his hands in tiny gestures. 'Y'know ... it happens. It happens all the time.'

'Who?'

'I figure the soldier-boy.'

'That Carter bastard?'

'I figure,' repeated Bobs.

From the floor of the sun lounge Wolff tried to speak but, as his teeth left his lips, a moan of agony took over.

'You wanna shove it?' enquired Cowboy, coldly. 'Or you want I should send another in, to keep it company?'

Wolff clamped his teeth on to his lips once more.

'You takin' over?' asked Bobs.

'How come soldier-boy's walkin' around?' asked Cowboy.

'Johnny said okay.'

'Yep?' Cowboy raised his eyebrows, fractionally.

'With Pinky,' amplified Bobs.

'Pinky ridin' herd?'

'Yeah.'

'That stupid louse, Johnny.' Cowboy breathed deep disgust. 'Don't he know Pinky? Don't he know he ain't too bright?'

Bobs said, 'He ain't too bright, right now,' and grinned.

Cowboy tilted the revolver.

He said, 'You laugh easy, friend. Maybe I should take a coupla front teeth out ... the hard way.'

Bobs stopped grinning.

Cowboy nodded his approval, and lowered the Colt.

'You takin' over?' Bobs repeated one of his previous questions.

Once more, Wolff tried to speak. Once more, the pain killed the words and beat the will, and only a sobbing moan came out.

Cowboy glanced at the wounded man, and drawled, 'Whoever else, he ain't.'

'It's his kid,' Bobs observed.

'Yep.'

'So?'

'Screw the kid.'

'You figure?' Bobs looked undecided.

'I'm here for dollars,' said Cowboy.

'Yeah. I, also. Everybody, I guess.'

'Except him.' Cowboy waved the Colt in the direction of Wolff. 'And he don't count no more.'

'I guess,' agreed Bobs.

'So, screw the kid.'

'Yeah ... I guess,' agreed Bobs.

'From here in on, it's dollars.'

'Yeah ... I like that.'

'And I,' said Cowboy, firmly, 'am takin' over ... okay?'

'I got myself a new boss,' grinned Bobs.

'Yep. The old boss.' Cowboy stood up from the chair and moved towards Wolff. 'He was reachin'. The right hip.'

Bobs used his foot to roll the wounded man on to his face.

Wolff opened his mouth to scream, then passed out before the sound could beat the blackness.

Bobs bent, removed the derringer from the hip pocket and handed it to Cowboy. Cowboy dropped it into the pocket of his jacket.

Cowboy said, 'Their outfit is sendin' a top man over, to parley. You should meet him, maybe. Bring him along to the saloon ... I'll be there, spellin' things out.' He holstered the Colt then, almost as an afterthought, added, 'That soldier-boy. You see him, stiffen him ... right?'

'Yeah ... sure.'

12.40 p.m. ...

'Volunteer'. It is such a nice, vague word. It can mean just about anything, from the you-you-and-you gag to the near-hero who puts his life in hock for his fellow-men. It can be a crusade, and it can also be a con but, unfortunately, (con or crusade) its worth is rarely capable of evaluation until things have gone too far.

Clemens almost wished he had not 'volunteered'.

He was worried about Wilson; and what might have happened to Wilson was playing his conscience up a little. He knew his way around Robs Cully; and, without a guide, Blayde might hash things up if the going grew tricky.

Nevertheless...

It was a feeling. A feeling he'd been sold something. A feeling he'd been hooked ... and that he hadn't, in fact, 'volunteered' at all.

Blayde said, 'Keep the thing straight, Clemens.'

Clemens said, 'Yes, sir,' in a very deadpan voice ... and wondered where the hell they'd found this bloody boat.

A 'Puffin', fibre-glass hull, sailing dinghy was rollicking fun on the flat waters of a lake, with a smooth breeze and the trim sail. It was *not* rollicking fun without the sail, in the racing waters of the Hewfraw and with only one paddle to work it from bank to bank. In such circumstances, a 'Puffin', fibre-glass hull, sailing dinghy became hell's own thing to handle ... something on a par with riding an elliptical merry-go-round.

Nor did Blayde, doing his 'Captain Bligh' act, help matters.

All right—he was a chief superintendent. All right—he had things on his mind. But (hell's bells) it wouldn't have brought down the monarchy if he'd grabbed the other paddle and doubled the manpower.

Clemens glanced at the opposite bank.

Two men (probably the two bazooka experts ... Clemens wasn't sure) watched their approach. Motionless and (from what he could see, at that distance) without expression. Threatening.

More than a little frightening.

They were two more reasons why Clemens wished he hadn't 'volunteered'.

'Up on your feet, my beauty.' Lennox waved the Luger, encouragingly. 'We're on our way.'

'Where?' Carter stood up from the bed.

'Across the road, to your place.'

Carter's face whitened.

'C'mon.'

Carter said, 'You must be out of your mind!'

'I need a telephone.'

'Look, I'm not...'

'A couple of 'em have left,' said the fat man. 'That leaves Wolff ... maybe one more, in case he needs a nappy-change. Two of 'em. That, at the most ... that's my guess.'

'*Your* guess. If you seriously think I'm...'

'I'm a good guesser.'

Carter said, 'Nobody—nothing on God's earth—will get me into that damned house. So, you might as well...'

'*I* will,' snapped Lennox. He waddled forward, lined the Luger on to Carter's chest and spoke without bluff. He said, 'Matey, I need you, to get into that *Yew Tree Bower* place. I need you—but I'm going ... with, or without, you.'

'Without me,' said Carter.

'The choice is yours. But, before you make it, remember the gun. The fancy gun you were lugging around not long ago.'

'The Dardick?'

'Your paw-marks. All over it. I squeeze this trigger, put the Dardick back in your fist, and swear it was self-defence ... you're with me, I hope?'

'Great heavens, man! That's...'

'Murder. Aye ... I know.'

'You—you wouldn't...'

'I'd earn myself a commendation, for committing murder. And, sonny, I'd take it, without blushing ... I'm that sort of bloke.'

Carter choked on an unintelligible whisper.

'You're getting the gist, I see,' murmured the fat man.

'No! You—you *wouldn't*.'

The fat man nodded, solemnly, and said, 'Believe me. I'd sleep like a log, every night, for the rest of my life.'

'You—you...'

'Try me.'

The fat man's finger closed around the trigger of the Luger.

'All right! All right!' Carter backed away. He caught the back of his knees against its edge and sat down on the bed, again. He held out his hands, palms forward, as if to shield himself from the Luger's bullets. He groaned, 'I'll go. I'll *go*. I'll do it. I'll go. I— I think I know a way. Into the back garden. Without being seen. If—if they're still in the sun lounge, I think...'

Lennox said, 'Fine. Don't just sit there. Let's move.'

As with all great schemes ... it was absurdly simple.

Cowboy opened the door of the 'Conference Room' and beckoned, with his head to Johnny.

Johnny knew that Cowboy was (in military parlance) Wolff's 'runner' ... that his duties included the carrying of urgent messages from the big man. Johnny, therefore, grunted quick annoyance before leaving the stage and joining Cowboy at the door of the 'Conference Room'. Cowboy closed the door, and they were alone on the landing.

'Somethin' happened?' asked Johnny, in a puzzled voice.

'Yep.'

'Okay ... what?'

'We forget the kid.'

'Ric? Wolff's kid?'

'Yep.' Cowboy nodded.

'Judas Christ! That's why we're *here*.'

'Nope.' Cowboy shook his head.

'Is that the goddam message?' exclaimed Johnny. 'Is that what Wolff sent you here to...'

'Nope,' drawled Cowboy. 'I can't rightly call it a message. Not from Wolff, that is. But from *me*? Yep ... that sure is the message from *me*, buddy.' The muzzle of the Colt .45 was hard against Johnny's ribs, as Cowboy continued, 'The chatter-shooter, friend. Just hand it over, nice 'n easy ... keepin' your finger well away from that little ol' trigger.'

'What the hell...'

'Nice 'n easy,' insisted Cowboy. 'Else you get one right where Wolff got his.'

Cowboy's fingers closed around the breech of the Stirling S.M.G. as Johnny's fingers loosened their hold.

'There, now,' said Cowboy, drily. 'That didn't hurt one little bit ... did it?'

'What the hell gives?' snarled Johnny.

'I kicked Wolff's ass outa things.'

'*You* did?'

'Yep.'

'Why the creepin' Jesus...'

'He was hittin' the booze too heavy. He was gonna screw us all down. An' all for some no-good, snot-nosed kid. So-o ... I quit.'

'Just like that,' sneered Johnny.

'He figured he could out-draw me,' said Cowboy, simply. 'He was digestin' a forty-five before he made it.'

'Oh!'

'Now *I'm* runnin' things.'

'Not with me around, you ain't. You think I'm gonna...'

Cowboy said, 'You ain't too important no more. Any fink who gets a nice guy like Pinky mashed ain't all that nice. An' ain't all that bright.'

'Pinky?' Johnny frowned.

'I figure soldier-boy.'

'Carter?'

'Yep.'

'Could be,' agreed Johnny, slowly. 'Yeah ... could be.'

Cowboy said, 'That was a crazy plan, Johnny. Carter and Pinky. You didn't even have the cream to give the poor slob a fair shake.'

'Could be you're wrong.'

'Yep. That, too, ain't somethin' that ain't happened before.'

'So, why not...'

'Turn around, Johnny,' said Cowboy, solemnly.

'You think you're gonna...'

'I think you have brains, Johnny. I think you're gonna turn around. You know the score. You have it comin' ... buffaloed, or plugged. Ain't no other way I can think of. The other guys—they'll go along ... greenbacks talk their lingo. You, I ain't too sure about. Like Pinky an' me. You an' Wolff were buddies ... so, you I ain't so sure about. Turn around, Johnny. Don't make me plug you.'

Johnny turned, slowly. He stood there, arms hanging loosely at his sides, and waited. There was a quality of stoical acceptance—a recognition of the inevitable—in his stance. Like every man in his own chosen, and twisted, world, he knew the rules . . . and accepted the penalty of failure.

Cowboy murmured, 'You wanna know? This is for Pinky.'

He brought the barrel of the Colt down, hard, across the back of Johnny's skull.

It was a long day, until darkness. A never-ending day. A day of highlights and a day of boredoms; a day of pain and a day of numbness. A day of contrasts—like any, and every, other day ... but, this time, the contrasts were greater and more nerve-tearing therefore, this time, the contrasts moulded themselves into local contemporaneous history.

A small lifetime of contrasts.

A forever of contrasts.

Contrasts; seconds—sometimes micro-seconds—of black imposed upon white ... eternity fragmented into needle-points of contrasted happenings.

12.45 p.m. ...

Blayde stepped from the dinghy. The tiny craft swung, Blayde missed his footing and one of his shoes squelched in shallow mud.

He muttered, 'Damn!'

'Easy, sir.' Clemens's warning came fractionally too late.

Blayde snapped, 'Keep it steady, constable.'

Clemens raised his eyes to heaven, but kept his mouth shut. He followed Blayde on to the bank and his shoe, too, sank into the shallow mud.

Blayde spoke to the hoodlum who had caught the thrown rope. He said, 'The man in charge. He's expecting me.'

The hoodlum moved his head in a wide arc; searching for something with which to anchor the dinghy to the bank.

'Here ... give it to me.' Clemens took the rope and knotted it to a sapling a few feet from the river's edge.

Blayde said, 'Don't let's waste too much time.'

'Oh, yeah ... yeah,' grunted the hoodlum.

Clemens glanced across the river, at the group of uniformed and plain clothes coppers watching and, for a moment, wished to hell *he* was one of the group.

Then he turned and followed the other two.

* * *

Cowboy stood, feet firmly planted, and surveyed the occupants of the 'Conference Room'. He held the Stirling S.M.G. easily. Professionally.

He tilted the barrel and squeezed the trigger in a quick, half-second burst.

The room exploded with noise. A cluster of holes appeared in the ceiling. Plaster flew and fell on the occupants of the room, captors and captives alike. A woman gave a single scream ... then there was silence.

The silence was so complete, everybody heard the last of the flakes of plaster hit the floorboards.

Cowboy said, 'To show I know which end the slugs come outa ... okay? Now ...'

12.47 p.m. ...

Lennox grabbed Carter's shoulder and pushed him down before he, too, ducked into a crouched position behind the beech hedge.

'Your friends,' muttered Carter.

Lennox touched Carter's spine, warningly, with the barrel of the Luger, and whispered, 'Quiet! They may be *my* friends. They're certainly not *yours*.'

They remained silent, and hidden, as Blayde, Clemens and the hoodlum walked along the road, and past *Yew Tree Bower*.

Carter murmured, 'Why?'

'Why what?'

'Why not here? This is where Wolff is.'

'There'll be a reason.' Lennox straightened, as the trio moved out of sight and beyond earshot. 'C'mon. We'll pay a call on Wolff, instead.'

'... this is a new deal, folks. So, listen good. Wolff ain't around any more. Which means we ain't interested in Wolff's kid. As of now, this is a straightforward hold-up. We talk dollars. We talk getaway machines. An' that's *all* we talk.'

Cowboy addressed himself to his fellow-criminals. 'Any o' you guys feel like takin' a powder, this is it. Walk outa here ... ain't nobody gonna stop you. Anybody linin' up behind me, I ain't sayin' but you're welcome. But no Wolf. No Johnny. This is my play. Okay ... anybody wanna call me?'

* * *

The road surface tore rubber from the tyres as the car braked to a screaming halt. The man was out, and racing for the entrance to Raine village hall, before any of the coppers could get within touching distance.

A couple of flashbulbs winked as two camera-boys snapped off a possible 'action shot'.

The man reached the counter and leaned, stiff-armed in front of the sign marked *ENQUIRIES*.

'My wife!' he gasped. 'She's in there. They tell me she's...'

'Your name, sir?' asked one of the policewomen.

'Kempton. Henry Kempton. I live at...'

'Ah, yes.' The policewoman consulted her list. 'Celia Kempton —your wife...'

'Is she *in* there?'

'Yes, Mr Kempton.' The policewoman's voice carried the professionally accurate union of sympathy and objectivity. 'I'm afraid your wife...'

'Just what the hell's happening?'

'Some criminals. They're holding hostages, for the moment. There's no need to...'

'What's happening? What are you people *doing* about it all?'

'There's no need to worry, sir.'

'For God's sake!'

'We're meeting their demands. None of the hostages will be in any way imperilled.'

'You—you...' The worry and anger almost choked Kempton. He snarled, 'You—you stupid bloody bitch!'

The policewoman looked wide-eyed and outraged.

Kempton turned from the counter and almost collided with Ruth Harris.

'It won't help, Mr Kempton.' The smile which went with the words was genuine. A sad smile; the smile of somebody equally tormented. She said, 'I know how you feel ... how you *must* feel. But...' The smile became even sadder. More wistful. 'We have to sweat it out. And pray a little.'

Kempton moved his arms, helplessly.

She said, 'Have some tea. Hot and sweet. That won't help, either ... but, for the moment, it's all we can do.'

Kempton nodded, dumbly and allowed himself to be led towards the far end of the counter.

Harris stood at the door of the Committee Room, frowning.

He'd seen and heard everything. The pronoun—the 'we' part of the exchange, between Kempton and his wife—had him puzzled. The emphasis had been deeper than it should have been.

12.55 p.m. . . .

'Your boss,' said Lennox, grimly.

They were in the sun lounge of *Yew Tree Bower*, and Lennox was on his knees, alongside the wounded and unconscious Wolff. Carter stood and watched. Did nothing. Said nothing.

Lennox unbuttoned the shirt, unbuckled the belt and unzipped the trousers. Despite gherkin-shaped fingers, he was both gentle and skilled. He eased the soaked cloth aside and examined the still-bleeding wound.

'A pad,' he muttered.

Carter remained motionless. Remained silent.

Lennox looked up, and snapped, 'A pad, man. Make a pad from something ... anything. Move!'

Carter shook his head; tiny, jerky shakes. Little more than twitches.

He breathed, 'Let the animal die. He isn't worth saving.'

Lennox pushed himself to his feet, waddled around the unconscious man's legs and stopped, less than a yard from Carter.

He said, 'Sonny, I haven't time to argue.' He yanked the Luger from the waistband of his trousers as he spoke. He growled, 'I never thought I'd enjoy doing this to any man.'

The barrel of the Luger slammed into the side of his jaw, before Carter had time to raise a hand to ward off the blow. He sprawled, and took a wrought-iron table and a potted rubber-plant with him.

'Stay there,' warned Lennox. 'Don't tempt me. Next time, I might not just *hit* you.'

He returned the Luger to his waistband, strode across the sun lounge and ripped the silk cover from a chair cushion. As he hurried back to the wounded Wolff he folded the material into a makeshift pad.

Cowboy eyed the young hoodlum suspiciously, and said, 'Boy, you on loco juice?'

'Naw,' lied the young hoodlum.

'I ain't too damn sure. You young punks ain't ...'

'Naw,' protested the young hoodlum. 'Jesus Christ, *naw*!'

'Okay—okay ... don't buck around too much. I gotta be sure.' Cowboy grinned a part-apology. 'Johnny's out there. Take him some place, and tie him good. But *good*. Then stand posse over him ... okay?'

'You scared?' mocked the youngster.

Cowboy said, 'We all have backs, boy. Johnny ain't gonna get near mine ... okay?'

The youngster muttered, 'Sure,' and slouched from the 'Conference Room'.

Bobs led the way. Two paces behind him, Blayde and Clemens walked, side by side.

'Not *Yew Tree Bower*,' said Clemens, softly.

Blayde's voice matched Clemens's in volume, as he said, 'So I gather. I noticed it, as we passed.'

'The pub,' guessed Clemens.

'Good. That's where the hostages are.'

Clemens flicked a quick glance at Blayde, for reassurance.

The divisional chief superintendent was outwardly calm and relaxed. He walked with his gloved hands clasped behind his back; easy paced, but with authority. His uniform wasn't his 'best blue', but it was still smart, and with creases in all the right places.

Blayde. 'Razor' Blayde—that's what he was sometimes called, behind his back ... but never to his face. He had flair. Not bombast—not shout, like Harris—but (by Christ!) don't let anybody try a flanker on Blayde. He'd have 'em. He'd cut 'em to ribbons ... cop, or comedian. When needed, Blayde could chop 'em *all* off at the knee-caps.

Clemens's lips moved into a barely concealed half-smile, at his own thoughts ... a wry smile.

The smile was accompanied by an addendum to the thoughts ... that, within the next thin wedge of contemporary history, Blayde would have an opportunity of living up to his reputation.

Cowboy was unlike Johnny.

He was far more relaxed ... and yet, in some subtle way, far more ready. His confidence wasn't too far removed from contempt. He didn't need no goddam Stirling spray-shooter to keep this bunch of hicks in line; he'd placed the sub-machine gun on the stage, then removed his jacket and tossed that, too, on to the floor of the stage. The shoulder-holster was there, for all to see. And, protruding from the mouth of the shoulder-holster, the butt of the Colt .45 revolver.

He sat, with one cheek of his backside on the edge of the stage. With one foot resting on the floor of the 'Conference Room'. With the other foot swinging easily, and rhythmically, along the front of the stage apron.

Less menacing than Johnny ... but, arguably, more dangerous.

Doc Pearson watched him, assessed him, but kept the conclusions of his assessment from his expression.

The police marksman grunted, 'This bloody grass is damp.'

'Dew.' His companion answered, without lowering the binoculars from his eyes; without interrupting the steady left-right-right-left sweep of his observation of the opposite bank.

'Dew, be damned.' The marksman shifted his prone position, slightly. 'It's the bloody grass. It's the soil. We'll have rheumatism—double-pneumonia—Christ knows what else, after this lot.'

His companion raised the glasses and scanned the sky to the west. He was weather-wise.

He said, 'We soon will be.'

'What?'

'Wet.'

'Eh?'

'It's building up. It'll piss down, before the day's out.'

'That,' said the marksman, glumly, 'is *all* we bloody-well need.'

12.57 p.m. ...

Pearson strolled across, smiled at Cowboy, and said, 'So, now *you're* the big cheese.'

'Yep.'

'Not like the other one,' probed Pearson.

'Uh?'

'Not like Johnny.'

'Nope.'

'More human, would you say? More humane?'

Cowboy said, 'I figure horses and dogs are nice people. What's eatin' you, friend?'

'That young woman.' Pearson motioned across the room, with

his head. 'They tell me you're the man who shot her in the shoulder.'

'Yep.'

'Nasty,' observed Pearson, drily.

'It weren't but an accident.'

'Really?' There was gentle mockery in the question.

Cowboy said, 'Ask the old-timer.'

'Nevertheless, you shot her,' insisted Pearson.

'Yep... I ain't sayin' I'm proud.'

'She's in pain.'

'Uhu.'

'And I'm a doctor. A G.P.'

'Yep?' For the first time, Cowboy showed interest.

'I need drugs... pain-killing drugs. I have some, in my bedroom. A first-aid kit, I always carry around with me.'

Cowboy picked his nose, reflectively, for a few moments.

Then, he said, 'Could be you're workin' somethin'.'

'I'm a qualified doctor,' said Pearson.

'Yep.'

'So, I'm...'

'Lemme tell you, doc. I have known some very two-timin' medicine-men in, an' around, my life.'

'Would my word be enough?' asked Pearson, quietly.

'Could be,' mused Cowboy.

'For what it's worth, you have it.'

Cowboy studied Pearson's face, then said, 'Okay. I gotta proposition you'd maybe put your brand on...'

12.58 p.m....

Lennox sent up a quick prayer that the increased agony would not overcome the bodily anaesthetic of insensibility, as he eased the belt a notch tighter over the makeshift pad.

From across the room—from where he still sprawled on the sun lounge floor—Carter sneered, 'You can't save him. You're wasting your time. In the stomach... thirty minutes, at the most. I know what I'm talking about. I've seen it happen too many times.'

'Shut up!' muttered the fat man.

He divided his attention between the wound and the wounded man's face; watching for signs of regaining consciousness;

watching for the flow of blood to ease, then stop.

The hell of it was that Lennox knew Carter was right; that a bad gut-wound needed immediate and very sophisticated surgery if the wounded man hadn't already bought a non-transferable, one-way ticket to a hole in the ground.

Slowly—with infinite care—Lennox tightened the belt one more notch.

'You're doing more harm than good,' said Carter, contemptuously. 'You're killing him. Not that *I* care ... but all you're doing is forcing the slug deeper.'

'Carter.' The fat man looked up. The sweat of concentration and terrible responsibility filmed his round, full-moon face. His eyes were hard with unaccustomed disdain. His voice was hoarse with alien repugnance. He croaked, 'Carter, don't push it. Please! I've never yet killed a man. But, God help me ...' He swallowed, and ended, 'Just don't push it. That's all.'

'... I ain't no likin' for gunnin' down women. But don't get me wrong, doc. That don't make me no pushover.'

'Your proposition?' murmured Pearson.

'The old guy. The old-timer.' Cowboy nodded towards Elliott. 'He can maybe fix the shoulder? Maybe stop it hurtin' bad ... wouldn't you say?'

'Possibly,' agreed Pearson. 'Given the instructions and the painkiller.'

'Okay. I wanna make sure about Pinky.'

'Who's Pinky?' asked Pearson.

Cowboy said, 'The Carter bastard. Johnny let him walk around. Pinky was ridin' herd on him.

'I think I know. The yob who left this room with Carter ... right?'

'Don't call my buddies names, friend. "Yob"—that ain't a ...'

'What else?' asked Pearson, impatiently.

'Carter jumped Pinky ... that's what I figure.'

'Really?'

'Mauled him ... maybe rough.'

'What am I supposed to do?' asked Pearson, sarcastically. 'Mourn?'

Cowboy used a hard voice, and said, 'You are gonna check, doc. You are gonna give the old-timer somethin' for the lady. Tell him how he has to fix things, so it don't hurt any more. Then, you are gonna mend Pinky ... okay?'

'And if he's dead?'

'He ain't *gonna* be dead.'

'But, if he *is*. What do I do? Perform the last rites?'

'Lookee, I ain't gonna ...'

'All right. Assuming he's in a bad way. What then? All I have is on-the-spot medicine. A few basic drugs ... nothing more. What if your friend needs something more sophisticated?'

'What we want, we get,' said Cowboy, harshly.

Pearson breathed deeply, and waited.

Cowboy said, 'That's it. That's the proposition. Mosey along. Get your box o' tricks. Tell the old guy what he hasta do, so the lady's shoulder don't pain her too much. Then find Pinky, an' fix him.'

'And if he *is* dead?' insisted Pearson.

'He ain't gonna be dead. No punk like Carter ain't gonna maul Pinky ... not that bad.'

Pearson faced facts, and said, 'If it's bad, I'll need equipment. I'll need drugs. I might even...'

'We get 'em ... *whatever*.' There was certainty in Cowboy's words. 'What he needs, we get.' Cowboy glanced beyond Pearson's shoulder, at the watching and listening hostages. He said, 'We got bargaining counters, doc. Pinky dies ... he is gonna have a nice escort.'

1.03 p.m....

Blayde and Clemens arrived at the 'Conference Room'.

They walked, Indian-file style, the length of the room. Bobs, followed by Blayde, followed by Clemens. In the watching silence, somebody breathed, 'Thank God!' ... as if a police uniform was the answer to all present problems and the warranty for all future safety.

Blayde played the morale-boosting gag; when every other trick was a waste of time, self-deception did no harm. He gave a quick, tight smile ... the smile of a victorious general relieving a beleagured town.

They reached the stage.

Cowboy looked at Bobs, and said, 'Okay, take the doc to Pinky.'

'Uh?' Bobs blinked.

'The doc.' Cowboy waved a hand, towards where Pearson was

with the Elliott-Hill group, taking phials from a small, black leather case, and giving quietly-spoken instructions to Elliott. Cowboy said, 'Take him along. See what sorta shape Pinky's in.'

'He's stiff.' Bobs stared. 'I already toldya. He's...'

'You some sorta medic?' asked Cowboy, coldly.

'Uh?'

'You arguin'?'

'Naw. But...'

'Check it out ... okay?'

'Okay.' Bobs shrugged. 'But what the hell am I gonna...'

'Pal.' Cowboy's eyes became hard and flat. 'You maybe figure you can do better than Wolff?'

'Naw. But...'

'We ain't raisin' no hands on it.'

Bobs blew out his cheeks, resignedly. He turned, collected Pearson and walked out of the 'Conference Room'.

Only then, did Cowboy seem to notice Blayde and Clemens.

He said, 'Yep?'

He'd picked the wrong man, in Blayde; now it was Blayde's turn to do a spell of 'deliberate ignoring'. The Beechwood Brook Divisional Chief Superintendent removed his gloves, patted his tunic pocket produced a packet of cigarettes, chose a cigarette, returned the packet to its pocket, took out matches, lighted the cigarette, then replaced the matches to the pocket from where he'd taken them. He didn't hurry and, all the time, he moved his head and his eyes; viewing the ceiling and walls of the 'Conference Room' and smiling gently, as if appreciative of some fine specimen of architecture and decor.

The silent pantomime lasted sixty full seconds.

Cowboy broke, first. He repeated his original greeting.

'Yep?'

'Eh? Oh ... ah!' Blayde gave the impression of reluctantly breaking off his reverie. He said, 'I'm here to talk with a man called Wolff.'

'That ain't possible.'

'Or nobody,' added Blayde, smoothly.

Cowboy said, 'The only way you're gonna meet Wolff, is if you beat him to hell ... that way, could be you'd bump into him, on the way back.'

Blayde drew on his cigarette and, with his eyebrows, silently asked for explanations.

'Wolff ain't around any more.'

'I see.'

'He ain't top man no more.'

'Really?'

'He ain't runnin' the show.'

'But you *are*?'

'Yep.' Cowboy nodded.

Blayde pondered the situation for a moment, then he smiled his tight, quick smile, and said, 'A question comes to mind. What are the exact odds in favour of another front runner?'

'Uh?'

'Which of these characters,' Blayde glanced swiftly over his shoulder, at the watching gunmen, 'is most likely to knock *you* from the top of the heap?'

'I ain't sayin' it can't be done,' admitted Cowboy, modestly. 'But the guy who can pull a faster trigger than this pappy's boy ain't around these parts.'

'Good.' Blayde nodded, approvingly.

'Uh?'

'I always like to deal, directly, with the top man.'

'That's me, friend.'

'I take it,' said Blayde, slowly, 'we can now forget Ricardo Wolff ... his father being a thing of the past?'

'Yep.'

'And?'

'Uh?'

'Instead?' asked Blayde.

'We-ell, now ...' Cowboy scratched his backside, meditatively. 'Ric Wolff goes back into storage ... okay? From now in on, we talk dollars.'

'A simple hold-up?'

'Yep.' Cowboy nodded.

'A simple hold-up.' Blayde repeated the words. This time, they were not a question. This time they were spoken musingly; they carried sadness. Wistfulness. He murmured, 'Simple ... but not quite so simple.'

1.05 p.m. ...

Lennox was telephoning from *Yew Tree Bower*. He was in the room adjacent to the sun lounge. He was holding the receiver in his left hand and the Luger in his right. The Luger was pointing at Carter, and Carter was sitting on a deep-cushioned sofa ... and Carter was even *breathing* very carefully.

Lennox said, 'Wolff. He's here, with a bullet in his belly. He's dying.'

Am I supposed to care?' Harris's voice came back, harsh and metallic, over the wire.

Lennox snapped, 'Yes ... you're supposed to care.'

'Lennox, let me remind you. That bastard ...'

'Is innocent, until proved guilty,' cut in Lennox. 'And, unless the law's been changed, within the last twenty-four hours, *you're* not yet judge and jury.'

'He's dying ... let him die.'

'You don't mean that, Harris.'

'The hell I don't mean it. As far as I'm concerned ...'

'You'd *better* not mean it,' warned Lennox. 'I'm making this official, brother-officer. Understand me? Official! The time is thirteen-zero-five hours, and I'm notifying you that I have a man here, in urgent need of hospital treatment. His life depends on it. Now, *do* something ... and, for your own sake, make it very zippy.'

Lennox dropped the receiver back on to its rest, before Harris could reply.

Carter risked his life by easing a twisted smile across his lips.

'Conscience,' he mocked.

'I know.' Lennox's voice was tired and heavy. 'It stops me from sitting back and letting Wolff snuff it ... just as it stops me from squeezing this trigger, and putting a bullet in *your* rotten guts, as long as you behave yourself. Don't knock it, son. It's the only reason you're still around.'

The 'Conference Room' held an audience, and never was an audience more interested in any performance; never was an audience more intent upon the duologue exchanged by two men. That half a hundred of that audience were captives, and that the handful of others were their captors, was not too important. For the moment, that relationship was ignored. Every man, and every woman, was a member of that one audience, and the audience was silent, and the audience listened.

The exchange between Blayde and Cowboy was as important as *that*.

It was important to the captives, because the ground had shifted since Johnny had been deposed; since Wolff had been toppled from his throne with a .45 bullet. Since then, the odds had lengthened; the certainty was not quite as near-absolute as it had been.

The original choice—a cheap, American dope-handler, for the lives of a roomful of innocent people—had been no choice at all. The decision had been obvious enough to make itself.

But cash, in large lumps, was a totally different can of beans.

The well-heeled residents of Robs Cully knew all about bread. Its importance. Its *real* value. Its *true* buying-power. They knew that, when the chips were down—when all the philosophies in the world had been aired and argued around—a pound note was the only voice left. It was the only note in the whole register which really meant anything. It was what they were, and why they were there. It was the difference between a desert and a rose garden. It was rotten, it was evil, it was corrupting—it was all these things ... but, at the final analysis, it was 'it'. And, when all the bluffs had been called, life itself could still be reduced to terms of hard cash.

And now somebody, somewhere, was being asked to *buy* them out ... with real bread.

Therefore, the captives listened. And the captives worried.

So did the captors.

They listened, and they worried, because there'd been a switch. Wolff and Johnny—a partnership they knew, and trusted—had been replaced by a single man. A Texan. A man so sure of himself, he kept his shooter housed pending the split-second moment when its trigger had to be worked. But (and at the same time) a man capable of smacking Wolff *and* Johnny, both, in the puss, and a man who talked dollars and not ideals ... which, maybe, made him *their* man.

Could be this guy—this 'Cowboy' cat—might pull the proverbial 'Impossible Dream'. Open the vaults of Fort Knox and buy them all out of this crappy, kill-or-be-killed life they'd all been slotted into.

Could be.

Therefore the captors, too, listened. And the captors, too, worried.

It was common ground, and the common ground was cash.

*   *   *

By five minutes past one o'clock, that afternoon, the nation had learned that there was a village called Robs Cully. That approximately fifty good and decent citizens of that village were being held at gunpoint, as hostages for a silly and unimportant reason ... in order that an unknown, and comparatively unimportant, American criminal might be granted a freedom to which he was not entitled.

The B.B.C. radio news-reader spoke the words with elocutionary perfection, and the listening millions were shocked ... and then relieved.

The gangsters could have their petty little colleague. Good riddance to him; he would no longer be a burden upon the United Kingdom tax-payers.

Ricardo Wolff was a nonentity.

But, at five minutes past one o'clock, that afternoon, 'money talk' had not yet moved beyond the river-locked boundaries of this village called Robs Cully.

Cowboy glanced at the people huddled around the walls of the 'Conference Room', and said, 'These folks. I want for you to put a price tag on their hides.'

'I can't do that,' said Blayde.

Cowboy said, 'I figure they're important. They carry some sayso. Else Wolff wouldn' picked this place ... okay?'

'Everybody's important.'

'Lookee, don't play dimes an' nickles with me, copper. I mean these folks are from the right side o' the tracks. They're *worth* somethin'.'

Blayde nodded, and drew on his cigarette.

Cowboy drawled, 'Okay ... the price tag. In *real* money. Dollars. How much you figure it's worth for all these nice folks to walk outa this thing?'

'If they don't you're in trouble.'

'Yep.' Cowboy paused, then added, 'They, too, are in trouble ... big, big trouble.'

In the silence, somebody breathed, 'For God's sake! Make him an offer.'

Cowboy grinned, sagely.

Blayde said, 'You don't put cash on human lives. It can't be done.'

'Friend, you have led one helluva sheltered life.' Cowboy's

mouth twitched into another quick, but humourless, grin. 'Lemme tell you. Who the hell it is, they have a price. Ain't nobody worth all the dough in the world.'

Blayde said, 'If you believe that, have it your own way. Put your own price tag on them ... but don't ask me.'

'Two?' suggested Cowboy. Then he shook his head, and said, 'Nope. I figured three.'

'Three?'

'Yep.' Cowboy nodded.

'Three what?'

Very quietly—very deliberately—Cowboy said, 'The big stake, friend. Million.'

There was a communal intake of breath, within the room ... then silence.

Blayde raised his cigarette to his mouth, inhaled tobacco smoke, dropped what was left of the cigarette on to the floor and, as he blew a feather of smoke, screwed the cigarette out with the sole of his shoe.

Then he said, 'You're off your head.'

'We are,' explained Cowboy, 'playin' this game for a man-sized pot. We ain't no time for barn-dance manners. Okay? An' we ain't assing around with no kid we want unlockin' from no local jail no more ... not any more we ain't. As of when Wolff boozed himself into thinkin' he could out-gun me, we moved strictly C.O.D. 'Tain't but good sense. I figure we number seventeen. Me, an' a sixteen-strong bunch. That makes for a lotta splits, friend. So, we ain't dealin' in no corn-pickin's. Three million, I guess ... else the local coffin-maker has a lotta work ahead.'

1.12 p.m. ...

On earth, puny men played the game of God.

In the sky, the clouds piled black, and high, along the horizon.

On Mount Olympus, Thor spat on his hands, reached for his hammer and contemplated which particular tune he might play on his anvil this time ... and how big, and terrifying, he should make the flying sparks.

* * *

'He's still alive,' lied Pearson. 'Alive ... but only just.'

The hoodlum called Bobs gazed down at the smashed corpse of what had once been Pinky, and breathed, 'Jeeze!'

Pearson straightened from his quick examination of the body. He positioned himself between the corpse and the dumbfounded Bobs, and pulled out all the subtleties of near-superstitious mystique with which any qualified medical practitioner can blind the dim-witted.

Why did he do it? Why did he tell this deliberate lie?

It was a feeling. A belief that Pinky was Cowboy's weakness; that this hunk of dead and battered flesh was an Achilles heel which must not be removed ... a pinpoint of hope, in a situation heavy with hopelessness.

It was a good enough reason to lie.

Nor was the lie difficult to maintain.

Bobs was scared of Cowboy; scared enough to wish life into a corpse which had once been Cowboy's friend. Pearson was the genie who granted that wish, therefore Bobs accepted the wish and was grateful. Pearson rapped out the orders, and Bobs obeyed them without question.

Nobody must touch the corpse, in case they felt the cooling of the body surface and the stiffening of the sinews. So-o—Pinky was 'in a bad way' ... therefore, nobody must touch him.

There was not the normal rise and fall of the chest, associated with the act of breathing. So-o—his breathing was very shallow ... but he was still alive, for the very good reason that a qualified doctor *said* he was alive.

It was a lie which fed upon itself. It multiplied and produced a back-up of lesser lies which, in turn, made the original lie an easily acceptable truth.

It was easy.

All you needed was the letters M.D. behind your name.

Clemens saw the effect of the conversation upon the hostages. He saw hope die, in some of their eyes. He saw emotional cracks appear in some of the expressions.

He saw these things, and he was suddenly very frightened.

Cowboy said, 'The deal is three million.'

'Dollars,' said Blayde.

'Yep.'

'Plus safe conduct, of course?'

'Yep.'

'And the deadline?' asked Blayde.

'Same deadline.'

'In beloved memory of Wolff.' Blayde moved his lips into the ghost of a smile, and the smile carried an aura of utter contempt.

'Why not? There ain't a better.'

Blayde nodded, and said, 'I'll pass your message.'

'The hell you will! You ain't gonna leave this...'

'I'm the messenger-boy. The go-between.' Blayde put real feeling into his words, for the first time. 'I didn't come with Wolff's son. I certainly didn't come with three million dollars-worth of loose change in my pocket. You claim authority here. Accept the responsibility. The responsibility to let me pass your terms to the men capable of meeting them.'

'You ain't leavin' here, pal,' said Cowboy, with finality.

Blayde looked bored, and waited for Cowboy to make the suggestion ... the obvious suggestion which would sound better coming from the opposition.

Cowboy made it.

He said, 'They have a phone ... right?'

'Who?' Blayde made believe not to understand.

'The guy you wanna contact. The guys with the dough.'

Blayde said, 'I can telephone my chief constable. I can tell him your terms ... and add that I think you mean what you say.'

'Yep. Do that.' Cowboy grinned. 'You got sense, friend. You 'n me ... we're gonna move this along real neat 'n easy.'

Blayde looked directly into Cowboy's eyes for a moment, then said, 'It's possible. Just don't start spending it ... yet.'

1.20 p.m....

Pinky was dead, and stiffening fast.

But Johnny was alive. He had hell's own headache, and he was in a murderously black mood ... but, sure as Christ, he was alive.

He was in a ground-floor room of *The Hind's Head*. The so-called 'Snuggery'; a small, lush-furnished room leading from the main lounge of the hotel. A room with comfortable, but very solidly-built, chairs, and Johnny was bound to one of those chairs. He was bound with wire; wire which had been ripped from two expensive stand-lamps which went to make up the decor of the lounge, beyond the door of the 'Snuggery'.

Thus Johnny, and Johnny was safe. But *safe*! He could just about breath, and he could just about think but, beyond that, his bodily movement was very restricted.

He had, moreover, a guard.

The guard was the young hoodlum whom Cowboy had detailed for the task, and the young hoodlum's name was Hoppy. Hoppy, because he was as unpredictable as a Mexican jumping-bean; because he was a hophead; because he was a combined main-liner and homosexual; because he was skin-popper-cum-joey. He had close, button-bright eyes. He giggled easily and handled a spring-loaded knife with true dexterity.

Robert Hill would have recognised him.

Jean Hill and Barbara Pickering would also have recognised him.

And Johnny knew him.

Johnny figured he knew him well enough—or, could be, *maybe* well enough ... because, with junkies, who the hell could ever be sure?

The first spots of rain came down. Slowly—almost lazily—and as big and as round as an old-fashioned florin. They polka-dotted the pavements and road-surfaces. They splashed the surface of the Hewfraw and Skew Beck and pockmarked even *their* turbulence.

The police marksman said, 'Jesus! It's coming.'

'A nice steady build-up.' His companion rested his eyes from the 'pull' of the binoculars for a few seconds. He squinted up at the darkening sky. He said, 'This one won't be a summer shower. This one's going to be a really bell-tinkler.'

'You are,' said the police marksman, sourly, 'just the sort of happy-go-lucky prick a bloke needs on a job like this. So bloody cheerful. So bloody optimistic.'

Ruth Harris didn't notice the curtain-raising drops to the on-coming storm. She hardly noticed the gradual darkening of the room, as the clouds thickened across the sunlight.

Ruth Harris was worried.

She positioned sandwiches on moulded-paper plates, handed the plates to an ever-growing crowd of coppers, newsmen, relatives, would-be-helpers and general rubberneckers ... and, at the same time, she worried.

She felt sick in the stomach; she wanted to throw up, every

time she allowed her imagination to hook itself on to a series of mental pictures of which she could not rid herself.

It was disgusting.

It was also ridiculous.

It was (she told herself) *ridiculous*. At her age. A married woman ... and a very happily married woman.

Robert would ...

Great heavens, Robert would be shocked. If he could have crawled into her skull, and watched those pictures, as they flitted across her consciousness—and listened to the thoughts, as they provided silent, background talk to those pictures ... he'd have been shocked. He would *be* shocked.

Because ...

Because she couldn't turn off the pictures. And she couldn't switch off the silent talk. And, together, they combined to make her sick with worry.

Worry about a man she ...

Hated?

Yes, damn it, hated. Hated, *hated*, HATED.

God! It was ridiculous, and disgusting ... at *her* age!

The telephone conversation was a little like a ball game.

Having left Bobs to supervise the 'Conference Room', Cowboy had settled himself at the tiny switchboard, behind the reception counter of *The Hind's Head*, and was the middle-man between a telephone conversation between Blayde and Grafton, and the conversational ball was tossed between Robs Cully and Raine and, each time, Cowboy tried to catch it—and each time he *thought* he'd caught it ... but, each time, he missed it without knowing he'd missed it.

It was a game, with certain rules—rank equalled truth, and 'Mr' equalled non-truth ... but, simple though the rules were, Cowboy didn't know them. Therefore, Cowboy couldn't win; the conversation ball swerved, in mid-air, and he *always* missed it.

Blayde said, 'The ransom price is three million dollars, chief constable. And the deadline is nine-thirty, tomorrow morning.'

'That's a lot of money,' said Grafton.

'Yes, sir.'

'Far more than any single, provincial bank is likely to hold.'

'I'd say so, sir,' agreed Blayde.

'It's doubtful whether it can be collected—organised—within the time period.'

Cowboy cut in, 'You do it, friend. Your man, here, will tell you. We're horsin' around none.'

'They mean it, chief constable,' said Blayde.

Grafton said, 'All right. We'll do our best. Are they to be trusted?'

'Yes, Mr Grafton, I think they can be trusted,' said Blayde.

'I see.'

There was a pause in the exchange.

Cowboy said, 'Pinky. Don't forget Pinky.'

'Who—or what—is "Pinky"?' asked Grafton.

Blayde said, 'One of the men here. One of the gangsters. There's a doctor here—a Doctor Pearson—he tells me he's injured.'

'He's mauled up bad,' interrupted Cowboy. 'He needs hospitalisation. I wanna be sure he gets it ... fast.'

'Doctor Pearson tells me he's in a bad way,' said Blayde. 'He asks me to give you his compliments, Mr Grafton, and to tell you that this man, Pinky, is still alive.'

'But mauled bad,' chimed in Cowboy.

'How—er...' Grafton hesitated, then said, 'How do we get him out? How are we *allowed* to get him out?'

Blayde said, 'That's up to our friend, here.'

'Helicopter?' suggested Grafton.

'Yep...' Cowboy sounded doubtful, then said, 'Yep. But no tricks. Okay? Any dealin' from under the cloth an' we start slingin' slugs.'

Blayde said, 'My advice runs parallel with that, chief constable. We can't afford to take risks with innocent lives.'

'An',' added Cowboy, 'I want Pinky back here, before we move out. Okay? Just patch him up—patch him up, good—then dump him back here. Okay?'

'Mr Blayde?' murmured Grafton.

'I think you'll be able to do that, Mr Grafton,' said Blayde. 'A simple collection, followed by a simple return.'

Cowboy said, 'Okay ... that's it. We give you a call later. Just collect Pinky, for now. An' move fast, at gettin' the dollars together. We call you later ... then you can say when we expect Pinky back.'

He jerked the plugs from the sockets of the switchboard,

and hung his receiver on its hook alongside the twin rows of sockets.

Blayde returned his receiver to its rest on the reception counter.

Cowboy smiled at the chief superintendent, and said, 'Didn't I tell you, friend. You 'n me. We are gonna move this thing along neat 'n easy.'

'I think you're nervous,' said Blayde, gently.

'Uh?' Cowboy stopped smiling.

'Jumpy.'

'Why 'n hell should I be...'

'I would be,' said Blayde. 'Anybody would be. The cards. You used an analogy ... dealing from under the cloth. They won't. They don't have to. You're already playing against a stacked deck.'

'You feelin' like one?' asked Johnny, softly. Teasingly.

The young hooligan called Hoppy gave a quick scowl and growled 'Shaddap!'

'You're feelin' like one,' said Johnny, with quiet confidence. 'It's startin'.'

'You gonna shaddap?'

'Sure.' Johnny mocked the younger man with his eyes. 'I ain't got ants crawlin' around under *my* skin.'

Hoppy tried to grin, but it came out a Jack o'Lantern leer. The grin held no humour; not even the cocky, contemptuous humour it had been meant to hold.

Johnny watched, and waited.

The moment—the split-second wafer of eternity—had to be caught. Then held. Then used.

Johnny watched, waited and prayed to his twisted gods that he'd recognise that moment, when it came.

1.40 p.m....

'There is,' said Grafton, 'a chopper on the way. A helicopter, from the Upstone Army Camp ... complete with rescue team.'

'I'll get some volunteers,' said Harris, grimly.

Grafton's voice was weary with disgust, as he added, 'To fetch out a dead man. As I understand Blayde, this Pinky character is already dead...'

'Guns and tear gas. All we needed was a foothold, on the other side of that bloody river.'

'... but his pal—this Cowboy comedian—doesn't know he's dead...'

'And now, we've got it.'

'There's also Wolff,' mused Grafton. 'According to what you say—according to Lennox—Wolff really does need urgent treatment...'

'We'll hit 'em fast, and we'll hit 'em hard.'

'... so-o, we'll have to do a switch. Somehow. We'll have to...'

'They'll be dizzy.'

'... substitute Wolff for Pinky...'

'They think they're tough.'

'... and have an ambulance standing by.'

'They don't know what the bloody word *means*.'

'What?' Grafton blinked the curtains of his musings aside, looked puzzled, and said, 'What word? I'm sorry, Harris, I wasn't listening.'

'With the helicopter,' said Harris impatiently. 'We'll cram it with men and equipment. We'll blast the bastards from their rat hole, and show 'em exactly what the word "tough" really means. We'll go through 'em like a dose of...'

'Christ in all His glory!' exploded Grafton. 'When will you get it through that thick skull of yours? We're not playing War Games, Harris. We're not fighting them. We're *paying* them. Anything! Everything! To a certain extent we have to bluff them ... into believing it's one wounded man we're bringing out when, in fact, it's another. But, for the last time of telling, chief superintendent, we are not—repeat *NOT*—starting a shooting war. Not with innocent people in the cross-fire.'

'I only hope,' sneered Harris, harshly, 'that they, too, hold the same humanitarian beliefs.'

Grafton used a flat, non-argumentative tone.

He said, 'Get on to Lennox. Tell him what's happening. Tell him to do what he can to help the switch. To have Wolff ready for lifting off.'

The spots diminished in size, but increased in ferocity. It was a gradual change; quality to quantity. The florins changed to shilling pieces, and the shilling pieces to sixpences ... but there was a hell of a lot of sixpences.

The police marksman grumbled, 'Send it down, David. We haven't enough bloody trouble.'

And, the harder it rained, the darker it became, until the light was little more than dusk. And, beyond the hills, the lightning shimmered and, like a muffled drum-roll, the thunder crept closer.

The lights of the 'Conference Room' had been switched on. Eight double-bulbed wall-lights—three along each side of the room and two, right and left, by the entrance—and twin, ten-bulbed chandeliers spaced, equi-distanced along the ceiling. In the 'Conference Room' there was plenty of light; garish and brilliant light which, because of the profusion of bulbs, cast no shadows.

Except for the stage. The stage lights had not been switched on and, by comparison with the rest of the room, the stage looked dowdy.

The mobsters leaned against the walls, at strategic points, and watched the hostages. The hostages stood, and sat, in groups and, apart from quick flurries of small-talk were silent; they'd said it all a score of times, and in a score of different ways ... all they could do, now, was wait.

Cowboy strolled slowly, up and down the length of the room, picking his nose and scratching his backside, and showing certain other external signs of nervousness.

Blayde and Pearson watched.

They had a job to do—a con to pull—and if anybody overplayed his part, or mis-cued an entrance or an exit, or even if the Gods rolled slightly loaded dice, the job was a non-starter and the con wouldn't work.

Blayde played the first move.

As Cowboy passed, he murmured, 'Why the nerves?'

'Uh?' Cowboy stopped his pacing, and scowled.

'You're bothered,' said Blayde. 'What about?'

'I ain't bothered,' growled Cowboy.

'You *look* bothered.'

'Lookee, I ain't gonna...'

'We could call it off,' chimed in Pearson.

'Uh?'

'The helicopter lift. We could ring up. Call it off. They could radio the helicopter to return to base. It's as easy as that.'

'He's your friend ... not ours,' added Blayde.

'Mind you...' Pearson stopped, after having put a world of meaning into the first two words of an unspoken sentence.

'Wassat?' Cowboy's eyes narrowed, suspiciously.

'Nothing,' sighed Pearson. 'It's not important, anyway.'

'C'mon. Lemme have it, doc. You know somethin' ... uh?'

'No.' Pearson shook his head.

'That things ain't on the level. That it?'

'How the hell...' began Blayde.

'Button it, cop!' snapped Cowboy. Then, in a friendlier tone, said, 'Doc, you done me one favour. Okay? Now, do me another. What's eatin' your guts?'

'In your position.' Pearson moved his hands, expressively. 'I'd feel like you feel.'

'I ain't catchin' it yet, doc.'

'Apprehensive.'

'I still ain't...'

Blayde turned upon Pearson and rasped, 'Why the devil should he feel apprehensive? He was there. He heard every word spoken. Why the hell should he...'

'You gonna button it, cop? Or maybe I should zip up that kisser o' yourn.'

Pearson said. 'I'm sorry,' and the apology seemed to be given to be shared, equally, between Blayde and Cowboy.

'Naw. C'mon,' urged Cowboy. 'I wanna hear.'

Pearson spoke slowly. Apparently unwillingly. Carefully, and with hesitation ... as if not wishing to offend Blayde.

He said, 'The American police. You—er—you know them better than I do, of course. The chief superintendent, here ... I suppose *he* knows them better than I do. But—y'know—with *them*. That helicopter. It would be filled with policemen. Guns. Everything. I suppose—in America ... I wouldn't trust the *American* police. That's what I mean ... I suppose. Only, I ... Truly, I don't think you need worry too much about that sort of thing in the U.K. It's only my opinion, of course. But, when they give their word, they *keep* it.'

'I know bulls, doc,' said Cowboy, bitterly. 'There ain't a goddam cop I'd trust with a lead nickle.'

'That's a damn fool thing to say.' Blayde aimed his mock-anger at Pearson. 'How the blazes can we expect any degree of mutual trust if you...'

'I said he could *trust* the British police, chief superintendent.

It was the one thing I emphasised. That he *could*...'

'Implications, man. Innuendoes. Good God, man, don't you *want* this thing resolved without bloodshed?'

'Of all the barmy accusations to make...'

'Hold it!'

'... I'm a doctor. I'm under a particularly binding oath to save life...'

'*Hold it!*'

'... not destroy it.'

'Then, why the devil don't you think, before you...'

'HOLD IT!' exploded Cowboy. 'Goddam it, how 'n hell can a guy think, with all this hasslin' goin' on?'

'There's nothing to think about,' growled Blayde.

Cowboy said, 'Maybe you don't figure so, friend. Me? I ain't so sure. Doc ... he's a guy I can trust a little. You ... I ain't too sure about you. An', sure as hell, I dunno the bastards across that damn river.'

'Cancel the helicopter,' said Blayde.

'That I ain't gonna do. Pinky's gonna be patched, before we move outa here.'

'All right. Surround the damn helicopter with gunmen, as it lands. Have enough gun-muzzles pointing at it, then you can be sure there's no...'

'Wouldn't you like that, copper?' sneered Cowboy. 'Ain't that somethin' you'd really like to see?'

Blayde shrugged his shoulders.

Behind his back, Pearson crossed his fingers, and prayed.

'Naw,' said Cowboy, slowly, 'we ain't gonna work it that way. We need the guns here, see? Here ... where all these folks are. Where we can blast a few guts, supposin' anybody starts assin' around with a straight deal.' He paused, pondered for a few moments then, in an even slower drawl, continued, 'Ain't nobody gonna get away with *nothin'* in this poker game. I got all the aces here, in this room. Okay? So, that's where they stay. An' all the guns. *Here*. Everybody keeps their paws on the cloth, nobody gets hurt ... that ain't hard to understand. But any fink wants a shoot-out ... that, too, is okay by me.'

'You—er—you have a plan?' asked Pearson, gently.

'Yep.'

'Without putting these people in any greater danger than they are already, I hope. I can't influence you, of course but, as a doctor, I must...'

'You don't wanna see anybody hurt ... right?'

'That goes without saying,' agreed Pearson.

Cowboy said, 'Okay. *You* meet the chopper.'

'Me?' Pearson pretended surprise.

'Yep.'

'Look—I'll be there, of course. To help them with Pinky. But...'

'Solo,' grunted Cowboy.

'I'm sorry. I don't understand.'

'Lookee.' Having made the decision, Cowboy scowled his impatience at the apparent inability of Pearson to follow the workings of his mind. 'I'm gonna send Bobs. Round the other guys up. All the guns here, in this room ... okay? The chopper comes, an' you meet it. Just you. I figure five minutes. That's all. Five minutes from touch-down, an' Pinky should be aboard and the chopper outa here. An' you back to say things are okay. Five minutes, from touch-down to your bein' back here.'

'That's not a long time,' said Pearson.

'That's all you're gonna get, doc.' Cowboy's voice was harsh with worry. 'After that, we start throwin' 'em outa the windows ... dead!'

'That is one hell of a...' began Blayde.

'Button it, cop!' Cowboy's right hand moved. Its speed was the end-product of years of practice. Near-unbelievable in its smooth precision. The thumb held back the hammer, the forefinger had already taken the full trigger-pull, the muzzle was less than twelve inches from Blayde's tunic buttons, and the Beechwood Brook divisional chief superintendent was within the lift of a thumb from sudden, and violent curtains. Cowboy's voice was tight with suppressed emotion, when he said, 'I ain't talkin' to you, cop. Like you say ... you are the message-boy. Nothin'! You ain't important no more. One more peep outa you, an' you ain't even *that*.'

'Easy,' murmured Pearson. 'Put the gun away. You're the boss. Nobody's disputing your authority.'

'Okay.' Cowboy took a deep breath. He eased the hammer down, then relaxed the pressure on the trigger. He re-holstered the Colt, then said, 'Okay ... just so's nobody ain't forgettin' that.'

Pearson said, 'I'll go. Alone. I'll see it's done ... exactly as you want it done. I'll have Pinky aboard, and be back here within five minutes of the helicopter landing. Right?'

'Yep.'

'Just trust me ... trust *somebody*.'

'Yep,' breathed Cowboy, again. He gave a quick, nervous grin, then said, 'Okay, doc. That's the way we do it. I'll get Bobs to round up all the other guys. Get all the guns in ... to show we ain't pullin' no goddam bluff.'

He walked away from Pearson and Blayde; towards the far end of the room, and to where Bobs was standing with one of the other gunmen.

The impression was that Blayde breathed, for the first time in five long minutes.

'We pulled it,' he whispered, without moving his lips.

'We pulled it,' sighed Pearson, softly. 'You bloody nigh got yourself killed ... but we pulled it.'

'*Shaddap!*' The young hooligan called Hoppy made it a soft, near-hysterical scream. 'This place—this ass-hole ... they ain't got nuttin' here.'

'Oh, yeah ... that they have,' murmured Johnny.

'You're lyin' man. You're lyin'.'

'I know where there's a spike,' said Johnny, softly. Teasingly.

'You're lyin'.'

'I know where there's some Miss Emma.'

'Naw. You know nuttin'. *Nuttin'*.'

In *Yew Tree Bower*, Lennox lowered the receiver and placed it carefully on to its rest. He chewed his lower lip, meditatively for a moment, then ambled across the sun lounge annex, to where Carter sat at one end of a sofa and nursed his swelling jaw.

'That,' said Lennox, 'was Harris.'

'Who's Harris, when he's at home?' asked Carter, sourly.

'You'll know him,' promised Lennox. 'Believe me, you'll know Harris better than you've ever known anybody else in your life ... eventually.'

'Another copper?' sneered Carter.

'A copper ... but, personally, I wouldn't describe him as *another* copper. He's a one-off job. They made him, then they broke the mould.'

Carter kept the sneer on his face, rubbed his jaw, gently, but said nothing.

'There is,' said Lennox, 'a chopper coming in. A helicopter, from one of the Army bases. It's taking Wolff out.'

'You're too late. I've already...'

'It's taking Wolff out,' repeated Lennox. 'It may also be taking out the body of the man you murdered.'

'Pinky? Why the devil should it...'

'And it's most certainly taking *you* out.'

'Oh!'

'Then, you'll meet Harris,' said Lennox, grimly.

'Just as long as...'

'Just as long as *nothing*!' Lennox bent forward, curled a fist around the lapel of Carter's jacket, hauled Carter upright and growled, 'Laddie, I will personally screw you solid if you even *try* to balls this thing up. Understand? There's a man in there—a man called Wolff—who's in urgent need of an operating table. This is his chance. His *only* chance. Deny him that chance at your peril, sonny. I swear ... you'll wish you'd never been born.'

'Look, I have certain rights...'

'Sod your "rights"!' snarled Lennox. 'Just between you and me, Carter, I don't give a monkey's toss about your so-called "rights". Just between you and me, you haven't even the right to be alive ... not in my book. We are doing this thing. Both of us. We're getting Wolff out of here. Carefully. Quietly. And without any argument ... *at all*! We're taking him to where you left Pinky. To where the chopper's going to touch down. Then—if you behave yourself—you are going to meet Harris. But, if you misbehave yourself—on my mother's grave—the only person you'll meet is your Maker.'

1.55 p.m....

Hoppy paced the 'Snuggery' like a newly caged wild thing. He rubbed the open palms of his hands against his upper arms. He scratched at his middle. The control of his muscles—the control of his nerve-ends—was going ... fast. He sweated; dope-craved agitation pushing moisture from every pore of his body. His face shone, as if from the surface of a shallow pond; white and with uncontrollable twitches ... tiny, insignificant twitches which would grow into a writhing, muscle-jerking urgency.

'Where?' He stopped his pacing, faced the bound Johnny, and rasped, 'Okay, bastard. You know where. Okay. C'mon ... *where*?'

'Friend.' Johnny smiled a reasonable smile. 'Needles and shit don't come cheap. They ain't hand-outs. They ain't *ever* hand-outs. You know that.'

'I need it,' muttered Hoppy, desperately.

'Sure ... and I need a deal.'

Hoppy exploded, 'Up your ass!' He resumed his pacing. His rubbing and scratching. His sweating. He mumbled, 'It'll pass. It ain't forever. Okay, it's rough—it's maybe gonna get a little rougher ... but it'll pass.'

'Yeah ... up *your* ass,' mocked Johnny.

'Naw. Naw. Come soon, I'm gonna get a shoot-up ... then I'm okay.'

'You're kiddin' yourself, kid.'

'Naw. I can ride this goddam thing. I can ride it. Who the hell needs H? Who the hell needs shit?'

'We-ell ... *I* sure don't,' agreed Johnny.

Hoppy muttered incomprehensibles to himself, and forced himself to stop his pacing ... but he couldn't stop the sweat, and he couldn't stop the itch.

'I should worry,' said Johnny, gently. 'I ain't sufferin'.'

'Shaddap.'

'Okay—I cork it—why not? ... I don't have to ride the goddam switchback all night.'

'Hey, man. What's with the...'

'Till thirty after nine, tomorrow.'

'Up you, bastard. Y'know ... up *you*.'

'With luck,' added Johnny. 'With one helluva lot o' luck ... which you ain't got.'

'No deal,' whispered Hoppy.

'Okay ... I ain't pushing. Chances are you are gonna puke your guts out for some few hours after thirty after nine, kid. Just don't forget that.'

'No deal.'

'Chances are it's gonna be all day. Maybe all another night. Lemme tell you, kid ... my guess is you are gonna be clawin' the skin from that good-lookin' face of yours, before you ever reach a spike and some shit again. That is *my* guess.'

'No deal.' Hoppy breathed the words, with his eyes closed and his clenched fists held tight against his outer thighs. He whispered, 'You bastard, Johnny. Man, are you a bastard? But—y'know—go screw yourself, bastard ... *no deal!*'

'Okay, kid.' Johnny smiled. 'I ain't goin' no place. I'll be around. Just lemme know when.'

The helicopter came in on a pendulum approach, across the rain-slashed surface of the Hewfraw. The down-thrust patterned the water, then the grass, and skewed the driving rain to one side until touch-down and until the blades slowed to a steady ticking-over.

The four Medical Corps men were out, almost before the skids settled on the turf.

Wolff was ready for them; Lennox had lashed the wounded mobster to a makeshift stretcher—a camp bed, he'd rooted from a boxroom of *Yew Tree Bower*—and the medics worked swiftly and smoothly for a quick loading and take-off.

Lennox screwed his eyes against the downpour and gathering darkness, and watched—hoped that Wolff was still alive ... hoped that, if still alive, that his life could be saved. Hoped, doubted but, at least, knew he'd done his best.

Pearson waved the army medics towards the body of Pinky and, farther along the turf, the body of Wilson whom they'd dragged from the river.

The medics doubled along the grass to the corpses.

'Five minutes.' Pearson held his watch close to his face, and shouted above the steady noise of the storm and the helicopter. 'I'll have to do the four-minute mile back to the boozer.'

'You'll make it.' Lennox returned the shouted conversation. He turned to Carter, and yelled, 'Get in there, lad. You aren't a stretcher case.'

Carter nodded, then sprinted, head and shoulders lowered, for the helicopter entrance.

'You too?' shouted Pearson.

'No ... here.' Lennox fished around in his soaked windcheater. 'Shove them in your little black bag. There's a couple in the 'Conference Room'—a couple of middle-aged blokes ... one of 'em was with the wounded girl. They know I'm a copper. Give 'em one each, if you can. Keep one for yourself.'

The 'them' of the shouted remark were firearms. One revolver, one Luger and one Dardick.

'Where the hell ...'

'I've been collecting 'em.' The fat man grinned into the rising storm. 'Pass 'em round ... like hymn books.'

'Not for me.' Pearson opened the first-aid case and stacked the handguns in, with the bottles and bandages. 'One for Blayde—the chief superintendent they've sent across ... I'm a doctor, not a mortician.'

'Please yourself.'

The Medical Corps men had loaded Pinky and Wilson and were standing, hesitantly, at the door of the helicopter.

Pearson held out his hand, and shouted, 'Wish me luck, Lenny. Then, in you get.'

'I'm staying.'

'That's stupid. You can't...'

'You'd be surprised, mate.'

'Look—I think you're unwise. The less...'

'How many minutes?' bawled the fat man, with a smile.

'Damn!' Pearson waved the helicopter to take off. He turned to Lennox and shouted, 'I've said it too many times to be wrong. You're a bloody fool.'

'Get your sprinting-blocks out, doc.'

Cowboy stood to one side of a window of the 'Conference Room'. The lights had been switched off, and every hostage was standing, facing the walls. The gunmen formed a line, down the centre of the room; guns out and ready for the word from the man at the window.

Cowboy glanced at his wrist-watch, then peeped out from alongside the window.

'There goes the whirly-bird,' he murmured. Then he chuckled, and added, 'Relax, folks. Here comes the doc ... an' ain't he travellin' some.'

An inaudible sigh of relief seemed to emcompass the whole room; captives and captors, alike. It was as if a high-pitched, nerve-tearing note had suddenly stopped ... and the balm of silence was already healing bruised nerve-tissue.

Somebody said, 'If we get out of this, that man gets an O.B.E. I'll see to it, personally.'

'With my recommendation,' added Blayde.

Less than thirty seconds later Pearson staggered into the 'Conference Room'. His hollow-cheeked face was dripping with a combination of rain and sweat. His clothes were soaked. He flopped into a chair, gulped air into his lungs and looked, questioningly, at Cowboy.

Cowboy said, 'Yep. You made it, doc. Ain't that somethin'?'

Unable to speak—still gasping for breath—Pearson nodded his relief.

'Pinky?' asked Cowboy.

'He ... He ...' Pearson took a lungful of air, then said, 'He's on his way. They'll—they'll let us know. When he's ready.'

'Ain't that somethin'?' repeated Cowboy, delightedly. He looked around, and said, 'Okay, folks. Ain't nobody gonna get hurt after all. I figure we could do a little light again ... till after this little ol' storm blows over.'

The Home Office man was doing five things, all at the same time. He was eating a boiled ham sandwich. He was sipping hot, sweet tea. He was smoking a cigarette. He was listening to Grafton's report of the latest developments. He was asking questions. Five things—and he was doing them all at once, and he was doing them all very elegantly ... and (as far as Grafton was concerned) he wasn't concentrating enough on any one of the five.

He was typical 'Home Office'. Typical bureaucracy. Typical chair-borne expertise.

Grafton was saying, '... and there's a certain—a certain ...' Grafton searched his mind for the appropriate phrase.

'Armed truce?' suggested the Home Office man, helpfully.

'No, sir,' said Grafton, heavily. 'The expression "armed truce" suggests a readiness to go to war. To fight it out. There are innocent lives at stake ... we can't afford to fight. Not an "armed truce".'

'Impasse?' suggested the Home Office man.

'Ye-es.' Grafton nodded, slowly. 'It could be called an impasse. A temporary impasse. This man who's apparently taken over—this Cowboy character—he has a certain ...' Once more, Grafton hesitated, then continued, 'Not honour. I wouldn't go so far as to call it "honour". But something akin. Something very much like. Some form of perverted pride ... that's the nearest I can get.'

'Upon what basis?' asked the Home Office man.

'Sir?'

'The assessment—that he's a man with pride—upon what basis do you make that assessment?'

Grafton said, 'He's—er—he's obviously capable of friendship.'
'D'you think so?'
'This man they call Pinky...'
'What ridiculous names these people give themselves.'
Grafton said, 'Every advantage we've gained, so far—what little advantage we *have* gained—is based upon the lie that this man Pinky is still alive.'
'Whereas, he's dead.'
'The—er—message... from Chief Superintendent Blayde. As I understood that message, the Pinky character was already dead.'
'I see.' The Home Office man popped what was left of a sandwich into his mouth, chewed, then said, 'Quite.'
'That's the—er...' Grafton moved his shoulders, resignedly. 'That's the picture, as of this moment, sir.'
'Quite,' repeated the Home Office man. He swallowed the chewed sandwich, drew on the cigarette, glanced distastefully around the Committee Room, and said, 'Not the ideal "Battle Headquarters", I suppose... but the best we can do, at a pinch, I suppose.'
'Sir.' Grafton kept his voice low, and controlled. 'This is not a "battle". Any more than it's an "armed truce". There are...'
'I know. Innocent lives, at risk. I'm appreciative of all that, chief constable. There's no need to labour the point.'
Grafton said, 'It's a point I try never to lose sight of.'
'Quite.' The Home Office man sipped tea, then bit into another sandwich. He said, 'This Ricardo Wolff, chap. Where is he?'
'On his way back to Wakefield. I notified them, and they radioed the vehicle in which...'
'Rather premature... don't you think?'
'His father isn't in control any more.'
'Quite. Nevertheless...'
'He's no longer a bargaining counter.'
'But useful... surely?'
Grafton said, 'I'm sorry. I can't think how.'
'Of their kind,' said the Home Office man, airily. 'Y'know... of their kind. You've already emphasised the weakness of this man, Cowboy. That he's capable of friendship.'
'But not universal, brotherly love,' said Grafton, impatiently.
'Nevertheless...'
'He shot Wolff's father. I see no reason at all to suppose that

he has friendship—*any* sort of friendship—for the son of a man he's tried to kill ... probably *has* killed.'

'Nevertheless...' The Home Office man moved his lips in a tight, condescending smile, and repeated, 'Nevertheless...'

He seemed to like the word. It was a word he used often. A damn sight too often, in the opinion of Grafton. It was a meaningless word; it made everybody else seem moronically-minded and yet, at the same time, added nothing in the shape of concrete proposals. It was a verbal exit ... a door through which governmental goons might make a quick dash for safety, supposing things went seriously wrong.

The Home Office man, swallowed, sipped tea, inhaled cigarette smoke, then remarked, 'Actually, they should be getting along quite well with each other, by this time.'

'Eh?' Grafton looked flummoxed.

'The bods in Robs Cully, and the gangster chaps.'

'Good God!' breathed Grafton.

The Home Office man said, 'There's a pattern in these things, chief constable. I know. I've had experience. Every time ... the same pattern. Captors and captives. They're *all* captives, really ... if you care to view it logically. Aren't they?'

'No,' said Grafton, grimly. 'One lot have guns. That makes one hell of a difference.'

2.30 p.m....

The storm reached its zenith. The met. boys, having consulted their records, named it as one of the three most violent storms of the century. The locals of Raine and district (and without having to consult any records) unanimously agreed that it was the most concentrated accumulation of thunder, lightning and water *they'd* ever experienced. It was a dinger. It was a right 'un. It was a one-hundred-per-cent crop-flattener ... and something they'd have to pay for, come harvest time.

Some of the more timid types in the 'Conference Room' looked scared and white-faced; they winced and ducked their heads a fraction at each nearby lightning flash and the ear-splitting crack which preluded a particularly loud thunder-roll. One woman squatted in a corner, her face buried deep in her hands; trembling and refusing either comfort or reassurance. Half a dozen of the hoodlums looked slightly worried—a worry which was spawned by superstitious fear of the unknown—and kept glancing out of the windows at a nature whose fury made their own ruthlessness dwindle into a needle-point of petulance.

It was some storm, and more than one person in that 'Conference Room' mentally calculated that, had the bridge not have been blown, the Hewfraw would, by this time, have done what the explosives had already done, and Robs Cully would still have been a river-bound island.

'Where?' The point of the knife eased itself into the flesh at the side of Johnny's neck. The blood trickled down and soaked into the collar of his shirt. Hoppy held his victim's head to one side, with the heel of his left hand against the side of the jaw, and croaked, 'You tell me where, fink. You tell me! Else you get skewered ... right through the gizzard.'

'That is gonna help, kid.' The only distortion in Johnny's voice was that brought upon by the stretched neck muscles. There was no fear. No pleading. Only mockery ... a mockery which rode, confident, upon certainty. He said, 'Where's the percentage, kid? The rules make me worm-meat ... that, already. You stiffen me. Okay ... I am gonna stiffen, anyway. The only way I am *not* gonna stiffen is if you want horse hard enough. Shove the sticker home, kid. An', up your ass, for all I care ... but you ain't gonna get no spike and no shit from a dead man.'

'I ain't bluffin',' whispered Hoppy.

'You are sure as hell *sweatin'*,' countered Johnny. 'Junkie-stink. An' I'm gettin' it right in the face.'

The lightning shimmered beyond the uncurtained window, the thunder cracked, like an overhead howitzer, then rolled as if ten-thousand empty barrels were trundling down the roof, the knife moved another whisker's breadth and the trickle of blood increased slightly.

'Up to the hilt,' scorned Johnny. 'Right through the swallow-box, kid. *You* ain't bluffin'. Punk—you think *I'm* bluffin'? ... lemme tell you, kid, you are gonna sweat blue piss within the next hour, wishin' you had been.'

Hoppy trembled, and the knife carried the tremble to the nerve ends in Johnny's throat. There was agony but, with a man like Johnny—a man who, all his life, had dealt in terror and the infliction of pain—agony was everyday coinage. It was what he handled. He gave it, he took it ... and, going or coming, it was part of his existence.

There was agony, and there was a cold-blooded weighing of odds.

He was due to die. That was the foundation upon which all logic had to be built. His own death. He could die, denying a junkie craved-for dope. He could die, via a slug through the head, and while still lashed to this damn chair. Or he could die trying to regain a throne which that fink Cowboy had pulled from under his ass ... maybe.

The 'maybe' was his only hope of salvation because, whilever there was a 'maybe' there was also a 'maybe not'.

In its own perverted way, it was a kind of courage. Given the right circumstances—within some other context—it would have won him acclaim. He was fighting ... but not even for his life. The only thing he was fighting for was a possibility. A 'maybe' ... or, to be precise, a 'maybe not'.

And why not?

'I crease you man ... uh?' breathed Hoppy. 'Y'know that? You ain't countin' on any screwin' around. Any screwin' around, and I handle this sticker. But good! You ain't gonna be the first to feel this goddam blade ... y'know that?'

'Do you hear me arguin', kid?' said Johnny ... and knew his 'maybe' had been won.

'You get the H and the needle. Okay ... we see what cooks from there.' Hoppy jerked the blade free from Johnny's neck. 'But, no deal. You get that man? This ain't no patsy game we're playin'. This don't mean we have any sorta deal.'

'We see what cooks from there,' agreed Johnny, flatly.

'Yeah ... we see from there,' whispered Hoppy.

He slashed with the knife; swift, up-and-down strokes. He could handle steel; the cutting edge went *exactly* where he intended it to go; the razor-edged blade parted the wire, without either scratching the chair's woodwork or snagging against Johnny's clothing.

Johnny stood up. He stretched his cramped muscles and flexed the fingers of his hands.

'C'mon ... move, man!' Hoppy made warning patterns in the air, with the knife.

Johnny shrugged.

He said, 'Upstairs, kid ... supposin' you can still make your legs do what you ask 'em to do.'

Harris elbowed his way from the squad car to the entrance to Raine village hall; he grunted 'No comment' a couple of times to the barrage of questions aimed at him by the crush of mass-media people. A uniformed constable, doing sentry duty, opened the door for him, then closed it on the still clammering news-gatherers.

He strode across the hall—past the chairs and tables, past the rain-soaked coppers and the waiting and worrying relatives and friends—and towards the door of the Committee Room.

He was intercepted by Kempton.

Kempton began, 'Excuse me, but...'

'Sorry, son. I haven't time.'

'I know them.' There was the desperation of near-crazed worry in Kempton's voice. 'Believe me ... I *know* them.'

'Eh?'

Harris stopped and eyed the younger man, suspiciously.

'You're—you're in charge here. Right?' stammered Kempton.

'One of 'em.'

'I have to see you,' pleaded Kempton. 'A minute. No more than a few words ... please!'

'It'll help?' asked Harris, doubtfully. 'Y'know ... not just a waste of time? I can sympathise, but this shoulder isn't for crying on.'

'It'll help,' insisted Kempton. 'I *know*!'

'C'mon. Let's find an empty table.'

Harris guided the younger man to a table, in one corner of the room. They sat down, and Harris waited.

'I'm—I'm a doctor,' said Kempton. 'Henry Kempton—a specialist, if you like ... I'm not a crank. Take it from me, I'm not a crank. I know what I'm talking about.'

'All right. You're not a crank,' said Harris, in a non-committal voice.

'My wife ... She's...' Kempton rubbed his mouth with the palm of one hand. It was a gesture of desperation; the act of a man on the brink of a breakdown. 'She's...'

'I know.' Gruff compassion and impatience mingled in Harris's tone. 'I saw you—heard you—talking to my missus, when you came in.'

'Oh!'

'Now—you say you know 'em. How do you know 'em? What do you know about 'em?'

'They're—they're a type,' stammered Kempton. 'They wouldn't be what they are, if they weren't. Normal men—with normal feelings—they couldn't stand the—the—the ... *dehumanising*. Normal men—when they make the mistake of thinking it's a career—get out of it. They spot the dangers. They...'

'Mobsters?' Harris interrupted.

'What?' Kempton stared, then rubbed his mouth again.

'Mobsters?' repeated Harris. 'We *are* talking about mobsters? The lunatics running riot in Robs Cully?'

'No! No!' Kempton shook his head, jerkily. 'The—the Whitehall types. There's one here ... just arrived. I spotted him...'

'From the Home Office. What about him?'

'They're the wrong sort,' said Kempton, desperately. 'The wrong *sort*!'

'Look, Kempton, you can't...'

'I can. I *can*.'

Ninety-nine times out of every hundred—nine hundred and ninety-nine times out of every thousand—Harris would have stood up, growled some disparaging remark and left the speaker to his own madness. But this was the odd time; the exception which emphasised the rule.

It was, perhaps, the absolute certainty of Kempton's tone. The anguish with which the younger man's plea for understanding and belief was made. Or it was, perhaps, Harris's own scorn for those who professed to 'know' ... but rarely knew 'how'. His inborn mistrust of the so-called 'expert' who came from nowhere, threw his inexperienced weight around and, having cocked everything to hell, returned to nowhere and left the practical men to pick up the pieces.

'All right,' said Harris, slowly. 'I'm listening. Now, take it gently—step at a time—and let's assume you know what you're talking about. Now, go ahead. Tell me.'

Kempton paused to light a cigarette. His fingers trembled and fumbled but, by the time he was inhaling tobacco smoke, he'd conquered much of his agitation.

He said, 'Look—I'm a specialist—not a psychiatrist ... not a head-shrinker. Psychosomatic illnesses. Hypochondria. That sort of thing. The brain—the mind—the link between the mind and the body ... and there is one, of course. The field encompasses social psychology. It *has* to ... people are ill, because they're subconsciously unhappy at their work. In their social environment. It's involved. The usual ... I suppose you'd call it "rubbish". But it isn't. Not all of it. A lot of it's based on hard, factual data and, if you keep your feet on the ground you can help. A doctor can help, if he understands. But he *has* to understand.'

He paused and watched Harris's face for the first sign of disbelief.

Harris said, 'Go on. I'm still listening.'

'The Civil Service,' said Kempton. 'It's a profession—a very good profession—for the right people. For the wrong people, it's hell. Literally, *hell*. They become ill—physically ill—because their personality isn't fitted for the disciplines of the Civil Service. Very often they don't realise the underlying cause ... which is where people like myself come in. But the others—the people with the required mental make-up—are happy enough. They even enjoy it. You—er—you believe me?'

'So far,' said Harris.

'You understand me?'

Harris said, 'I think I do more than understand you. I think I'm ahead of you. The men who fit—the ones who don't become ill—make the grade. They're promoted. Or, if you like, the square pegs in round holes *don't* make the grade. They're *not* promoted.'

'Thank God!' sighed Kempton.

Harris said, 'All right. I'm with you. Expand it a little.'

'He's a senior civil servant,' said Kempton. 'The man who's just arrived ... right?'

'Pretty important. Which means—by your reckoning—a round peg in a *round* hole.'

'Without imagination.' Kempton leaned forward, across the table. There was urgency—a life-or-death desire to be understood—in his voice. He said, 'Look ... Westminster and Whitehall. Generalities, you understand. It's all we've time for ... generalities. But the general picture. Westminster provides the dreams. Whitehall tries to destroy the dreams. It's checks and balances. A part of Democracy ... what makes our sort of Democracy work. The politicians have the visions, and the civil servants provide the facts ... the cold water, which they pour on those visions. A Cabinet Minister, left to run wild, would be self-destructive. A Whitehall department, without a kick up the backside from Parliament would be sterile.

'This man—this civil servant they've sent up here, to deal with this thing—he has a sterile mind, and he's expected to handle an emotional situation. And he *can't*. He can't even *understand* it.'

'That's putting it strongly.' For the first time, doubt showed itself on Harris's face. 'You don't know him ... do you?'

'No.'

'Nor do I.'

'But I know his kind.'

'Look, Kempton, you can't ...'

'Generalise?' Kempton ended the sentence, then said, 'We can't afford *not* to generalise. All right, men with hearts *are* in the Civil Service. Some hold high office. But, in the main ... Good God, man, can't you see? It's *because* a civil servant is a cold fish—*because* he can "negotiate"—that he has the advantage over a—a ...'

'Fighter?' suggested Harris.

'They don't fight,' said Kempton, heavily. 'That's what scares me. They don't fight ... they wear down. They call it patience. You and I know it as "time". And that's one thing we haven't got. Time!'

Kempton had said his piece. He smoked his cigarette, and waited for a reaction, and the fingers holding the cigarette trembled slightly.

Harris pursed his lips, raised a half-sceptical eyebrow and, for a few moments, watched the worried expression on the younger man's face.

Then, he said, 'Son, I could believe you. Maybe because I *want* to believe you ... that's what's worrying me. You've used psychological flim-flam to reinforce a personal bias.'

'I'm not biased. I'm merely ...'

'*My* bias. I don't like 'em, either.'

'And if I'm right? ... and I *am* right,' said Kempton.

'I dunno.'

'I do.' Disgust. Worry. Anger. Defeat. They were all there, in Kempton's tone. They were all there, reflected in his face. 'There'll be a killing. A mass killing. Decent people—innocent people—are going to be slaughtered, while some Home Office man buggers about "negotiating" nit-picking terms.'

2.35 p.m. ...

For the second time, within five minutes, the lights of the 'Conference Room' flickered, faded, then returned to full power.

'That grid system's taking some stick,' remarked Hill.

'They'll go,' murmured Elliott. 'And when they *do* ...'

'Nothing,' murmured Pearson. 'Please! It isn't yet time.'

'If you think I'm going to ...'

'Cool off, Bill.' Robert Hill added his argument to that of Pearson's. "If they go now, there's still light—enough daylight ... we haven't a chance.'

Elliott grunted reluctant acceptance of a valid point.

They were grouped around Elizabeth Elliott. Pearson (still wearing rain-saturated clothes) Elliott, Hill and his wife, and Flora Aimes. They were going through the motions of examining Elizabeth Elliott's shoulder.

The bandages were off, and Pearson was probing the flesh around the wound with gentle fingers.

The nearest gunman was almost four yards away.

Pearson leaned forward, peered at the torn flesh and, in a whisper as light as swansdown, breathed, 'Mrs Hill. Open your handbag ... and be ready to close it.'

Jean Hill blinked, frowned, then turned her back on the gunman and thumbed open the catch of her handbag.

Pearson lifted his first-aid case from the floor, placed it on Elizabeth Elliott's knees, opened it and took out a pad of cotton-wool ... and the Dardick.

The Dardick was in the handbag, and the handbag closed, before the cotton-wool was in position at Elizabeth Elliott's shoulder.

Within minutes, the shoulder was re-bandaged, and the arm was resting in a broad sling, formed by a triangular bandage ... and, behind the arm, and hidden by the bandage, the Luger hidden ready for use.

Elliott and Hill watched the smooth delivery and hiding of the weapons with glints in their eyes.

'Where ...' began Elliott, in a whisper.

'Quiet!'

'Lennox,' breathed Hill.

'Who the hell's...'

'Quiet!' repeated Pearson, warningly.

'He's a copper.' Hill answered Elliott's question, without moving his lips. 'The fat man.'

'Oh!'

'When *he* says.' Pearson busied himself with the knot of the sling, and breathed the words into Elizabeth Elliott's shoulder. 'Understand that. When *he* says ... not before.'

Grafton's palms were sweating. That was the degree of his concern; that he was worried stiff that this Home Office official might not agree ... might snarl everything up, and jeopardise innocent lives.

He said, 'They're professionals, sir. We have to understand that. They're *professionals*, and if we don't ...'

'Are you suggesting that we're *not*?' The Home Office man smiled, gently. 'Are you suggesting that we're amateurs, chief constable?'

Grafton said, 'They have fifty innocent people in there. Most of 'em women. They're demanding three million dollars, by ninethirty tomorrow morning...'

'Which is utterly impossible, of course.'

'I would hope it *isn't* impossible,' countered Grafton.

'Apart from it being a ridiculous sum—outrageously large— apart from that...'

'You can't balance human life against hard cash. It isn't...'

The Home Office man held up his hand, to silence Grafton's protestations, then continued, 'Apart from it being a ridiculous amount, it would set a precedent. The precedent has already *been* set, by some countries. Wrongly, in my opinion. H.M.G. can't possibly follow suit. Blackmail—and this is a form of blackmail, chief constable—is an expanding crime. H.M.G. can't become a party to it ... obviously. If it's allowed to start, it will grow bigger. Greed is the motive-power, and once a greedy man finds something upon which he can batten his greed, he can't stop. Other greedy men will repeat the formula ... if we allow a precedent to be established. There'll be no end to it. It's what I'm here to prevent, chief constable. To make quite sure a precedent is *not* established.'

The wisdom (or stupidity) of the Home Office man's opinion was there, in the 'Conference Room'. Grafton might not have believed it ... but that made it no less true. Captors and captives were, by this time, 'getting along quite well with each other'.

It is possible that the rage of the storm helped things along; that its sheer size dwarfed their own microcosm of bickering, constrained their threats and withered their fears. It is more than possible that Pearson's 'reliability' did much to help; the captives trusted him, because he was one of them, and the captors trusted him, because he had done exactly what they had required him to do.

Their common denominator, however, was boredom. Boredom and inactivity ... gradually (very gradually) it was eroding the invisible partition between the two groups.

Technically, they were opposites. Two separate and conflicting companies. Captors and captives. But they were, in effect, (and, again, as the Home Office man had pointed out) all 'captives ... at least, for the moment.'

They were also all *people*.

Which meant they all had some degree of curiosity. They were interested in each other ... as all people are. There was an odd desire to 'communicate' ... as there always is.

They were 'getting along quite well with each other', because they were people, and because they were becoming bored to hell.

They were also becoming increasingly hungry.

Blayde detached himself from a group which included Celia Kempton and Charlotte Douranby, strolled across the floor and spoke to Cowboy.

'Are *you* hungry?' he smiled.

'Yep,' admitted Cowboy.

'It's nice to know you're not unique. So is everybody else.'

Cowboy said, 'Ain't much I can rightly do about it, buddy.'

'You could feed them,' suggested Blayde.

'Uh?'

'Feed them. Tea and sandwiches.'

'Nope.' Cowboy shook his head, sadly.

'Why not?'

' 'Tain't possible.'

'Your own men must be hungry,' said Blayde.

'Yep,' agreed Cowboy.

'They, too, would like something to eat.'

'Yep.'

'So, don't be a damned fool.'

'Lookee...'

'We've co-operated,' said Blayde. 'Everything you've asked for. Nobody's tried any fast moves. What else do you want?'

'Not a thing,' admitted Cowboy. 'But I aim to ride this little ol' thing *ve-ery*...'

'Carefully?' suggested Blayde.

'Ain't that a fact.'

'Windily?'

'Uh?'

'Because you're scared?'

'Lookee...'

'Because you aren't the man you thought you were? Not big enough to handle the situation?... now it's arrived.'

'Easy, friend,' warned Cowboy. 'We ain't thrown slugs around, yet. But that don't mean...'

'Wolff would have had food organised.'

'How 'n hell do *you* know...'

'Anybody capable of organising a thing this big would have had food organised... for his own men, if not for us.'

'Wolff ain't handlin' this thing no more. I reckon...'

'You're scared,' taunted Blayde.

'Lookee...'

'That's the impression. That you're strutting around, with a gun under your armpit... scared to hell.'

'Uhu.' Cowboy shook his head. His eyes were hardening, dangerously.

'*My* impression.'

'Buddy, you ain't been more far wrong since you sat on your ol' daddy's knee.'

'An impression your own men might share.'

'Lemme tell you,' drawled Cowboy. 'While I'm ridin' herd on this thing, we ain't gonna risk no stampede... okay?'

'We aren't cows,' murmured Blayde.

'Uh?'

'Cattle.'

'Steers.' Cowboy grinned. 'You're meanin' steers, friend. Okay ... you ain't steers. So, what you're provin'?'

Blayde said, 'That we have brains. Opinions. And that we're hungry. All except those men you used to patrol outside, earlier on. They're not hungry. They'll have gorged themselves stupid

...while those in here—those doing the *real* work...'

'You're workin' for a split, buddy,' interrupted Cowboy. He smiled, knowingly. 'You're easin' a wedge into a crack that ain't there.'

'It soon will be. They're all listening. Some might already have worked it out for themselves.'

Cowboy eyed the uniformed chief superintendent. At first with suspicion, laced with anger then, gradually, the suspicion and anger melted into reluctant admiration.

His mouth twisted into a wry grin, and he drawled, 'Buddy, you're either callin' spades on an empty deck ... that, or you are one smart gringo. You could be so damn right, friend.'

'I'm right,' said Blayde.

'Okay,' invited Cowboy. 'Gimme how.'

'Tea and sandwiches. Coffee for those who don't like tea. Cigarettes. The landlady—Mrs Aimes—I'm sure she could fix things. My man—Constable Clemens—could help. That's all. I'm not suggesting a banquet.'

'Ain't nobody gonna leave this room to eat,' warned Cowboy.

'Of course not. Trays *have* been invented.'

'An' a coupla my boys walk along behind ... checkin' out any goofy play.'

'I'd have been disappointed if you hadn't suggested it.'

'Okay.' Cowboy nodded, slowly. 'We eat, friend. Fix it. Just tell the bull ... uh? An' tell him. Anythin' crazy, an' nobody ain't gonna need no tea an' sandwiches. Just tombstones.'

2.40 p.m....

Flora Aimes sliced the bread, the tongue and the ham. Police Constable 2728 Wallace Clemens busied himself with the Thermos tea-urn and the wheeled trolley upon which the snack-meal was to be taken up to the 'Conference Room'.

That this scene, enacted in the kitchen of *The Hind's Head* and, in many ways, a scaled-down version of the scene being enacted at Raine village hall, might have brought a smile to the face of a particularly sour-minded cynic was something of which Flora Aimes and P.C. Clemens were not aware.

But the cynic would not have smiled for long.

The man Bobs and the man Beaumont would have wiped the smile from the make-up of a clown.

Bobs, because of his fear of Cowboy, was hair-trigger-happy ... and looked it.

Beaumont (scared for life by the foresight of the Stirling S.M.G., minus his beloved Lugers, still carrying the remains of a headache from where Lennox had belted his skull with Dutch's revolver, and his face webbed with tiny scratches from broken glass) looked crazy ... and probably *was*.

They were both ready to kill, for the sheer kick of taking life.

Bobs carried his own gun; a Colt .45 automatic pistol. Beaumont held the Stirling S.M.G., whose foresight had carved a path across his face. Each man was on edge. Each man had a finger curled firmly around the trigger of his weapon.

Flora Aimes sliced bread, tongue and ham. P.C. Clemens messed about with the tea-urn and the wheeled trolley. Such mundane and ordinary tasks ... but, when performed within the orbit of split-second horror, elevated to the status of mild heroism.

'I would like,' said Harris, 'an undertaking, by you, that my orders will be obeyed ... and without question.'

'Sir?' The uniformed chief inspector looked startled.

'Without question,' repeated Harris, sombrely. 'Blind obedience ... from you, and from everybody else, down the line.'

'Of course, sir.' The startled expression stayed on the chief inspector's face. 'Has somebody disobeyed an order, sir? Queried an order, perhaps? If so...'

'No.' Harris chewed his lower lip, then said, 'I—er—let's say...' He paused, then murmured, 'Self-preservation.'

'I'm sorry, sir.' The startled expression changed to one of puzzlement. 'I don't understand.'

Harris seemed to mentally shake himself from a brown study.

He said, 'I want volunteers, chief inspector. Good men. Hard nuts. Good swimmers. Men who can handle firearms. Men who can use themselves.'

'I'll pick them, sir. I know the type...'

'*Volunteers*,' emphasised Harris. 'And that includes yourself.'

'You'll have them. With me. How many, sir?'

'Twenty—thirty, if you can get 'em ... including as many qualified marksmen as you can get. I want 'em down there, at the bridge. Out of sight, and waiting. Understand?'

'Understood, sir.'

'I don't know *when*. I just want them ready. No questions. No speculation. Nothing! Just down there, on the start-line. Talking to nobody.'

'Yes, sir.'

'Any questions?' asked Harris.

The chief inspector said, 'You've given an order, sir. No questions.'

Harris nodded, approvingly.

The chief inspector hurried off and, more slowly, Harris made his way towards the telephone kiosk.

At the last bedroom Johnny knew the hoped-for 'maybe' had become a burst bubble. The dream had disappeared, with reality when the first-aid box wasn't on the last bedside table.

It had been worth a try. The dice had been there, in his hands, and he'd have been a mug not to have rolled them ... but, okay, the throw had been jinxed from the first wrist-shake.

He faced the youngster called Hoppy, twisted his mouth into a lopsided grin, and said, 'Kid ... they call it kismet.'

'Uh?'

The point of the knife made tiny threatening circles. Hoppy's thumb was along the flat of the blade, in the classic fighting hold.

Johnny said, 'Okay. You ain't gonna believe this, but...'

It was as good a place as any, in the sentence, to make his play, so he made it. He grabbed at the knife arm, half-caught it, lost it as Hoppy danced back, sideways, then forward, then clamped his teeth together as the blade ripped home.

To die tough. To take it—however it came—without a squeal. To deny the ice-man the final pleasure of hearing what he wanted to hear.

The prayer of every yob and every mobster ever spawned.

And Johnny blew it!

The blade went hilt-deep, between the ribs, then twisted, and the agony was something Johnny would never have believed. It opened his mouth, threw back his head and sent a high shriek of anguish echoing through *The Hind's Head*.

Cowboy said, 'Freeze!' and, before the scream died into silence—before the single-word warning had time to register—the revolver was clear of its shoulder-holster and in his fist. His eyes darted, like a snake's tongue, he was perfectly balanced on the balls of his feet and his legs were bent slightly, at the knees. The stance was perfect. The stance of the champ, watching for the opening through which he could deliver the kayo punch ... the stance of the old-time gunfighter at the show-down. He said, 'Watch 'em. Anybody try anythin' ... start shootin'.'

The 'all-pals-together' routine scurried into the nearest mouse hole. A curtain dropped, and they were captors and captives; terrorists and hostages; killers and victims.

In the kitchen, Flora Aimes and P.C. Clemens did not need to be told. They 'froze' into an immediate and motionless tableau. Flora Aimes stopped the saw of the bread-knife part-way through a slice. Clemens kept his hands resting, wide-fingered, on top of the tea-urn.

They watched the gunmen, and the gunmen watched back. The Colt automatic and the S.M.G. seemed to strain, like thoroughbreds at the starting-gates, anxious for that infinitesimal pressure which would flash the cordite and throw faster-than-sound sudden death from their muzzles.

'Check it,' grunted Beaumont.

'Yeah.'

Bobs gave cold-eyed warning to the landlord's lady and the copper, then turned and hurried from the kitchen.

2.45 p.m. ...

Harris silenced the pips by thumbing coins into the kiosk's slot.

He said, 'Harris. I'm calling from a kiosk.'

'I gathered. What's up? More Post Office problems?' Lennox's voice was as round and plummy as ever—as round and bouncy as the man himself ... but with the hint of tension.

'No.' Harris answered Lennox's question.

'Trouble?' asked Lennox, gently.

'You could say that. How did you guess?'

'From the tone,' said Lennox. 'Not quite the—er—Harris bark ... if you see what I mean.'

'I'm undecided,' said Harris, heavily.

'That makes a change.'

'Lenny, I'm worried. I've just been convinced—part-convinced—that we're doing this thing all wrong. That we're in for a bombing, if we don't change tactics.'

There was a pause, and Harris waited. The rain hit the tiny panes of the kiosk, exploded into miniature waves and allowed gravity to take over. Up above the clouds were charcoal grey, and thick enough to give the impression they went on forever. The lightning still sizzled from cloud to cloud, and cloud to earth. The thunder rolled, like surf, and hammered on the eardrums.

Lennox said, 'All right, Bob. Let's get together. Let's work something out.'

Grafton thought he could see the weakness in the Home Office man's premise. The H.O. man thought he was dealing in politics; that this hold-up situation was on a par with splinter-group political fanatics and their terrorist activities.

And the H.O. man was *wrong*.

Politicians compromise ... even fanatical politicians. Compromise—the very art of politics—was the name of their particular game.

But not crooks. Not genuine, one-hundred-per-cent killers. These bastards meant it. Every word. Every punctuation mark.

They wanted three million, plus safe conduct, and they wouldn't settle for one dollar less.

Grafton tried to explain all this to the Home Office man.

The Home Office man listened, looked bored, then said, 'You're being very pessimistic, chief constable. In these sort of confrontations nobody means what they say ... not *really*. They ask too much. We offer too little. Then, we build a bridge, and meet somewhere, midway.'

'What do we build the bridge of?' asked Grafton, sourly. 'Bodies?'

'They won't kill,' said the Home Office man, and he sounded supremely confident. 'The threat. That's all they have. If they carry out the threat, they have nothing left with which to bargain.'

At that particular moment, Cowboy killed ... twice.

He edged along the corridor, leading from the 'Conference Room' to the hotel bedrooms. He moved carefully and with his back to the wall; the heavy revolver was in his hand and ready to blast at the first thing that moved.

The first thing that moved was Johnny.

Johnny was dying, anyway. He stumbled from the open bedroom door, caught at the upright of the jamb, twisted as his knees bent ... then hastened into the hereafter as two .45 slugs smashed into his chest.

The punch of the bullets lifted him and sent him back, through the bedroom door, and into the shins of the following Hoppy. Hoppy stumbled forward, into the corridor ... and he, too, died.

The first shot took Hoppy in the groin, and the second in the face. Then he, too, was merely bleeding meat staining the carpet of the corridor.

As the confined roar of the two double-explosions faded, a voice said, 'Jeeze!' then, as Cowboy whirled, Bobs gabbled, 'No! It's *me*. I ain't gonna...'

'Fink.' Cowboy's voice was piano-wire taught. 'Why 'n hell ain't folk where they shoulda been?'

'I—we—we heard the yell. Y'know ... We...'

Cowboy jerked his head.

'Move on out,' he snapped. 'Make the passage at a run. We take the damn bedroom from both sides.'

'You—you think, maybe...'

'I aim to be sure. That greenhorn, hopped-up kid. Who knows? I ain't forgettin'. We are light one fat-gutted bastard who maybe ain't so goddam dumb as he acts. I ain't takin' chances.'

The 'fat-gutted bastard' was itemising the pro's and con's to Detective Chief Superintendent Harris.

He was saying, '... in the pub. They're still there. All of 'em, as far as I can make out. This weather helps ... that way, too. Nobody's likely to feel like taking a stroll till this lot eases.'

Harris said, 'Give me an hour. I'll have 'em across, then set up the other thing.'

'Darkness,' suggested Lennox.

'Midnight,' said Harris. 'A nice, easy-to-remember time.'

'Aye. It'll give the Home Office wallah enough time to come up with *his* brainwave.'

'I wish to God...' Harris's worry choked he sentence short.

'Bob.' Lennox's voice was strangely sombre. 'This thing has to be finished. Our way, if nobody can come up with an alternative. People are going to get hurt. Let most of 'em be coppers ... it's what they're paid for.'

Harris said, 'I'll see you in...'

'No!'

215

'What?'

Lennox said, 'Somebody has to be there. On the outside. Making damn sure the switch is thrown ... dead on midnight. Not the Home Office type. You!'

'Look, I'm not going to...'

'*You!*' repeated Lennox, urgently. 'We'll have enough weight at this side. We could be isolated, between now and midnight. If we aren't sure—one-hundred-per-cent sure—it's a half-cock thing. You stay outside, or I want no part of it.'

'For Christ's sake! What sort of a ...'

'*Or I want no part of it*,' repeated Lennox, harshly. 'That's the price. Don't worry ... you'll suck the hammer, if it doesn't work. Don't kid yourself, Bob. I'm not handing you a cushy number. I could be a hero. You could, very easily, be drummed out of the Brownies.'

'Think I don't bloody-well know?' growled Harris.

'So, you stay that side.'

Harris's sigh of capitulation could be heard over the wire.

He said, 'So be it. I'll stay this side of the river.'

'The Home Secretary,' said Grafton, tentatively.

'He wishes to be kept informed,' said the Home Office man.

'He could override your decision ... that's what I mean.'

The Home Office man said, 'I haven't yet *reached* a decision.'

'About the three million dollars they're ...'

'That's out of the question,' interrupted the H.O. man, impatiently. 'When I make my report I'll advise him on that.'

'That it's out of the question?'

'That H.M.G. can't be blackmailed. That *that's* out of the question. It's something he won't need telling.'

Grafton's expression reflected his thoughts. Sadness and defeat. The sour experience of personal humiliation.

'It's what some people claim,' he said, bitterly. 'I've spent my life denying it ... but I've been wrong. And they're right. The law values property more than it values life. When the crunch arrives—when the choice is really *there*—wealth has the edge.'

'Bolshevik claptrap,' snapped the H.O. man.

'That's what I thought ... until now.'

'Chief constable—I keep telling you—H.M.G. can't be...'

'The hell with H.M.G.!' exploded Grafton. 'H.M.G. spends its whole damned life being blackmailed. By the oil sheiks. By trade union trouble-makers. By capitalist money-grubbers. Don't tell me H.M.G.—*any* H.M.G.—can't be blackmailed. It's blackmailed, from the time the ballot-boxes are emptied till the next General Election. It's *all* blasted "blackmail" ... but the right name's never used. This time, a spade's being called a spade. That's what you don't like. That dirty language is being used to name a dirty game. But there are people there. People! Not just names. Not just statistics. Not just potential voters. *People!* And you've just put a price on those people. Less than sixty thousand dollars a head. Dollars ... not even pounds. Less than it takes to plan a new pedestrian precinct. Plan it ... not even build the damn thing. And fifty people—the lives of fifty people—don't add up to a bundle of plan drawings in some architect's office.'

'You're getting over-emotional about this thing, Grafton,' said the H.O. man in a dead voice.

'I find it an emotive situation.'

'*Too* emotional.'

'I doubt if that's possible.'

'Too emotional to remain objective,' amplified the H.O. man.

Grafton knew what was coming. He waited for it. Silent ... and, to his secret shame, a little glad.

The H.O. man said, 'I have the authority, chief constable. I was specifically given that authority, before I left ... in case it was needed. I think it *is* needed. I'm suspending you from duty, until further notice. I'll take over, here.'

Grafton sucked in air, and let out a long, heavy sigh. It was like the release of an almost unbearable tension.

He said, 'I'll stay.'

'I've already explained. I have the ...'

'As a civilian,' added Grafton.

'If you must,' said the H.O. man, sourly.

Grafton said, 'To watch. To make sure that the right man gets blamed for any mistakes.'

4 p.m. ...

The killing of Johnny and Hoppy had been an episode. It had been a warning; that the cooling lava upon which the hostages stood was paper-thin and that, beneath that slender crust, the volcano still bubbled and could erupt, and slaughter if anybody was foolish enough to tread too heavily.

That the gangsters had, so far, only killed each other, merely underlined the obvious. That they put no value on human life. That, if killing became necessary—if corpses were needed as bargaining counters—they would, undoubtedly kill.

The hostages (those who had had doubts; those who had clung to a tattered belief in the ultimate decency of *all* men) settled down and accepted one more sad fact of life.

The checks and balances thing gradually slipped into gear, again.

Captives and captors. They ate together. They stood around, in the 'Conference Room', together. Gradually—very gradually—they talked together.

Normality—the normality of a prolonged hi-jack situation—returned.

Blayde had refused the gun.

The opportunity had presented itself, at a few minutes past three o'clock. Blayde had been relaxing; half-leaning half-sitting at one end of the kerb of the stage; alone, and with nobody within four or five yards. He'd been smoking a cigarette, sipping the remains of a cup of tea and (no doubt) thinking secret thoughts.

Pearson had strolled across. He'd placed the first-aid case on the edge of the stage. Casually. As if to give temporary freedom to both hands, in order that he, too, might light a cigarette.

Having lighted the cigarette, he'd exhaled smoke, and murmured, 'Bored, superintendent?'

'Er...' Blayde had pushed his thoughts to the back of his mind with a quick smile, apparently noticed Pearson for the first time, and said, 'A little like chess, don't you think? Boring for the spectators ... unless, of course, they're fanatics.'

'And we're spectators?'

'Of a sort,' Blayde had agreed.

'Pawns,' Pearson had suggested.

Blayde had said, 'It must be equally boring for the pawns.'

'I suppose so.' Pearson had drawn on his cigarette and, this time, as he'd exhaled the smoke, he'd murmured, 'In the first-aid case. There's a revolver.'

Blayde had sipped tea, and said nothing. His expression had remained impassive.

Pearson had murmured, 'Move your back to the case. I'll open it. Nobody'll see you take it.'

'Thanks ... but, no.' Blayde had tilted his head to eye a far corner of the ceiling. 'I don't happen to believe in shoot-outs.'

'There has to be one.' Pearson had allowed his gaze to follow that of Blayde's. 'These people mean what they say.'

'So do I. It's why I'm here.'

'I'm sorry ... I don't follow.'

'Because I don't believe in guns.'

'Oh!'

'And don't try Clemens,' Blayde had added, softly. 'I might be tempted to tell them.'

Blayde had drained his cup, walked away from the stage and returned the empty cup to the trolley, by the door.

By four o'clock, twenty-five coppers had crossed the river, and were in Robs Cully. The uniformed chief inspector, two C.I.D. sergeants, a uniformed sergeant, fourteen uniformed constables and seven detective constables. Hand-picked hard nuts, and every one a volunteer.

They'd crossed the river at the bridge; wading, sometimes chest-deep, through the boiling Hewfraw and clinging, for their lives, to the shattered structure of the blown bridge.

They'd made it. Soaked to the skin and, some of them, with revolvers, rifles and tear-gas cartridges, in waterproof plastic bags, taped to their bodies. Without opposition ... Lennox had been right—the sheer fury of the storm had kept the opposition out of harm's way, in *The Hind's Head*.

Somebody had retrieved the bazooka, and the box of remaining anti-tank shells, from the river bank.

Lennox had been waiting for them, in *Yew Tree Bower*.

As they'd arrived, Lennox had given the same order to every man.

'Right. Keep out of sight ... well away from the pub. Hunt around. Break in, if you have to. Find towels and clean clothes. Report back here, dry and ready for action, at four o'clock.'

At twenty minutes to four, Harris had telephoned, from the farmhouse, midway between Robs Cully and Raine—the farmhouse Rufus Aimes had telephoned from, at 9.30 a.m.—and had given Lennox the final details.

The times ... and the houses.

'Then, midnight,' Lennox had verified.

'On the nose.'

'We'll be ready.'

Harris had said, 'Good luck, Lenny. Pass it to the others,' and had hung up.

The storm circled. It was like a beast, imprisoned by the surrounding hills, and it forked and hammered at its geographical confinement, as if trying to flatten the land and escape. It grew, and diminished, then grew again; each time more angry, each time more wild. It hissed its hatred in lightning, and roared its passion in thunder ... and the rain drove, in solid rods of water, until the timid crossed themselves and prayed that this was not the second deluge.

Four times, the lights of the 'Conference Room' flickered, went out, then came on again. At five minutes past three. Then, ten minutes later, at three-fifteen. At half past three. And at ten minutes to four.

At the fourth time, Bobs had remarked, 'Those cables are takin' some punch.'

'Yep.' Cowboy had frowned slight worry.

'Could be they ain't gonna take much more,' Bobs had suggested.

Cowboy had nodded, and said, 'Take the dame who runs this joint. We maybe need back-up lightin'. Fix it ... okay?'

Lennox faced his 'army'. Twenty-five assorted adult, male homo sapiens, all wearing clothes which were not their own ... and some of the clothes not fitting too well. They were gathered in the room leading from the sun lounge of *Yew Tree Bower*. They filled the room. Every chair, plus a couple of chairs brought in from the sun lounge, had its occupant; every wall had its quota of men, leaning against it and listening; three men squatted on the carpet—backs against occupied easy chairs, pulled-up knees encircled by arms—and looked up, as the fat man talked.

'... the houses. This one—*Yew Tree Bower*. *Green Gables*—that's down the road, a piece ... the home of a family called Mitford. *Woodvine Manse*—that backs on to *Green Gables*, at a bit of an angle. The owners are a family called Elliott—father-in-law, daughter-in-law ... both of them hostages in the boozer ...'

Some of the men were smoking. Mostly cigarettes, but a couple had pipes puffing away, comfortably. Lennox was smoking one of his cheroots, and waving it around as he passed on the detailed plan worked out by Harris and himself.

'... Then there's the Hills' place—*Sunny Corner*—across the road, and a bit nearer to the boozer, than *Green Gables*. The Hills—man and wife—are among the hostages. *Conte Lauba*—that's only about fifty yards from the front gate, here—owned by a couple called Douranby ... he's at work, but she's inside *The Hind's Head*...'

He talked. Easily, and without rhetoric. But, and despite his comic appearance, with authority. He was a cop, with the trained retentive memory which all successful coppers need, and he named a dozen houses, in Robs Cully, without notes. Where they were situated, in relation to *The Hind's Head* and *Yew Tree Bower*. More often than not, the owners of those houses and whether, or not, people from any particular house were being held hostage in the 'Conference Room'.

The men listened, and they, too, memorised. They, too, were cops. And they were conscious of the fact that any lapse of memory—any point missed in this briefing—could mean loss of life ... and that the life lost might well be their own!

'... ten minutes to five. After that, we can get to work. I want you working in pairs. These ...' Lennox waved a podgy hand at the assortment of tools, on the carpet of the room. 'I've raided a few garages. Adjustable spanners and hacksaws. Help yourself, before you leave. Break into the houses, if the doors are locked ... then get to work...'

With lesser men—or, to be slightly more accurate, with less complete men—there might have been a build-up of tension. An excitement which, if not controlled, would have been a liability.

With these men, there was a stoical calm. They were not merely volunteers, they were hand-picked volunteers ... and the uniformed chief inspector, who had done the picking, knew his men and the personalities of those men. They each had that which, in the vernacular of the force, was known as 'style'; the God-given gift of knowing when to be angry, when to be frightened and when to be ruthless ... with the correlative instinct of knowing when anger, fear and ruthlessness were wasted emotions.

The moment—this particular moment—was all that mattered. Future moments could be handled, when they arrived. At this particular moment they were dry, warm, comparatively comfortable and in no apparent danger.

Therefore, they were calm.

Their job was to listen ... and not to forget.

'... and twist the ends together. Open the fronts of a few fuse boxes. Then get back here ... you should all be back, within an hour. We'll do this place, last. Then, it's a matter of waiting till dark, keeping our eyes skinned, deploying ourselves with a certain amount of cunning ... and keeping our fingers crossed, at midnight. Any questions?'

Nobody asked any questions.

4.50 p.m....

In the 'Conference Room' the lights flickered, went off, came on, flickered again, went off a second time ... and stayed off.

Cowboy growled, 'Goddam it!'

In the semi-gloom from the darkened sky, the gunmen watched the hostages for the first sign of revolt. Elliott and Hill tensed their muscles, ready to snatch any splinter of advantage offered by this sudden distraction. Elizabeth Elliott moved closer to her father-in-law, and held her slinged arm an inch or two clear of her body. Jean Hill thumbed open the snap of her handbag.

At that particular moment, it could have happened. The shooting, the screaming, the concentrated carnage—the gloriously suicidal, but doomed-to-failure-before-it-started counter-offensive —could have been triggered, at that precise moment.

Blayde de-fused it.

He said, 'Nobody do anything stupid. Please! We sweat this thing out. The money gets paid. And we all live to tell our grandchildren what it's like to be held to ransom by American gangsters.'

'You got brains, pal.' Cowboy turned to Bobs and added, 'Okay ... get the back-up lightin' workin'.'

The Home Office man said, 'Damn!'

He frowned up at the dead light bulb, in the Committee Room, as if that innocent and inanimate globule of glass was personally responsible for this tiny inconvenience.

He said, 'How long, I wonder?'

'If a pylon's gone...' began Grafton.

'Secondary lighting should have been arranged,' snapped the H.O. man, petulantly.

'Something, perhaps, *you* should have thought of ... being in charge,' murmured Grafton.

The H.O. man waved a hand towards the telephone, and said, 'Get on to them. Ask them. Tell them I want the current restored, as soon as possible.'

Grafton looked as if he might refuse, then shrugged his shoulders, picked up a battered directory and looked up the number of the local Electricity Board. He dialled and, within the confines of the Committee Room, there was half a telephone conversation.

'Chief Constable Grafton, here. The electricity supply has just failed here, at Raine. When can we expect it back on again ... Oh! ... I see ... Yes—of course. You—er—have my authority. And the authority of an official from the Home Office. He's here, with me, at this moment ... Quite so ... Yes—of course—I must insist that you do your very best. It's important ... Good ... Good ... I'll rely on you then. Thank you.'

Grafton replaced the receiver.

'When?' asked the Home Office man.

'Midnight.'

'Good God! We can't...'

'It's a major repair job. I've made them promise to have it finished by midnight. Not a minute later.'

'This is very inconvenient,' grumbled the H.O. man.

Grafton said, 'I'll arrange for oil lamps and candles.'

He left the Committee Room.

5 p.m. until 10 p.m....

Gradually—almost reluctantly—the storm crept away, beyond the hills. It left the rain, as a reminder—a continuous downpour which arrived like never-ending clouds of spray—but the thunder slowly diminished, until it was little more than a series of muffled rolls on a distant timpani, with the glow from the lightning playing 'stage effect' from beyond the humps of the surrounding range.

The sky lightened a little. Slowly. Imperceptively. From charcoal grey to gunmetal. From gunmetal to dirty-white. And, for an hour before true dusk, it was lighter than it had been since noon. A harsh and brittle lightness. Neon-bright, and without shadows. A meteorological absurdity to the continuous, drenching rain.

Harris returned to Raine village hall.

He was soaked. The rain dribbled from his hat, and the shoulders and back of his mac was stained dark with rain. He walked with his hands deep in his pockets, and with his head bent. He looked as near defeat as it is possible for such a man ever to look.

He slumped into a chair at the table which he'd left; the table at which Kempton still sat.

'Have you...' began Kempton.

'Don't ask!' Harris's voice was rough with pent-up emotion. 'Don't ask questions, son. What I've done, I've done ... and I'm not looking for an excuse to pass the can.'

'I advised you,' said Kempton, gently.

'Aye.' Harris nodded, heavily. 'Remember that, if you have to bury your wife.'

There was a silence.

Around them, coppers, reporters, cameramen and general helpers moved and jostled in a hubbub of activity. Candles, storm lamps and a couple of strategically-placed Tilley lamps gave adequate lighting and, in their warmth, wet clothes steamed until the room had an atmosphere reminiscent of a laundry; a warm, damp smell which, somehow, added to the heightening realisation that, three miles away, fifty people were awaiting slaughter.

'They'll—er—they'll do *something*?' said Kempton, plaintively.

' "They"?' Harris's come-back question was bitter.

'I mean—y'know ... they won't let it *happen*?'

'Son,' said Harris, wearily, ' "they"—if, by "they" you mean the people *I* mean—don't part with three million dollars very easily.'

'It's only money.'

'Don't try to convince me, son ... try arguing with *them*.'

'Look—but, that's all it is ... money.'

'Aye.' Harris's mouth twisted. 'Now tell that to the Treasury.'

Kempton breathed, 'Oh, my God!'

'You've told me how their minds work.' Harris pulled a well-used pipe from his pocket, as he talked. He rubbed the dampness from the outside of the bowl, then charged the pipe with ready-rubbed flake from a zip-topped pouch. 'Now I'll tell you how *they* work. Bluff ... it's their way of life. The deliberately leaked rumour. The double-talk. The "yes" which, when the crunch comes, can be made to sound like "no". It's known as "diplomacy". They're great guns at it. The trouble is, they think everybody else is playing the same game ... even the bastards out there, at Robs Cully.'

Harris returned the pouch to his pocket, took out matches, and held the match, unstruck, as he continued, 'Come nine o'clock, tomorrow morning, they'll learn. That top villains don't bluff, because they can't *afford* to bluff. It's not politics, with them. It's keeping at the top of the heap. Being heavy enough to mean every damn word you say.' Harris let loose a long and heavy sigh, then said, 'They'll start killing, at nine o'clock, tomorrow morning. Not everybody ... but enough. Enough to show the clown-dogs they mean business.'

'Unless, of course, something happens before. Say—er ... midnight.'

Grafton was standing by Harris's right shoulder.

Kempton looked startled ... then oddly guilty.

Harris scraped the match, and stroked the flame across the surface of the tobacco.

'Harris?' said Grafton, gently.

'Come midnight,' growled Harris, between puffs, 'it'll be another day.'

Grafton said, 'The Home Office is in charge, now.'

'Were they ever *not*?'

'I've been ... suspended.' The last word took some saying.

'Makes a change.' Harris waved out the match. 'A little like the public hangman being sentenced to death.'

'Harris.' Grafton's voice was tight with a plea for understanding. 'Why do you hate me so much?'

'Hate you?' Harris turned in his chair, stared up into Grafton's face, and said, 'Sir, with respect ... I don't *like* you enough to hate you.'

'Trust me, Harris,' begged Grafton.

'Up a duck's arse!' growled Harris.

'When the lights went. The Home Office man asked me to check with the Electricity Board. They told me.'

Harris grunted, 'A slip on my part.'

'What's happening?'

'Nothing ... now.'

'What's going to happen?'

Harris thumbed the smouldering tobacco, in the bowl of his pipe, and said, 'People are going to get killed. What else did you expect?'

'I ...' Grafton rubbed the back of his hand across his lips. 'I won't tell anybody. I swear.'

Harris smiled across the table at Kempton.

'I swear,' repeated Grafton.

'Should you *be* here?' asked Harris, flatly. 'Y'know—having been suspended ... should you *be* here? I don't think you should. I know damn well you shouldn't be questioning a senior detective officer.'

'I want ... I want ...'

'*I* want something to eat.' Harris cut across the stumbling plea of Grafton. He pushed his chair back, stood up and spoke directly to Kempton. He said, 'Come on, young 'un. I'll introduce you to my missus. She can feed us a few sandwiches. We can be just as scared on filled bellies.'

They worked in pairs.

There was no need to break in; each house had already been visited by a duo of Wolff's men, and each house had one door which was not locked. There was no need, therefore, for noise.

Each pair concentrated upon one house. Getting there, unseen; they acted as if the place was alive with hoodlums—as if the villains were *not* holed up in *The Hind's Head* ... which was how Lennox had instructed them to act. They checked each corner, before they turned it. They moved behind hedges, and below walls. From leaving *Yew Tree Bower*, they disappeared until, two at a time, they ducked into the earmarked houses.

Then, one stood guard while the other went to work with the spanner—with the hacksaw ... and, where necessary, with his teeth.

They were conscientious.

They weren't experts, but they knew that, providing *they* didn't stop at half-measures—providing *they* didn't place too much reliance on hope and ignorance—the experts would make it work.

And it had to work, or else ...

'My wife,' said Harris.

'We've met.' Ruth Harris smiled at the worried and helpless Kempton. 'Mr Kempton ... right?'

Kempton nodded.

Harris scowled, and said, 'Ah—er ... yes.'

Ruth Harris placed cups of tea and a plate of cheese and tomato sandwiches on the trestle-table counter, in front of the two men.

She said, 'Mr Kempton's wife is in there. He's obviously very distraught.'

'Thanks.' Kempton lifted a cup and picked up one of the sandwiches from the plate. He tried a timid and weary return smile, and added, 'Your husband's a great man, Mrs Harris.'

'Really?' She looked startled.

'I think so.'

'I—er—I suppose I'm too close to ...'

'Decision-making, ma'am.' The way Kempton used the last word gave it dignity, without subservience. 'Some men have the ability. Others just do what's already *been* done. They use history as a pattern, and hope it'll repeat itself. Fortunately, it often does.'

'I'm sorry. I don't ...'

'In the last war.' Kempton warmed to his subject; he enthused, as if, by means of a self-imposed enthusiasm, he could rid himself of the nightmare churning around his brain. He said, 'Montgomery. Eisenhower. Set-piece battle men. Even Rommel ... although he had moments of intuitive inspiration. Good soldiers —good commanders—don't get me wrong ... but without the flair of, say, Wavell. Or Wingate. Or Patton. Or Lawrence, in the First World War.'

'And he's ...' Ruth Harris looked at her husband, with something akin to wonderment in her expression. 'And he has *flair*? Is that what you're saying?'

'Lawrence,' growled Harris, self-consciously, 'was a bloody poofty ... as I've read.'

Kempton said, 'The courage to know he's right. When everybody else—and the book or words—insist he's wrong.'

'Oh!'

'You have an extraordinary husband, ma'am.'

Harris raised his cup, grinned his embarrassment at his wife, and said, 'You might remember that ... next time I forget to clean the bath, after I've used it.'

Grafton was *not* an extraordinary man.

As late afternoon ticked its way into evening—as dull daylight brightened a little, then settled into the thickening gloom of dusk—Grafton became aware of his true size. He became, in effect, a man and a microbe ... the one examining the other. And what he saw, under the glass, was something of which he was not proud.

He had had respect. But (come to that) every chief constable who'd ever drawn breath could make the same claim. Respect—it came with the rank ... it was stitched to the epaulets, along with the crossed tipstaves and the laurel wreaths. Respect, because of what he was, but not because of *himself*.

The truth—the truth which Grafton worried out of himself, like a terrier dragging a rat from its hiding place—was that pips, crowns and stripes did not, of themselves command respect ... not *real* respect. Obedience, perhaps—and not always that—but never respect. That an idiot remained an idiot, irregardless of the baubles hanging from his jacket. That, in the eyes of complete men, trinkets did not add stature to other men ... that they sometimes merely added ridicule.

And now, he'd been temporarily stripped of his trinkets!

The truth, when it eventually came, was hurtful. It burned, and it was shaming. But the burn was deep, and it cauterised; it destroyed the rotten tissue, and there was (he hoped) healthy flesh underneath.

He left Raine village hall.

He pushed his way through the throng of media-men; not answering their questions, not even hearing them ... hardly aware of their clamouring presence.

He walked—not consciously, but unerringly—towards Robs Cully. Towards where the road ended, at the broken bridge. He walked in the downpour, and the rain soaked his clothes until its cold dampness touched his flesh and made goose-pimples on his skin.

A small man—a man who, until that moment, had been a self-important man—coming to terms with himself ... and, in the process, exchanging self-importance for self-disgust.

'Don't these people *know*?'

Clemens asked the question of Blayde. It was a question shot with amazement. A puzzle, to which Clemens could find no possible answer.

They were apart from the rest, in the 'Conference Room'. The mobsters were lounging by the door, and along the walls. Some of them were even parts of tiny knots of chattering people—captives and captors, together—behaving like oddly assorted guests at some macabre cocktail party. A kinky cocktail party, where the lighting was provided by oil lamps and Calor gas mantles.

'Don't they *know*?' repeated Clemens.

'They choose to ignore,' said Blayde, gently.

'I'm sorry, sir. But, how the hell *can* they? At half past nine, tomorrow morning, they'll...'

'It doesn't exist,' insisted Blayde.

Clemens said, 'It doesn't make sense. They're mad. They're...'

'Or sane,' interrupted Blayde, softly. Cynically. 'They could be right, constable. Now—this moment in time—is the only moment worth worrying about. The rest—past and future—either isn't, or hasn't. These people have been indoctrinated. Ignore it, and it'll go away... money will buy it off. You pay people to do your worrying for you. Lawyers. Accountants. Business managers. Even coppers. You sign a cheque, and the experts build a wall around you. A wall against worry.'

'But, sir, they must realise...'

'They don't *wish* to "realise". Therefore, they don't.' Blayde moved his lips into a slow, sardonic smile. 'It's a state of mind, constable. It has certain advantages.'

'If so, I don't see them.'

Blayde said, 'The end... it's twelve hours away. So, why worry? Twelve hours from now, you're going to be killed... if you think about it. You. Me. Any of us. But that's twelve hours away. Who knows? You could die, anyway... before the twelve hours are up. A coronary. A stroke. Anything! It *could* happen. The odds are it won't... but it's a possibility. So, why worry? Enjoy the moment, constable. Do what they're doing—enjoy the moment ... it could be the last moment of your life.'

'That, sir,' said Clemens, 'is a lunatic philosophy.'

Blayde said, 'It's the only philosophy they have left. Mad, or sane, it's *their* philosophy... one they've lived by, for years. Some of 'em, all their lives. It works... with them, it works. Don't destroy it, Clemens. If you destroy it...' Blayde didn't end the sentence. He shook his head, sadly.

'You destroy them.' Clemens ended the sentence for him.

The Home Office man was telephoning. He was 'reporting' to his immediate superior ... a bowler-hatted, pin-striped-panted individual whose position on the Whitehall ladder of hierarchy was three rungs lower than the Home Secretary.

In fairness to the Home Office man, it must be emphasised that he truly believed every word he spoke. His was a cold-blooded, objective analysis of the situation, complete with an equally cold-blooded and objective series of suggestions via which that situation might be resolved.

The Home Office man was saying, '... we can, of course, ignore such outrageous demands. They're in an impossible position. If they do anything silly they'll only make matters worse for themselves. We can safely assume that even *they* can see that.'

'There's no chance of them making a break for it?'

'Not a chance, sir,' said the Home Office man. 'They're completely isolated. The river is, virtually, uncrossable ... especially after this rain. We can simply sit back, and starve them out.'

'That will take time, of course.'

'Yes, sir. Not too long, though. Estimates put the number at about two dozen. A few days, and they'll be feeling the pinch.'

The man at Whitehall said, 'Those people—the house-owners of Robs Cully—they'll have deep-freezers ... don't forget that. There may well be food enough to withstand a long siege.'

'Possibly,' allowed the Home Office man, reluctantly.

'And, of course, if the Press decide to make a major issue out of this thing. Some back-bencher is bound to take it up ... try to make a name for himself. I don't want the Home Secretary embarrassed.'

'That's understood, sir.'

'I think,' said the man at Whitehall, meditatively, 'you'd better give this whole thing as low a profile as possible ... provisionally.'

'Of course, sir.'

'Twice daily press releases, I think.'

'No more than twice daily,' agreed the Home Office man.

'Starting ... when would you suggest?'

The Home Office man didn't hesitate. He said, 'Tomorrow morning. At their own ridiculous deadline. Emphasising that it *is* their deadline, and that we've called their bluff.'

'Quite. As I recall, it's been done before.'

'Some of the foreign hi-jack incidents.'

'Very effective.'

'The only way to handle these things,' said the Home Office man.

'Quite. I'll leave it to you, then.'

'Yes, sir.'

'Just don't let the yobs get away with it ... what?'

'I won't let them get away with anything, sir.'

Charlotte Douranby had given it much thought. The pain from her bruised temple had eased, the initial terror had quietened to a cold, hard appraisal of the facts and she had reached a decision.

These animals were capable of *anything*. They would kill, at the blink of an eyelid. There wasn't one good reason why they shouldn't ... and there was three-million-dollars-worth of good reasons why they *should*.

Charlotte knew the value of cash; not its true value, but the value which she, and her kind automatically placed into the Number One slot. Cash was there to spend. Not to earn, and certainly not to save. Cash was a loot-lined eiderdown, under which she could snuggle against periodic blasts of minor inconvenience. It was something all 'nice people' had; something bank managers manipulated; something tax men tried to steal.

She remembered...

The boring, never-ending squabbles with the aforementioned bank managers and tax men. And all for a measly few hundred quid. The threatening letters. The paltry-mindedness. The prolonged bickerings by these money-grubbing little men ... and for a sum hardly capable of buying her a new evening gown.

My God!

Three million (even dollars ... however much that represented, in civilised money) would have them throwing fits. They'd be talking about 'collateral' till next Christmas. They'd *never* agree.

Therefore...

She had a body, and she wanted to live. Roj—even supposing Roj ever found out—would understand. He'd want her to live ... of course he would! She was young—they were both young— and it wasn't yet time to book a plot in the nearest necropolis.

Therefore...

Why she chose Beaumont nobody will ever know. It may have

been because, having had his beloved Lugers removed from his person by a particularly crafty detective superintendent, he was the only mobster there without a firearm. He'd tossed the Stirling back on to the stage, when he'd returned from the kitchen and, thereafter, had remained apart from his brethren; scowling, in one corner of the 'Conference Room' and nursing the ignominy and the hurt from his smashed face. Her choice may even have been guided by that very injury; the near-horrific tear of facial flesh and muscle which slashed, diagonally, across an otherwise moderately handsome set of features. Or her choice may have had a deeper significance—a more Freudian basis ... for indeed (and apart from the injury) Beaumont's looks were not a hundred miles apart from those of Tony Mitford. There was a distinct resemblance. And (possibly) that resemblance rubbed away at a memory and transformed that memory into a subconscious wish.

She chose Beaumont.

She walked up to him, and hesitated. Then, when he looked up, she said, 'I'd like a bath.'

'You'd ...' Beaumont frowned, and the frown stretched the muscles of his face and hurt his injury, so he cleared the frown, and said, 'You crazy, lady?'

'I'm grubby,' she said, in a perfectly controlled voice. 'Your friends arrived before I'd had time for my morning shower. I'm in need of a bath.'

'Look—we ain't got time to ...'

'I don't expect to be allowed to go alone.'

'Aah!' His eyes sought her face for confirmation of the innuendo he thought he detected in her words.

She said, 'People are going to the loo, all the time. With an escort. We could pretend ... that that's where *we're* going.'

'Yeah.' He still watched her face, as he nodded.

'Just the two of us,' she said.

He nodded a couple more times, said, 'Okay ... I'll fix it,' then strolled across the room towards Cowboy.

Grafton stood to one side, and unnoticed. He stood in the saturated verge grass, within the shadow of a massive, two-hundred-year-old oak; cold, but without feeling the cold, soaked to the skin, but without being aware of the wetness, alone, but without being conscious of his loneliness.

He was sad. He was sadder than he'd ever thought it possible to be; sad at his own weakness—at his own ineptitude—at the priggishness which he'd once mistakenly called 'pride'. There was self-searching within his mind ... but no self-pity. Disgust was there. Boiling anger, directed against himself and the past years of self-delusion which he had enjoyed.

But, most of all, there was sadness.

He watched the men, ahead of him, at the road block by the broken bridge ... and he was silently heartbroken. They were coppers—C.I.D. and uniformed, motor patrol and scene-of-crime specialists—all, and every, type and rank, from inspector down ... but every one a copper.

Law-enforcement men, and he was their chief.

And (with this soul-tearing blaze of hindsight) he knew they despised him. The discipline of the force demanded that they accept his orders ... even though they spoke his name with a curl of the lips.

And, because of this—because of *him*—because he wasn't a big enough man to handle this catastrophic situation—half a hundred people, beyond that broken edge of the bridge were going to be slaughtered.

He breathed, 'For God's sake, Harris. Whatever it is ... *Whatever* it is ...'

It was a soft-spoken prayer, but a prayer without an ending.

Grafton's own sadness provided the only appropriate ending to his prayer.

Beaumont carried a four-battery torch and guided Charlotte Douranby along the darkened corridor. At the far end of the corridor the last of the daylight grey-tinted the panes of a bow-topped window.

Her voice was steady, and controlled, when she said, 'We'll have to look. I don't know where the bathroom is.'

'Bathrooms come later, lady.' He tightened his fingers on her elbow. 'First thing we're needin' is a bedroom.'

He felt her quick tremble, grinned ... then stopped grinning as the pain hit his face. He flashed the beam of the torch along the carpet of the corridor and, for the first time, she saw the rag-doll shapes of Johnny and Hoppy. She'd led a sheltered life—they were the first corpses she'd ever seen—and the jointless, blood-soaked abomination of human life brought a quick intake of breath which might have preluded a scream.

Beaumont increased his grip on her elbow.

He said, 'They ain't gonna hurt you none. It's a bedroom... it'll be jake for what we need.'

He turned her, and she stepped over the bodies without looking at them. He gave her a tiny push into the centre of the bedroom, moved the stiffening limbs clear, with his foot, then closed the door.

'We—we...' She stood there, moistened her lips and watched him with widening eyes.

'First, we screw, lady.' He walked past her and placed the torch on the bedside table. 'Why the hell else are we here?'

'I—I...' The words stopped, before they were clear of her throat.

'Yeah?' he mocked.

'I—I don't want to die,' she whispered. 'That's what I...'

He waited, mocking her with his prolonged silence.

'You're—you're going to kill us... aren't you?'

'A sweet bimbo like you, kid?'

'You are... aren't you?'

'I ain't top cat in this alley, lady. Cowboy makes the play. I just go along.'

'Help me,' she pleaded, in a little-girl voice. 'If you do, I'll—I'll...'

'Yeah?'

'W-whatever you want. Whatever it is you want.' She was panting as the enormity of her own stupidity hit her.

'You ain't,' said Beaumont, gently, 'gonna try any tease-mamma tricks with me, lady. Not unless you got pebbles up there, in your skull. You asked me, did I wanna lay you... an', okay I wanna lay you.'

'I—I *didn't*. I said I wanted a...'

He hit her in the mouth, and she fell back, on to the bed.

In the gloom of the bedroom, he stood and stared down at her.

He said, 'I like to see my way, lady. Move the glim a little... please.'

She reached out a hand, and turned the torch until its beam fell, diagonally, across her body. She was weeping, silently... but was unaware of her tears.

'Okay. That's nice.' His voice was hard, and without emotion. 'Now lemme see the goods. I don't do deals with coy broads.'

She unbuttoned the coat, unbelted the dressing-gown and wriggled her arms free of the sleeves, without getting up from the bed. And, all the time she watched his face; watched his eyes search out every secret place of her body.

'You'll—you'll help me,' she sobbed.

'Yeah ... sure.' He was unbelting and unzipping his trousers, as he spoke. 'On your back, kid. I ain't for the kinky ways ... you wanna be glad.'

She dropped back, on to the bed, drew up her legs and waited, with closed eyes.

Dear Roj—darling Roj—please understand ... *please understand!*

As he mounted her she made a final plea.

'Don't let them kill me. Please! ... don't let them kill me.'

'They ain't gonna kill you, kid. Believe me. They ... ain't ... gonna ... kill ... you.' It was pure lust. Savage and fast. Hard and deep. As he ejaculated, his fingers found her throat, and tightened. He growled, '*They* ain't gonna kill you, kid. Ain't nobody else gonna kill you. Just me.'

She was purple-faced, big-tongued and quite dead before he drew himself from her.

10 p.m. ...

Lennox eyed the men, and said, 'Right. Everybody happy?'

A couple of the men murmured, 'Yes, sir,' most of them contented themselves with a grunted, 'Aye,' and some merely nodded.

'Those with firearms,' said Lennox, 'safety-catches on, until the last moment ... then *off*. No wild west antics. As little shooting as possible ... but, if you *have* to shoot, be damn sure who you're shooting at, and shoot to kill. Understood?'

There was another muttered round of syntony.

'Those with staffs and handcuffs,' continued Lennox. 'Get into that room ... fast! You're the lads who can make it, or break it. Give 'em a second wind, and these comedians will try a shoot-out. I want 'em disarmed and in bracelets, while they're still groggy.'

'If there is a shoot-out?' asked the chief inspector. 'We don't want one—I realise that ... but if there *is* one? What then?'

Lennox rubbed his bald head, and looked worried.

He said, 'Don't even think about it, old son. If there's a shoot-out, it means we've come unstuck. It means they've a few more hostages.'

'We *surrender*? Without a scrap?' The questioner was a burly front-row-forward type. Eager for the fray, and obviously outraged at the thought of capitulation while still perpendicular.

Lennox treated him to a lopsided grin, and said, 'Old lad ... there's a lot of women in there. Middle-aged women. Some of 'em elderly women. These bloody apes won't hesitate. They'll use 'em as a shield ... and we're *not* going to shoot our way through *that* shield.'

The front-row-forward type looked disappointed ... but convinced.

'Speed,' murmured the chief inspector.

'Everything hinges on it,' said Lennox.

'The—er—the bazooka?' The tentative query was voiced by a raw-boned Scot. He had blazing red hair, and those magnificent forget-me-not-blue eyes which are so often a complement to a scarlet thatch. His voice was soft, with an Argyllshire lilt. He said, 'Ye're asking a lot, sir. I'm no' a bad shot wi' the things ... but ye're asking a lot.'

'The gable-end. The top cornice.' Lennox's tone was demanding; it held no qualification through which an excuse might wriggle. 'You've used 'em before, son. You'll have your mate with you, to help you steady the thing. Take the top corner off ... to about twenty bricks down. Not the whole bloody wall, laddie. Just chip the corner off ... gravity should be on our side, from then on.'

'I'll do ma best,' said the Scot.

'You'll take the top corner off ... to twenty bricks down,' growled Lennox.

The Scot hesitated, then said, 'Yes, sir. Ta twenty bricks down.'

Lennox looked at his miniature 'army'; twenty-five ordinary blokes, squatting around in the lamp-lit glow of that lounge of *Yew Tree Bower*. Twenty-five men. Some good. Some (he had no doubt) stamped by the community as 'wrong 'uns'; bastards who—fortunately for that critical community—had elected to channel their bastardy along law-enforcement lines. Some with slabs of muscle, others of the whale-bone-and-wire build. Each a personality—each a copper, in the true sense of that word.

Lennox (a man not given to too much emotion) knew that this

moment was one of the highlights of his life. Win, or lose—victory, or defeat—this moment of sheer, choking pride could never be snatched away from him.

He cleared his throat, then said, 'All right ... to re-cap. We go into the boozer. Three of us, at first. Back door—through the kitchen—up the stairs, and into my bedroom. With luck, there shouldn't be lights ... and we use pencil torches, as little as possible. Fingers crossed that there's no opposition ... that they're all in the 'Conference Room'. If there *is* opposition, we deal with it. Fast and quiet ... then pray.

'One man stays in the kitchen. One man stays under the stairs. I go up to the bedroom ... to the corridor. We're lucky, about the bedroom. There's a double-corner between it, and the 'Conference Room'. Unless they have guards, all we have to do is use our nuts and walk on tiptoe.

'Five minutes later, one more man comes in. As far as the kitchen. The man in the kitchen relieves the man under the stairs. The man under the stairs joins me, in the bedroom. Same relay-race, every five minutes, until you're all in the bedroom ... except for the bazooka boys.

'One at a time. Never more than one at a time. And if anybody gets nabbed, he keeps his mouth shut. And the rest of you play it by ear. But, as many as possible in that bedroom ... without the yobs *knowing* we're in the bedroom.

'Once we're in the bedroom, no noise. No talking. We leave the start-line ten seconds to midnight ... it's going to be as tight as *that*! Into the 'Conference Room', just as the balloon goes up. Straight down the middle. All women are on our side. All men with guns are on *their* side. That's the only guide-line I can give.' He paused, then ended, 'Some of you might get hurt. Badly hurt. If you do, it's your own fault ... you've either made too much noise, or you haven't been fast enough. Speed and silence. Enough of each, and it should be as easy as pissing through a porthole.'

The vulgarism—although it was a gross exaggeration—eased the tension, and made this last briefing sound a little less like karma-kharzi farewell dinner.

The men stood up, stretched and gathered their respective weapons from one corner of the room.

The red-headed Scot hefted the bazooka, looked at his pal, and murmured, 'Ta twenty bricks down. Ye're sure he wouldn' like us ta gi' him a quick shave wi' the bliddy thing?'

11.05 p.m. ...

Celia Kempton said, 'Where's Charlotte?'

'What?' Blayde blinked aside his thoughts and, momentarily, stopped the merry-go-round of answerless questions with which he was plaguing himself. He smiled, and said, 'I'm sorry. I was miles away.'

'Charlotte,' repeated Celia Kempton. 'Charlotte Douranby. I haven't seen her for a while.'

'She went out.' Jean Hill answered the implied question. 'With one of the roughnecks. That was ... oh, it must have been an hour ago.'

'Where on earth is she?' Concern etched lines across Celia Kempton's face.

'That one.' Jean Hill moved her head in a single nod, indicating the lounging, solitary Beaumont. 'That's the one who went out with her.'

'Well ... where is she?' Celia Kempton searched the groups of hostages, with her eyes. 'He's back. But where's Charlotte?'

Blayde said, 'Stay here. I'll ask.'

He walked to Beaumont and, as the gangster eyed him, quizzically, Blayde said, 'About an hour back. You played escort to a young lady—the one with the bruised temple ... where is she?'

'Does it interest you, pig?' countered Beaumont, contemptuously.

'I wouldn't be asking, otherwise.'

Beaumont said, 'She asked to take a walk ... okay?'

'To the toilet?' pressed Blayde.

'Could be,' said Beaumont, in a bored voice.

'I want an answer. Did she ask to use the toilet?'

'Hey, pig. What's it to you, eh? I mean—y'know ... what the hell is it to you?'

Blayde said, 'Her friends are worried.'

'Yeah?'

'So am I.' Blayde strung barbed-wire around the three words. 'I wouldn't trust bastards like you with a dead tom cat.'

Beaumont's eyes narrowed, above the open wound which made his face mis-shapen and repulsive. He chose his words carefully —deliberately—and delivered them with mocking arrogance.

He said, 'Okay, pig. You wanna know. She was hot-assed. She

asked that I should screw her ... see? She was feelin' like a little excitement, so she asked me. Bein' a nice guy, I obliged. We took a walk, and I laid her. But good! An' she ain't gonna be laid no more. No more, pig. Get me? No more ... not unless some fink likes screwin' dead meat.'

In a soft, flat voice, Blayde said, 'You raped her? Then killed her?'

'Yeah ... you could say that.' The boredom returned to Beaumont's voice.

Blayde clenched his fists, then took a long, deep breath. It was an effort ... but he held on to himself.

'You feelin' like being some sorta hero?' asked Beaumont, gently.

Blayde swallowed, then whispered, 'Not at the moment.'

'Ain't that somethin'?'

'But later,' promised Blayde. 'Later ... be assured.'

'You figure?'

'What's your name, animal?' asked Blayde, gently.

'It ain't important.'

'Oh, yes.' Blayde nodded, solemnly.

'Ask around,' suggested Beaumont. 'Some fink might say.'

'Your name?' insisted Blayde, quietly.

'Then what?'

'I wish to know your name.'

'It ain't gonna do you no good, pig.'

'Your name?'

'Okay.' Beaumont shrugged. 'Beaumont. That's my name ... Hugh Beaumont. So, what?'

Blayde said, 'If we get out of here alive—you and I—I'll stand you in a dock, for what you've done, here ... in my division. I'll hit you with every charge I can dig out of the book, Beaumont. I'll make it my personal task to throw you behind bars, until the day they bury you.'

'Is that a fact?' sneered Beaumont.

'Yes.' Blayde nodded, slowly. 'That is a fact.'

11.30 p.m. ...

In the darkness, the man edged along the wall. He ducked through the partly-open door and into the kitchen.

The slim beam of a pencil-torch flicked on and off.

The second man whispered, 'Okay?'
'Okay,' breathed the first man.
'I'm on my way.'
'Good luck, mate.'

The second man moved silently from the kitchen. He used a split-second flash of the pencil-torch to check the position of the tables, then eased his way, carefully, through the dining-room. In the hall, he ducked under the slope of the broad and banistered stairs.

He whispered, 'On your way, boy.'

The third man touched the second man's arm, in greeting and goodbye, then left the shelter and took the stairs, two at a time. Silently, and in a semi-crouch. He hesitated, for a moment, at the top of the stairs, where the faint backwash of lighting from the 'Conference Room' spilled from around a corner to his right. Then he made two quick strides and rounded a corner to the corridor, to his left.

The door opened fully, from a few inches, as he reached it. He stepped into the darkened bedroom, and Lennox closed the door, again.

A second pencil-torch flashed on and off, long enough for him to see the other occupants of the bedroom, and the corner of the bed reserved as his sitting place.

In the darkness, Lennox whispered, 'Fine. Fine. Keep praying, lads. But quietly.'

The Calor gas mantles were eye-searing and, by contrast, the yellow-flamed oil lamps were almost insignificant. The few candles added nothing, and were already beginning to end their life, one at a time, in a spluttering pool of melted wax. The 'Conference Room' was a place of black shadows, saffron-coloured pools and brilliance. The people (hostages and guards, alike) kept their eyes averted from the white-hot mantles—stood with their backs to the brilliance—and created the elongated shadows. There was, therefore, light ... and *not* light. Contrasts, to which the eyes had become accustomed. Gloom, to which the pupils of those eyes had adjusted.

Blayde was holding a low-voiced conversation with Pearson. The exchange was a tiny ripple of sound, lost and indistinguishable in the sea of mutterings which filled the room.

'The gun,' murmured Blayde. 'The revolver.'

'Yes.' Pearson looked away from the Beechwood Brook divisional officer as he spoke.

'You still have it?'

'Yes.'

'I've changed my mind,' said Blayde.

'Oh!'

'How can you get it to me?'

'Why the change?' murmured Pearson.

'Is it important?'

'No ... I suppose not.'

'Just get it to me,' insisted Blayde, softly.

Pearson muttered, 'Like last time. Walk to the stage. I'll follow, in a few minutes.'

11.35 p.m. until Midnight...

It was a nice night. The sickle-moon played host to a series of scudding clouds but, by this time, the storm was a thing of the past. Away from the industrial haze, the stars showed their true brilliance and number. The term 'midnight blue' was not an empty expression; the sky, between the stars and away from the moon, *was* blue—lighter than navy, but darker than royal ... 'midnight blue'.

On the road, breasting the hill, and looking down upon the darkened village, the car was parked, without lights. Harris and Kempton stood by the car, watched, waited and hoped.

'It'll come off?'

Kempton asked the question which, strictly speaking, was not a question. It was a plea for reassurance.

'Lennox is a good man,' growled Harris.

'Yes—I've no doubt—but...'

'How the hell do *I* know?' The savagery of Harris's interruption was proof of his own state of mind. Then he said, 'Sorry ... don't take what I say too much to heart. For what it's worth, *I* think it'll come off.'

There was a silence, during which Kempton lighted a cigarette. He fumbled a little, and the match flame trembled as he held it to the end of the cigarette.

Harris said, 'Y'know what I wish? I wish the stupid bastard who built those houses, *and* the stupid bastard who gave him planning permission were down there with the stupid bastards who bought 'em.'

'Me,' grunted Kempton, without anger.

'Eh?'

'I'm one of the stupid bastards who bought one.'

'Oh! Aye ... sorry.'

'I, too, wish I was down there.'

Harris checked the time with his wrist-watch; he held the dial close to his face in order to see the luminous figures.

'How long?' asked Kempton.

'Twenty minutes ... just over.'

Kempton said, 'The timing. It's linked in?'

'Aye. To the second. The Speaking Clock ... everybody's watch has been set.'

'Oh!' Kempton smoked his cigarette for a few moments, then said, 'Look—shouldn't we be...' He stopped.

'What?'

'Y'know. Down there? Ready to...'

'No!' Harris's voice was harsh and uncompromising. 'There's twenty-five men in there ... twenty-eight, counting Lennox, Blayde and Clemens. It's enough. It either comes off, or it doesn't come off. What we *don't* want is a war ... anything that even *looks* like a war. We have one trump card. Surprise. We play it ... and that's the end of the game.'

'Win, lose or drawn,' muttered Kempton.

'No draw,' said Harris. 'Win, or lose ... that's all.'

In an upstairs room of a house adjacent to *The Hind's Head* the Scot squinted along the sights of the bazooka for the umpteenth time.

'We're taking a lot for granted,' he complained, to himself.

'What's that?' His companion was standing on a chair, unscrewing the bulbs from a ceiling light.

'The bliddy sights,' complained the Scot. 'Ta twenty bricks down ... and I dinna know how true the bliddy sights are.'

'It knocked Clemens's van for a burton.' The man stepped down from the chair. 'It can't be too far out.'

'Aye.' The Scot nodded reluctant agreement. Once more he bent, and squinted along the sights of the bazooka. He grumbled, 'I only bliddy-well *hope* so.'

The snout, and the first twelve inches, or so, of the bazooka, was poked from an upstairs window of the room. Its weight was held by the window-ledge and a heavy, and very expensive sideboard, which had been dragged to the window. Nylon clothes line held it firm to its anchorage and, as an added counter to its recoil, cushions and pillows had been packed tight along the sides of its length.

It was aimed at the gable-end of *The Hind's Head*. Tilted slightly, to slice off the top corner of the gable ... 'to twenty bricks down'.

'It's no' a two-two rifle,' said the Scot, pessimistically. 'It's made ta hit a tank ... no' a table-tennis ball.'

'Cheer up, Jock.' The second man chuckled. 'They'll not complain if you only take nineteen layers off.'

Kempton breathed, 'Oh, Jesus!'

'What's up, now?' said Harris.

'A thought's just struck me.' Kempton waved his arms a little in his sudden agitation. 'Oxygen. The damn stuff has to be mixed with oxygen, otherwise it won't...!'

'Shut up!' The interruption was an explosive snarl. Harris was near to breaking-point. His voice was ugly with savage indecision, as he said, 'The experts, Kempton. We're in their hands. They know what they're up to. They know what we're after. Christ Almighty, when things go wrong, it happens. They know *why* it happens. Surely to God they can *make* it happen.'

The night wasn't cold, but Grafton was chilled to the bone. He hadn't moved for more than two hours. The longest and most solitary two hours of his whole life. From the shadow of the oak, he'd watched men, and vehicles, move to and from the phalanx of coppers and newsmen by the broken bridge. He'd watched, with a dead face and dead emotions.

He shivered as his soaked clothing cooled his body temperature.

Somewhere, among the racing turmoil with which his mind was filled, a thin thread of thought suggested the cynical possibility that *his* total contribution to the night's events might be a bout of pneumonia.

The thought came, and went—like a hair in a hurricane—and, either way, it didn't matter a damn.

* * *

'What's it like?' asked the Home Office man.

The uniformed sergeant said, 'It's not bad. It's not The Hilton ... but it's not bad.'

'I'll need a meal,' said the Home Office man. 'I'll need a decent meal—and a drink—before I retire.'

'I dunno about that, sir.' The sergeant looked doubtful. 'Village pubs—y'know ... they don't often go in for top-class catering.'

The Home Office man put on a bored, and long-suffering, expression, and said, 'Fix it, sergeant. Give them a ring. I'll be over, within the next half hour. I need a meal—plain, but substantial—and a drink. Then a warm bed. And I want a call at seven o'clock, in the morning.'

The H.O. man walked out of the Committee Room.

The sergeant sighed, 'You'll be lucky!' and moved towards the telephone.

'So far, we've had luck.' Lennox breathed the words in the gloom of the bedroom. His 'army' had reached its first objective ... and that, of itself, was a minor miracle. He whispered, 'Let's hope to hell we haven't used up *all* our luck.'

'We'll make it now, sir,' said a voice, from the darkness.

'I hope so. My God, I only *hope* so!' He seemed to be talking to himself, in a soft whisper. Convincing himself. Arguing himself into a continuing belief in something which, until this moment, he had not doubted. He breathed, 'Wolff wouldn't have made it as easy. He was a leader ... he'd have had pickets out. Rain, or no rain, he'd have had men outside. Watching for moves. Ready for whatever we tried to pull.'

Somebody said, 'This other bloke's a mug.'

'*He's not a mug!*' There was urgency in Lennox's whispered rejoinder. 'Don't underestimate. None of 'em are mugs ... Wolff wouldn't have brought 'em, otherwise. A bit slack. But no more than that. We've had luck ... since Wolff was shot, we've had luck. We've been riding on its back, every inch of the way, so far. For Christ's sake, don't insult it by calling these comedians mugs. Otherwise, it might turn round and bite.'

The voice muttered, 'Sorry,' from the darkness.

Lennox switched on a torch. He held his pudgy hand over the glass, and let the light filter through his fingers in a red glow. He held his wrist-watch in the glow and watched the sweep second-hand, as if hypnotised.

He said, 'Ready lads. Safety-catches to the off. Thirty seconds, before we move in on 'em. You blokes with the staffs ... get the thongs good and fast round your wrists. Twenty seconds. Now —when we move out—fast, quiet and no buggering about. Good luck, lads ... see you in church. Ten ... Nine ... Eight ... Seven ... Six ... Five ... Four ... Three ... Two ... One ... *Move!*'

WEDNESDAY, June 26th

Midnight...

Reduce time to micro-seconds. Take unimaginable speed—the speed of light, and the speed of electricity—and freeze its action. Do these impossibilities, and only then can the true size and scope of Harris's plan be appreciated.

For example...

Fifteen miles from Robs Cully a local Electricity Board expert watched the wall clock, above the dials and switches in a power station. As the minute hand touched the dead-centre of the twelve mark—as it became in perfect line with the hour hand— he operated a switch. One switch, on a long, neat manual of switches.

The needles on the dials flickered, then steadied.

He spoke to a second Electricity Board technician, who was standing by his side.

He said, 'That should make 'em cough.'

In a local Gas Board regional office a trio of men also watched a wall clock. They looked worried.

One of the trio had a telephone receiver to his ear, and was listening to the steady drone of the Speaking Clock. At the third pip of midnight he nodded his head, took the receiver from his ear and strained forward in his chair, as did his companions, as if waiting to catch the echo of a distant sound.

One of the men began, 'Damn! It hasn't...'

Then, because the office was ten miles away from Robs Cully, and because sound travels relatively slowly, they heard it.

A rumble which grew, rattled the windows, then faded.

'It *has*,' said the man, and dropped the receiver on to its rest.

One of his companions sighed, and said, 'And how the hell do we sell North Sea Gas, after *this*?'

Seconds before the Gas Board officials heard it, Harris and Kempton heard it ... and saw it. Momentarily, it terrified them. The whole of Robs Cully seemed to spew flame and debris, as if the village was one huge fire-bomb, and it seemed impossible that any living creature down there—lawless, or law-abiding—would not be instantaneously barbecued.

Kempton held his forearm to his face, and gasped, 'Oh, Jesus!'

The blast raced up the slope, hit them, plucked at their clothes and rocked the car.

Then the fury of the initial cloud of flame contracted into a dozen roaring furnaces; furnaces which gradually—but with discernible movement, even from that distance—spread and enveloped larger and larger areas.

Harris peered down into the rising and thickening smoke.

He said, 'We're in luck. The main power-line hasn't gone ... not yet. I can see lighted windows. My money says it's *The Hind's Head*.'

'God, I hope you're right,' croaked Kempton. 'I only hope you're...'

'Come on.' Harris turned to the car. 'Let's see the Fire Service sort *that* little lot out.'

In retrospect, it had been so easy. Even obvious. As Harris had so rightly pointed out ... 'they' (the experts) always knew *why* it happened, therefore they could *make* it happen.

All it had needed was care, and split-second timing. The volunteers—Lennox's army—had paired off, and visited the various houses with gas-fired central heating. They'd turned off the gas, disconnected as many joints as possible and sawn through a few pipes. Then, they'd fused positive and negative wires on the various electrical circuits, opened fuse-box covers, for good measure, turned on the gas again, and left.

Eleven very expensive dwelling houses—including *Green Gables*, including *Woodvine Manse*, including *Sunny Corner* and including *Conte Lauba*—had been turned into potential bombs. And, before they'd left, Lennox and the chief inspector, had done the same with *Yew Tree Bower*.

Twelve multi-storied bombs, with fuses primed and ready for

detonation at the throwing of a switch, fifteen miles away. Each bomb carefully chosen—strategically chosen ... not *too* near, or in direct line of blast, to *The Hind's Head*.

Harris had thought up the scheme. Harris had chosen the houses. Harris had fixed things with the local Electricity Board.

In retrospect, it had been both easy and obvious. As simple and as uncomplicated, as a wheelbarrow ... but, at some moment in time, somebody had first thought up a wheelbarrow.

Wheelbarrows work.

Harris drove down the hill, and hoped to God *his* 'wheelbarrow' had worked.

The doubtful Scot didn't have to fire the bazooka. It virtually fired itself. His finger was curled around the trigger, the weapon was loaded and ready ... and the multiple-explosion did the rest.

His finger jerked, involuntarily, and the peak of the pub's gable-end disappeared in a cloud of dust and falling brickwork.

The mobsters had held the 'Conference Room' of *The Hind's Head* for fifteen long hours. They lost it, in less than fifteen seconds ... and, to some of them, they were the most frightening fifteen seconds they ever lived through.

Three things happened, at once.

The lights came on, and they were temporarily blinded.

The whole world seemed to be blowing up around *The Hind's Head*.

The room was suddenly filled with ready-for-action coppers.

Any one of these things the mobsters might have handled. Any two of them (and because, and despite their wickedness, they were neither weak nor easily frightened men) and they would have fought back, and there would have been carnage.

But *three*!

To be blinded, to be deafened and to be overwhelmed, and all this simultaneously, meant, for most of them, a throwing down of firearms and a throwing up of hands. The set procedure was there, on the last page of The Book of Rules, and it had been enacted too many times in the Hollywood gangster-movie era ... the precise point when the shooters were tossed aside, and the bad guy yelled, 'Okay coppers. I'm comin' out.'

Not, this time, in words, of course. The vocal effort would

have been wasted in all the noise. Nevertheless, guns hit the floor of the 'Conference Room'.

For some seconds the room was a Kaleidoscopic cacophony of light and sound. The blast hit the windows along one side of the room and shards of glass flew, in all directions, at head and chest height. It sliced faces, necks and hands. A woman took a dagger-shaped splinter, just below the eye; it drove deep, severed an optic nerve and, for the rest of her life she was half-sighted, half-blind. One of the mobsters was sliced open, at the back of the neck; less than one inch to the left, and the carotid artery would have emptied his body of blood within minutes. Other hostages—other gangsters—were hit, and cut, by the flying glass ... not fatally but, in some cases, badly enough to need stitch-work when they eventually reached hospital.

The chandeliers swung and spun in the blast but, miraculously, kept every last one of their bulbs blazing.

And, with the blast and the blinding light, came Lennox's 'army'. With near-choreographic precision, straight down the centre of the room, then left and right and at the men holding guns. The gun-hand was smashed down with a single swing of a truncheon; here and there a revolver, or a rifle, was used, instead of a truncheon, and the revolver or rifle was rammed unceremoniously into the mobster's gut.

Only one of the mobsters was missed. Beaumont. He hadn't a gun ... therefore (and especially in view of his smashed face) the coppers took him to be a hostage.

He dived for the stage, fingers reaching for the Stirling S.M.G. He didn't make it. Cowboy's hands moved faster than sight could record. They were a blur. The left hand knocked the rifle away from his chest, the right hand found the grip of the Colt .45, drew the revolver from its holster, aimed and squeezed ... twice. The first slug took Beamont in the leg, just below the knee. The second missed.

Beaumont yelled, once. Then a shunt of broken bricks from the shattered gable-end came through the ceiling and clattered around his head and body.

The detective sergeant, whose rifle had been knocked aside, stared as—and with the same smooth, eye-defying speed—Cowboy reversed the revolver and held it, butt foremost, in token of surrender.

Cowboy said, 'Ain't no sense in tradin' shots with a cavalry charge, friend.'

The D.S. took the revolver, and moved the muzzle of the rifle on to Cowboy's chest once more.

Then, there was comparative silence.

It had taken less than fifteen seconds, and two shots—one of which had missed its mark ... and nobody had been killed.

Lennox waddled up to Cowboy, and said, 'You the bloke in charge?'

'Yep.'

'The bloke who shot Wolff?'

'Yep.'

'You almost made *that*, too,' said Lennox, drily.

'Uh?'

'He'll live ... with luck. And bastards like him always have luck.'

Cowboy controlled his expression, and said, 'Pinky?'

Before Lennox could answer, Blayde and Pearson made it a quintet. Blayde introduced himself, held out the revolver he'd smuggled from Pearson's first-aid case, and said, 'Take it. I might still be tempted.'

'On whom?' asked Lennox.

Blayde jerked his head at the unconscious Beaumont, under the debris of the gable and ceiling. He said, 'Murder and rape ... he boasted about it. I'd call that a confession. Wouldn't you?'

'These things,' said Lennox, sadly. 'However it happens—however careful—somebody always gets hurt.'

'Pinky?' said Cowboy.

'I didn't know.' Pearson looked shocked.

Blayde said, 'She'd have been no less dead...'

'No. But...'

'... and we had troubles enough.'

Lennox glanced out of the window, to where the tall flames, and sparks from the fired houses, reached for the night sky.

He said, 'I think we should let 'em know. We need some sort of an air-lift, out of here.'

'Pinky?' asked Cowboy, for the third time.

Pearson answered the question. His voice carried genuine sympathy.

He said, 'I'm sorry. I lied. Your man, Bobs, was right ... he was dead.'

Cowboy's face remained impassive. He lowered his head, looked at the rifle, still levelled at his chest, then said, 'I ain't ever gonna ask but one thing. Gimme the soldier-boy. An' my iron ... an' just one more squeeze.'

Blayde smiled, grimly.

Lennox said, 'Have a word with the judge, son. He might fix you both up in the same jail.'

'Yep.' Cowboy nodded. His eyes narrowed, and he said, 'Yep ... that, too, would please me good.'

They disposed of their dead.

Charlotte Douranby was given a flower-bedecked send-off, at a posh crematorium. Her parents, the Kemptons and the Hills were among the mourners. The Elliotts were asked, but the Elliotts declined ... they were at another interment.

Wilson was buried at Raine village church. His body was lowered to join that of his wrongly-beloved mother. Clemens and Rufus Aimes helped to carry the coffin. Blayde saluted the body as it descended into the clay. And Babs Pickering watered the coffin with a few tears.

The U.S. Embassy covered the expense of planting Johnny, Hoppy and Pinky. They were all three planted together, in the same hole in a public cemetery. They were sent on their way the same day (and within thirty minutes) of Charlotte Douranby's final curtain-call. There was an invited audience of two—strictly for Pinky—Bill Elliott and Elizabeth Elliott ... by special request of Cowboy, who was otherwise engaged.

As they strolled from the grave, the minor U.S. Embassy official, who had been detailed as 'obligatory mourner' asked, 'Why?'

'Friendship,' growled Elliott.

'For those three?' The U.S. Embassy official jerked his head at where the grave-diggers were already heaving earth over the coffins.

Elliott said, 'No. I'm standin'. For a man whose friendship for one of 'em is why we're here.'

'Oh ... I see.' The U.S. Embassy official nodded, sagely ... and wondered what this old donkey was on about.

For a few days the Robs Cully business was fresh enough to fill a few columns of every front page, but when (six weeks later) Roger Douranby joined his wife in their new, and heavenly

Conte Lauba, his passing wasn't mentioned in a single newspaper.

There was a public enquiry about the episode and, as a result of this enquiry, the Home Office man was congratulated upon the sagacity of masterful inactivity, Grafton was crucified as a man 'lacking the moral fibre necessary for chief constableship', Lennox was recommended for an O.B.E. (which he never received), Harris was criticised for 'placing in jeopardy the lives of a great many innocent people', Blayde was mentioned as little more than a bit-player and the North Eastern Gas Board was solemnly warned to double-check their appliances.

The Home Office man was moved up, one more rung of the Whitehall ladder.

Grafton resigned.

Lennox and Harris went out and got drunk.

Blayde put his feet up, watched *Z Cars* ... and wished to God bobbying was a little more like *that*!

And, as the Gas Board official said, in a world-weary voice, 'Damn it all—the stuff's *supposed* to burn ... and it did *that*.'

If you know the way—if you take the right road, and continue on, through Raine—you will come to the end of a secret, steep-sided, blind-ended valley; a wind-sheltered sun-trap in summer, and a cosy corner of rural England in winter. The Hewfraw tumbles down from the tops, flattens out at the valley floor, then makes a sickle-bow of racing, foam-spangled water. The points of the sickle are joined by Skew Beck—not noticeably less deep nor less fast-running than the Hewfraw itself—and the two waters combine to form a private island.

Robs Cully—at one time, just about the most loot-laden piece of land in the North of England.

Now an island of burned out buildings and weed-choked gardens.

Dead, and without human habitants ... a place of once-upon-a-time violence, and the brain-child of a man called Robert Bottom.

Also available in Magnum Books

PETER WAY

Super-Celeste

The year is 1982. Behind the cool façade of international aviation, a deadly contest is taking place. Euro-Aviat, headed by Henri Levitte, the grand old man of French aviation, is battling with the American giant, North-West Aerospace, for the big Australian order which will guarantee its future. But can the Super-Celeste, Euro-Aviat's superb new jet fighter, win the vital order? Or must both sides resort to trickery and threats in the deadly battle for survival which is the reality of modern aviation?

For Henri Levitte there are family problems too, for he has created a family which hates him. His adopted son – who was to fly the Super-Celeste – is shot dead. His daughter commits suicide. And his remaining son vows a terrible revenge...

FRANKLIN BANDY

Deceit and Deadly Lies

Kevin McInnes is the Lie King. An expert with the Psychological Stress Evaluator, he can reach into the mind to discover the truth behind the lies. Politicians, businessmen, the police, are all eager to pay the high fees his expertise demands. But one mistaken judgement leads to a man's death and McInnes begins to question his skill and motivation until he's asked to save the life of a political assassination target – identity unknown. An error now could precipitate national disaster...

PATRICK ANDERSON

The President's Mistress

Ben Norton is determined to uncover the truth about the murder of his former girlfriend, Donna Hendricks. With the aid of a brilliant, if eccentric, Washington reporter he begins to penetrate the tangle of deception surrounding the affair. But each time he gets a lead there is someone around to put him off the scent. Powerful White House officials, corrupt senators, his own one-time friends in the Washington social set, as well as the dirty tricks department, all conspire in a massive cover-up operation – with bribery, blackmail and sudden death. Why? Because Donna Hendricks was the President's mistress, and Norton's enquiries seem to be leading straight to the Oval Office itself.

The Senator

Charles Pierce epitomises the American Dream – young, handsome, rich. But when he becomes the Senator, something goes wrong, his world crumbles against the backdrop of the JF Kennedy assassination, the Vietnam war, the hippy era, and the increase in drug addiction and racial tension. His loyalties are split by his personal experiences and his role as the Senator. He has to choose between his true conscience and bettering his career.

JOHN D. MACDONALD

Soft Touch

Jerry Jamison had married a beautiful, spoiled child, and she had stayed that way. He had joined his own small business to her father's, and found frustration. After eight years the marriage had gone sour, the business become boring. Jerry was ripe for temptation.

It came from Vince, a war-time buddy. He arrived suddenly from South America, with a proposition. Millions of dollars were being smuggled out to buy arms. Vince intended to intercept the next cash delivery, and he needed a partner he could trust...

That was the first temptation, and there were more to come...

Dead Low Tide

Her name was Mary Eleanor – the boss's wife. She was one of those dark-haired Alabama girls and had on a sort of blue denim play suit. She slouched in the chair and crossed her brown legs. 'Will you find something for me?' she asked. 'Will you find out what's wrong with John?'

Andy McClintock had no wish to start spying on his employer, and said so firmly. Nevertheless he became involved, and still further involved. The clincher was the body on the sand with a harpoon barb through the throat.

PETER DICKINSON

King and Joker

If Prince Eddy hadn't died in 1892 a quite different Royal Family would now occupy Buckingham Palace: King Victor II, a qualified doctor prevented from practising by the TGWU; a lefty Prince of Wales who is also an amateur zoo-keeper; and Princess Louise who attends Holland Park Comprehensive. There is also a practical joker at the Palace, who seems harmless enough . . . until the discovery of a most bizarre and unpleasant murder there.

'Wry, witty, irresistible'
Financial Times

Walking Dead

Sent to a remote Caribbean island to experiment on rats, research scientist Dr David Foxe becomes enmeshed, ratlike, in a maze of politics, corruption and voodoo. In one of his most entertaining novels yet, Peter Dickinson weaves his usual brilliant web with skill, originality and cool intelligence.

'His most delightful imaginative exercise yet'
The Observer

Other top thrillers available in Magnum

	Patrick Anderson	
417 0227	The President's Mistress	£1.25
417 0299	The Senator	£1.25
	Franklin Bandy	
417 0387	Deceit and Deadly Lies	£1.25
	Tasman Beattie	
417 0212	The Zambesi Break	80p
417 0195	Panic Button	90p
	David Beaty	
417 0261	Cone of Silence	95p
417 0262	Excellency	95p
	O. J. Currington	
417 0393	A Bad Night's Work	90p
417 0392	Break-Out	95p
	Peter Dickinson	
417 0185	King and Joker	70p
417 0276	Walking Dead	95p
	Frank Parrish	
417 0266	Fire in the Barley	80p
	Peter Way	
417 0218	Super-Celeste	90p

These and other Magnum Books are available at your bookshop or newsagent. In case of difficulties orders may be sent to:

Magnum Books
Cash Sales Department
P.O. Box 11
Falmouth
Cornwall TR10 109EN

Please send cheque or postal order, no currency, for purchase price quoted and allow the following for postage and packing:

U.K. 19p for the first book plus 9p per copy for each additional book ordered, to a maximum of 73p.

B.F.P.O. & Eire 19p for the first book plus 9p per copy for the next 6 books, thereafter 3p per book.

Overseas customers 20p for the first book and 10p per copy for each additional book.

While every effort is made to keep prices low, it is sometimes necessary to increase prices at short notice. Magnum Books reserve the right to show new retail prices on covers which may differ from those previously advertised in the text or elsewhere.